2/6

ROUND THE RUGGED ROCKS

Round
the
Rugged Rocks

by

DAVID NIVEN

LONDON
THE CRESSET PRESS
MCMLI

For
HJÖRDIS, DAVID
AND JAMIE

First published in 1951 by
The Cresset Press Ltd., 11 Fitzroy Square, London, W.1
and printed in Great Britain at
The Chapel River Press, Andover, Hants
10.51

Round the Rugged Rocks
The Ragged Rascal Ran . . .

*Old-fashioned nursery saying for children
who have trouble rolling their Rs*

AUTHOR'S NOTE

This, heaven help me, is *not* an autobiography.
All of the characters who appear on these pages
are imaginary . . . unfortunately.

D.N.

CHAPTER ONE

'BILL,' SHOUTED JOHN HAMILTON, lieutenant, commanding 'C' Troop, 23rd Reconnaissance Regiment.

'Yes, sir?' answered William Parkinson, sergeant of the same outfit.

This easy familiarity between officer and non-commissioned officer was the outcome of six years of battles that had taken them together through desert, olive grove, bocâge and now to the cross-roads marked X236410 on the map of Germany (Hanover District).

The young officer who was standing up in the turret of his armoured car continued to address the sergeant, who, thirty yards away, was relieving himself on a bush of wild lupins.

'Just because the war is nearly over, it doesn't mean that open mutiny is next on the list—so why the bloody hell doesn't someone bring *me* a mug of tea, too?'

'Right away, sir,' grinned the sergeant; and from the way he said it, and from the nods and winks of the soldiers within earshot, it would have been obvious to an outsider that mutiny was about the only thing that never could happen to 'C' Troop.

'Trooper Blossom,' yelled the sergeant, and the cry was passed down the line of men waiting with their tea mugs. 'Blossom! Blossom! the Sarnt wants yer.'

The sergeant listened to the shouts and sucked his teeth. 'Gawd, wot a bloke!' he observed to no one in particular . . . 'Supposed to be a bloomin' orficers batman and all 'e does is to spend six years chasin' ruddy rabbits.' He spat on the dusty road.

'Lookin' for me, Sarnt?' inquired Trooper Blossom mildly.

He had appeared silently from nowhere: and as was his wont, he was in close touch with animal life; this time it was a fat, white farmyard duck that bulged beneath his tunic; its head and neck lolled grotesquely out from between the second and third buttons.

7

Blossom was a little man with a wrinkled and humorous brown face: in peace time he was a Norfolk poacher and he had kept his hand in at the game ever since he had been called into the service of his King. 'I found this 'ere bird, Sarnt, proceedin' down the road . . . it was limpin' quite bad so thinkin' it might be classified as "walkin' wounded" I knocked it orf to save it a walk.'

'That is loot, Blossom,' said the sergeant, 'and as such is punishable by death; 'owever, pluck the bastard and 'and it over to the cook.'

'Very good, Sarnt.'

'And get a move on and take 'is Nibs a cuppa, 'e's screamin' blue bloody murder up there.'

'Yes, Sarnt.'

Blossom dashed off to do as he was bid and in a matter of seconds John Hamilton was handed an enormous tin mug filled with the sweet scalding tea that only the British soldier can make.

''Ere's the gunfire, sir.'

'Thanks, Blossom, and where, may I ask, have you been?'

'I was makin' a short reconnaissance for the cook, sir. . . . Seein' that it's all over now, bar the shoutin' that is, 'e reckoned as 'ow we all ought to 'ave a nice change of diet.'

John Hamilton grunted, he was not really listening, instead, over the rim of his tin mug he watched the endless stream of field-grey shapes as they shambled past the armoured car on their way back to the prisoner-of-war cages. There had been a heavy shower a short while before and now a hot May sun was causing a visible steam to rise from the damp hot sweaty mass of Germans that flowed unendingly past. Some of the faces turned wonderingly towards the armoured cars of 'C' Troop; as always in the mass surrender of an army, a large proportion of the soldiers involved were catching their first glimpse of the enemy; but apart from this small flicker of interest, they tramped stolidly along without even looking up, obeying a general order to hand over their weapons and ammunition and keeping moving west . . . always west.

8

Their expressions were completely blank or stamped with fatigue, but on the morrow, after a rest, their minds would begin to live again, and then, for each one would start the daily torture of the prisoner of war—fear for the safety of wives and children, the realization of the dreadful uncertainty of his own future, the apparent awful finality of his case.

As John looked down on them he was surprised that he felt so little emotion. 'I suppose I ought to be gloating or something,' he thought. . . . 'After all, this is IT, this is the moment which for years we have all been fighting and praying for—total, complete, smashing victory. This is exactly what "The Old Sweat" at the regiment depot had always said *would* happen—"when the rot really sets in they will just pack up in millions."' . . . Well here was the rot with a vengeance! . . . A few small pockets of resistance left, perhaps, but everyone knew that Monty had received a surrender offer somewhere farther north, and now it could only be a matter of hours before it was all over. . . . 'Over?' His mind took a different turn. That would mean being sent to Japan or being demobilized and sent out into the world to earn a living having gone straight from school into the army. 'A grisly prospect,' he thought. . . . 'At twenty-five I don't know a damn thing except how to run an armoured car, how to kill people and how to look after my men's feet—that'll get me a hell of a long way in civvy street.' He grinned to himself. . . . ' "The Aunts" will be glad to see me though:' his mind flickered fondly towards the two old ladies who had brought him up since his father and mother had been drowned in a fishing boat off Margate whither he had been taken for the summer holidays at the age of nine.

'The Aunts' were not really aunts in the true sense of the word—they were two septuagenarian spinster sisters who had been devoted family friends for years; and, who, when the tragedy of the drowning had taken place, had at once stepped forward and taken complete charge of the only child—John.

He owed everything to 'the Aunts' and the little Queen Anne house in a fold of the Wiltshire Downs near Devizes was the only home he had ever really known. It was there that his thoughts now turned—to the beautifully proportioned little house of rose-coloured brick with its high white window frames making a smiling countenance of the façade—to the enormous chestnut trees in the two large meadows in front of the house beneath which the six or seven jersey cows and the two or three horses would be shading themselves—the horses standing head to tail and flicking the flies out of each others' eyes, the cows lying placidly, just chewing and gazing out over the yellow carpet of buttercups towards the river. . . .

The river! His heart tightened as he saw himself standing beside one of the best chalk streams in the world, the rooks were making their homely clamour in the high elms behind the house, a snipe was drumming in its springtime joy above the water meadow and on the other side of the stream he caught, out of the tail of his eye, the flash of a king-fisher. . . .

'Beg pardon, sir,' said Sergeant Parkinson from the road below, 'a message 'as just come in from the C.O. 'e wants to speak to you.' John shook himself and groaned inwardly. 'All right,' he said, 'hand me up the gadget.'

After a few preliminary crackles the commanding officer's voice came clearly through the earphones. 'John, there is still resistance coming from the area around the farmhouse at X236410. Go and investigate and if you can't put a stop to it yourself we'll get some other stuff sent up. . . . It doesn't seem to be much except small arms fire, but they are in a pill-box and could hold up some motorized units of 2nd R.B. who have orders to pass there shortly. . . . Don't worry beyond that one point . . . it now seems clear all the way to Nienburg and that is our limit.'

John acknowledged the order, then leaned over the edge of the turret and said, 'Take over the troop, Sergeant Bill, go on collecting the stuff and keep these Boches moving. . . . I'll be back directly but I may need some help, so keep listening out on 624, that is the clearest channel.'

As the big armoured car, with its name—Mae West—painted on its side, lumbered along the dusty side road towards the farmhouse John thought grimly to himself, 'Well, here we are, about to get mixed up in the last remaining vestige of resistance of the whole bloody German army. I'll probably get knocked off just as they are blowing the final whistle for the whole game to end . . . what a life!'

As they approached the danger area, however, his mind became fully occupied with the technical points of the business in hand and he had no further qualms. He took a careful look through his binoculars at the farmhouse, one of the typical red and white variety, then he examined the pill-box. It was not a very formidable object and had probably been hastily erected by local labour to help the Volksturm to guard the railway bridge which, according to his map, lay out of sight around a bend of the road to the right. His practised eye soon saw on his left a useful piece of dead ground in the shape of a big clamp of potatoes standing some eight or ten feet high. He pointed this out to the driver and the armoured car was quickly sited behind the clamp—its big turret-gun able to bear comfortably on the pill-box some 400 yards away, its machine gun ready to deal with any sudden appearance of the enemy on either flank.

The first round just missed the target but the second and third hit it squarely and judging by the shower of debris that shot up into the air it must have been extremely unpleasant inside—at any rate a square of fluttering white appeared almost immediately from behind it. John ordered the gunner to cease fire.

The figure carrying the surrender token approached uncertainly, being sure only of the general direction from which the shells had come; he advanced a hundred yards or so before he saw the turret of the armoured car just showing above the potatoes, then he turned straight towards it. 'Looks like a proper von Stroheim,' said the gunner, who was an ardent but rather antidated movie-goer.

'Looks like one of those S.S. bastards, too,' muttered the driver.

'Whatever he is keep him covered every minute,' said John grimly, '. . . and we won't open the lid . . . we don't want him popping any hand grenades in here at this stage of the game.'

The German was now fifty yards from the vehicle and as the gunner had said—he was a tough and brutal-looking customer with a thin line for a mouth and a sneering, arrogant face: this was a type the crew of 'Mae West' knew well and towards which they had no reason for charitable reactions.

He spoke slowly in tolerable English, 'As we have now run out of food we are forced to surrender—only that would make us stop fighting—is that understood?'

John answered through an observation slit 'Perfectly, and we will gladly give you some K-Rations; so you can get the hell back in there.' The gunner and driver chuckled. 'Cheeky bastard,' said the gunner under his breath.

The German's face worked and he made an involuntary move forward; then without another word he turned on his heel and waved his arms in the direction of the pill-box. Eight, ten, and finally sixteen figures emerged with their hands clasped behind their heads; they stumbled across the field at a half run.

The lieutenant gathered them together into a dispirited, scared-looking huddle, then he turned to the 'Mae West' for instructions.

'Straight down this road for three miles,' said John, by now standing up in the turret, 'at the crossroads turn west and keep going . . .' he grinned and added, 'you will be among friends.' The S.S. lieutenant spat on the ground as they marched away.

John walked down the road and removed the fuses from the demolition charges which, as he had expected, he found beneath the railway bridge; next he destroyed the arms which they found inside the pill-box by the simple method of piling them on the ground and driving 'Mae West' over them; then he gave some butterscotch to the inevitable horde of tow-headed children that came rushing out of the farmhouse and lastly reported by radio to his commanding officer that all resistance in that area had ceased.

'Well done, John, now you had better go back to collecting that stuff again and I'll relieve you as soon as I can—oh! and incidentally, the official order to cease fire has just come through. . . . I thought you would like to know.'

'Thank you, sir,' John said quietly.

The end!—the official end of six years of struggle, tension, fear, boredom, discomfort and electric excitement. He felt strangely tired and let down, and had a great longing to go away somewhere and sit quietly by himself: he felt he wanted to digest this slowly. What he did, in fact, was to order 'Mae West' to set upon her return course to the Troop waiting at cross-roads X236410. As they lumbered along they passed the little band of S.S. tramping stolidly up the dusty road, the glowering lieutenant at their head—another tiny tributary of the great flood of field grey that was flowing west. They did not even look up as the Armoured Car went by.

Once back with the rest of his Troop John called the men around him. A smiling circle of twenty brown, confident and friendly faces looked up at him; he told them the news of the cease fire. As he spoke he speculated upon what this piece of information would mean to each individual. Naturally there was a chance of all of them being sent to take part in the closing phase of the war in the Far East, but from what he had heard this seemed most unlikely. The units needed for this had long since been withdrawn from the Western Front and had for many months been undergoing special training for this very different kind of warfare. He could visualize the entire Navy, the Air Force, all Airborne units, many infantry and commandos being involved, but he just could not imagine 'Mae West' hacking her way through steamy jungles. No, it looked very much like a spell of police duty in Germany, then home to a replacement centre to await demobilization. Big Bill Parkinson, his Troop sergeant, would go back to his wife and six kids in Balham and would again become a conductor on the red No. 14 bus that plies between Putney and King's Cross; his kindly battered cockney face would peer over the back of the bus and observing a very large man in a very small sports car he would inevitably raise two fingers in a questionable V sign and call out 'Wot-cher—cuckoo in the bleedin' nest. . . .' One of the best N.C.O.'s in the regiment, and a friend for life.

Franks, his best radio operator, would go back to his wireless and cycle repair shop in Rochdale, and Davis, who had somehow kept 'Mae West' running smoothly from the beach at Arromanches all the way to cross-roads X236410 would go back to his vocation—a wall of death motor-cycle rider at the county fairs. Wilson, the Durham miner, who had turned a deaf ear to all the Government's appeals for men of his craft to accept release from active service in order to swell the thinning ranks in the pits, would, John knew, stick by his avowed intention—never to go below ground again except in a six foot wooden box. Charters, who had landed in Normandy with a number four iron secreted somewhere in his kit, would joyously go back to being the assistant pro of a Sussex Golf Club: His famous report when he returned wounded from a near-fatal reconnaissance would remain a regimental classic . . . 'tell 'em to stay on the fairway—there's a hell of a lot of Boches in the rough.' Perks the Troop cook, an enormous smiling giant (who had caused mass indigestion on more than one occasion) would once more become Ben Ali the lion tamer, and complete with turban, whip and chair, would draw Oooh's and Aaah's from the squirming females of the circus audience.

Finally, Trooper Blossom—well, he had already confided to John, that owing to the scarcity of food, pheasants should be fetching two pounds apiece in the open market by Christmas, so his future seemed assured.

When John finished his short announcement of the official end of the war in Europe, the voice of Perks spoke up, 'Sir, seein' that old Adolf 'as decided to put up the shutters and go out of business, wouldn't this be a nice time to 'ave a little nip of that whisky we liberated in 'olland?'

Unanimous cries of assent greeted this most intelligent suggestion: a nod from John, and Perks produced, from the depths of his bed-roll, two bottles of Haig and Haig. Mugs were filled and raised, and thus, against the ever-present back-drop of shuffling field-grey figures and to the accompaniment of half-embarrassed murmurs of 'Good Luck', 'All the Best', 'Good 'ealth', 'Cheerio' and 'Good Old Johnny', did the war end for 'C' Troop.

CHAPTER TWO

IT ALL HAPPENED pretty much as John had expected. The Americans having unleashed two atom bombs on the mainland of Japan, the war in the Far East ended abruptly, and any possibility of his being sent in that direction was removed. A few weeks of policing a docile and flattened Germany and of coping with thousands of heartbreaking dis-placed persons fell to his lot, but by midsummer he was returned to England to await demobilization.

His beloved Troop was scattered to the four winds and he found himself kicking his heels in utter boredom, surrounded for the most part by complete strangers.

As he was a country lover, it was his great good fortune to be sent to the West Country and there to a beautiful early Georgian house in Somerset called Blagthorpe Hall, the country seat of Sir Arthur Prentice Bart. Unlike most of the buildings in England of any proportions, beauty or interest, Blagthorpe had, during six years of war, been neither battered down by the enemy nor defiled and devastated by the de-fenders. The official reason for this last phenomenon was that the water supply was insufficient for it to be requisitioned as billets. John found this difficult to understand as on the estate there were at least seven large lakes or ponds bountifully fed the year round by a strong clear stream which had flowed in those parts since the end of the ice age. Sir Arthur Prentice, however, was not the son of Alfred Prentice for nothing. Old Alf Prentice had made his fortune in the 1914–18 war, manufacturing so-called jam on government contract. After a brief scandal a discreet shade had been pulled over the rumours that he operated a special machine which gave a more lifelike quality to his gooseberry preserve by the insertion therein of the bristles from very old toothbrushes, and he had concentrated quickly and profitably on plum and apple.

Blagthorpe became his in 1918 by the simple expedient of acquiring the mortgage and foreclosing on the owner—the impoverished widow of a Colonel of the Grenadier Guards. Enormous gifts of jam to schoolchildren had later helped unload his surplus stocks and had earned him a Baronetcy. Old Alf would no doubt have approved of his son's war record in the Second World War. At the start of the conflict, faced with conscription, Sir Arthur, a soft twenty-two, had evinced a sudden burning interest in farming; so great was his determination to help fill the national larder that he fired old Tom Preston, whose family had farmed the six hundred acre Grove Farm on a tenancy for five generations, and officially became a farmer himself, thereby achieving classification as an untouchable as far as the fighting services were concerned. He did, however, take an active interest in local defence, and although he himself was unfortunately too busy with his farming to join the Home Guard, he had the farm workers build a good solid air-raid shelter in the gardens of Blagthorpe Hall.

As more and more men streamed across the Atlantic to prepare for the great offensive across the Channel, even the Squire of Blagthorpe could not fight off the billeting authorities forever. It is true that through the good offices of a friend at the Ministry of Information he arranged for the records of this strange wartime circus to be sent there for safe keeping and thus managed to keep the rude and licentious soldiery out of the house proper, but he finally bowed to the inevitable and with much head-shaking over the question of the water supply he had watched Nissen huts being erected beneath the trees in his Park, for the accommodation, in the acutest discomfort, of some five hundred fighting men.

When John arrived at Blagthorpe, he was blessedly accompanied by Trooper Blossom. The King had pinned a Military Cross on his left breast as soon as he had arrived in England; and he had also been home on leave for a fortnight during which time 'the Aunts' had fussed and clucked over him and made him feel as though he had won the war single-handed. But alas! he had found himself increasingly restless during this leave, and it had soon begun to dawn upon him that he would take a long long time to unwind and settle down to civilian life. It was with a feeling almost of relief that he had packed his bags at the end of the two weeks and returned to his regiment.

One-half of the regiment was billeted in the Nissen huts at Blagthorpe, the other half was more comfortably accommodated in a village some three miles away. The whole outfit was a sort of glorified transit camp, with a skeleton crew of officers and N.C.O.s running it.

The regiment, in the general contraction of a huge wartime army into a small peacetime force, was being amalgamated with two other armoured car regiments: a few recruits were being trained in a desultory sort of way as replacements for the British Army of the Rhine: vehicles were being handed in to the great Ordnance Depots—piles of equipment were being packed and sent away to Army Surplus—documents were being filed or burned, and the whole was being carried out with the same degree of enthusiasm as that displayed by sleepy waiters in a night club when, in the small hours of the morning, one small group of patrons is preventing them from going home to bed. The military elastic had long since been stretched to the limit.

As demobilization was on the basis of age plus length of service, officers and men came to regard themselves and each other as 'points' and 'age groups' instead of as human beings. John's group was not due for release until the end of the year. He may have looked forward to his freedom with misgivings but he certainly viewed the intervening months with the utmost distaste.

The only bright spots as far as he could see were the beauty of his surroundings, and the fact that Trooper Blossom was still with him. He had, however, reckoned without Oglethorpe.

It was just before dinner one August evening when he first spotted Oglethorpe. John was sitting in a dilapidated armchair, in the hut that did duty as an officers' mess, and was flicking through the pages of a vintage *Sphere*, when Oglethorpe appeared.

Oglethorpe was a subaltern of thirty who looked fifty: six feet six inches in height, with a moustache which could be seen from behind (on a clear day): he was very very thin indeed and his chin was non-existent. He stood in the doorway of the hut. He was beautifully drunk.

'I would like,' he announced to the room in general, 'to have a stoop of meade or a posset of burnt sack—I would also like to park an amber jet in some convenient pot.'

The colonel, a new importation to the regiment, shot up from his chair like a jack-in-the-box. 'You are drunk, young man.'

Oglethorpe clicked his heels. 'You are right, sir.'

The colonel was obviously shaken by this candour, but he was an old regular soldier and had dealt with young puppies of subalterns before: he was damned if he was going to let a little simple war service go to their heads now. . . .

'Who the devil are you?' he barked.

'Oglethorpe,' said Oglethorpe.

'Well, what are you doing here?'

'Sir,' said Oglethorpe with the patience usually reserved for backward children . . . 'Mr. Churchill once said, "in every great world conflict one finds the little folk who trot beside the Juggernaut car of the God of War!" . . . Well, I have been beside that bloody car for six years and now my trotting days are nearly done: I was ordered to come here to be demobilized: . . . I did not argue: I did not complain: to gratify some foolish military whim I came, I saw, and,' he concluded, with a sly backward glance toward the door and a forefinger pressed against the side of his nose . . . 'I stopped for a bottle of yoghurt.'

The colonel glared balefully for several seconds before he spoke. 'Go to your room, Oglethorpe, and consider yourself lucky not to be under close arrest. . . . I'll deal with you in the morning.'

The long thin man opened his mouth to make a further pronouncement, but John got quickly from his chair and taking him by the arm propelled him away from the presence of his snorting commanding officer and out into the cool of the evening.

By the time the hush of late summer was upon them, John and Oglethorpe had become inseparable. For all his thirty years, Oglethorpe was a true Edwardian. His clothes, that is to say his civilian clothes, were as outrageous as his moustache. His tweed coats were of fabulous length, full-skirted and indentated all over with slanting pockets; cuffs were turned back at the wrist and trousers were mere drain pipes encasing long thin legs. There were far too many buttons on everything. In London he sported a little round bowler, from Lock's; in the country a deerstalker was the order of the day. The fact that he was still in the army and supposed at all times to be in uniform was something that Oglethorpe recognized only in the immediate vicinity of the camp; even then a shepherd's crook had mysteriously been added to the military ensemble.

Oglethorpe's reputation as the most imperturbable officer in the Western Desert had clung to him till the end: legendary had become his observation during three days of heavy shelling at Halfaya Pass. . . .'Like everything Teutonic this goes on far too long.'

The new colonel, who was a good man at heart, soon grew to learn that the subalterns of his day must cease to be the mental yardstick by which he should measure such wartime products as Oglethorpe and John Hamilton. This change of attitude could, of course, have been brought about by his young blonde French wife; John, who had a heart like an hotel, had turned his attentions to her as soon as he had set eyes on her.

He had not meant any real harm, but the young and luscious wives of vintage colonels had always held a fatal fascination for him; they presented a challenge which it was beyond him to ignore.

It had all started over a bottle of champagne at Salisbury Races. This in due course had been followed by surreptitious meetings by the lakes at Blagthorpe and finally by the laying of intricate plans for a week-end to be spent together at an hotel in Bournemouth.

This particular campaign of John's came to an untimely end when one morning, before lunch, the colonel asked in clear bell-like tones which were heard in every corner of the mess. . . . 'By the way, Hamilton, are you very much in love with my wife?'

John clutched the corner of the bar and paled somewhat. 'Oh, no, sir—er—thank you, sir—I—er—no—not at all.'

'Well,' said the colonel, looking him straight in the eye, 'if you're *not*, then be a good chap and don't go on telling her you *are*—it upsets her, you know—Lunch?'

After one of the most embarrassing meals of his life, John went in search of Oglethorpe: he had a knot of indigestion in his stomach and a whole new attitude towards wives in general and colonels' wives in particular.

Oglethorpe was comforting and helpful. 'Married women,' he said, 'a jumpy game at best . . . always a risk, old man . . . not for Oglethorpe. I learnt my lesson during the era of the flying bombs, old man. I was safely tucked in the feathers with the wife of a B.B.C. announcer; now on paper that would seem safe enough, wouldn't it? There he was on the air talking a lot of balls about our Russian allies having liberated over a thousand towns and villages in the past three days, and there we were having a spot of mum and dad in the fourposter: well, suddenly there was a hell of an explosion and the next thing I knew the side of the house had gone and we both had to climb down a ladder stark naked, with half the London Fire Brigade looking up at us.'

John felt better. 'Anyone killed in the house?' he asked.

'No, I don't think so. I couldn't stay long because being dressed in a sheet I didn't fancy meeting the B.B.C. bloke on his demolished threshold. A fireman got my clothes, or what was left of them, and then went up after an old lady who lived in the flat above—she was still up there looking for something, poking about in the rubble—I heard him talking to her. ". . . . Wot are you lookin' for, Ma?"

"I'm looking for my false teeth."

' "Wot the 'ell do you think they're droppin' round 'ere— 'am sandwiches? . . ."

'Wonderful blokes, those firemen, most grateful I was for that sheet.' Oglethorpe paused. 'No, old man, never again— not married women.'

The army had very little work for officers awaiting de-mobilization and, as the colonel was generous about leave, London saw a good deal of the two friends. Oglethorpe had an elderly uncle who lived in Pickering Place just off St. James's Street and thither, as soon as they arrived in the city, they would invariably repair so that Oglethorpe might change out of his hated khaki. Oglethorpe's uncle announced one day that he proposed to make them a present of entrance fees and five annual subscriptions as members of Quennell's—his club in St. James's Street. In the time of Beau Brummell there had been six or seven coffee shops in St. James's Street. Mr. Quennell owned one and enjoyed his own clientele of young bucks; so did Mr. White, Mr. Brook, Mr. Boodle and the others; later their patrons had formed clubs on their premises and the ultra-exclusive establishments bearing their names are today's monuments to their hospitality and good cheer.

John and Oglethorpe were elected to Quennell's at the midsummer election; probably as Oglethorpe put it, 'because they don't know us well enough to blackball us; otherwise the ballot box would look like caviare.'

They made their first appearance a week or so later. The first person they encountered was Wills, the hall porter. This great man had been enthroned in his glass-covered booth just inside the front door for over forty years: the club was his whole life, the welfare and well-being of its inmates his crusade. He escorted the two new members around and, as it was four o'clock in the afternoon and many of the older members were sleeping off their post-luncheon tipples of Cockburn's '08, it was in an awed whisper that he pointed out the various items of interest.

'Here, gentlemen, is the dining-room. Like the rest of the club—genuine Adams. Note the Wootons and the Stubbs upon the wall: beautiful pictures, gentlemen, beautiful pictures. . . . There is no smoking in here until after two o'clock and, of course, we always dress for dinner.' He pointed with pride to an Angelica Kauffmann hanging above the beautifully carved staircase, and then to the Fifth Duke of Axminster's racing colours, preserved in a glass case. Rings of sweat stained the silk beneath the armpits, the result, confided Wills, of Fred Archer's superhuman efforts to bring in his fifth Derby winner. In another glass case in a corner of a lovely panelled room were relics of the club; these included shoe buckles belonging to Beau Brummell, a snuff box said to belong to the Scarlet Pimpernel, 'who really existed, gentlemen, he held his councils of war in this very room'; and in the place of honour, the wager book.

Wills tapped it reverently. 'All bets, gentlemen, must be entered in this book, duly witnessed by two other members.'

He showed them the record of the famous wager of one thousand guineas taken in 1785 by His Grace the Duke of Aylesbury, that he would walk from his house in Regent's Park to the club at high noon on the 4th of June—stark naked. The wager had been witnessed and according to the book the Duke had collected in full. Wills smiled, he was full of information on this subject.

'It seems, gentlemen, that His Grace ordered the floor boards of his coach removed and the curtains pulled, then once he was inside, he took off his clothes and ordered the coachman to drive very slowly—oh! he walked down here to the club, all right.' He shook his head a trifle sadly. 'Yes, those must have been wonderful days in the club, wonderful days.'

As they entered the big downstairs smoking-room, Wills offered a discreet word of advice: 'Some of the older members are a little crusty, but don't let them upset you—their bark is worse than their bite. . . . For instance, that gentleman over there'—he indicated a huge sleeping purple mass adorned with a bristly white moustache—'be careful with him, he is Sir Frank ffollett and he likes everything just so; why, he even looks upon that chair as his very own property, of course he has spent a great many years in it . . . we on the staff take great pains not to upset him.'

The dear old man smiled beguilingly. 'Now gentlemen, I hope I won't be speaking out of turn if I say how pleased I am to see a little young blood coming into the club. . . . I'm sure you young gentlemen will cheer us all up a bit.

'Of course, some clubs have a small room set aside so that the members can entertain their ladies, but not here, not in Quennell's. When I first came here the lady friend of one of the members took a bet that she would get into Quennell's and she did—it was quite dreadful really—she ran right in, dashed upstairs and through the dining-room in the middle of lunch, too, then downstairs again and out into her carriage and drove away . . . oh! it was a terrible day, gentlemen . . . a terrible day, and poor Mr. Scott-Andrews, that was the member whose lady friend she was, he had to resign of course. It appears that she would not marry him unless he resigned from his clubs, and she went all over London doing the same thing till he had nowhere left to go, poor man; I imagine he more or less *had* to marry her.' A telephone bell rang in the distance.

'One word of warning, gentlemen, please be careful in the Silence Room.' He sighed sadly. 'It is always causing friction— that room.' He bowed and withdrew.

'I take it,' said Oglethorpe, 'that we ought to have a look at this Silence Room.'

John agreed. They found and entered the holy of holies.

There they saw a big fireplace within a semi-circle of deep leather armchairs. Other groups of sofas and chairs were dispersed around the room and there was a long table upon which was a leather-bound book containing the names and particulars of prospective candidates for membership and all the weekly papers in addition to *Horse and Hound, The Field, Country Life, Punch, Truth, Who's Who* and the *A.B.C.* Against the walls were several small writing tables with little green-shaded lights upon them.

In spite of the bright sunny afternoon outside, this room, being at the back of the building and facing a brick wall, was very dark. It was also restful, cool, peaceful and apparently deserted.

Oglethorpe looked around carefully and then did a strange thing. He planted his feet wide apart, put his hands on his hips, inhaled a great breath, tilted his head back, opened his mouth and let out an earth-shaking cheer. 'Hip . . . Hip . . . Hoorah,' he yelled. The scene in the Silence Room changed rapidly: heads shot up from the depths of every chair: ferocious and baleful eyes peered out of the gloom; moustaches bristled from every corner. The two new members turned and fled.

'Leaving so soon, gentlemen?' asked Wills as they shot past his sanctum.

'Yes, we have to,' said John, as he grabbed his hat. ' . . . er . . . a little something came up.'

They allowed several weeks to elapse before they returned to Quennell's. Upon the occasion of their second appearance they decided to lunch there. They arrived at about a quarter to one: Wills was at his post and greeted them, they thought, with a little less enthusiasm than he had displayed upon the first occasion, but they rose above this and pressed bravely forward.

In the hall affixed to what appeared to be a church lectern was the menu of that day's luncheon. Owing to the large number of members who still owned country estates, the dreary diet of this small section of the long-suffering British people was often enlivened by fish and game from these various retreats; but today was not a lucky day in this respect. As John and Oglethorpe were glancing interestedly at this

24

announcement of gastronomic promise, a gruff voice boomed behind them, 'Can't read a damn word, what's it say?'

They turned to find Sir Frank ffollett.

'First of all, sir,' said Oglethorpe, 'there is Moules Marinières.'

'Good God, what an outrage,' roared Sir Frank, beating on the floor with his walking-stick, 'the damned Labour Government has got us eatin' moles now.'

John hastily translated this particular dish into English, but the thought of eating mussels seemed to infuriate the old man even more.

'Never would have happened if Winston had got in . . . I'm goin' to lunch at the Turf . . . comin' Charlie?'

Charlie then emerged from the shadows, an elderly admiral, his blue seaman's eyes slightly rheumy now; together they made a muttering exit.

Outside on the pavement the admiral hailed a taxi, or rather he commanded it to halt in the same tones he would have used in bygone days to address the captain of a Chinese junk: the two old men climbed aboard. It was at this point that the ever-watchful Wills came running out with Sir Frank ffollett's hat.

'Your hat, Sir Frank,' he called as the taxi ground its gears into place. 'You left your hat, Sir Frank.'

Suddenly the poor man slipped, his feet shot from under him and he came to a slithering stop, sitting bolt upright in the gutter of St. James's Street; the hat still in his hand. Sir Frank ffollett, at last realizing that some kind of commotion was taking place, peered out of the cab and observing the venerable Wills sitting in the road, he turned to the admiral.

'You know, Charlie, we shall have to be gettin' rid of Wills, he has taken to leavin' the club like some of the members do.' Without a backward glance he settled in his seat, and they drove away.

John and Oglethorpe helped the forlorn hall porter to his feet and back into his cubby hole in the cool dark of the club;

he was still worried about his members being seen about London improperly dressed.

'Sir Frank will be most upset when he finds out he has left it behind.' Sadly he placed the black homburg on a hook in the hall.

John and Oglethorpe walked into the dining-room; there they noticed, with interest, that although every table was occupied, it was, in most cases, by only one member. They held a hurried consultation in the doorway and selected the least hostile-looking of those present as their lunch-time companion. He was a small, very bald, old gentleman sitting alone at a large table in the far corner of the room. With the aid of a bottle of Rhine wine he was methodically disposing of a large fish cake. On the table and just beyond the fish cake was a book-rest: on the book-rest was a masterpiece entitled 'Horses I Have Known'—he was devouring this with his eyes while his jaws and hands dealt rhythmically with the fish cake.

John and Oglethorpe seated themselves and ordered their lunch: the old man never looked up. They talked together in low tones, keeping a weather eye on the activities of their fellow member. At last the old gentleman finished his fish cake and became for the first time aware that he was no longer alone: appalled by the realization of this, he laid down his fork and treated them each to a long and penetrating stare. John, mistaking this stare for a look of interest, thought that the moment had come to start a nice chatty conversation; as an opening gambit he selected an easy subject.

'Do you live in London, sir?' he asked.

The unwinking stare which for some moments had been fixed on Oglethorpe's moustache now switched over like a searchlight to John. Through pure nerves, he repeated the question.

'—er—I was wondering, sir, if you lived in London?'

'No,' came the reply in a strangely shrill voice. 'I do not.' The searchlight remained upon him and John heard himself add a second asinine query.

'Oh, then you live in the country?'

The red-rimmed eyes bored into him for several seconds before the answer finally came.

'I live,' said the old man, 'so far out in the country that the owls come and rodger my chickens.'

Fighting down their laughter they gulped the rest of their meal and stampeded from the table. At the door John and Oglethorpe turned for a last look—the searchlight was still upon them.

Downstairs in the smoking-room a scene of great activity met their eyes. It appeared that the incumbent of a foreign throne had once mentioned to the president of the club, an old and trusted friend, that she would be most interested to inspect the wonderful new dishwasher which, he had told her, some American friend had sent: it had been arranged that, in order to see it, the old lady should pay a purely unofficial visit to the club's kitchen on this very afternoon. This she had been doing while luncheon was being served upstairs, but now the inspection was over, and she had suddenly and without the slightest warning expressed a desire to see the rest of the club as well—pandemonium was reigning supreme.

Waiters were dashing about tidying the rooms and Wills was personally assessing the capability of various members to withstand the shock should they suddenly see a royal personage sailing majestically through the ante-rooms. Gently he shook a magenta-coloured general who was sleeping peacefully beneath *The Times*.

'The Queen will be in in a minute, general.'

The old soldier roared with impatience.

'Well, tell the harbour-master, you bloody fool.'

Such matters were slowly put to rights (although old Lord Bembridge was convinced that the Japs had landed and had to be locked in the lavatory until it was all over): the royal personage was shepherded quickly through the downstairs rooms and everything went off beautifully. John and Oglethorpe happened to be standing in the hall when she was about to leave: Wills was there, too, he had been presented to her and was glowing with pleasure. Suddenly out of the brightness of St. James's Street two figures loomed in the doorway—Sir Frank ffollett and Charlie were back from the Turf club: they blinked as they peered into the gloom of the interior.

'Just imagine, Charlie,' Sir Frank ffollett was saying, 'members of the Turf eatin' whale! . . . don't know what we're comin' to—it's that bloody fool Cripps, must be an appallin' bounder—old Wykehamist too, I believe.'

Dimly across the hall he spied a pink figure with a parasol. 'Wills,' he hissed, 'what's this? Women in the club?'

'Please, Sir Frank,' pleaded the agonized hall-porter in a hoarse whisper, 'it's the Queen.'

The old baronet immediately bowed in deep and courteous obeisance, but John could have sworn he heard him mutter, 'It's the thin end of the wedge.'

As the summer moved gloriously into autumn, John managed to enjoy himself more and more at Blagthorpe. His military duties were almost negligible, the colonel was becoming humanized, and Trooper Blossom had declared open war upon Sir Arthur Prentice who had abruptly refused permission to anyone from the camp who asked if they might catch a fish in his lakes or shoot a pigeon in his woods.

'You mark my words, sir, by the end of November I'll 'ave all 'is partridges put away and 'e'll be lucky if 'e finds a cock pheasant for 'is Christmas dinner.'

Far more important to John, however, was the fact that he met Carole. Carole Parker was a beauty with corn-coloured hair and large violet eyes; eyes so disturbing that they made most men overlook the fact that she also had a somewhat hard mouth above a most determined chin. When she first laid those violet eyes upon John, she was a young actress of great promise and was just finishing the summer season in the Bournemouth Repertory Company.

At the precise moment of their meeting John had hardly been looking his best. A large fancy dress ball was taking place in the Grand Hotel and, the affair being in aid of the local charities, was graced by the presence of minor royalty. It was the high spot of the Bournemouth season. John and Oglethorpe arrived very late and had consumed a considerable quantity of martinis *en route*. They were dressed as goats.

They entered the hotel just as the contestants for the prizes for the best costumes were lining up two by two, like the animals going into the Ark; the Grand March was about to start. The goats joined on the end of the procession. They had draped themselves in the most noisome and motheaten fur rugs: antlers, which Trooper Blossom had borrowed from the Prentice Arms in Blagthorpe village in exchange for a dozen of Sir Arthur Prentice's finest trout, were affixed to their heads : and as they started the first circuit of the ballroom it was noted with mounting horror by those present that between the legs of each a football dangled: a pair of gloves was sewn to the under surface of each football.

John and Oglethorpe made about one and a half turns round the floor before they began to feel dizzy. Then oblivious of the fact that they were now the focal point of all eyes and directly in front of the judges, Oglethorpe issued a loudly-whispered instruction.

'Now squat.'

'Now what?' asked John.

'Go on—squat, you bloody fool.'

John obeyed as best he could and placing his hands on the ground in front of him arched his back and awaited developments. He did not have long to wait for Oglethorpe as his *pièce de résistance* produced a brown paper bag and sprinkled black olives on the floor immediately behind him.

For a full ten seconds there was a stunned silence in the huge hall. Then pandemonium broke loose. A fat woman dressed as Nell Gwynne fainted and several people trod on her oranges: one of the judges tried to shield the eyes of the minor royalty and stepped gallantly into her line of vision; unfortunately he stepped too far and toppled backwards off the dais and had to be carried away by two clowns: the orchestra leader lost his head completely and confusing the situation with that of a theatre catching fire struck up the National Anthem. This action undoubtedly saved John and Oglethorpe, for, as the majority of the occupants of the hall instinctively stiffened to attention, they made their dash for the exit. Running as best they could, though somewhat hampered by their costumes, they managed to reach the open street; but there a glance over his shoulder for possible pursuers was fatal for John. He tripped and fell sprawling to the ground.

Oglethorpe, whose huge strides had taken him well ahead, did not hear the fall and John sat up just in time to witness the grotesque spectacle of a six and a half foot goat disappearing at high speed round a corner clutching its horns in one hand and its udders in the other.

Two red-faced commissionaires and a policeman were bearing down upon John and all had seemed lost when Carole's cool voice came from the interior of a Bentley that had moved silently to the curbside.

'Hop in.'

Without further ado John hopped and the sleek car slid smoothly away.

'Well,' said Carole as the Grand Hotel dropped behind, 'where do you want to go now?'

John looked at her and heartily approved of what he saw. She was dressed as a French apache dancer and the tight black skirt, white silk shirt and beret of that profession made it easy to see that she had a superb figure.

'I'm a little shaky after all that,' he said. 'Don't you think we might have a drink together somewhere while I make up my mind?'

'My dear man, you may have been chased away from the party, but it may interest you to know that I haven't even arrived at it yet.'

'I can promise you,' said John, 'that the best is now over; so if you are hoping to enjoy yourself you'd better have a little nip before you go in.' He caught the laughter in her eyes. 'Oh, I'll take my tits and things off if you're ashamed of me.' Carole laughed outright. John thought it was the most delicious laugh he had ever heard.

'No, honestly I can't,' she said, 'there are some people waiting for me and I'm dreadfully late already.'

'Some dreary boy friend, I suppose,' said John. 'I bet he's dressed as Mickey Mouse or a Pearly King—boy friends always are.'

'No, as a matter of fact, he has gone as Humpty Dumpty.'

'Oh, my God! How awful.'

' . . . and I really must go and join him. This is his car for one thing.'

'I've only seen one other Bentley since the war,' mused John, playing for time, 'and that belongs to the frightful twerp who owns the place we are billeted in.'

'Where are you billeted?' she asked with a flicker of interest.

'Blagthorpe—it's about thirty miles from here: actually we are not in the house itself because this frightful twerp did some fiddle over the water supply and the place was never requisitioned, so we are in a dreadful sort of hutted camp thing under the trees in the park.' A soft chuckle came from the semidarkness. 'Perhaps,' said Carole, 'I could persuade the frightful twerp to ask you up for a drink or something this week-end. . . I shall be bringing his car back on Saturday night.'

'Oh, Christmas!' said John grinning, 'I am sorry. . . . That would happen—old Mother Fortune doesn't let you get away with it for long, does she? There I was, picked up out of the gutter by a beautiful girl in a Bentley, saved from the oncoming flatfoots—probably from lynching—driven mad by the nearness of her and the intoxicating wafts of her Chanel 5. . . . Then just as things begin to look promising she tells me that the Bentley belongs to her boy friend who is waiting for her dressed as Humpty Dumpty and that he is none other than Sir Arthur Prentice.'

'Well, at least she told you that she might be spending the week-end within about four hundred yards of you,' said Carole with a long look out of the violet eyes.

John brightened. 'Yes, that's right. . . .' He studied the

lovely face in the orange light of the street lamps. 'Good old Mother Fortune, I knew the old bag wouldn't let me down.'

Carole looked away. 'Now really you must get out or tell me where you want to go. . . . We've been driving round and round without making any sense.'

'Where are we?' he asked. He looked out of the window. 'Oh, yes, Pantile Street. Anywhere down here will do fine: we have our car parked in a garage somewhere here . . . Thanks so much.' He fumbled with the door handle: 'I really am grateful, you saved me from a fate worse than death.'

John climbed out into the street, his antlers in his hand, his football still dangling, and bent down to say good night. Carole leaned across from the driving seat to look up at him, her silk shirt fell away slightly from her body and he caught a glimpse of her firm, uptilted and beautifully-moulded breasts.

He raised his eyes with an effort. 'Er . . . tell Humpty Dumpty to take it steady up on the old wall, won't you? . . . We don't want anything to happen to him, do we?'

'Don't we?' asked Carole softly as the Bentley moved away.

He watched the car glide smoothly down the road: he could just see her silhouetted through the rear window: as it rounded the corner at the end of the street, she turned and waved: he felt as though he had champagne in his knees.

Oglethorpe was waiting for him in the garage.

'Come along, old man. What happened to you? . . . I thought you were right behind me. I came whizzing in here about five minutes ago and I've been talking to myself ever since . . . most inconsiderate, old man, most inconsiderate.'

'I was picked up by the most beautiful girl in the world.'

'Oh, Crippen! here we go again. . . . What was her name?'

'I forgot to ask her,' said John in a dreamy voice.

'She must have made a hell of an impression on you. Let's get going. I feel we are persona on the slightly non-grata side in Bournemouth tonight and there is much to be done else-where before closing time.' As they divested themselves of the more tell-tale portions of their attire, Oglethorpe was pensive.

'I can't understand why the local inhabitants took such

exception; the last time I did the goat act it went down like a dog's dinner.'

'Where was that?' asked John.

'In an Australian sergeants' mess, old man, just outside Mersa Matruh.'

Late that night, as they approached Blagthorpe, the conversation swung for the hundredth time to the subject of 'the girl in the Bentley'.

'I tell you,' said John, 'that this is it . . . this is the one for me.'

Oglethorpe sighed. 'That you have said on eleven separate occasions during the short time I have known you, including, if I remember correctly, a regrettable moment when you thought that "the one for you" was the wife of our long-suffering commanding officer.'

'I know, but this is different.'

'You'll get over it. . . . Anyway she's got this drip Prentice sniffing round her . . . what are you going to do about him?'

'Well, I think the poor girl is dazzled by that Bentley and he's probably been showing her photographs of the ancestral home to impress her.'

'I don't want to be old-fashioned, old man, but I suggest that he has probably been showing her a good deal more than that. Incidentally, it's only a small point I know, but today is Wednesday; she said she was bringing the car back this week-end. Now don't you suppose that he is going to be in it, or do you think he is the sort of fellow to come back to Blagthorpe by train in order to spend three days on his flat feet?'

For the first time in his life, John felt the green, icy fingers of jealousy closing round his heart.

They arrived at Blagthorpe and parked Oglethorpe's small car under the trees.

'Good night, fellow goat,' said the tall man as he tied the tarpaulin sheet in place. 'Don't let that apache costume spoil your beauty sleep.'

The shadowy figure of Trooper Blossom materialized from

the darkness of the huge trees. 'Good evening, sir, I 'ope everything passed orf all right.'

'We did not exactly win the prize, Blossom,' answered John. 'In fact, we very nearly ended up in the cooler.'

'Furthermore,' said Oglethorpe from his great height, 'Mr. Hamilton has found a new girl,' he winked, '*The* girl.'

'Oh, my Gawd, sir, not again! . . . Pretty soon there won't be no new girls left—Mr. 'amilton will start meeting some of the old 'uns the second time round the course.'

John chose to ignore this sally. 'It was a most instructive evening, Blossom, and it's very good of you to have waited up to see us safely home.'

'No trouble at all, sir,' said Blossom. 'As a matter of fact, I 'ad a couple of odd jobs to finish orf afore I turned in.' He bade them good night and disappeared among the trees where he retrieved the two cock pheasants which he had cached there earlier in the evening.

The next morning the commanding officer sent for John and Oglethorpe: he was in no mood to be tampered with.

'Look here, you two, I'm getting pretty fed up with you . . . what the hell do you mean by breaking up a Charity Ball in Bournemouth? . . . I know you both had a damned good war and did very well, but that is no excuse for behaving like a couple of spoiled schoolchildren now that it's all over. How do you expect the army to maintain any discipline if the officers who are waiting to leave it behave like this all the time? . . . I've a damned good mind to send you both up before the general—goats, indeed!' he snorted. 'And Sir Arthur Prentice, who saw you there, telephoned me and said that you were both drunk into the bargain . . . drunken goats, indeed!' he snorted again. 'Sir Arthur also said that you knocked several people over as you fought your way out of the place. All I can say is—thank the Lord you weren't in uniform.'

They smiled encouragingly at their commanding officer.

'Damnit, there is nothing to laugh about,' he raved. He sat for a full minute shuffling some papers. Then having arrived at a decision he leaned forward with his elbows on the desk.

'You are both due to leave the service in three months' time and, by God, you'll behave as though you are still in it until you are out of it . . . understand?' Without looking up, the colonel then addressed the adjutant who had been hovering behind them near the door. 'It is obvious, Hawkins, that these two officers have too much time on their hands; for the next month they will do extra orderly officer on alternate days.'

'Very good, sir,' said Hawkins.

John and Oglethorpe realizing the interview was at an end took a smart pace backwards, saluted in unison, turned about and marched from the room.

'The trouble with the army today, old man,' said Oglethorpe as they walked away from the orderly room, 'is that it has too much time on its hands.'

'I feel sorry for that commanding officer of ours,' said John. 'The poor old poop was commissioned just as the last war was ending so he missed that; then he spent twenty years in India getting ready for this one to start; when it did, he was too old for it, so he spent six years in an office in Whitehall. Now the poor bastard is back where he was at the end of the first one . . . getting ready for the next . . . no, I really do feel sorry for him.'

'You feel sorry for his wife, old man.'

'Yes, I suppose I do.' A reflective pause. 'Do you suppose they do everything by numbers?'

'Talking bedroom shop,' said Oglethorpe, 'does not alter the fact that we are stuck with doing extra orderly officer every other day for a month.'

John chased and caught a leaf as it fluttered to earth. 'If you do that—catch a leaf before it touches the ground I mean —they say you will be married before the following autumn.'

'In that case, old man, I shall take the greatest precautions to see that no falling leaf comes anywhere near me. . . . Let's walk across the fields.'

They turned through a gate and out across a large stubble field. The harvest had been a heavy one and the weather had been gloriously un-English; now, although they were not yet

35

in the last week of September, the yield had nearly all been collected.

In a few fields the stooks of barley were still standing, but these would soon become part of the growing rows of stacks around the farm buildings. As they walked across the broad acres of stubble a farm cart came towards them, pulled upon its creaking way by a huge grey cart horse straining forward into his collar, his great shaggy iron-clad feet stamping into the hard ground. On top of the load was a little boy with a mop of red hair and a little girl wearing a pink sunbonnet; both were apple-cheeked and both were sucking straws. They waved to the two officers.

John looked out over the smiling English countryside. 'God! How I love all this,' he thought. 'Why can't all countries be happy? . . . Why can't all people be happy?' Cumulus clouds like towering galleons were sailing in the infinite blue above his head, the wooded ridge on the horizon was shimmering in the heat and at his feet the young clover, early-sown between the rows of barley, was already coming up fresh and green. He felt his Anglo-Saxon blood rise in his throat.

Whirr! A covey of partridges got up at his feet. He watched the little butterbrown birds skim across the field, make ready to land in the corner, think better of it and with a 'corrup' of consternation and a last minute beat of wing arch up over the cut-and-laid fence and settle on the far side.

'There is nothing like nature for helping you get things back in proportion,' he mused aloud.

Oglethorpe glanced down. 'You sound like an elderly female schoolteacher. . . . What the hell are you talking about?'

'Oh, I was just thinking that here we are getting depressed because a dreary colonel is going to twist our tails for the next month. What does it matter anyway? At the end of that time we'll be free. You'll be growing mushrooms in Norfolk, living in a nice little cottage on your uncle's land and being sued by old ladies in Norwich when they get ptomaine poisoning and I . . .'

'Well, what about you?'

'Well, I'll be free, too; a grateful government will have placed almost £150 in my pocket, so I'll be rich as hell for a while.'

'What will you do? Live with the "Aunts"?'

'No. I suppose if I got ill or something, I could always go there. They want me to go and live there, but I've got to get out and do something, though what the hell I *can* do I don't know. I thought of taking out an ad. in *The Times*. . . . You know, "Young ex-officer, keen, clean, intelligent, willing to go anywhere, do anything legal" . . . that sort of thing.'

'Old man, as a *Times* reader I hate to disillusion you, but there are not only hundreds of those in every day, but also there is a waiting list of three months before the ad. even gets into the paper. Come and grow mushrooms with me! they say it's a snip! all you do is fill an old cellar with manure, sprinkle a few bags of mushroom spawn around the place, then wait a day or two and make a fortune.'

John smiled. 'Well, I will if I get stuck . . . thanks awfully.' And he meant it.

They breasted a hill and saw nestling in the fold below them the little hamlet of Nettlebed: Oglethorpe pointed down.

'If I am not mistaken, there is an excellent place down there called the Castle and Ball. Let us therefore descend and touch off a pint or two of old and mild. . . .'

Neither of them was of a mind to return to the Mess for lunch; so it was with great delight that they accepted the landlord's suggestion that a hunk of bread, a slab of cheese and some pickled onions might go well with their beer.

They passed a pleasant afternoon.

On the following Saturday it was John's turn to be orderly officer, so he had no chance personally to find out whether or not the Bentley had returned. Trooper Blossom was pressed into service and lurked all day long near the lodge gate so that he could report on its arrival and give a description of its occupants.

By dinner-time John was in the depths of despair. Blossom had seen nothing, but had learned from a housemaid (with whom he had formed a most beneficial liaison) that Sir Arthur Prentice had been away in Bournemouth for several days. He was expected back any minute.

Shortly before midnight Blossom's patience was rewarded and from his hideout in the rhododendrons beside the big wrought-iron gates he was able to get a clear view of the occupants of the big car as it swung into the drive. Prentice, whom he knew by sight, was driving and beside him sat a very pretty girl with fair hair. The back seat was occupied by another couple. Blossom reported that the owner of Blagthorpe had arrived 'with a nice little bit of muff', and John slept better that night.

The next day his captured Zeiss field-glasses stood him in good stead and from an observation post in a tree John had a clear view of the group of deck chairs on the lawn outside the French windows which appeared to open out from the drawing-room of Blagthorpe Hall. At about twelve o'clock a butler came out with a tray of bottles and glasses and placed them on a small table: the stage was set for the pre-luncheon cocktail. John shifted his position slightly and waited.

The unknown couple came out first, then came Carole followed closely by Prentice. John was glued to the eye-pieces. Carole looked wonderful, her hair was shining in the sunlight and she tossed it out of her eyes as she laughed at something Prentice said. She was wearing a bright green shirt and a white pleated skirt: she had a beautiful figure and moved with a sensual grace. She seemed very attentive to Prentice, holding on to his arm and laughing up at him. John could not see her eyes, but he knew how provocative they could be, and a wave of resentment swept over him at the thought of Prentice having her all to himself. He watched her every move through the glasses and prayed that she would feel the force of his thoughts reaching out to her on the green lawn.

Then, as if in answer to his prayer, he saw her, still holding on to Prentice's arm, turn round and face the camp. She pointed directly at John. He drew back instinctively. Although over a quarter of a mile separated them, for one uncanny moment he felt as if she were looking right into his eyes. He did not want to be caught spying. Prentice turned back to the table and busied himself mixing the drinks, but for a long while the slim blonde girl stood staring intently towards the camp.

The party remained on the lawn for perhaps half an hour and during that time John never took the glasses from his eyes. When they finally stood up to go inside he watched with minute attention: he saw Prentice slip his arm round the girl's small waist and together they disappeared through the big windows. John swallowed with disgust.

He climbed down from the tree to find the faithful Blossom waiting at the foot of it. Long since taken into full confidence, he was bursting with information.

'I've 'ad another chat with my young lady, sir, and the followin' is the situation . . . the three guests are all members of a theatrical troupe from Bournemouth . . . they will be stayin' till tomorrer lunch time and the fair 'aired one you fancy is called Carole Parker . . . er—my young lady reports that Sir Arthur Prentice seems to fancy 'er too.'

There were further details of the sort to which housemaids have special access, but these Blossom did not impart. Being a sensible man he saw no point in sowing the seeds of disillusionment so early in the proceedings.

John brushed some pieces of lichen from his trousers and pulled some twigs out of his hair. 'Do you think your friend at the house could slip Miss Parker a note?'

'That she could, sir, and furthermore, I've already warned 'er to be prepared for that kind o' duty.' He handed his officer a pink Royal Corps of Signals message pad and a stub of pencil.

John grinned. After considering several different approaches, he settled for a straightforward statement of facts.

'Dear Miss P.:
   1. There is a place called The Grotto on the far side of

Ten Acre Lake. (It's a sort of waterfall and rock
garden combined and is very easy to find once you
have arrived at the lake.)
2. There is a path at the far corner of the tennis court
which leads through the wood to this lake.
3. The tennis court is just beyond the lawn where you
were having a drink before lunch.
4. The grotto is very beautiful.
5. It is open twenty-four hours a day.
6. Please come.

The Goat.'

As soon as Blossom had left on his errand of mercy, John
went to the grotto. At first he felt sure she would come, but
as the time dragged slowly by, he began to feel less confident
till at last his watch told him it was almost five o'clock and
his heart descended to his boots.

He had spent the time visualizing just how she would come,
how he would first see her walking down the path, looking
out across the lake and searching for the grotto—in his
imagination, he had followed her as she walked round the
far side and he had rehearsed a hundred times what he was
going to say to her when she finally arrived. He was going to
be gay and lighthearted, to put her at her ease. He would
suggest a little walk perhaps. He put one foot on a low rock
wall and stared moodily down at some small perch sunning
themselves in the sandy shallows a few feet below him. His
thoughts took a defeatist turn . . . quite obviously she had
never had any intention of showing up . . . what a mug he
had been to send that note . . . at this moment it was probably being read out at the tea-table . . . he could almost
hear the derisive and condescending laughter . . . he hated
them all . . . the fat, common face of Prentice, the other
couple, too, he had no idea what they looked like, really, but
in his imagination he saw a slimy blue-jowled Shaftesbury
Avenue type of man and a frizzy-haired chorus girl with an
over-painted mouth and a shrill laugh. He started to build his
mental defences. . . . Anyway Carole Parker is not so hot,

she must be pretty cheap to go about with ghastly people like that . . . she's probably been having an affair with Prentice anyway—Oh, no! I'm really well out of the whole thing . . . why should I want to be mixed up with a tough little actress anyway? He heard a sound behind him and turned his head. Carole stood at the entrance to the grotto, the afternoon sun was backlighting her lovely hair and making a transparency of her white skirt. For a second they stood, looking into each other's eyes and then with a little breathless sound she was in his arms.

John kissed her full and long: her mouth went soft and her lips parted slightly in an expert way, her body pressed against his and seemed to fit there. At long last she pulled her mouth from his, returned it again for one brief second, then snuggled the top of her head beneath his chin.

'I knew it . . . I knew it the first moment I saw you lying on the pavement with that awful smelly rug all over you. . . . I knew it when my knees went all funny as I said good night . . . Oh! darling, things like this just don't happen to me.'

'Nor me . . . nor me,' murmured John.

They kissed again and now the tip of her tongue ran round the inside of his lips: when she pulled back her head to look up at him her eyes were bright and wet-looking. He lifted her up then, and carried her to a little grassy slope, lush and inviting, that lay between the azalea bushes. Her arms were about his neck and her lips stayed on his as he carried her.

Later they lay side by side and hand in hand and the shadows crept towards them over the grass. Carole turned on her side and kissed the tip of his nose. 'Give me a cigarette, darling. I have to pull myself together.'

CHAPTER THREE

JOHN'S LOVE AFFAIR with Carole was handicapped by two things. First, her season in Bournemouth ended with the advent of October and she returned to London to open in a musical comedy at the Adelphi: second, as had clearly been the colonel's intention in the first place, he had to be orderly officer every other day, and was therefore more or less chained to the camp. Nevertheless he made his way to London several times and Carole's little flat in Kent Terrace, Regent's Park, became the scene of many a chilly departure in the small hours of the morning to be followed by a desperate dash to Paddington Station and a falling gummy-eyed into the guard's van of the milk train that would deliver him back in time to inspect the soldiers' breakfasts in the draughty mess hall beneath the now yellowing trees.

Their month of penance was almost completed when a further occurrence very nearly sent John and Oglethorpe back for a further period of incarceration.

It was a Saturday afternoon and once again it was John's turn for extra duty. Oglethorpe was the only other occupant of the mess and together they were dealing in a desultory sort of way with a bottle of vintage port. Suddenly a strange major sporting a General Staff armband stepped into the hut.

'Where is the orderly officer?' he asked.

'Here, sir,' said John.

'The new area commander is outside and wants to see over the camp.'

John grabbed his forage cap and made for the door in the wake of the stranger.

Outside was a most impressive sight. The general, a gaunt, cadaverous type of ex-cavalryman, was standing surrounded by a court of brigadiers and full colonels: all had notebooks, pencils and purposeful expressions. John shuddered and saluted the General.

'Here is the orderly officer, sir,' said the major.

42

'Good afternoon,' said the general briskly.

'Good afternoon, sir,' said John.

'Is the camp commandant here?'

'No, sir . . . I believe he and the adjutant went to play golf.'

'H'm. . . . Well you'll do. . . . Show me round.'

'I beg your pardon, sir?'

'Don't gape at me. . . . Show me round the camp . . . I want to see it.'

'Oh, yes, sir,' said John and then in an explanatory vein as they moved off. 'Er . . . there is nothing much going on this afternoon, sir. Saturday afternoon is left free . . . I mean there are no parades or classes to see.'

The general looked at him patronizingly. 'I don't like set pieces, young man. I like to inspect the units under my command when they do *not* expect me . . . in that way I see what I want to see and not what is put on specially to impress me. Do you understand?'

'Yes, sir.'

John felt that this was very intelligent; he decided to be bright too.

'The way they don't do in Russia, sir?'

'What's that?'

'I mean the tourists in Russia only see things laid on by the boys in the Kremlin, don't they, sir? I mean they never get a chance to sort of pop down and look at the slums and things.'

The general did not answer, he just shot John a quick glance.

John wished he hadn't had so much port and hoped desperately he would be able to answer the many technical questions which he knew would be coming his way. Later they did come, but he acquitted himself fairly well, and as the afternoon wore on every nook and cranny was poked into; men in various stages of Saturday afternoon undress were questioned; vehicles and radio equipment were inspected and checked; ammunition stores were opened and closed. John had only one bad moment and that was when Trooper Blossom, luckily unnoticed, passed quite close to them carrying a hare. The general's staff, like foxhounds, feathered about the buildings, questing and seeking everywhere: pencils flew across the buff-coloured army notebooks.

The general seemed well pleased. Suddenly he looked across the grass field that did duty as a parade ground and raised his eyebrows.

'Who is that officer over there?'

John turned and saw the unmistakable figure of Oglethorpe slinking from the cook-house: his friend had obviously been organizing a little last minute spit and polish in the one department for which he, as messing officer, was directly responsible.

'Oglethorpe, sir, he is the messing officer. . . . Do you want to see him, sir?'

'Yes.'

'Mr. Oglethorpe,' called John.

Oglethorpe ambled over and unloosed an elaborate salute in the general direction of the general. To John's practised eye is was obvious that the bottle of port which they had been sharing together and which he had last seen half-full must now very definitely be among the empties.

The general was not so observant; by now he was in an affable mood.

'Good afternoon, Oglethorpe. . . . Hamilton here has been conducting a Cook's Tour. Perhaps you would take us round your section—that is the messing. Am I not right?'

'Too true, sir,' said Oglethorpe, 'Too true. . . . Pray follow me.' With a headwaiter's bow he led the way towards the mess hall. The general frowned a little, but followed.

John waited in some apprehension till they emerged again but things seemed to be going quite well.

'Thank you,' he heard the general saying, 'that is very good. You seem to have that running very well.'

'Thank you for coming, sir,' said Oglethorpe with another *maître d'hôtel* inclination of the head.

The general's frown deepened, but Oglethorpe's expression was guileless.

'Well, Hamilton, I suppose that's all you have to show me?'

John, with great relief, was framing an affirmative answer when an elderly full colonel, who looked like a dentist, ruffled the pages of his notebook. 'We haven't been shown buildings 32 and 33, yet, general,' he piped.

'Oh . . . where are they?'

The staff major indicated two wooden sheds barely visible behind a thicket of laurel bushes.

'That must be them over there, sir.'

'Come along then, Hamilton . . . show us the way.'

John for the life of him could not remember ever having seen those particular buildings before. As the little procession walked round the laurels he racked his brains—what could they be? Surely they had covered everything usually seen in a camp by now? He was grateful that Oglethorpe had joined the little band and would now be at his side in case of emergency, but he still felt uncomfortably like Sidney Carton mounting the scaffold at the end of 'A Tale of Two Cities'. The dreaded question came.

'Well, what is that building, Hamilton?'

John looked helplessly at Oglethorpe who framed his lips with what John took to be the word LIBRARY. He sighed with relief.

'That is the library, sir.'

'Ah, good! Let's have a look at it.'

The concourse moved towards the long shed and through the open door, but it was soon painfully obvious to all that far from being a library it was in fact—the lavatory. Rows of feet were protruding beneath doors: khaki trousers and grey woollen army pants encircled ankles: John panicked, and heard himself ask in a loud voice:

'Any complaints?'

The occupants of the stalls, not knowing that the place was full of members of the General Staff, yelled their replies to this tactless question. The general beat a hasty retreat. Once outside he turned on John with a dreadful look.

'I thought you said that was the library?'

45

'Terribly sorry, sir . . . I . . . er . . .' He had a brain wave. . . . 'That is the men's nickname for the place, sir . . . er . . . quite a lot of reading goes on in there, actually.' He accompanied this statement with a sickly grin.

The general glared at him. 'Oh God,' thought John, 'still one more building and in a minute the man is going to ask me what is in *that*.' He did.

At first John looked helplessly at the squat wooden structure, then waves of relief swept over him: he wanted to wring the general's hand, to dance, to sing—for above the door in bold red letters a foot high were the words, 'FIRE HOUSE'.

'The fire engine, sir,' he answered with the air of a man laying down five aces.

'Get it out.'

John's world began to crumble. Who had the key?

'Yes, sir.' He played for time. 'It's not a very special model . . . I don't know if you want. . . .'

There was now a hint of steel in the general's voice.

'Get it out.'

'Yes, sir.'

It had to be done then, but how? Oglethorpe, he noticed, had suddenly become interested in something in the far distance; he was also humming quietly to himself. This was too much for John: if he was going to sink, then Oglethorpe should go down with him. John turned to him.

'Mr. Oglethorpe, the general wants to see the fire engine. . . . Get it out, please.'

Oglethorpe's shocked surprise was so comic that in spite of the thinness of the military ice upon which he was now skating John felt the laughter welling up inside him: he felt much better, too, as he saw the faces of the general and his staff now swing towards Oglethorpe. But he had under-rated his man: his partner in crime was, once the initial shock had worn off, quite equal to the occasion. With tremendous authority the tall man beckoned to the orderly sergeant who had been hovering in the background.

'Sergeant Fulsome.'

46

'Sir.'

'The fire engine—get it out.'

Sergeant Fulsome's face was at first, by the very baseness of this action, blasted of all expression, but he too rallied, and with a 'two can play at this game' expression, he yelled to a shadowy figure in the middle distance.

'Corporal Hodgkinson.'

'Sarnt?'

'Get the fire engine out.'

Like the chain concussion set up by the shunting of a goods train the cry was taken up round the camp.

'Get the fire engine out . . . get the fire engine out . . . get the fire engine out,' till finally it died away into silence.

The general by now was very, very angry: he had turned an ugly mauve.

John thought it best to fill in time while someone was looking for the key and certainly it would seem that the less opportunity the general had to ponder upon what might happen to the camp in case of fire, the better. . . .

'It's a very good engine really, sir,' he opened chattily.

Oglethorpe took up the cue.

'Yes, sir, it's got a lot of brass on it and a big coil of hose stuck on the back.'

John tried desperately to remember some of the finer points of fire engines and added rather hopefully, 'And it's got Merryweather and Co. written on the front, too.'

The general began to hop up and down.

'Get it out,' he roared.

His staff edged nervously away from him, as people do when someone starts shouting and making a scene in the National Gallery.

'Yes, sir,' John looked desperately round and saw to his relief that a man from the quartermaster's stores was approaching at high speed. So great was his relief that he developed a sudden great love for the fire engine and started once more to enumerate its achievements and to sing its praises.

47

'It put out a big fire in the village a short while ago, sir.'

Oglethorpe joined in again. 'Oh, yes, sir, undoubtedly our engine saved considerable loss of life. . . .'

'To say nothing of property,' added John.

'To say nothing of property,' repeated Oglethorpe.

'Get it out,' stamped the general. His eyes had become bloodshot—like a runaway horse.

The man from the quartermaster's store dashed up, and John with a feeling of pleasurable anticipation put out his hand for the key. He was handed—a screwdriver.

'Sorry, sir, key can't be located, sir,' said the man.

The general made a noise like boiling water—his face had turned a mottled grey, but the ignominious task had to be done: John turned to Sergeant Fulsome.

'Take the lock off,' he said in a toneless voice.

While this embarrassing operation was in progress, he turned once more to the area commander.

'Another good point about this particular engine . . .' he got no further.

'Don't talk any more . . . just get it out.' These last words were said in the 'water for the love of Allah' tone—a sort of croak—the man was at the end of his tether.

At last the lock was off—the sergeant moved back—the staff crowded forward—John looked at the general: the general stared bleakly back.

John stepped up to the door and applied a little trial pressure. . . . Yes! it would open nicely now . . . he swallowed nervously and turned what he hoped was a bright and confident countenance towards the general, then like the major-domo of an embassy, he announced:

'Sir—the fire-engine. . . .'

With quite a flourish he gave the double doors a push and they creaked open. A bat flew out. John paled and peered into the gloomy interior: he was aghast at what he saw—no shiny red engine stood there, with Merryweather and Co. written on its front; instead, leaning against the far wall, their tyres flat, their rims rusty, were two very old bicycles—

48

women's bicycles: a bucket of hard and cracked whitewash stood in one corner and in the middle of the floor upon a pile of broken flower pots lay an old Christmas tree with some battered and yellow ornaments still upon it.

The general turned on his heel. Without a word he strode away. John noticed that the back of his neck looked quite swollen.

The month of alternate orderly officer was almost up and the leaves were nearly all off the trees. If there had been any unpleasant repercussions from the fire engine episode, then they must have descended on the long-suffering head of the colonel and there been absorbed; at any rate John heard no more about it.

One Saturday night, after the theatre, Carole motored down for a week-end. John found a room in a nearby farmhouse, but the expedition was not quite the success he had expected it to be—she did not seem to fit into the countryside as well as she had before. Her tweed suit was a little too loud; her makeup seemed thicker than usual and it was with a sense of shock that John realized that her lovely corn-coloured hair had in reality been most skilfully bleached: however, these little things were quickly forgotten when they were together in the warmth and comfort of the room.

They went for a long walk together on Sunday afternoon and as they turned back towards the farmhouse the hedgerows stood out blackly in the thin frosty air. Blue smoke was spiralling straight up from the cottage chimneys and the wood pigeons were coming into the big woods to roost after feasting on beechnuts at their favourite day-time haunts. The golden Bath stone of the buildings in the villages turned a lovely pale yellow as the ground mists rose to join the smoke from a score of garden bonfires. John breathed deeply, savouring the smell of the burning leaves, and feeling the first wintry sting in his nostrils. His feet rang on the rough country road. He was utterly content. 'God,' he thought to himself, 'how I love this.'

'God,' said Carole out loud, 'how I would hate to live in the country . . . it's all right for a week-end with you, darling, but I'd loathe it as a steady diet.'

John didn't say anything just then, but it was there, unmistakable and no bigger than a man's hand, the first small cloud in the sky of his contentment: the beginning of his disenchantment.

That evening after supper they sat with the farmer and his wife in the big cosy kitchen where they had been invited to drink some excellent home-made cowslip wine. As John heard Carole addressed as 'Mrs. Hamilton' he felt as though he were cheating at cards; something of his feelings must have shown in his face because Carole mentioned it as soon as they were upstairs.

'Why did you look so grumpy down there, darling?'

'I felt guilty lying to those sweet people about us being married, that's all.'

She seemed irritated. 'Well, you shouldn't. . . . I bet they know we aren't anyway, and besides it's none of their damned business.'

He left it at that. They had never had an argument, and he had no intention of provoking one now. He changed the subject.

'Tell me more about the play. . . . You're really pleased with it?'

'Well, of course. Jennifer is a frightful bitch and tries to upstage me all the time and treads on my lines, but I don't let her get away with it. . . . She has always had affairs with her leading men and now she's jealous of me because Roger is always coming into my room and gossiping. The joke is, of course, that Roger is a roaring queen and has a beau in a strong man act at the Palladium: but she's so dumb she still keeps on trying and Roger comes and tells me all about it. Oh, you'll love Roger.'

'I very much doubt it.'

'He'll probably make a pass at you, darling, then *I* shall be jealous. . . .' She prattled on. 'There's a scene in the second act that I have with Jennifer and it never fails that every time I make my exit, I get a round.'

'Get around. Where?'

'A round of applause, stupid, and Jennifer is left there with egg on her face and it makes her furious.'

He kissed the back of her neck. 'I wonder what you'll be like when you are a star. You'll probably be a frightful bitch, too. If you are, I'll smack your bottom.'

'I'd love that.'

When the light was out and he felt the touch of her satin skin down the whole length of his body, he forgot that her incessant theatre shop bored him. He forgot everything.

One evening at the beginning of December the colonel sent for John. He never entered the orderly room without a feeling of impending doom. But this time, as he opened the door, he found the commanding officer in a jovial, even paternal, mood.

'Ah! Come in, Hamilton, and don't look so guilty. . . . You haven't done anything wrong for once as far as I know, though I don't doubt you've been doing plenty I haven't heard about. Ha! . . . ha! . . . ha!'

'Ha! . . . ha! . . . ha! . . .' said John.

The colonel walked over from behind his desk and looked out into the darkness for a minute before he spoke.

'In another month or six weeks you'll be a civilian. Have you made up your mind what you are going to do? Of course, it's none of my business, but I don't like the idea of someone your age . . . how old are you?'

'Twenty-five, sir.'

'Twenty-five, going out into the world with no plans and no money. . . . Have you got any money?'

'No, sir. I live on my pay.'

'You live on your pay? Well, you should get a gratuity of about a hundred and fifty pounds, but that won't get you far.'

The colonel's eyes twinkled. 'You don't want to stay on in the army by any chance, do you?'

'No, sir. I don't somehow think I would be any good at peace-time soldiering. . . . Do you?'

'Confidentially, no, but it is my duty to ask all officers before they leave; so there it is—consider yourself asked.'

'I thought I might get a job in the country somewhere learning to farm,' said John vaguely. 'I love the country, sir. I could never settle down in an office.'

'No, I don't think I could, either,' said the Colonel quietly.

There was an awkward pause. The colonel cleared his throat. 'Well, there it is, Hamilton, you'll soon be a civilian and if there is anything I can do to help you get settled, or if you think I can give you any good advice, don't hesitate to come and see me. Good night.'

'Good night, sir.'

Outside, John pondered upon this strange interview and realized that in his bluff soldier's way the colonel had been trying to be fatherly; his heart warmed towards his superior officer, and he even had the grace to feel another pang of remorse over the little blonde French wife.

At that moment Blossom approached.

'Any trouble, sir?'

'No thanks, Blossom. Everything's under control.'

'Well, that's a relief anyway. I 'eard you'd been sent for and I says to meself—'ere we go for another little dose of extra orderly dog.'

They walked together down the muddy track through the camp and Blossom continued.

'I've just about cleaned out 'is Nib's partridges, thanks to a new net a pal o' mine sent me down from Norfolk, but there's still a lot o' pheasants and believe it or not that river's full o' salmon,' he sucked his teeth reflectively. 'I've 'ad 'em out of the 'ampshire *Avon* and the *Dart* in Devon, but I'd like to get 'old of a salmon in Somerset. Of course, the only way I can get to them is wiv a little touch o' dynamite. Well, we'll 'ave to leave that till just before we are pullin' out of 'ere for good.'

Blossom's voice grew lyrical. 'Marvellous stuff that 'igh

explosive . . . marvellous stuff . . . I remember, sir, in one of them there Baedeker raids. Poor old Norwich bought it proper. I was there on leave. There was a lovely little boy about five years old lived in our street, curly 'aired little bastard 'e was, wiv bloody great blue eyes like bleedin' saucers . . . well when they found 'im 'e'd been stretched out about fifteen feet long . . . marvellous, wasn't it, sir?'

At the vehicle park they parted.

John stood alone for a while beside a huge armoured car, one of the few still kept at the camp for training purposes. With a start he saw in the bright moonlight that it was 'Mae West.'

Memories crowded in upon him . . . Dunkirk, a smoking holocaust with men waist deep in the Channel patiently waiting their turn to be signalled aboard the *Island Queen* or one of the other pleasure craft that had raced, sailed or even rowed across from England to save a British Army from utter destruction. As he stood quietly under the trees he heard again the jokes of men filling their minds with trivialities in order to stifle the ever-present dread that something would happen to prevent them from being pulled on board to safety.

'If I'd known it was goin' to be like this, mate, I'd 'ave brought me wife and kids,' said one.

'Oh, 'ow I like to be beside the seaside,' sang another.

' 'and me a shrimpin' net, there's somethin' ticklin' me toes,' said a third.

Corporal Hamilton, Sergeant Hamilton, Second Lieutenant Hamilton—all passed before his eyes. The desert battles came and went. The desert! . . . 'miles and miles of dung-coloured austerity, Oglethorpe had called it! Standing there under the safe and peaceful chestnut trees he felt again the unbearable heat of the African sun blazing down from a brassy sky. 'Tommy Cookers!' they had called out to some Tank Corps men who passed them in their newly arrived Shermans—they had had a bad reputation for catching fire when they were hit, those Shermans.

The ebb and flow of those battles came to him again: he saw the great chase of the routed Africa Corps. . . . 'Good hunting,' Monty had said.

Back to England, then, to train for the final assault across the Channel: back to a little England the size of the state of Idaho, trying manfully to digest a million and a half young men from every State in the Union.

He saw Rainbow Corner, and Piccadilly Circus and was inspired afresh. American G.I.s in their myriads, Norwegians, Free French, Belgians, Czechs, Dutch, Poles, all joined with men from every corner of the British Isles and Commonwealth —it could not fail! Nor did it.

He watched once more as the blackened-faced paratroopers and glider troops climbed aboard—tough, gay men who painted No. 13 on the fuselage of their machines in a final gesture of bravado: eight hours before D-day.

He remembered supervising the waterproofing and loading of his own Troop. He glanced up at 'Mae West' and thought again of Davis, her driver, pushing his kit on board.

'What have you got in that parcel, Davis?'

'That's me dartboard, sir.'

'What the hell do you want to take a dartboard for?'

'Well, we've got to 'ave something to do when we get the other side, 'aven't we, sir?'

He grinned anew at the thought—'something to do when we get the other side'—they had had plenty! Somewhere in the woods behind him he heard a night bird call and remembered how the nightingales that first night in Normandy had refused to be silenced by the sounds of D-day. The agony of the slugging match at Caen with four-fifths of the German armour concentrated against the British: the sudden relief as the American Third Army broke out on the right: another chase of a defeated German Army. . . . 'Good hunting,' Monty had said again.

Brussels, wild with joy, was all round him in the darkness now. The smiling, waving thousands were dancing in the streets.

54

The clean Dutch farms came clearly into his vision and the flooded, muddy, slushy, seemingly endless winter of 1944 passed before him with its series of frustrating, rain-soaked and costly battles. The casualties had been heavy, but in common with all fighting men he had become hardened to the sudden disappearance of friends and companions. Replacements came up and the army churned forward. 'The last big heave,' Winston had growled. The air had filled with noise as the hundreds upon hundreds of troop carriers and gliders had crossed the Rhine, then the broad river was flowing beneath a barge carrying 'C' Troop itself. . . . 'Good hunting,' Monty had called for the last time.

It didn't seem possible that the end had come only six short months ago: it all seemed, now, to belong to a different age.

John looked at 'Mae West' as she stood there, ghost-like, in the moonlight. Her gun was silver-tipped: she looked very proud and erect. He put out a hand and touched her—he felt absurdly sentimental.

On the 8th of December, 1945, Mr. John Hamilton walked out of the demobilization centre at Chelsea Barracks with a cheque for £150 in his pocket. In his hand was a chit entitling him to draw from the clothing centre at Olympia:—one suit; one pair shoes; two pairs socks; two shirts; four collars; one tie; one hat; one overcoat or waterproof and one civilian ration book.

He presented himself at Olympia and stood in line for a considerable time before he was able to make his choice—the shoes and socks would come in useful. But the rest—the dreadful austerity suit (no flaps, no cuffs, no turn-ups), the badly made shirts, the ghastly tie, the appalling hat apparently made of three-ply wood and the waterproof which the attendant had confidentially described as 'being all right, provided it doesn't rain'—these he sold in the street outside to a little man with a barrow above which conspicuously displayed upon a board was a set tariff for the various articles. To make even this simple transaction John had to stand in a queue—two queues in two hours!—he was not at all sure that he liked being a civilian. He decided to go and see Carole.

On the way to Kent Terrace he bought a bottle of champagne with which to celebrate. Although it was almost midday when he arrived, Carole was still in bed; so they drank the warm wine out of a tooth tumbler. It was matinée day, so Carole had to get up and dash to the theatre at half-past one, but before she went she mentioned quite casually that she was going to stay with Arthur Prentice the following week-end at Blagthorpe: Carole excused this action to John by saying that she hoped to wheedle Prentice into financing a play for her.

'You wouldn't want me to miss a chance like that, would you, darling?'

'No, of course not—er—does it mean you have to sleep with him?'

Carole laughed her gay, easy laugh but there was a certain wariness in her eye.

'That's the old-fashioned way of raising money. Anyway, if you don't trust me, why don't you come down and stay too. He told me to bring anyone I liked—you could keep an eye on me.'

John liked this idea, not only for the more obvious reasons, but also because he had several things to pick up which he had left behind at the camp.

So it was arranged, and after the curtain came down on Saturday night John went backstage to Carole's dressing-room. He had seen the show several times before, but he never failed to get a thrill when Carole made her entrance on to the stage. She did not have a very good part, but it was the second lead and she sang and danced her way through it with an easy charm and a clear voice. Some women can walk into a room full of people and every man present will immediately be aware of them. Carole had this quality in real life; on the stage it was magnified a hundred times, and John always felt a possessive delight when he watched the faces of the men in the audience; every male eye in the house would be upon her.

The usual twittering crowd of acquaintances came back-stage after the show.

'Darling, you were wonderful . . . you acted Jennifer Joy right off the stage . . . we loved your songs . . . you were wonderful . . . wonderful . . . wonderful."

Most of the visitors were theatre folk with other friends and acquaintances in the cast so, after a while, the mass insincerity flowed out of Carole's room and continued down the line of dressing-rooms. John helped himself to a large whisky and soda and sat in the wash-basin till the last 'wonderful' had died away.

'What a bore all those people are,' sighed Carole when at last they were alone. But John knew they didn't bore her and guessed rightly that they never would.

Sir Arthur Prentice was waiting up for them when at one o'clock in the morning his Bentley deposited John and Carole on the doorstep of Blagthorpe. He eyed John with obvious misgivings, but offered him a nightcap and some sandwiches before showing him his room.

Any hopes which John might have entertained about the sleeping arrangements at Blagthorpe were quickly dispelled when he realized that in order to reach Carole he would have to navigate the entire length of the enormous house in total darkness with a very fair chance of ending up in the wrong bed at the end of the journey.

The next morning he rose early and walked down towards the familiar huts beneath the trees: Blossom was overjoyed.

'Wot a bit o' luck seein' you again, sir. It's me last day today, of course, I 'ave some unfinished business to tidy up 'ere, then it's up to good old Chelsea Barricks termorrer and *Mr.* Blossom it'll be from then on. Now don't forget if you should ever want me for anythin', sir, Alf Perkins, 'e's the landlord of 'The Rose Revived' at Diss—'e'll always pass the word along.'

Besides Carole and John there were three other house guests, two rather dim middle-aged Americans—Mr. and Mrs. Elmer S. Dimbleby—and a nondescript young Stock Exchange sportsman who talked incessant and complete rubbish on every subject to do with the countryside.

Mr. Dimbleby was the founder and head of the famous Dimbleby Dog Food Corp.: he was full of information on the subject.

'Yes, sir,' he told the little pre-lunch circle, 'I woke up one morning and I said to myself, "Elmer Dimbleby," I said, "there's a lot of money to be made out of dog food," and I started right in there and then to make it.'

He smiled at Clarice, his wife.

'Mrs. Dimbleby and I have been married now for twenty-two years—without a cross word.'

Mrs. Dimbleby beamed through her pince-nez and the rest contributed polite murmurs.

'. . . and we reckon that the dog food did it.'

'Why,' continued Mr. Dimbleby, 'we were so busy as young folks collecting the neighbours' scraps and titbits and working out different ways of binding them together that we never did have time to disagree over family matters. Now we have a Dimbleby plant in every State in the Union and the greatest distribution organization of its sort in the world. . . .'

Mr. Dimbleby warmed to his work.

'. . . We have special refrigerator cars on all the railroads and we have horsemeat buyers in every area. Yes, sir, it took a lot of organization to bring it to a point where over 15,000 veterinaries all over the country telephone our local representative the moment a horse gets sick. From then on that horse is tabbed and watched, and sooner or later . . . well . . .'

He spread his hands in a gesture.

'. . . there's a hell of a lot of competition in the horsemeat business and by getting in there early we have been able to cut costs to a point where we can deliver to your doorstep an

58

ice-cold, gift-wrapped and dated package of dog food for just 28 cents a pound.'

An announcement that lunch was ready cut short further dutiful cluckings of appreciation and wonder from the other guests; they filed into the dining-room.

John was placed next to Mrs. Dimbleby, and as soon as he was seated she took up where Mr. Dimbleby had left off.

'Mr. Dimbleby,' she said, 'is very excited because *Fortune Magazine* is doing an article on him next month. It's going to be called Kibble Kingdom. . . . Don't you think that's just wonderful?'

John thought it was just awful, but he said, 'It must be very exciting to know that so many dogs in the world are grateful to you and Mr. Dimbleby.'

Carole gave him a stony look, which he pretended not to see: Mrs. Dimbleby was just hitting her stride.

'Do you know,' she continued, 'when I've been walking along with Mr. Dimbleby back home many is the time that I have been positive that dogs knew him and were grateful for all he had done for them. . . . It seems almost as though he had an aura round him—the little fellows just seem to sense it.'

John helped himself liberally to roast beef and said, without daring to look in Carole's direction:

'How do you advertise the dog food? Do you have little posters on convenient places for dogs to notice them . . . lamp posts and trees, and things like that?'

Mrs. Dimbleby didn't get it; she put down her knife and fork, her eyes shone behind the pince-nez—she leaned across the table—

'Go ahead, Elmer, you tell.'

Mr. Dimbleby cleared his throat.

'Well folks, Mrs. Dimbleby and I came to Europe for one reason . . . for one great reason . . . and yesterday we concluded the deal.' He looked proudly round the table. 'We now own,' he paused dramatically, "Sledmere, Queen of England".'

The long silence which greeted this mysterious announcement was finally broken by the stockbroker sportsman.

'Congratulations, that is a great horse,' he said.

'Sledmere, Queen of England,' said Mr. Dimbleby fixing the unfortunate young man with a withering look, 'is an English bulldog. In fact, I might go as far as to say that she is THE English bulldog.'

John couldn't resist it. He put on an innocent expression.

'Surely the female of bulldog would be bullbitch, wouldn't it?'

He could feel Carole's eyes boring into him. Sir Arthur Prentice at the end of the table coughed.

'That's very interesting, Dimbleby. Does the purchase of this dog have any connection with your business?'

'Why sure it does!' cried Mr. and Mrs. Dimbleby in unison.

'Please, Clarice, I'll tell,' said Mr. Dimbleby, sternly.

'Very well, Elmer.'

Mrs. Dimbleby sighed and went on with her lunch with an aggrieved expression. Mr. Dimbleby continued:

'My whole purpose in buying the "Queen of England" was so that we could have a whole new publicity campaign for our product starting in the New Year. All over the country we will have big twenty-four sheet posters with her picture on it, and a big splash caption: "THE QUEEN OF ENGLAND EATS DIMBLEBY'S DOG FOOD".'

'I think it might be nice to check with Buckingham Palace first,' murmured John as he bent over his plate.

Suddenly there was a deafening explosion. The French windows were blown in with a crash of broken glass: the butler dropped the roast beef on the floor and Mrs. Dimbleby's pince-nez fell into the mashed potatoes.

John shaking with laughter acted with considerable aplomb.

'Quick, under the table everyone,' he shouted.

The lunch guests, the butler and the maid, who miraculously still balanced a dish of brussels sprouts, all flung themselves to the ground. Arthur Prentice was white and shaking with fear.

'What is it, Hamilton? Oh, whatever is it?' he squeaked.

'Was it a bomb?' asked Carole.

The others were huddled together.

'Yes, I think so,' said John, trying to keep a straight face. 'We'd better stay here for a few minutes—in case any more go off.'

'Who is bombing us?' croaked Prentice.

'I can't imagine,' said John '. . . it might be an old German one that's been here without anyone knowing it had even been dropped. They will be going off all over the country for years.'

'Did they drop many round here?' whispered Mr. Dimbleby.

'No, thank God,' said their host. 'They used to fly over here on their way to London though.'

'Well, that's probably it,' said John. 'They unloaded one here one night and it didn't go off—you all stay here and I'll go out and see what's happening.'

'Do be careful,' said Prentice.

'Yes, do,' echoed Mr. Dimbleby between pale lips.

John ran out, and raced straight across the lawn to the river. The tale there was plainly told: the once clear water was now a cloudy yellow, trailing weed hung in the nearby bushes and the unmistakable smell of cordite was in the air. John composed his expression and walked slowly back to the dining-room.

'It's all right, everybody. You can come out now.'

Scared faces appeared from beneath the table, making a human fringe to the white tablecloth. Arthur Prentice was much braver now. . . . 'I don't know why you ordered us all under the table like that, Hamilton. It wasn't very close anyway.'

'What was it, Mr. Hamilton?' asked Dimbleby as he settled himself once more in his seat.

'Just as I thought,' said John, 'an unexploded bomb that had fallen in the stream sometime during the war.' He turned to Prentice. 'Must have been at the bottom of the big pool.'

'Did it kill any of my salmon?' asked Prentice.

'There are none floating about,' said John with truth.

After lunch a still shaky butler handed John a buff-coloured envelope. . . .

'This was sent up from the camp, sir.'

Inside John found the familiar pink message form of the Signal Corps. On the form was written: 'Today's bag: five large salmon; twelve small trout. D. Blossom, gamekeeper.'

For the rest of the week-end the subject of dog food was always just around the corner and during one of the many times it came out into the open John asked Mr. Dimbleby whether he intended purchasing any more well-known dogs during his European visit.

'Well, sir, I had intended to purchase the champion poodle of France, the champion St. Bernard of Switzerland and the champion Saluki of Afghanistan, then our publicity campaign would be along the lines of the one conducted by Ponds Cold Cream, but whereas Ponds use ladies with titles we would have dog-world royalty selling our product. But I shall have to make another trip in order to do that because I must take the Queen back at once so that my advertising branch can get to work on her right away. The big campaign starts January 1st. Mrs. Dimbleby is very disappointed as she had looked forward so much to visiting Paris and Rome and I had it in mind to pick up a few of those Impressionist pictures that everyone back home is collecting right now, though I don't reckon any of them can hold a candle to Grandma Moses, do you?'

'It might be funny if they tried,' said John, who was not really concentrating; in his mind a vague plan was forming. 'Who is your favourite Impressionist, Mr. Dimbleby?'

'Well this fellow Utrillo seems to have plenty on the ball with all that white paint and stuff. Mrs. Dimbleby thought one of those would look dandy in the bathroom. . . . Yes, it's a great disappointment to us both that we can't send the Queen back to the States alone, but someone must go with her and we have no one over here we could trust to do it for us—so I guess we're stuck with it.'

'I'll take her over for you,' John heard himself say.

Mr. and Mrs. Dimbleby were at first dumbfounded, then completely overjoyed at this suggestion: the rest of the day was spent in completing the arrangements.

John was to pick up the Queen in London on the following Wednesday morning: he would be sailing in the *Queen Elizabeth* and would arrive in New York four days before Christmas. The Dimblebys, who were nothing if not thoughtful, started writing a sheaf of letters of introduction to people who, they assured him, would be delighted at the prospect of a total stranger sharing their Christmas dinner with them. Then Mr. Dimbleby broached the subject of expenses.

'Mr. Hamilton, I cannot tell you how grateful we are to you for this magnificent gesture, and believe me, I don't want you to be out of pocket one red cent as a result of your kindness. I'll make all the arrangements for your travel and knowing how tough your British regulations are about taking pounds out of England, I'll have one thousand dollars put in your name at the Chase National Bank on 79th Street in New York City. . . . That way you'll be able to enjoy yourself during your visit. Of course, my Vice-President, Mr. Schumann, will meet you and take care of your hotel and anything else you may need. But this way you'll have a little spending money to get along with.'

John's brain reeled at the realization that for taking a dog on a free trip to New York he would be paid more than twice as much as his army gratuity after six years of war service.

When Carole cornered John alone, she was furious.

'I think the very least you could have done would have been to ask me first. After all I have done for you, I surely deserve some slight consideration.'

John was staggered by the onslaught.

'After all you have done for me?'

'Well, who brought you to Blagthorpe in the first place?'

'The War Office.'

She stamped her foot.

'That's typical. You make fun of everyone and everything. You were downright rude at lunch to the Americans and you

63

haven't addressed a civil word to Arthur since we came here. You've been perfectly odious.'

'In that case you ought to be very happy that I am going away for a while.'

She stamped her foot again and her eyes filled with tears. 'Oh, you're insufferable.'

John had a feeling of relief. He never had liked possessive women; they gave him claustrophobia. The spell which this one had cast over him was beginning to show definite signs of wear and tear. He smiled at her.

'I suppose we have now arrived at the point where I tell you how lovely you look when you are angry.'

Her voice was becoming shrill. 'I don't care what you tell me any more. You are spoilt and useless. . . . What have you ever done in your whole life?—Nothing!—for anybody!'

John let this pass.

'And now you have started sponging off Americans. . . . I think you are despicable and hateful. . . . I don't know why I wasted my time on you. . . .'

She waited for him to reply, but John said nothing; he stood looking at her with a little half smile. The silence became unbearable for Carole. She slammed out of the room. Later a maid came down with the news that she had retired to bed with a headache. John said farewell to his host and to the young man from the Stock Exchange whose name he had never quite caught, then, with the gratitude of the Dimblebys still ringing in his ears, he departed.

He dropped in at the camp on his way to the station and discovered that Trooper Blossom with a sack full of fish among his effects was also travelling up on the evening train. They left the camp for the last time and rode away together on the back of a truck.

Blossom was most interested in John's forthcoming trip with 'the Queen,' and also inquired tactfully about the romance with Carole. John looked at the wise leathery face and smiled.

64

'It is drawing peacefully to its close.'

After much fumbling in strange pockets (usually reserved for woodcock and snipe), Blossom produced a dreadful blackened old briar pipe. He lit it, and blew out a cloud of foul-smelling smoke before carefully pronouncing his judgment.

'That's good!' he said.

At Devizes John decided to leave the train so that he could see 'the Aunts' before his forthcoming trip: he had a funny hunch that he might be away for quite a long time.

As the train slowed up to make the stop he turned to say a final good-bye to this little soldier who would soon be plying once more his doubtful civilian trade. He remembered with warmth the loyalty, bravery and cheerful obedience which Blossom had unfailingly displayed during the past six years. The second and most heartbreaking of the desert retreats had been the supreme moment of their comradeship. All had seemed lost when Blossom had appeared with an enormous tin mug of scalding sugar-sweet tea.

"Ere, drink this, sir, it'll cheer you up. We'll come out of this orlrite. We weren't born in the good old English climate for nothin'. We're used to disappointments, we are. Why when we was kids and we 'ad a nice little old picnic all arranged for Saturday afternoon, as sure as fate it rained and the bleedin' picnic was put orf again. . . . This 'ere picnic's just been put orf, that's all. . . .'

The train jerked to a halt and John stepped down on to the platform. Blossom leaned out of the window: the two men shook hands and smiled: into both their heads came a voice out of the past, and simultaneously they spoke—'Good hunting.'

'The Aunts' had grown used, during the war years, to his sudden appearances and departures, so when John announced that he and a bulldog were travelling to New York it caused hardly a ripple on the surface of their calm. They inquired about his warm underwear, gave him a brandy flask for Christmas and went back to planting their tulip bulbs.

On the day John was to pick up 'the Queen', Oglethorpe, who had been demobilized a week earlier, came down from Norfolk to see him off.

After a luncheon at Wilton's, suitable to the occasion—they each had a dozen and a half of the finest Whitstable oysters and shared a delicious bottle of Hock—they proceeded to the seventh floor of the Dorchester Hotel. John knocked upon the door of Mr. Dimbleby's apartment.

All was in readiness—Mr. and Mrs. Dimbleby and 'Sledmere, Queen of England', were waiting for him. Oglethorpe was introduced and immediately launched into a lengthy dissertation on the finer points of bulldogs—a subject about which, it soon became apparent, he knew absolutely nothing.

The Queen herself looked to John's unpractised eye exactly like any other bulldog he had ever seen. He did not particularly like the breed, but as he felt he owed a certain amount to this particular beast, he approached her with a false smile and gently patted her on the head. The Queen looked up from the bone she was gnawing and fixed him with a dreadful red-rimmed eye.

'Good dog,' said John as an opening gambit.

The hackles on the Queen's back rose stiffly; she emitted a fearsome warning.

These preliminaries having been concluded, John retreated to the far end of the room and the dog turned once more to her interrupted grinding and crunching. Mr. Dimbleby laughed.

'Isn't she a character?'

'I hope she'll grow to like me,' said John, 'after all, we are going to spend a certain amount of time together.'

'Oh sure, you haven't a thing to worry about.'

John looked doubtfully across at the Queen.

'What does she eat?'

Mr. Dimbleby produced a sheaf of papers from a folder.

'Right here is her diet—every meal for every day from now until she arrives in New York. We have even worked out a couple of reserve days in case you run into bad weather and the ship runs behind schedule. You will notice that each day she is to have a little bit more of Dimbleby's Dog Food and a little bit less of the rest. Right now she only takes a few ounces daily, mixed in with the other food, but by the time you see the Ambrose Light Ship she will be eating it exclusively.' He paused and tapped another folder. 'Now . . . here is your ticket, and all the necessary papers, including her pedigree: as I told you, my Vice-President, Mr. Schumann, will meet you in New York.'

The few minutes of polite conversation which followed were occasionally marred by the fact that Oglethorpe insisted on referring to 'Sledmere, Queen of England' as 'the old bitch.'

The Dimblebys expressed again and again their gratitude to John, and Mrs. Dimbleby waxed almost coy on the subject of the clothes she would now have the opportunity to buy in Paris. Then the car that was to take John to Southampton arrived: the last good-byes were said.

John managed to persuade the dog to follow him out of the room by the simple method of showing her a lamb chop which he had thoughtfully brought with him in case of emergency.

Downstairs a large Rolls Royce awaited him in which the dog's luggage was already stowed. These paraphernalia included several spare collars and leads, some blankets, a most embarrassing dog's coat made from a Union Jack, and a package containing a dozen large tins of Dimbleby's Dog Food.

John and Oglethorpe sat in the back; the Queen sat placidly at their feet. They drove to Quennell's, where John picked up his own large suitcase containing most of his worldly goods and over a farewell glass of port Oglethorpe presented him with his latest invention—a small pigskin case inside which, in specially fitted green-beige slots, reposed a bottle of Scotch whisky, a horn mug and a large bottle of aspirin.

'That,' announced Oglethorpe with pride, 'is to be known as "the Dypsomaniac's Delight". . . . I am working on another little thing, too, which is designed to save thousands of officers' lives in the next war. It is a shoe lace, old man, on a spring . . . there is a small electric battery which is carried in the hip pocket and the top fly-button is in reality a switch. When some bloody fool says something ambitious like "over the top" or "charge" all you do is press the top button, the shoe lace immediately comes undone and you say "On, on, men, don't wait for me." Should prove a positive boon, old man.'

A stirring and heaving on the sofa behind them heralded the fact that this conversation had been overheard; after a few shattering grunts the face of Sir Frank ffollett appeared over the back.

'Don't know what the army's comin' to,' he said, 'in my day fellers fought to the end, no shoe laces came undone—anyway, we wore boots.'

'I suppose you've seen a lot of action, sir?' asked John politely.

'Yes, all over the world. Worst experience was in the Sudan in eighty-two, got ambushed by the Fuzzy Wuzzies, all the men got killed and all the blacks, too, except one great big ugly feller. Well, this feller came at me with a spear and as I had no ammunition left, I just had to wait for it. He flung the spear at me and it went right through me stomach and pinned me to a yam yam tree.'

There was a long dramatic pause which John ended with a somewhat feeble inquiry.

'. . . er . . . didn't that hurt terribly?'

'Only,' said Sir Frank ffollett, 'when I laughed.'

The face disappeared.

At the front door Oglethorpe shook John's hand.

'Now have a good trip, and when you come back let me know if you want to get into the mushroom business—and oh, yes! . . . you might bring me back a few pairs of nylons, will you?'

John's eyes widened.

'What are you up to?'

'Nothing definite—nothing definite, but it's always sound practice to sprinkle a little ground bait about the place. . . . Good-bye, old man.'

He turned and disappeared purposefully in the direction of the bar.

As the Rolls slipped through the gentle Hampshire countryside the Queen slept heavily. John looked out of the windows and had the same strong premonition that much time would elapse before he would again see England.

After many tense troopship departures it was a pleasant relief to board the giant liner at Southampton with every likelihood of still being alive at the end of the trip; he looked up at the vast black hull towering above him and the sense of adventure was strong within him.

Once aboard he took the Queen to the luxurious kennels and handed her over with her diet sheets to the attendant.

'I'll come and see her a couple of times a day and let me know if she gets seasick.' He pressed one of Mr. Dimbleby's pound notes into the man's hand to give weight to these instructions.

Then, unaccountably lonely, he went to the radio office on the sun deck and sent a telegram.

'Carole darling, miss you very much, back soon, all love. John.'

It didn't make much sense in view of the terms on which they had parted three days before, but he felt much better when he had sent it. Suddenly the faintest tremor came up from the deep bowels of the ship—the great engines were turning. John went out on the deck and looked down. Like the severing of the umbilical cord between mother and child, the gangplank had disappeared . . . the tin coverings of the customs' sheds were slowly, ever so slowly, slipping away below him, and the pale wintry afternoon sun beautified the bomb-battered face of the town beyond.

The seagulls wheeled overhead crying their intention of escorting the ship as far as the open sea, where at nightfall they would peel off, and turn again for home.

John stayed on deck while the light lasted. The huge ship glided down Southampton water, past Netley Hospital with its hundreds of war-blinded inmates, past Calshot with the silver R.A.F. flying boats moored off the Spit, past the red lightship at the point, then on with gathering speed down the Solent with the gentle downland of the Isle of Wight on one side and the bustling naval dockyard of Portsmouth, a haze of smoke and a forest of cranes, on the other.

As she rounded the Nab Tower at dusk and turned into the open sea the giant Cunarder gave her first great convulsive heave as a huge swell gathered beneath her belly. John shivered and went below. Later that night he was very sick indeed.

CHAPTER FOUR

THE SECOND DAY out from Southampton found John, none too robust a traveller, walking gingerly around the promenade deck. A hearty fellow passenger wearing a beret and smoking a long black cigar, impressed by the size of the ship, smote him between the shoulder blades. 'I wonder when this place gets to New York,' he said. '. . . Ha-ha-ha.'

John smiled feebly and went below again.

On the third day the sea relaxed a little so he visited the Queen: she seemed more friendly than before. The kennel steward reported that she would eat anything he gave her, but that she positively refused to touch the dog food which John had so specifically instructed be worked into her diet. John was pensive.

On this day also the fourth cablegram from Carole was delivered. 'MISS YOU DREADFULLY DARLING. PLEASE HURRY HOME. THREE LITTLE WORDS. CAROLE.' He threw it, with the others, into the waste paper basket.

In mid-Atlantic the weather became positively summery, cloudless sky and glassy sea. John entered the ping-pong tournament and reached the final, where his opponent was a Mrs. Polliniri, a very attractive American of thirty-six or -seven, meticulously and miraculously preserved. He allowed her to win.

Patricia Polliniri was the divorced wife of Mario Polliniri, the hotel multi-millionaire of the Middle West. Born Patricia Malony, she had at a tender age immigrated from County Wicklow to New York: there she had graduated through two previous marriages and had managed to find time to be the mistress of an ex-Tammany politician on the Broadway side of the Hall.

Now she was returning to New York having completed the routine by falling in love with her ski-ing instructor at Davos. She told John that she had been in Paris *en route* and he noticed that she had also picked up several other little particles of the local tongue *en passant*.

She was great company and her native Irish wit had not withered and died beneath the mink coats and the diamonds which had, from time to time, enveloped and encrusted her.

John took her to dinner in the verandah grill, where they ate exactly the same food as they would have done in the main dining saloon, but paid a cover charge for the privilege of sitting a great deal nearer the propellors.

Patricia Polliniri, her teeth chattering from the vibration, told him how much she preferred dining *à deux*. 'It is so much more *chic* here than dining *en masse.*'

Over cocktails she told him about her first husband: while dealing with a Dover sole she brought him up to date on her second: the lover from Tammany Hall took a little longer so he came with the *filet mignon*: the third and last husband, Mr. Polliniri, was brushed off during the *crêpe Suzette*, with a poignant observation.

'The only thing he and I had in common was that we both wanted his money.'

The ski-ing instructor, *la pièce de résistance*, came with coffee, and liqueurs. Of him she painted a beautiful word picture, and as she talked John could just imagine the strong white teeth in the brown smiling face; the swooping graceful tempo turns of the Arlberg School; the gay Viennese waltzes in the evening; the lifted stein of beer, the arm around the waist—he could see it all. But looking further ahead he could also visualize the inevitable visit to New York in the spring when the snows would have melted; an ill-fitting blue serge suit; a clumsy walk on the strange streets, an unhappy, lost expression on a face, now greenish from night clubs and lack of exercise—he sighed as he listened.

'. . . Of course,' continued Patricia Polliniri, 'I don't expect we shall get married for a long time. . . . François will have to find his *milieu* first, but we might live *en famille* for a while and see how it works. After all he must never feel *de trop* and that is *très simple* when you are living . . . er'—she faltered for a beat but filled in by waving her wrist in an expressive, continental gesture, then finished triumphantly, '*ex patria.*'

John looked at the luscious creature beside him and then at his watch: it was eleven-thirty and high time he entered into the conversation.

'*Voulez vous coucher avec moi?*' he said.

Patricia Polliniri stood up and turned so that he might slip her silver fox cape snugly about her white shoulders.

'Let's go,' she said and led the way to her cabin.

The rest of the trip passed quickly, and before he knew it John was standing beside Patricia Polliniri gaping with admiration at his first sight of the New York skyline.

It was a cold, hard, crystal-clear day with an ice-blue sky. The thermometer was glued to the zero mark and the overflows from the heating systems made white streamers blowing off the tops of the skyscrapers.

The downtown section passed slowly by, the canyon-like streets between great towering cliffs of buildings etched sharply in the wintry sunshine and pure air. John was speechless—he had never seen anything like this. He had imagined it, seen photographs of it, films of it, but he was still unprepared for the real thing; the Empire State Building, the Chrysler Building and in the distance the Waldorf Towers were pointed out to him by the mink-clad figure at his side. Patricia Polliniri was different now, the foreign phrases had long since ceased to flow from her lips, her eyes were shining with pride and her voice shook with genuine emotion.

'Gee! . . . it's great to be home,' she said quietly.

John was looking at Radio City. He spoke in an awed voice. 'I just don't believe that was made by man.'

The tugs, efficient and precocious, started fussing about the huge ship. Patricia Polliniri glanced up at the rapt face of the tall young man beside her.

'Good-bye, John. . . . Have fun with your old bulldog and thank you for a lovely trip. If there's anything in the world I can do to help you, you know where to find me.'

He tore his eyes away from the buildings.

'I'll see you on the dock, won't I?'

'I'd rather you didn't. . . . I like you much too much and it might show . . . er . . . I'm being met.'

John turned her towards him and pecked her on the cheek.

'We are a dreadful couple, aren't we?' he said.

They both laughed quite unselfconsciously and parted.

As the ship was turning slowly into her berth, John went down to the main saloon to complete his landing card for the immigration authorities. The cavernous gilded place was transformed: gone were the orchestra and the watchful stewards, no longer were little parties of various nationalities huddled together like partridges in the snow as they sipped their after-dinner coffee. Instead bustling grey uniformed government officials were seated at desks and passengers were being herded into waiting lines.

One of the purser's assistants approached a ferocious-looking old gentleman standing next to John.

'Are you a U.S. citizen, sir?' he enquired.

The old man swung around as though shot.

'Good God, no!'

'Then you must be an alien?'

'An alien! . . . Certainly not, man . . . British.'

He was led away fuming.

John was soon through the necessary formalities and was

73

presented with a landing card for himself and one for 'Sledmere, Queen of England.'

He went to collect the bulldog. She seemed genuinely friendly now and submitted quietly to the strapping on of the Union Jack coat, and the affixing of a heavy leather and brass collar which would have looked much better on a cart horse. The kennel steward was quite sorry to see her go.

'A real lady, sir, and apart from spoiling the stewardess's stockings that first night, no trouble at all really, but,' . . . he lowered his voice confidentially, 'if I was you, sir, I'd throw the rest of that Dimbleby Dog Food away. . . . She'll never touch that stuff and I don't blame her.'

John thanked him and led the Queen down to his cabin.

A man was waiting for him there: a short, fat man with a cigar, a Derby hat, a blue overcoat with a velvet collar, rimless octagonal glasses, too-even teeth and a hearty manner.

'Well . . . well . . . well,' said the man seizing John's hand and pumping it up and down. 'My name is Schumann and I'm certainly glad to meet you, Mr. Hamilton. . . . Yes, sir! Elmer Dimbleby cabled me that you were bringing the dog over for him and I came right down here this morning as soon as I got up so that I'd be on the dock when you stepped ashore.' He winked. 'However, I managed to pull a few strings at the gangplank so here I am right up on board to bid you welcome.'

Mr. Schumann became aware that the Queen was staring impassively at him. He stooped to pat her head.

'Hi, there, pooch,' he said gaily. 'How's tricks? . . . You look great, kid.'

He poked the Queen in the ribs. The great jaws snapped together and the teeth missed his wrist by a fraction of an inch. Mr. Schumann leaped on to the bed in terror.

'Jesus!' he said, 'that's one hell of a way to greet one of your employers.'

John soothed the animal.

'She's a bit tricky with strangers. She scared me to death the first time I met her, but we are great pals now . . . aren't we, old girl?'

The dog did not reply.

'Well, for Christ's sake, keep a good hold on that lead, Mr. Hamilton,' said Mr. Schumann. 'If she starts biting the reception committee, we're going to wind up with a lawsuit instead of a publicity campaign.'

He climbed nervously down from the bed; the Queen watched his every move closely.

'Yes, sir, we have a great little reception waiting for you on the dock—twenty Powers Models, the most gorgeous dolls you ever laid your eyes on, and a twenty-five piece brass band. . . . Then we have an escort of motorcycle cops to take us to the hotel. And have we got a great gag there! We've taken the bridal suite and we've organized a male bulldog! Now these two are supposed to be engaged—get it? . . . So, she comes all the way over from England to marry this male dog and we have arranged to cover the wedding breakfast on television—both dogs sitting up in bed with their breakfasts on a tray and what do you suppose they will be eating?' He slapped John on the chest with the back of his hand. . . . 'Why, Dimbleby's Dog Food, of course. . . . Isn't that great?'

John's brain reeled. 'I don't know whether she'll like so much attention,' he said weakly.

'Oh sure she will. . . . Let's get going.' Mr. Schumann looked warily at the Queen. 'I think you'd better lead the way.' He stood aside to let John and the dog pass.

Looking back on the next few minutes, John never could summon more than a hazy recollection of what actually took place: it all happened with incredible rapidity. He was slowly leading the way down the steep incline of the gangplank, holding a small suitcase full of dog food in one hand and the dog's lead in the other; he paused at the foot of the gangplank because a man rushed forward and said:

'Hold it there, Mr. Hamilton.'

Then thirty or forty flashlight bulbs went off in his face, leaving him in a temporary state of total blindness. One minute he had been standing there looking at the scene in the customs' shed . . . the next he was staggering back unable to see anything at all except thirty or forty bright green discs imprinted on his eyeballs. The reaction of the Queen was electric. She jumped straight up in the air with her legs absolutely stiff; when she landed, she let out a fearsome roar and took off like an express train. John was pulled off his feet and for several seconds, like a game jockey clinging to the reins of his late mount, he was towed along the ground. As he whizzed between trunks and golf bags his sight slowly returned and he had a momentary glimpse of a dreadful cardboard kennel built to look like Buckingham Palace: DIMBLEBY'S DOG FOOD was emblazoned on a royal standard which fluttered at the masthead. Stationed around the palace, and carrying toy rifles, was a bevy of unbelievably beautiful girls all dressed in the uniform of the Brigade of Guards. There also was a large brass band which at that instant saw fit to strike up 'There Will Always Be An England.' Then the real shambles started—a powerful square-jawed woman in tweeds aimed a whack at the Queen's head with an umbrella, she failed, however, to make any allowance for movement and the blow landed with its full force across the back of John's hand. Uttering a yelp of pain, he unclenched his fist and the Queen was free.

Scrambling to his knees, John saw the female Guardsmen break and run. Two of them tried to get into the kennel at the same moment, bumped heads in the entrance, and sat sobbing on the ground. Silken ankles were all about him as the girls hurdled over him in their efforts to climb to safety up the steep sides of packing cases. Dreadful wailing noises issued from the brass band as one by one its members saw the approaching danger and ceased to put any further wind into their instruments—they huddled together like sheep.

Snarling and snapping, the Queen tore straight into the band. They panicked. A snowstorm of sheet music filled the air as the wretched group stampeded from the scene. Half of them tried to find sanctuary on the ship, but the master-at-arms on duty at the foot of the gangplank, finding himself suddenly rushed by a uniformed mob, became convinced that an armed party had been sent around from the Soviet Embassy to seize the ship.

'Repel Boarders,' he roared and floored a wild-eyed saxophonist with a tremendous haymaker. More sailors dashed down the gangplank and a pitched battle ensued. People at the far ends of the customs' shed, hearing the sound of strife, hurried up to discover the cause of it, only to clash head on with those dashing blindly away from the maddened animal which by now was rending blue serge and destroying nylons in a frenzy of rage.

Several subsidiary fights broke out: and a near riot was on when the shrill blast of a police whistle rent the air. John picked himself up. Those round him were far too busy hiding behind each other to notice him, so he retired discreetly into the background and awaited events. The police arrived and order was gradually restored; but, judging by the number of people receiving first aid of the 'minor-cuts-and-bruises, smelling-salts-and-lost-false-teeth' variety, the casualty list was high. A sack was thrown over 'Sledmere Queen of England' and she was carried away by two men wearing thick leather gloves. From behind a pile of wooden boxes John watched with mixed feelings as Mr. Schumann was led away by detectives.

As he waited for an official to look for cocaine in his two small suitcases, he examined his own situation. He was in a strange city in a strange country: he had fulfilled his obligation to Mr. Dimbleby—he had delivered the bulldog to Mr. Schumann in New York: the fact that the bulldog had caused pandemonium on arrival was certainly not his fault: he held a return ticket to England and he had been led to believe that $1000.00 had been deposited in his name at the Chase National Bank: it was three days before Christmas: he was twenty-five and sound in wind and limb. He considered the situation to be sound, and fraught with possibility.

His luggage was finally stamped; and with a last look at the vast black hull of the *Queen Elizabeth*, John passed into the pulsating hurly-burly of New York and hailed a taxi.

'Where to, Mac?' asked the driver.

'The Chase National Bank, 79th Street,' said John.

As the bright yellow cab slipped in and out of the honking traffic John was fascinated by what he saw. The stately beauty of Park Avenue and the grandeur of Fifth; the cleanness of the huge buildings rising out of the squalor of others: shops filled with a Christmas-time abundance, quite staggering to his eyes after the drabness of London's war-time window displays: the hurrying, well-dressed, parcel-laden throngs passed endlessly by. He was absorbed by the sight of a bell-ringing Father Christmas collecting for charity on each of the main street corners. He noticed the red Irish faces of the ear-muffed cops, the beautiful women in their mink coats and the sleek and shining limousines. Michael Ranfskeicyk (whose name and photograph from two angles adorned the inside of the cab) proudly provided the running commentary.

'Jees, it's a great city, the greatest on earth, I guess. . . . They ain't got nuttin like this over there.'

This was said as a simple statement of fact. There was no offence in that.

At the bank John was gratified to find that the money awaited him. He drew it out—all of it—one thousand dollars.

'Where to, Doc?' asked Michael Ranfskeicyk.

'I tell you what,' said John, 'I have only been in your country a few minutes and I'd like to have a drink. Will you join me?'

'Sure will, feller,' said Michael, 'be glad to.'

'Well, let's find a little bar somewhere and we'll get to work,' said John.

Work started in Michael's favourite haunt—a dirty saloon on 3rd Avenue, where they shouted their orders as the elevated trains clanged overhead. It ended several hours later in Michael's three-room tenement flat overlooking 9th Avenue, with Mrs. Ranfskeicyk, fat and jolly, insisting that John share the evening meal with the four rollicking children.

After supper Michael drove John to a little hotel on Lexington Avenue at 52nd Street, the Claybourne. It was clean, he said, inexpensive and in a useful central position. They nearly came to blows over the question of the cabfare.

78

Although the clock now said $14.00 Michael stoutly refused to let John pay it.

'You Goddamn stuck up limey sonofabitch . . . you can't give me your lousy money.'

'All you bloody Yanks are the same,' said John, 'trying to impress people with how rich you are.'

'Well, I'll tell you what I'll do. . . . I'll take what I have to hand in to the company, but, you British heel, if you try to make it more—I'll bust you right on the snoot.'

John was learning fast.

'Oh yeah?' he said.

'Yeah!'

'Okay.'

'Okay.'

After further noisy haggling, he parted from his new-found friend, checked into his room, pulled on a pair of pyjamas and fell into bed. His last waking thought on this, his first day in America, was—'if you can judge a country by its taxi drivers, then this one I'm going to love.'

Three days later Christmas morning dawned.

Clear, bright and cold. There had been a heavy fall of snow during the night and a silencer had been placed upon the city—what little traffic there was, was noiseless, apart from the occasional 'slap slap' of a broken chain. John woke late, ate his usual massive breakfast, listened to the church bells, and decided he was rather lonely.

He found the number that Patricia Polliniri had given him and telephoned her to wish her a Happy Christmas. She was delighted to hear his voice, but from the tone she used he gathered that, at the moment, she was not alone.

'What are you doing today?' she asked.

'I am going to deliver a few presents,' John told her, 'then I am going to wander about and see how the locals spend their Christmas.'

At the other end of the line American hospitality and warmth came quickly to the boil.

79

'Do you mean you are all alone today?'

'Yes, I suppose I am . . . but please don't worry about me . . . I'll find plenty to do.'

A giggle, then: 'Yes, that's what I'm afraid of. . . . Hold on a minute.'

John heard a whispered consultation. Then:

'A friend of mine is going to drive me down to Long Island for lunch,' said Patricia Polliniri; 'I know he'd be very happy to have you join us. . . . You stay right where you are, we'll pick you up in about an hour.'

John was easily persuaded.

He got up, dressed quickly, found a lone taxi and drove soundlessly over the snow to the tenement home of Michael and Betsy Ranfskeicyk. They were overjoyed to see him and the presents he had brought were greeted with shouts of delight from the whole brood. There was a handbag and a big bottle of eau-de-cologne for Betsy; an expensive pair of fur-lined driving gloves and a couple of bottles of Scotch whisky for Michael; innumerable toys and boxes of crystallized fruit and candy for the children.

Michael opened one of the bottles—half filled three china mugs and grinned.

'Happy Christmas, you stuck up limey bastard!'

John grinned back. 'Good luck, you Goddamned Colonial.'

Betsy's eyes shone with pleasure, 'All the best fellers,' she said; and the mugs were emptied.

They pressed him to stay for Christmas dinner, but he persuaded them that he had to get back to the hotel, so another great beaker of whisky followed the first and he descended somewhat dizzily into the street.

Patricia Polliniri arrived at the hotel looking most attractive in a leopard-skin outfit. The car was a giant Cadillac and the owner-driver, introduced as Mr. Armstrong, was the quiet, serious-minded and extremely wealthy President of the great Armstrong Oil Corporation of Houston, Texas.

As they swung out towards Long Island over the Triboro Bridge, John commented on this masterpiece of engineering:

Patricia said she considered it to be both '*formidable*' and '*merveilleux*,' and he knew that the French phrases were back with a vengeance.

Mr. Armstrong told John that they were taking him to lunch with some friends of his named Despard who lived near Westbury.

'Lovely people,' he said, 'with a gorgeous home . . . aren't they, honey?'

'*Très sympathique*,' replied Patricia as she snuggled closer to John.

On Long Island the countryside lay quietly under its mantle of snow and John noticed with delight the well-kept paddocks and gardens as they passed the fine houses.

'Yes,' said Mr. Armstrong, 'you'll like Jake Despard. Of course, his wife's a bit rough when she's hitting the bottle, but she's a great kid just the same. Jake and I roomed together in college. . . . He was probably the greatest end we ever had.'

John looked blank. 'The greatest what?'

'The greatest end.'

'Was he really?'

'Sure—all American.'

John was still looking blank when the car drove up to the house.

Jake Despard was a huge man in his early fifties. He had an enormous stomach, several double chins and hands like bunches of bananas with which he slapped every back within reach: he roared with laughter most of the time.

'Well, you old son of a gun . . . wadda you know?' he boomed to Mr. Armstrong. Then he lifted Patricia Polliniri high above his head and kissed her on both cheeks on the way down. He turned to John. . . . 'And I'm certainly glad to know you, Mr. Hamilton, and welcome to America . . . delighted you could come down and a Happy Christmas to you.'

One of the bunches of bananas descended with the force of a sledge hammer between John's shoulder blades, all but battering him to the ground.

'What do you think of our little country?' Down came the bananas again, and John's knees buckled.

'I love it,' he said weakly.

'Good boy! Well, we'll have to show you around. . . . Come on in folks, Janet is inside with the Tom and Jerries.'

They followed their host and a maid took their coats. The house was so full of people that it was difficult for John to get much of an idea as to how it was furnished, but it seemed attractive and comfortable in a chintzy sort of way—it was as hot as a blast furnace.

Life seemed to be revolving around a huge silver bowl. Everyone had glasses in their hands containing a thick yellowish mixture. This they replenished from time to time with a ladle from the bowl while trying to make themselves heard above two grand pianos being played simultaneously: the din was terrific.

A small faded blonde with round blue eyes detached herself from the group. Janet Despard greeted her guests in a vague way and waved towards the bowl.

'Come and get a Tom and Jerry.'

John sampled the stuff and found it delicious—warm, sweet and potent. His hostess nudged him and whispered hoarsely in his ear. 'When you go to the can, leave one in there for me, I'm on the wagon.'

He was introduced to those nearest him, but the noise was so deafening he never did discover who they all were. He helped himself to another Tom and Jerry and gazed at the scene through eyes smarting from cigarette smoke.

Jake Despard bore down upon him, but, wiser now, John backed against the nearest wall and managed to take a glancing blow on his shoulder.

'How's it going?' roared his host.

'Fine,' John yelled back, and then, to make polite conversation. 'How is your end?'

Despard didn't get it. 'My what?'

'Your end—your all American end?'

Despard got enough to take it as a compliment.

82

'Want to come to the game next Saturday?' he shouted. 'Should be great!'

'I'd love to,' John screamed.

A group of people joined them and someone filled John's glass again.

'Why did you kick Churchill out after all he'd done for you?' asked a man with red hair.

'If you have ever seen a bird face to face,' announced an attractive dark girl with a mole on her cheek, 'you'd agree with me. . . . In profile birds are beautiful, but face to face they're just plain mean.'

John smiled and nodded at them both. They seemed satisfied and went away. By three o'clock in the afternoon he found himself stunned, deafened, half drunk, faint from hunger and suffering from a bad attack of claustrophobia. He was relieved when a young couple asked him if he would like to go skating on their pond: they lived next door, they said, and would love to have him go along with them. Outside he inhaled the fresh air gratefully.

A very poor skater at the best of times, and his natural balance having been badly upset by the vast quantities of Tom and Jerries which he had consumed, John thought it prudent to borrow a cushion; this he strapped to that portion of his anatomy least likely to succeed. For the most part the skating was a very lighthearted affair, but one or two people seemed to be taking it rather seriously. One very pretty girl had even gone so far as to bring with her an orange. This she had placed on the ice and round it she was performing the most intricate manoeuvres.

It was inevitable that John, being easily the worst skater present, should in one of his spasmodic dashes across the pond cut this orange in half. Worse than that, this collision with a piece of soft fruit proved too much for his already faltering balance, he fell; and, like a drowning man clutching a straw, he brought the girl crashing down with him.

At first she was justifiably annoyed, but it was Christmas Day and she was very pretty, and John quickly told her so,

83

so she ended up by giving him a skating lesson and they spent the rest of the fading light skating round hand in hand as the icicles formed on the fir trees round the pond.

She told him she lived in New York and when he asked her for her telephone number, her face dimpled deliciously.

'You'd never remember it if I gave it to you, but you can try. My name is easy—Windsor, like the Duke—you can find it in the phone book under my father's name, Dennis Windsor, 983 Park Avenue.'

'Then I'll call you tomorrow,' said John, 'may I? Will you be back by then?'

'Not till Wednesday night.'

'Then I'll call you on Thursday morning early . . . good-bye and I'm so glad I ran into you . . . in every sense of the word.'

She smiled very prettily indeed as she shook hands and said good-bye.

Back at the Despards' house things seemed to have quieted down a little: more than half of the guests had gone home and Janet Despard, leaving a row of empty glasses on the window-sill of the downstairs lavatory, had retired to bed.

Patricia and Mr. Armstrong were ready to leave.

'I'll call you about that game next Saturday,' Jake Despard boomed to John, 'and I'll get an extra ticket in case you want to bring a girl.'

'Thanks so much, I'd love to come and thanks for the party too . . . that's one of the best Christmases I've ever had.'

'Well, we couldn't have you sitting all alone in an hotel, could we, Armie?'

Mr. Armstrong wilted under a tremendous wallop in the region of his kidneys.

'Sure couldn't,' he gasped.

Patricia was hoisted high into the air and kissed again.

'Good-bye, honey, and keep an eye on Armie now,' he nudged her in the ribs, 'we don't want him getting into any *more* trouble in the big city, do we?'

This must have been an obscure allusion to some past

84

misdemeanour on the part of the President of the Armstrong Oil Corporation for he looked extremely sheepish and Jake Despard went into a paroxysm of mirth, slapping his own thigh so hard it was a wonder he didn't cripple himself for life.

Patricia Polliniri and Mr. Armstrong climbed into the car and John turned to do likewise. As he did so he realized that he had made a grave tactical error: with the same fortitude as that displayed by French aristocrats awaiting the knife of the guillotine, he braced himself for the blow. With appalling force it landed squarely in the middle of his back; he fell forward into the car.

'See you Saturday,' yelled their host, '. . . and if you can't be good be careful.'

As they moved down the drive the frosty evening air vibrated anew with a parting roar of laughter.

They crossed back over the Triboro Bridge and John had another view of the magnificent skyline. The lights were on inside the giant buildings and the city seemed to have come out in a rash.

John insisted on taking Patricia and Mr. Armstrong out to dinner. For Patricia's benefit he found a delightful little French restaurant where she made a promising, if lucky, start by exclaiming, when she spied the menu, 'Ah!—*la carte.*'

In the morning while dealing with his usual huge breakfast John looked searchingly into his financial status and was very little surprised to discover that he was only just afloat. The thousand dollars from Mr. Dimbleby had, in four days (and more particularly in four nights), been subjected to a process of dehydration; also his hotel bill had yet to be paid. Carefully he selected the crumpled currency from among the crumpled telephone numbers and addresses that seemed to have accumulated in every pocket of his two suits.

He removed an amount sufficient to cover his hotel bill to date: then he gathered up and counted what was left—forty-eight dollars and eleven cents. He picked up the telephone and asked to be connected with the offices of the Cunard White Star Steamship Company.

'Cunard White Star? . . . Passenger bookings please . . . Good morning . . . I have the return half of a round trip ticket from Southampton . . . When is your next sailing? . . . Tomorrow midnight? . . . Yes, that'll do fine . . . Plenty of room? . . . Thank you.'

He gave his name and particulars and hung up. It was now ten o'clock on Wednesday morning so he had roughly thirty-six hours before sailing time. He picked up the forty-eight dollars and extracted thirty-five for his expenses on the voyage home. Thirteen dollars left—Yes!—that should do it comfortably.

John had a wonderful day wandering all over the city. The weather was still cold and a further snowfall had brought out large gangs of men with shovels. He went to the top of the Empire State Building and looked down at the little ant-like figures in the streets nearly a quarter of a mile below him. In the evening he saw a burlesque show on 8th Avenue and sat delightedly through the rough and tumble of an ice hockey match at Madison Square Garden. After the game was over he walked down Broadway and mingled with the crowds pouring out of the theatres and movie houses, while above his head a myriad electric bulbs winked and twinkled out their exhortations to drink this, smoke that or purchase an antidote to the effects of both.

He dropped in at a bar for a nightcap and a sandwich and found warmth and friendliness inside. 'I shall be sorry to leave these people,' he thought, and reflected with sadness that by the same time the following night he would be gone.

When he woke on the morning of his last day in New York, John lay in bed for quite a while before ordering a light breakfast.

Thursday! There was something he was supposed to do besides leave the country. . . . What was it? It worried him through orange-juice, eggs, bacon, kidneys, tomatoes, toast, marmalade and coffee. . . . He could not for the life of him remember.

It came to him while he was shaving.

Of course! Windsor! He was going to call up 'Miss Dimples' of the ice.

There didn't seem much point in doing so now that he was leaving, but at least it would be nice to chat on the telephone for a few minutes—but what was her telephone number?

He remembered that she had said it was under her father's name—Dennis he thought . . . and that it was a high street-number on Fifth Avenue or somewhere. He ran his finger vaguely down the W's—'8oo hadn't she said?—Windsor—Charles B. Windsor—Cuthbert Windsor—Here we are!—D. Windsor, 893 Fifth Avenue—that must be it.' He asked the operator for the number and a female voice answered the phone.

'How are you?' asked John.

'Just fine, thank you,' answered the voice.

'What time did you get home last night?'

'Who is this?'

'John Hamilton. —er, the man who ran over your orange.'

'The man who did *what*?'

'Ran over your orange . . . on the ice . . . on Christmas Day, remember?' There was a pause. Things were not going too well.

'Mr. Hamilton, I think you must have the wrong number.'

'Don't you remember me? . . . I had a cushion strapped on my behind.'

'I beg your pardon?'

John began to sweat.

'. . . Skating at Westbury. . . . You had an orange and I ran over it, and I had a cushion strapped on . . . er . . . in case I fell down.'

'Mr. Hamilton, I don't know what you're talking about. I've never been ice skating in my life. I have never been to Westbury and furthermore I loathe oranges.'

John pondered over this.

'Well, I'm terribly sorry, but you are Miss Windsor, aren't you?'

'No. I am Mrs. Windsor.'

'*Mrs.* Windsor? Are you quite sure? . . . Well, I'm terribly sorry. . . . I must have called the wrong number. . . . Please forgive me.'

There was a musical laugh from the other end.

'That's quite all right—'

John thought it was a very nice voice indeed and was loath to close the conversation.

'. . . you see, I've only been in this country for a few days,' he went on. 'It's a jolly fine place . . . I'm from England you know.'

She laughed.

'That's funny, you sound as though you're from Kansas City. . . . What made you call this number anyway?'

'Well, the character you are supposed to be, or rather the one I was trying to call, said I could find the number in the book under her father's name, Dennis Windsor at 983 Park Avenue, and, incidentally, I still think that's what I found.'

'No—what you found was *Donald* Windsor at 893 *Fifth* Avenue. . . . That puts you roughly one block west and eight blocks north of where you are supposed to be. . . . Well, it's been nice knowing you, Mr. Hamilton. . . . Good-bye.'

'I love that voice,' said John to himself. Out loud he said. 'Is Donald your father?'

'No. Donald is my husband.'

'How is he?'

'He's very well, thank you.'

'Is his business going along nicely and everything?'

'Yes, I understand it's going very well indeed.'

'Where is it?'

'Where is what?'

'His business.'

'Well, his office is downtown if that's what you mean.'

'A long way downtown?'

'Yes . . . Wall Street. . . . Why?'

'Then we could have lunch together somewhere uptown, couldn't we?'

A pause, John waited.

'I think you have a colossal nerve,' came the voice from the other end. 'Why I've never even laid eyes on you.'

'That's probably as well, but it's a pity though,' he sighed down the telephone, 'All you middle-aged women are the same . . . no sense of adventure, no fun out of life, no . . .'

'I'm not middle-aged. I'm twenty-two.'

John grinned to himself.

'Then that makes it much worse. You'll probably share a lettuce leaf with three dreary girl friends and spend the rest of the afternoon drooling over some ghastly dress show.'

'I really don't know why I don't hang up . . . I don't know who you are, or what you are, and there is certainly no reason why I should listen to you telling me how to run my life.'

John plunged in deeper.

'Please have lunch with me . . . I'm very harmless and I am going back to England tonight.'

'Certainly not! You . . . you might be a kidnapper or something.'

He had a flash of genius.

'I tell you what, I will stand on any street corner you care to name, at one o'clock, and I will wear a blue scarf with white spots on it round my neck. To make doubly sure I will also wear a red carnation in my button hole.'

'What am I supposed to do?'

'Well, then you can walk by, or drive by in a taxi if you like. You will know me, but I won't know you and when you have had a look you can make up your mind whether I'm a kidnapper or not . . . and if I look a trustworthy type, then come up and tell me so, and we'll have lunch together . . . er . . . uptown.'

There was a long pause.

'Come on,' said John. 'Be a sport. . . . There's no risk. I'll never even know which one you are, unless you want me to.'

'I'm thinking,' she answered, and then, 'all right, but it's all very stupid.'

'Wonderful! Name your corner.'

'Madison and 79th, but make it one-thirty as I have a lot of things to arrange before I see you.'

John was delighted.

'Fine . . . Madison and 79th Street at one-thirty. . . . I'll be there and I do hope you will be, too.'

'Good-bye, Mr. Hamilton.' She hung up.

John spent a morning of pleasurable anticipation. He took special pains with the knotting of his tie and the arrangement of his handkerchief, he tried hard to copy Mr. Truman and have all four corners of it sticking out of his breast pocket at once, but it was beyond him. At twelve-thirty he completed his ensemble with a blue and white spotted scarf and at one o'clock he was on the corner at 79th Street and Madison Avenue, or rather he was at the intersection of the two big thoroughfares wondering which of the four corners he ought to be on.

He selected the one outside a bank. At one-fifteen he remembered that he had failed to buy a red carnation so he dashed madly off in search of a flower shop, found one, bought a red carnation and in a burst of zeal bought a dozen red roses as well, thereby ruining the planned economy for his return trip to England.

At one twenty-nine he was paying for a double martini in a nearby bar—'a nerve steadier,' he told himself—and at a fraction after one-thirty he was at his battle station.

As the minutes dragged by and nothing happened John began to feel supremely foolish. Several people stared at him as he stood with chattering teeth, in the sub-zero weather, a dozen red roses gripped in a blue fist.

The martinis faded within him and were gone. He felt like the famous Snaffles picture of the miserable jockey in the Grand National—'the wrong side of Beechers and the drink died out o' me.' He wished he had never dreamed up the whole thing, then someone spoke at his elbow.

'Would you like an orange, Mr. Hamilton?'

He looked up and beheld a tall, smiling girl holding out a paper bag. He whipped off his hat.

'Mrs. Windsor?'

'No . . . I'm Mrs. Smith. . . . Good-bye.' She walked on down the street. Before he had time to recover he was accosted again.

'Going skating today?' A short girl this time, also with laughing eyes.

He doffed his hat. . . .

'Mrs. Windsor?'

'No . . . I'm Mrs. Smith. . . . Good-bye.' She too went her way.

John paled.

'Yoo Hoo! . . . Mr. Hamilton . . . Hammy . . . Yoo-Hoo,' came a chorus of voices. He spun round. A big black limousine was passing slowly by: he caught a glimpse of four laughing girls inside it.

He swayed on his feet; this was not going according to plan. Giggling girls started to stream past . . . three were on bicycles, two loads of them passed in carriages driven by coachmen wearing top hats, one was on a horse.

'Yoo hoo, Hammy! . . . Where's the cushion, Mr. Hamilton? . . . Yoo hoo! . . . D'you want an orange. . . . Yoo hoo!'

Other people began to take an interest. Three small children approached.

'Are you a movie star—may we have your autograph?'

'No. . . . Run away.' John hissed through his teeth.

'Aw, he's a phoney,' said one of the horrible infants as they departed.

Snow began to fall heavily: defeat was in the air; John decided to leave the field of battle. He turned to go.

'Mr. Hamilton?' said a voice, a male voice this time.

Four youths and two girls all dressed in the mud-coloured uniforms of Western Union employees stood round him in a circle.

'Yes,' he croaked, 'that's me.'

'We have a greetings message for you,' said the leader, 'to be delivered on this corner at one-thirty.' He stamped his foot on the pavement. 'One-two-three—Happy Meeting tew yew,' they warbled, 'Happy Meeting tew yew, happy Meeting dear Hammie, hap . . .'

'Stop it! For God's sake stop it!' John burst out of the harmonizing ring and made for the open country with the speed of a welshing bookmaker: straight down Madison he ran, the red roses held aloft like the Olympic torch in the hand of the final marathon runner—in his ears the cries grew fainter—'Happy Mee-ting tew yew . . . Yoo hoo! . . . Hammy! Yoo, hoo!'

He found the place he wanted and dived in.

'A quadruple Vodka,' he gasped to the man in the white coat: he was shaking like a leaf. He drank deeply. As the fiery liquor covered and anaesthetized the nerves of his stomach he became calmer.

'Where shall we have lunch?' said a quiet voice at his side.

He spun round to face his latest tormentor.

'No, please, I give up,' he said laughing.

The girl laughed too: a gay, tinkling laugh. She had a slim, graceful figure and beautiful hands and feet. She stood beside him with the chin of her perfect oval face tilted down a little so that she looked up at him from beneath long, thick lashes. Her eyes were not green exactly and not brown either, they were wide apart, large and sort of tawny-coloured. They were dancing with merriment. Her golden hair curled out deliciously from underneath a ridiculous little hat—she was lovely.

John climbed off the bar stool and faced her.

'I am Ann Windsor,' she said as she held out her hand. . . . 'Please forgive me . . . I think we went too far.'

'I was lucky to be let off so lightly,' smiled John.

'No . . . it was a horrid trick, but you took it so well I had to come and apologize.'

'Who were all those various Mrs. Smiths?' grinned John.

92

'Oh, all my girl friends. I spent a couple of busy hours rounding them up and rehearsing them after you called.'

'They were beautifully rehearsed,' said John. 'Would you like a drink?'

They found a little table in the corner and she ordered a glass of Dubonnet. 'I think I ought to be buying drinks for you after what you went through for me.'

They laughed again and John said.

'The Western Union idea was a masterpiece . . . by the way . . . where were you all the time?'

'Oh, I stood across the street and watched the whole thing . . . it was terribly funny,' she giggled. 'Please forgive me.'

'Good Heavens! There's nothing to forgive . . . and incidentally are you going to stick to the bargain and have lunch with me?'

'If you still want me to. . . . Where do you want to go?'

'Anywhere you say. I don't really know New York.'

'You seem to have found a very sweet little place. Why don't we just stay here?'

'Wonderful! Let's do that.'

She took off her coat and as he helped her he caught a glimpse of a delicious profile with a little uptilted nose and a sweet sensitive mouth above a firm rounded chin. She looked at John and smiled.

'I suppose I ought to feel embarrassed, but I don't.'

'Nor do I,' said John. He offered her a cigarette. '. . . er . . . does your husband mind you having lunch alone with people? . . . I mean, are you sure you won't get into trouble if anyone sees you here?'

She laughed out loud and put a hand on his arm.

'Oh, I invented him. . . . After all you were behaving so strangely at your end of the telephone, I decided to play the same sort of game. . . . Aren't I awful?'

'You mean he doesn't exist?'

'Good Heavens, no. . . . I'm not married.'

'Then who is the mysterious Mr. Donald Windsor who is responsible for me making such a fool of myself?'

'That's Uncle Don: I stay with him when I'm in New York. My home is in North Carolina.'

A waiter came up and took their order, and John, who was acutely conscious of the few dollars left in his pocket, was immensely relieved when she announced that all she ever had for lunch was a salad.

'Tell me about yourself,' she said. 'When did you come over? . . . What are you? . . . Where do you live . . . or am I too inquisitive?'

She laughed till she cried when she heard about 'Sledmere, Queen of England,' and listened with genuine interest when he told her about 'the Aunts' and the lovely Wiltshire countryside.

'I've always wanted to visit England,' she said. 'Daddy goes over once in a while. . . . He's just crazy about it.'

Then it was her turn and she described her happy childhood in the little town of Tryon, North Carolina, and described the colours of the trees in the fall when the feet of the Smoky Mountains are bathed in gold. She told him of her sweet old-fashioned parents and how she spent two years with uncle Don's help persuading them to let her come to New York to earn her own living.

'I'm nothing much, just a model, and not a particularly successful one at that, but the girls I work with are all just dreamy and the work is interesting and not too hard: if I'm lucky I may be on the cover of *Redbook* next month, which will give me a terrific boost. Anyway, I love New York . . . it's so exciting and I just had to see it and live in it before I settled down.'

John longed to ask her what exactly she meant by that, but he didn't.

'You still haven't told me what you will do when you get back to England,' she said.

'I wish I knew,' said John. 'I suppose I shall have to get a job in some dreary office in London.' He sighed. 'How I dread it. The trouble is I don't really know anything—I went straight from school into the war and that went on for six years.'

They talked on and on. There seemed to be so much to say; so many questions to ask. Suddenly she jumped up.

'Good Heavens, it's after four o'clock. . . . We've been here for hours. . . . I must dash.'

He helped her on with her coat.

'What time does your ship sail?' she asked.

'Midnight . . . from Pier 59.'

He looked at her as she was putting on her gloves.

'It's very strange,' he added, 'I really do feel as though I have known you all my life.'

Ann kept her head bent and there was quite a long pause before she answered.

'Yes, it's funny, I have been thinking the same thing.'

Another pause and John said:

'What an odd way to meet.'

'Yes,' she said slowly, 'Yes, it was. . . .' And then, because a funny little silence had fallen between them, she went on more quickly, 'Oh, dear, I really must go. . . . I'm terribly late now. Will you walk part of the way with me? It's only a few blocks.'

'I'll walk all the way if you don't mind,' smiled John and she smiled back.

He paid the check and they walked out together into the freezing air of the late afternoon.

Some silences are empty and cold, others are not: they are warm and cosy and much fuller and more comforting than small talk. In silence they walked along Madison Avenue. It had stopped snowing while they had been having lunch, and now the lights from the bright shop windows, beginning their victorious battle over the fading light of the December day, were reflected in a million little sparkling stars in the snow at their feet.

When Ann at length broke the silence she spoke with a soft North Carolina voice accented just a little by the time she had spent in New York. It was a delicious voice, and when she mentioned anything that particularly interested her, or talked about the people she loved, her beautiful face lit up with pleasure. She was completely unspoiled, completely unaffected and she brought with her to the busy streets a breath of the clean open countryside. They were completely engrossed in each other, and when their hands brushed together once or twice as they walked John was very conscious of the fact.

At last their walk was over and outside a big office building Ann stopped.

'We're there,' she smiled.

'I wish I didn't have to go tonight,' said John wistfully.

Ann did not meet his eye.

'Maybe you'll find some job in England that will bring you back here soon.'

'Will you meet me on the street corner again when I come back?'

'Yes. I'll always remember our corner . . . will you?'

'Always,' said John, and he meant it with all his heart.

She faced him.

'Well, I suppose I had better say good-bye.'

'Unless I see you again before I sail?'

'I wish you could . . . I really do, but I have to work now, and it's Uncle Don's birthday, and I've promised to go to the theatre with him. So . . . I'm afraid. . . .'

'This has been such a wonderful day,' said John softly. 'Thank you so much.'

'I've enjoyed it too . . . more than I thought possible. Good-bye, John.'

'Good-bye, Ann.'

John watched her pass through the big doors of the office building. He watched her look at the directory on the wall. He watched her walk to the elevator. Then the doors were closed by a white-gloved elevator man.

He wandered aimlessly down the street: suddenly he remembered that he had never given her the roses which he had bought: he toyed with the idea of going back and collecting them from the place where they had had lunch and then following her into the big building and presenting them to her with a flourish. But, even if he could find her, it all seemed a bit cheap and theatrical now: he felt desperately depressed: all the fun had gone out of life.

'One thing,' he said to himself, 'sticks out a mile, I have got to see Ann again and I can't do that if I am in England.'

A bum approached him.

'Say Doc, can ya spare a guy a dime for a cuppa coffee?'

John gave him a dollar in an absentminded way and the amazed man stood rooted to the sidewalk staring after him.

John mused on—'If I am to see Ann again, then I must stay in America . . . in order to stay in America, I must not sail to England . . . in order to avoid sailing to England I must not go on board the ship tonight . . . it's simple,' he said out loud, 'it's obvious.'

'I beg your pardon?' said an elderly lady wearing a hat like a Christmas cake.

'I said it's simple—obvious,' said John with explanatory gestures.

'Oh,' said the elderly lady and passed hurriedly on.

John's mind was made up—he took a taxi to the offices of the Cunard White Star Steamship Company and fifteen minutes later he emerged again with a check for $300. The fact that he had burned his only bridge was a matter, to him, of the completest indifference. He felt happier than he had done for years.

Back in his hotel room he mapped out a simple plan of campaign.

First of all he must find cheaper quarters, and secondly, he must find a job.

His telephone rang.   It was Jake Despard.

'Hello there.' John held the phone some distance from his ears. 'Hello,' he called back.

'Everything is all set for the game, day after tomorrow . . . are you going to bring a girl with you?'

'Yes, I'd love to,' said John crossing his fingers. 'Thank you, so much.'

'I'll be in town Saturday morning,' yelled Despard, 'so I'll

pick you both up at the hotel around eleven o'clock . . .
we'll take a picnic lunch.'

'I'll look forward to it. Thanks awfully.'

'Should be a great game,' roared Jake.

'It certainly should,' screamed John, wishing he knew which
sport they were discussing.

'Good-bye.'

'Good-bye.'

Should he telephone Ann? He spent a good half hour
debating this point: twice he got as far as picking up the
phone and once he even got as far as asking for the number,
only to hang up again when a male voice answered. 'Uncle
Don, I suppose,' he thought. 'No—I'll just call her very
casually tomorrow morning and ask her to the game, whatever
it may be. . . . What a shock she'll get.' He hugged himself
at the prospect: then feeling very happy and very rich he
treated himself to an excellent dinner and went to bed.

He awoke early, ordered a more moderate meal than usual
—'must cut down on expenses now,' he told himself—
finished it and immediately phoned down for another order
of everything; then he began to pore over the 'jobs vacant'
columns in the morning newspaper. It was wasted effort—
most of the vacancies were for domestic help, for linemen,
pressers or for salesmen, nothing into which he could readily fit.

He looked at his watch—ten past nine, too early to call
Ann yet . . . but she may go out to work at nine-thirty,
so I'd better call her at twenty past nine.' He went back to his
perusal of the morning paper.

'I might be a butler,' he thought.

But if anybody required a butler they were keeping it dark;
there was no word of their need in the paper.

'Chauffeur? . . . No—I can't find my own way about
New York on my feet yet. . . . What I really need,' he
admitted to himself ruefully, 'is for someone in a black
overcoat and a bowler hat to come here every Wednesday
morning with a big suitcase full of hundred dollar bills, empty
it on to the bed and go away without a word.'

Nine-fifteen—only five more minutes and I'll call. . . .
What shall I say? . . . I missed the boat? No, that's no
good. . . . I decided to stay because I could not bear the
thought of going away and leaving you here in New York?
That, of course, is the truth, but probably the best way to
frighten her all the way back to North Carolina. . . . No,
I'll stick to my original plan—just call up and ask her to this
mythical game and see what happens.'

He looked at his watch again—seventeen minutes past nine
—he grabbed the phone, put it down again, and then, for no
reason, went into the bathroom and brushed his hair. When
he came back he finished up the syrupy dregs at the
bottom of his coffee cup . . . then with a pounding heart he
asked for Ann's number.

The sweet voice answered the phone. All the nonchalant
opening phrases which he had concocted flew out of his mind;
instead, in a voice which he hardly recognized as his own,
he said:

'Ann, it's John . . . I'm still here.'

'Yes,' she answered, 'I know. . . . I went down to the ship
last night to see you off.'

CHAPTER FIVE

For a blissful second John pondered this then blurted
out, 'Will you come to a game with me on Saturday?'

A silvery laugh came down the phone.

'Is that why you changed your mind—so that you could go
to the game? . . . Why I'd just love to.'

'And will you have lunch with me today, please?'

'Yes, please.'

'Well, good-bye.'

'Good-bye.'

In four seconds he had called her again.

'Sorry. . . . I forgot to say where. . . . Same place all right with you? One o'clock?'

'Yes, I'd like that.'

'Well. . . .'

'Well. . . .'

'Good-bye.'

'Good-bye.'

After he had hung up he sat for a long time on his bed—all thoughts, all sane and sensible thoughts driven from his mind: 'She went to the boat to see me off,' he kept repeating it to himself. He was bathed in happiness.

There was a knock at the door and a large man in overalls carrying several huge spanners and wearing a heavy woollen muffler round his throat came into the room.

'You Hamilton?'

'Yes.'

'Did you by any chance turn off your radiator last night?'

'Yes, I did,' said John.

'And could you by any chance have left the window just above it—open?'

'Not by chance, I assure you,' said John. 'I always sleep with the window open . . . fresh air, you know.'

'You always sleep with the window open?' the man's eyes narrowed and he nodded his head to punctuate each word. 'Fresh air? Well, it might interest you to know, that it was fourteen degrees below zero last night and as your radiator is now filled with a solid block of ice the heating system for the entire building is out of order.'

'It doesn't look,' observed John, after a long moment of reflection, 'as though I shall be staying here much longer, does it?'

'You can say *that* again,' said the man.

Downstairs the hotel lobby looked like a scene from 'Nanook of the North,' porters, bell captains, elevator men, cashiers, house detectives and guests all were bundled up to the eyebrows: the room clerk wore ear muffs.

'I'm checking out,' said John in a matter-of-fact tone. 'Room 1907. . . . May I have my account, please?'

'What name?' asked the man through clattering teeth.

'Hamilton,' said John and a cloud of steam billowed from his mouth.

The effect was impressive.

'Hamilton?' The cry was taken up round the lobby. 'Hamilton . . . Hamilton . . .' at the sound of the hated name faces turned everywhere towards him: the glass door, with OFFICE written on it, opened, and the manager came slowly forward; his blue nose quivered with indignation: a coon-skin coat covered the black morning coat and striped trousers of his profession: his patent-leather shoes were encased in snow boots: on his head was a Daniel Boone hat.

He spoke not a word: he just stood and glared at John—everyone glared at John.

John paid his bill, grabbed his change, picked up his suitcases and turned to go. Hostile eyes from all over the lobby bored into the back of his neck—nobody moved. As he started to walk towards the big revolving door, the manager spoke and his voice was like the hiss of steam now so sadly lacking in his establishment.

'Good day, Mr. Hamilton.' The heart of Quisling would have been warmed by the way in which he spat out the words.

Outside John found a taxi and gave the address of his friend Michael Ranfskeicyk.

Mike was out driving and two of the children were at school, but Betsy was there and delighted to see him.

'Hi there, Limey darling,' she said and gave him a smacking kiss on the cheek. Her hands were covered in flour and she smelt of baking.

As John ate some of the cookies she had just made, he brought her up to date on his movements.

'Betsy, may I leave my suitcases with you for a few hours? . . . and when Mike comes back ask him if he knows of a job I could get. I've decided to stay right here in New York.'

Betsy smiled happily. 'Why that's just great, Limey. Sure, we'll look after the stuff. What sort of a job have you in mind?'

'Oh, I'll do anything so long as its moderately honest and provided I don't have to work next Saturday . . . er . . . I'm taking someone to see a game.'

'I knew it,' cried Betsy thumping him on the shoulder and leaving the perfect imprint of a hand upon his coat. 'It's a dame?'

'I'm not telling,' said John grinning. 'I'll be back for the bags sometime this afternoon. Good-bye, Betsy, and thanks very much.'

' 'Bye, Limey, and give the gal a break, will you?'

John spent a couple of hours trying to find a place to live. At the third try he found something he thought would do— a room in the basement of a brownstone house on West 55th Street: it had probably once been a janitor's room when the street had known better days, but it was clean and there was a minute gas stove in one corner on which he could cook things when he had to.

The bed, which had big brass balls on top of each post, was large and seemed fairly comfortable and the room was kept warm by the fact that the boiler was next door and the hot water pipes for the flats above passed through it.

'How much?' he asked.

'Seven dollars a week,' said the landlady, a thin depressed woman. 'Two weeks in advance and no dogs. . . . There's a phone in the hall above.' She wiped her nose on her apron.

John gave her fourteen dollars and went out to meet Ann.

They arrived almost simultaneously. John was just turning into the doorway of the little bar when he saw her walking down the street from the opposite direction—it was ten minutes to one. He stood still and watched her as she came towards him, and his heart tightened as he saw, again, the fresh, open beauty that was hers.

When Ann saw him she ran the last few yards. John took both her hands in his and they stood for a long moment on the sidewalk just looking at each other and smiling; then they went inside out of the cold.

The table they had had the day before was unoccupied; so they sat down and looked at each other and smiled again.

'Thank you for going to see me off,' said John.

Ann laughed softly, 'I just wanted to make quite sure you left the country . . . you can imagine my disappointment when they said you had cancelled your passage.'

A waiter who had been hovering beside them for some time now began to move things around on the table in an expectant sort of way; without taking their eyes off each other, they ordered something, and he went away.

After lunch Ann went with John and he showed her his new home next to the boiler room. She set to work at once and tidied the place up; then they went out and John bought a bunch of flowers for Ann, and sent a cable to 'the Aunts' asking them to forward his letters. At four o'clock Ann left him to keep an appointment with a photographer, and John, lightheaded with happiness, made a token effort to find a job. He walked up and down Seventh and Eighth Avenues, peering at the notices posted in the windows of the employment agencies, but the next morning when Ann came to meet him he was still very much a gentleman of leisure. They had arranged that she should come to his dungeon at ten o'clock and that he would cook breakfast.

The breakfast was the usual male one—burnt bacon and broken eggs, blackened but scraped toast, weak coffee, and cream that had been much too near the hot water pipes. Ann said it was the most delicious meal she had ever eaten and they smiled happily at one another through the haze of blue smoke which filled the room.

'What time is your friend coming to pick us up?'

'Eleven,' said John. He jumped to his feet. 'Oh, my God!'

'What's the matter?'

'He's picking us up at the hotel. . . . I forgot to tell him I'd moved out. . . . Come on, we'll have to run for it.'

They grabbed coats and hats and dashed out.

'After the radiator,' panted Ann as they neared the Claybourne, 'you'd better wait outside and try to catch him.

I'll go in in case he's arrived already. . . . What does he look like?'

'Oh, huge and noisy,' said John vaguely.

Ann made a quick survey of the lobby, saw no particularly big or noisy men waiting there and rejoined John outside; they did not have long to wait: a great roar of welcome came echoing down the street followed a few seconds later by Jake Despard himself, mountainous in a huge coat. He was alone in his car.

'Janet sent her love. . . . She couldn't make it; so we're on our own. Glad to meet you, Miss Windsor. Climb in front will you? . . . John, you get in back with the food, and don't drink all the Bourbon before we get there. Gee! . . . what a great day for a ball game. How've you been, John? How did you ever find a beautiful girl like this?' He prattled gaily on with all the delicacy of a pneumatic drill, and Ann decided he was a lovable Teddy Bear.

They drove out into New Jersey and arrived at the stadium half an hour before the game was due to start. After picnic lunch in the car park (Jake had brought enough to feed an army) they fought their way through the entrance to the ground, bearing rugs and the bottle of Bourbon as protection against the frosty air.

They took their seats, the two men flanking Ann, and wrapped the rugs about them. Jake proffered the bottle, Ann refused, but John joined him in a little corrective before he leaned forward and looked with amazement at the spectacle around him.

Having at last discovered that he was about to witness a football match between two college teams he had rather naturally expected the same sort of intimate setting as that in which Oxford annually confronts Cambridge; he was quite unprepared for what he now saw. Ninety thousand people were present, and the green arena itself was occupied, at the moment, by what appeared to be a military parade of enormous proportions. Ann explained that one of the teams represented a military academy and that members of that establishment were now running through a little drill as a curtain raiser.

John's military eye was delighted with the precision with which marches, counter-marches, wheels and turns were executed.

Finally, to thunderous applause, the swarm of uniformed young men left the field and took up their seats in a giant square block in the middle of the stadium, exactly opposite where John, Ann and Jake were sitting.

Once they were seated, they produced pieces of different-coloured pasteboard and by holding these to the front presented, for the benefit of the spectators seated on the opposite side of the ground, the silhouette of a giant tank, its gun belching fire. Tremendous applause greeted this achievement.

An even louder burst of sound issued from ninety thousand throats when, a few minutes later, upward of a hundred young men in football clothing and all of incredible physique dashed on to the field. They proceeded to rush madly about clasping footballs to their chests, throwing, kicking and scrambling. Some, John noticed with interest, seemed to be indulging in simple Swedish exercises on their own, while others just ran up and down with the utmost velocity, their knees pumping up under their chins. . . . All wore deadly serious expressions.

He turned to Ann. 'Who are all these people?'

'Oh, those are the reserves, but I don't expect many of them will get into the game.'

'I see,' he said blankly.

Another ovation from the crowd, and another four score and ten young gladiators entered the area. As soon as he saw them Jake roared like a bull.

Down on the field the air became thick with flying footballs and hurtling bodies. John watched spellbound. At a given signal both sets of giants left the centre of the field and arrayed themselves on benches along either side of it. Attendants covered them up with blankets and offered them water—they were brushed angrily aside.

As John was looking down on the owners of the hundred broad, blanketed backs beneath him, they all rose suddenly to their feet, flung away their coverings and started to clap: some, beating their enormous hands together, advanced to the very edge of the field. Jake went into a paroxysm of delight and leaped, yelling, to his feet. The man seated immediately in front of John did likewise, thereby completely obliterating his line of vision. He asked Ann for information.

She smiled and formed the words with her mouth.

'Their team is just coming out.'

By the time the people around him had settled back in their seats the two teams were lined up in the centre of the field facing each other, but more surprises were in store for John. Down below him in front of the bottom row of seats he now perceived five young men in spotless white, dressed, apparently, for tennis. They were standing to attention and staring up at the crowd with fixed and purposeful expressions.

A great hush fell upon the vast concourse.

Out in midfield the opposing teams were poised on tip-toe ready for the coming conflict. The ball lay unsuspecting on the turf between them. Slowly at first a helmeted mammoth commenced a long loping run towards it, and two brass bands, one on either side of the stadium, struck up simultaneously, each with the battle song of one of the rival teams.

Down below the tennis players were galvanized into furious action. They turned into whirling Dervishes and began turning handsprings and cartwheels with great rapidity. 'Cheer leaders,' Ann explained. In midfield the mammoth, running swiftly now, was almost upon the wretched ball, a great spiked hoof was drawn back, and from ninety thousand throats came a mighty shout which rent the heavens. . . . The kick-off! John leaned expectantly forward, but the man in front stood up again and he saw nothing but a large expanse of tweed.

For the first quarter of the game he sat in a daze. That is to say, for the first quarter of the game he went up and down like a dazed jack-in-a-box. Whenever anything exciting happened everyone leaped to his feet and John found that as the game progressed he became trigger-kneed, and his legs coiled beneath him like a spring, ready to propel him aloft at the first sign of an upward surge from in front. It would be idle to suppose that he understood the game, but he enjoyed his occasional glimpses of it enormously.

He was fascinated by the committee meetings which were held before each play. The circle of gleaming helmets pressed together during the whispered consultations reminded him of the start of a Maori war dance which he had seen performed by some New Zealand troops before the battle of Sidi Barrani: he winced at the grinding crash as the two lines of heroes met with appalling force.

Occasionally after some particularly horrifying collision one body would remain writhing on the ground and a strange ritual would follow.

First, one of the attendants, who had been spending his time keeping the ungrateful shoulders of the reserves covered with horse blankets, would grab a white bucket in one hand and a sponge in the other and dash to the side of the fallen hero.

Sometimes this first attendant would be joined by another, who rushed out pushing before him a small white handcart, reminiscent to John of the 'Stop me and Buy one' ice cream wagons of sultry English Augusts.

After frantic spongings, flappings and slappings, the prone figure might rise and go staggering bloodily back into the maelstrom; if not, then the ministrations of the slaves had failed and they would signal desperately towards the benches from whence a man in a dark blue overcoat would run forward with a slithery motion caused by wearing smooth black leather shoes on a field already churned to mud by spiked football boots.

A swift examination by this expert would follow and the maimed fighter would then either be carried off, inert, on a stretcher, or would be assisted from the battlefield, cradled in the muddy arms of two of his comrades, to be dumped unceremoniously in a casualty clearing station just over the touch line. Whatever happened the Dervishes would exhort the crowd to give the unfortunate young man a special cheer and as he contemplated the weeks that lay ahead of him with his leg strapped to the ceiling, it surely warmed the cockles of his heart to know that 90,000 people approved of what he had done for dear old Alma Mater.

Slowly John began to catch on to the game. In point of fact, his neighbours all around, having heard Ann's patient explanations in reply to some of his more naïve questions, took it upon themselves, in the warm-hearted fashion of their race, to make absolutely sure that a foreigner in their midst, seeing a game of American football for the first time, should be afforded every opportunity to enjoy and understand it.

Even the man in front, as he went up and down with the frequency of an elevator in a busy hotel, took to pointing out plays, blocks, and tackles.

John came to realize that unlike rugby football or soccer, the man with the ball was only slightly more important than the other members of the team, and he grew to appreciate the superhuman efforts of the mountainous men of the line, and to appraise the beauty of the teamwork as a swathe was cut through the opposition for the benefit of the ball carrier. It took Jake and Ann and all the neighbours quite a considerable time, however, to convince him, when he heard a pistol shot ring out, that it was indeed the signal for the end of a period of play and not one of the players being put out of his agony.

The afternoon passed all too quickly for John. Jake's team won and the only untoward incident was at the very end when John, during an exciting moment, dropped a hot dog on to the seat of the man in front of him. The man, of course, was standing: when he sat back there was an ominous squelch and yellow froth appeared between his knees.

Back in New York, Jake Despard left them outside Ann's apartment building: he was worried, he said, about his Janet getting lonely unless he hurried home.

'Come on up,' said Ann when Jake had gone.

It was not a large apartment but it was comfortable in a dark brown, *café au lait* and leathery sort of way—a bachelor's apartment pure and simple.

'Uncle Don is away till Monday. He had to go to Chicago on business, so he said, but he had a funny look in his eye when he left.' She laughed. 'You'll love Uncle Don.'

They lit cigarettes and sat side by side on the sofa.

Another of their special silences fell between them: each was thinking so much about the other that it seemed ridiculous to spoil it by embarking on a conversation about something which was bound to be uninteresting by comparison: so they just smiled at each other, a tiny bit self-consciously, and though the silence lasted for a long time it never became unbearable.

Later they foraged in the ice box and found a can of corned beef. John peeled some potatoes and Ann chopped an onion: together they fried the corned beef, the potatoes and the onion in a big pan, then with a couple of poached eggs on the top of it and a bottle of chili sauce beside it, they bore the result in triumph into the living-room.

They sat on the floor and ate in the firelight. There was no silence now. They talked and talked of everybody and everything, and everybody and everything seemed important.

At eleven o'clock John rose to leave.

'Sunday or no Sunday, I've got to start job hunting in earnest tomorrow, and you won't have a job either if you sit up gossiping all night and get bags under your eyes.'

Ann walked with him to the door and helped him with his coat. With one hand on the door handle John turned and looked down at her. Ann held her chin down a little so that she looked up at him from under her dark lashes—the same way she had looked at him when he had first laid eyes on her in the little bar off Madison Avenue. His heart thumped against his ribs. Gently he took her shoulders.

'I am not going to shake hands and say "Good-night, Miss Windsor, thank you for the best day of my life. . . ." I am going to kiss you once, very quietly, and then go home without saying anything at all.'

Ann did not move. John took a half step towards her and kissed her very softly, very gently, on the lips. He kissed her just once, then turned and walked to the elevator: at that instant, they both knew—for sure.

The next morning, John received a cable and a note: they were both lying outside his door when he went out. He opened the cable. 'MUSHROOMS TOO TRICKY . . . EN ROUTE BERMUDA TO TRY LILIES . . . JOIN ME ANY TIME . . . ADDRESS C/O BUTTERFIELD'S BANK. OGLETHORPE.'

The note, which was from Mike Ranfskeicyk, was written on a page of a notebook.

'Dear Limey:
    Why in hell don't you get up in the morning? Gus has got a job for you if you know anything about wine, told him you were okay on spirits! Get the hell down there, Limey, and see Gus if you want the job. Betsy sends best.
                                                                Mike.
    P.S. It's Gus Weinkopf, he used to be a bootlegger. Now it's called Weinkopf's Wine and Liquor Store, 684 3rd Avenue.'

Gus Weinkopf was a squat little man, bald and fat, with grim eyes beneath thick glasses and teeth like a row of buttonhooks. He got right down to business.

'You got plenty of contacts?'

'Oh, yes, I know quite a number of people really.' John waved his hand airily. 'Long Island, you know.'

The grim eyes gleamed behind the lenses.

'Now see here, Mr. Hamilton, this joint of mine is going to be a classy joint. . . . I want Jock Whitney to come in here with maybe the British Ambassador or that South American doll—what's her name?—Perona?—some name like that . . . them's the type customers I want to see ordering their liquor in my joint.'

John inclined his head gravely. 'In that case I take it you have a tasting room where we can receive them?'

Gus looked suspicious.

'A tasting room? . . . What the hell kind of a set-up is that?'

'A small room, preferably with good Jacobean oak panelling, where we can let the customers taste the various wines before they decide which they want to buy.'

Gus slapped him on the back.

'Say, that's a great exploitation idea! Give 'em half a dozen free shots and they won't know what the hell they're buying anyway! That's great!'

John winced.

'Okay, Hamilton, you're in,' continued Gus Weinkopf, 'start today?'

'Fine,' said John.

'Forty bucks a week and ten per cent on any orders you bring in over four hundred a week.'

John was still at the stage where he had to convert dollars into pounds before he had any idea of the price or value of anything.

Gus mistook the serious expression caused by this mental effort of calculation for the outward and visible sign of indecision.

'Okay,' he said 'Fifty a week. . . . Now you satisfied?'

John nodded in stupefied agreement.

Gus showed him round the premises. It was a typical liquor store, counter and till at the far end and flanked on either side by the usual shelves reaching from floor to ceiling. It was presided over by a seedy-looking individual with a heavy scar across the lower half of his face.

'Glad to know you, Hamilton,' said the seedy-looking individual, and what did duty for a smile lifted one side of his face in a terrible leer.

It did not take John long to persuade Gus that the little store room at the back would make a perfect tasting room.

'All we need is a few chairs and a few small basins.'

'A few small basins?' Gus looked alarmed. 'What the hell are they for?'

John explained.

'The true wine taster does not swallow. He rolls it around with his tongue so that his palate is given every opportunity to appreciate the body or the dryness of the wine, then, so as not to spoil his taste for the next sample, he spits it out. . . . A good layer of sawdust on the floor is one way of handling this, but personally I favour the basin—the "individual deep dish" so to speak.'

Gus had a reverent expression on his face now.

'Gee, that's great, Hamilton. I can just see all them big shots in here. Big guys from Washington, Park Avenue, Wall Street, Hollywood—all sitting in here and spitting into little basins. . . . Why that would be just beautiful, and when they get knocked off and cool we could have a window display: "In Here Spat Huey Long"—that type thing. . . . Jees! we're going to make a lot of dough out of them spitting ideas of yours. . . . I'm sure glad I met up with you, Hamilton.'

Gus went out to buy the basins which John had suggested. Soon after he had gone four sinister figures sauntered into the store: they announced that they owned a restaurant and wanted to purchase some wine. The man in the front of the store, the one with the scar, looked vaguely alarmed when he saw them and passed them on to John. John asked them if they would like to taste some wine and took them into the little back room. He suggested that they try some Maison Cheval Blanc, which 'Scarface' happened to have handy, opened a bottle and poured some into each glass. One of the men asked John to join them; so, to make them feel at home, he poured some out for himself and started to taste it in the approved manner. At the identical moment that he spat his out, however, the customers all swallowed theirs. This caused quite a stir. They coughed and spluttered and accused him of trying to poison them and said that he had no right to give them bad liquor. It was no good trying to explain; so John opened a bottle of Bêcheville and with his help they drank it down to the last drop. A bottle of Pontêt Canet and a bottle of Mouton Rothschild followed in quick succession, then they switched to champagne. Three bottles of Charles Heidsieck were quickly disposed of.

Finally as they were tottering out of the store, John nervously asked them what their selection had been. Scarface was giving him some pretty dirty looks by this time so it was to his great delight that they ordered fifty cases of champagne. They wanted it delivered at once, they said, to their restaurant.

Scarface was watching him closely and John was more than ever determined to make good in this, his first big business deal.

'Fifty cases at sixty dollars a case, that would be three thousand dollars.' He felt very businesslike.

'Would you be paying cash?'

'By cheque,' said the biggest and ugliest of the men. 'Certified banker's cheque. That okay? You just send the stuff round right away to the restaurant—The Captain's Table is the name—just east of Broadway on 54th Street. One of us will be there with the cheque.'

When the truck had been loaded with the fifty cases of champagne, John climbed on to it and gave the driver the address of The Captain's Table: he was determined to pick up that certified cheque himself.

He arrived at the restaurant to find all four of the wine-tasters standing outside waiting for him: they were very friendly and even gave him a hand with the unloading.

'Just dump it right here on the sidewalk,' they told him. 'We'll take it in later—we have to make room in the cellar.'

When the unloading was completed, John was presented with a cheque for three thousand dollars: it was as impressive as only a certified banker's cheque can be. Everyone shook hands. John mounted the truck and, flushed with success, returned to the store.

Gus was there when he got back: a different Gus. Gone was the eager advocate of the tasting room: his eyes were glinting

113

evilly and the buttonhooks were snapped back into a thin blue line.

Scarface too was a changed man: he was shalky white and his teeth were audibly chattering: he was cowering in a corner behind the long counter. John sensed a certain tension.

Gus regarded him with loathing. 'Give me that cheque,' he snarled. John handed it over. Gus grabbed it, examined it minutely, held it up to the light—tore off a corner of it and peered at the exposed tissue: then very deliberately he folded it in half and tore it across and then across again. He repeated this several times and all the while his eyes never left John's face. As the fragments fell from his fingers, he moved slowly forward.

'You stupid sonofabitch,' he hissed. 'That cheque was forged by Kramer . . . Kramer!' His voice rose. 'Kramer who used to work for *me*. . . . And now you—you half-baked jerk— you have to sell Kramer three thousand dollars worth of *my* liquor. . . .'

John did some quick thinking. 'Surely all we have to do—if you're quite certain the cheque is a dud, is to pop along to the restaurant and ask for the champagne back: they probably haven't even taken it inside yet.'

Gus pushed his suffused face to within half an inch of John's nose. He spoke with venom, and his breath was dreadful.

'Listen Sonnyboy—you're damned right they haven't taken it inside yet: they never had any intention of taking it inside. That restaurant never had a goddamn thing to do with their order for champagne. Five seconds after you left three thousand dollars worth of my liquor lying on the sidewalk, Kramer and the others picked it up, loaded it on their own truck and now it's half-way to Jersey City—you—you'—he paused, gesticulating and inarticulate, '. . . get out of here, before I break your goddamned neck.'

John was determined not to be stampeded: he moved with dignity towards the door.

'Mr. Weinkopf,' he said, in measured tones, 'I understand

that I have been dismissed—however I hold no animosity towards you on that score, and as a demonstration of my good faith, I now intend to become a customer.'

He took a bottle of gin from the shelf and placed a five dollar bill on the counter.

'I understand you prefer cash.' A bellow of rage followed him into the street.

Ann was quiet when John related the saga of the tasting room but at the thought of an ex-bootlegger having his champagne hi-jacked in broad daylight, Uncle Don laughed until the tears ran down his cheeks.

Uncle Don was round and merry: a huge watch chain hung across his ample midsection.

'I reckon you're a pretty lucky young fellow. In the good old days they would have dropped you into a barrel of cement and heaved you into the East River!'

The next day John looked for a job and the day after that he looked again: the search became a permanent feature of his stay in New York. Ann helped him look, so did Mike Ranfskeicyk. Sometimes he found jobs—small jobs for a few dollars; sometimes he didn't. He registered as a spare butler with the Diamond Domestic Agency and several times was employed by the night to assist at parties.

Ten dollars he was paid for six hours, but the hire of a dress suit was two dollars and by the time the party was over he would often forget that he was a hired help and not a guest and take a taxi to one of the night restaurants and there do himself proud, arriving home in the small hours of the morning with a couple of dollars in his pocket, and the riches of Crœsus in his heart.

Every Saturday morning Ann would make him go through his accounts; and every Saturday night John would insist on declaring a dividend. Anything left over after the next week's rent had been deducted would have to be spent before Monday morning.

'I like to start fresh, darling,' he would say. If the dividend was a handsome one, then a carefully ordered dinner would be part of the evening's entertainment; if the dividend was a small one, then fearful smells of cooking would emanate from his tiny dungeon next to the boiler room.

On Sundays, if the weather was fine, they would run out into the country in Ann's little red roadster and go for long walks through the fields and woods. Sometimes they went to the sea and walked for hours along the beach. They were completely happy together wherever they were.

Ann's friends welcomed John open-heartedly into their circle and invitations of various kinds were constantly appearing in the mail box of the brownstone house on West 55th Street.

One of these invitations marked the end of John's days of butlerhood. He had been bidden to what Ann warned him might turn out to be a stuffy dinner party in a house on East 81st Street.

He had also received a call to work that night from the Diamond Domestic Agency, so putting business before pleasure he refused the invitation to dinner and accepted the employment.

After arriving at the service entrance, dressed in his butler's regalia, he was given a tray of *hors-d'œuvre* by the cook and shown the door into the drawing-room, where twenty odd guests were assembled, martinis in hand.

John put on what he fondly imagined to be his 'butler face': raised his eyebrows in a disdainful arch, balanced the tray as lovingly as though Salome's head had been nestling amid the parsley, and passed majestically through the door.

The first person he saw was Ann. The second was Jake Despard, and the third and fourth were Patricia Polliniri and Mr. Armstrong—all looked stunned.

Jake was the first to recover: he let out a whoop of joy.

'What a great gag,' he yelled.

Then he seized the unsuspecting host and hostess and dragged them over.

'Hi! Martha . . . Pete! . . . This is the man you wanted

to come to your dinner and here he is—Mr. and Mrs. Winthrop—Mr. Hamilton.'

John stood rooted to the spot. The tray began to feel heavy: out of the corner of his eye he could see Ann's agonized expression.

Mr. Winthrop rallied magnificently.

'Well, thank goodness you could come after all . . . we're a man short.'

'What a lovely joke,' said Mrs. Winthrop. 'So glad you are here. . . . Jake has told us so much about you.'

Jake grabbed the tray. 'Hey, let me take this.'

Mrs. Winthrop took his arm and he was propelled, scarlet-faced, round the room to be introduced to the other guests.

Patricia Polliniri was delighted to see him, and so, apparently, was Mr. Armstrong: Ann dissolved into helpless laughter and had to sit down. The rest of the people seemed to take it all as a matter of course; and in a few minutes the tide of the party was again flowing smoothly along.

Just once the hot and harassed face of the cook appeared at the door. She saw John, the butler, sitting on the sofa between Mrs. Winthrop and Ann; he was toying with a dry martini and talking gaily about ski-ing at the time. She gave him a terrible look and withdrew.

John, a little worried now in a professional way as to who would actually serve the dinner, asked Ann what was going to happen.

'I told Jake the truth,' she whispered back, 'and he has fixed it: he called up for someone else. They said they would have a man over in five minutes.' John's pride was a trifle hurt.

'Didn't they ask what had happened to me?'

Ann giggled. 'Yes . . . Jake told them that you were acting like a Communist and that you were unsuitable!'

'Oh, my God,' he groaned, 'there goes another job.' He was right and the following Saturday evening the smell of burned food again permeated the lower floors of the brownstone house on West 55th Street.

Ann's career as a photographer's model was beginning to hit its stride. Her beautiful face smiled from the bookstalls where it adorned the covers of several national magazines: she was much in demand. This meant that John saw less and less of her during the daytime, and most days while she was nibbling a sandwich in some fitting-room, he would be searching for a cheap place in which to eat in solitude. That was when he discovered the Restomat. The Restomat was a large help-yourself restaurant on Second Avenue. It operated on the nickel-in-the-slot principle. John had never seen one of these before, but jobs had been hard to find and the need for watching pennies, let alone nickels, had finally been borne in upon him.

The first time he entered the Restomat he did not notice the slot machines against the walls. The place just looked like a large, clean, unlovely restaurant, but the prices displayed in the window were a big attraction.

He sat at a small marble-topped table and looked round for a waiter. No one approached. After several minutes he rapped impatiently upon the surface of the marble and a large loose-mouthed individual moved across. He jerked his head in the direction of the walls. 'If you want anything you'd better go get it.' John followed the direction he had indicated and there beheld the customers, buying their midday meals at a row of slot machines—everything was priced 5, 10 or 25 cents.

He thanked the man and approached a machine labelled COFFEE—5 cents. He put a nickel in the slot and waited—he waited for quite a while. Presently he felt a warm dampness in the front of his trousers. He looked down. A thin stream of coffee had been playing upon him for a considerable time. He moved soggily away in search of a cup.

The next try was more successful. He caught the jet of coffee in the cup but steam from the first effort was still rising from his trousers and he was none too happy.

'Food,' he thought, 'that is the next move.' He placed his cup on a nearby ledge and went off to make a reconnaissance.

That was where he made his second mistake—placing that cup on the ledge. The ledge, in point of fact, was the dirty plate conveyor which moved every fifteen seconds: it moved now, and John turned just in time to see his cup of coffee disappearing through a hole in the wall.

Although depressed and wet and deeply resenting the fact that so far he had spent 10 cents for nothing, he was determined not to give up. He looked along the row of slot machines. A notice caught his eye—*Club Sandwich 25 cents*.

He advanced upon the machine. There was his sandwich, enormous and luscious-looking, staring out at him from behind a glass window: all he had to do was to put 25 cents in the slot and this vast quantity of food would be his! He checked the machine carefully to make quite sure where the sandwich would appear. There was only one possible exit: the operation appeared to be foolproof. With confidence he placed his quarter in the slot. There was a 'click,' a whirring noise and a minute sandwich slithered down the little launching ramp into his hand.

John held it up and inspected it. It seemed very small indeed. He looked back at the machine whence it had come: the next sandwich had moved up into the window and was now looking out at him—huge and luscious.

So that was it! A magnifying glass! Tricked again! He looked at the little thing in his hand, and his stomach grumbled: small, it was true, but good white bread covering bacon, tomato, chicken and lettuce. A wave of hunger swept over him. He raised it to his mouth and was about to sink his teeth into it when a voice spoke sharply at his elbow, 'Hey!' He looked round. The large loose-mouthed individual was with him once more. He wore an aggrieved and accusing expression. 'Hey!' he said again, 'new here, ain't you?'

'Yes,' said John.

'Well, take it easy then,' said the man. He took the sandwich out of John's hand. 'This is mine.' He nodded at the machine. 'Yours comes out next.'

'Oh! I'm terribly sorry,' said John. 'I didn't know—please forgive me.'

'That's okay, feller,' said the man. 'You'll learn.' He moved away munching steadily.

John turned back to the machine and waited; his stomach was rumbling ominously. He waited a long time but nothing came out. He banged on the glass front—the sandwich inside looked out at him impassively, but it did not move. A horrible suspicion entered his soul: he whirled round just in time to see the man with his sandwich disappearing through the swing door into the street. The man waved his hand in a farewell salute.

John sank down at a nearby table. 'I must not panic,' he thought: 'I must keep my head. It must be possible to get a meal here: it must be.'

For a long time he sat gathering his reserves for a fresh assault upon the machines, then when at last he felt able to try again, he took a coffee cup from the rack and stealthily approached the machine which had so basely drenched him before. In went his nickel and out came the coffee. He caught it all in the cup.

'There,' he told himself, 'it's perfectly simple when you know how to do it.' He carried the cup triumphantly to a table, sat down, added some sugar from the container and stirred the strong, brown liquid expectantly—at last he felt master of the situation.

An old man with a violin case under his arm and carrying a small brown paper bag materialized; he smiled hesitantly.

'Do you mind if I dunk?'

'Do I mind if you what?'

'Dunk,' said the old man.

John hadn't the faintest idea what the old man was talking about, but he seemed harmless enough.

'Dunk on, old fellow. In fact,' he added magnanimously, 'have a good dunk.'

'I'm most grateful I assure you,' said the old man.

Then with much rustling of paper he produced from his bag

a large doughnut which he plunged into John's coffee. Slowly and gravely he stirred the doughnut round inside the cup, while John sat like a dog watching a snake. At last the old man took out the doughnut and put the brown dripping end of it into his mouth.

'Ah!' he said with a sigh. 'Delicious! . . . I am most grateful, sir. Good day!'

'Good day,' said John in a high cracked voice. He looked down at his coffee—several crumbs and a currant were circulating slowly on the surface.

He got up, and disregarding a final growl of protest from his stomach, passed haughtily through the swing doors into the street.

CHAPTER SIX

IF, IN THE YEARS to come, John had looked back on his life, it would have been difficult for him to enumerate the turning points: in all probability he would have said that, like policemen, various people at various times had directed the traffic of events.

Certainly if he had not met Oglethorpe he would never have been dressed up as a goat; if he had not been dressed up as a goat, he would never have met Carole; if he had not met Carole, he would have gone through life without making the acquaintance of Mr. Dimbleby and 'Sledmere, Queen of England', who, in turn, had led him to New York. New York had provided Ann, and Ann was the sole reason why he was now walking down Park Avenue on a bright April morning four months later. It was Ann's birthday and John was going to buy her a present. He had twenty-five dollars in his pocket and he fully intended to spend every cent of it.

He walked briskly. The champagne air of springtime New York seemed to have affected everyone. The crowds were smiling, and even the traffic cops on the corner looked benign. With the first warm sunshine of the year, pretty girls, like butterflies newly hatched from the chrysalis, had sloughed off the furs and tweeds of winter and were testing their wings in their gaily-coloured frocks. His heart sang as he walked. He smiled happily, and this very smile brought about one of the most important turning points of all.

'What's so funny?' demanded a belligerent voice.

This jarring note brought John quickly back to earth. He perceived, standing squarely in his path, complete with ten gallon hat, high-heeled boots, blue jeans, shirt and neckerchief —the first cowboy he had ever laid his eyes on.

'What the hell's so funny?' this rugged man of the West now demanded.

At first John thought that someone immediately behind him was being questioned and he looked over his shoulder to see who this might be.

'No. . . . You,' said the cowboy and he poked John hard in the chest with his forefinger. 'What the hell were you laughing at?'

A small crowd began to collect.

'Believe me,' said John hurriedly, 'I was not laughing at you. . . . In fact, until you spoke to me I hadn't even seen you. I was miles away.'

'Is that so?' said the cowboy. 'Well, listen to me, stranger . . . the next time you are miles away take my advice and don't grin like a baboon at folks from out of town, or you'll wind up with a new set of uppers.'

'Thanks,' said John. 'I'll watch it in the future.'

'Okay,' said the cowboy. 'No hard feelings, pardner.' He paused and his voice became softer, almost wistful. 'Let's you and me take a shot of rye together.'

John could never resist 'characters'.

'That's an idea,' he said.

'Let's go then,' said the cowboy.

He turned to lead the way, but his spurs locked together and he fell into John's arms.

'These goddamn things,' he muttered, 'I don't know why the hell they invented them anyway.'

John propped him up again on his high heels and they walked off together in search of a bar. As they went along John took stock of his new acquaintance. He had seen cowboys on the screen, of course, and like millions of youngsters all over the world he had, at one time, formulated a pretty strong idea of the prototype of these lean, rugged characters. Milton Myers, for as such he had by now introduced himself, did not quite measure up to the specifications. His fortyish figure was short and tubby, his round thighs under the tight blue jeans did not look to John to have spent many years gripping the leather of the saddle; and the very definite paunch bulging beneath a red silk shirt seemed to be as far removed from steer wrestling and broncho busting as were the small white hands with the manicured nails, the blue chin and the carefully clipped black moustache. The rolling gait of the horseman who has spent a lifetime in the saddle was absent too, and disillusionment was complete when, seated at last upon a bar stool, instead of the promised shot of rye, he ordered an Orange Blossom cocktail. He was perspiring freely from the short walk. He swivelled round to face John.

'Have you got any dough?'

The question came suddenly but in a voice resigned to the negative answer: the emphasis was on the 'you'.

'I have twenty-five dollars in the world,' said John, 'unless you are expecting me to pay for these drinks, then I have twenty-four . . . or twenty-three if we order the other half.'

Milton Myers shook his dark Semitic head sadly.

'No, I mean real jack . . . around twenty-five grand.' He sighed. '. . . and it's such a beautiful idea too.'

John cast about for a way to open up the conversation a little more. He tried being technical.

'What idea? Some new way of fattening beef . . . er . . . on the hoof?' He didn't know what he was talking about, but it sounded knowledgeable.

Milton Myers looked lost and disconsolate.

'Beef on the hoof? Listen brother, the only beef I have ever seen has been on a plate. I've never been west of Central

Park. . . . I'm scared stiff of horses and,' he added with venom, 'I hate these goddamn clothes.'

He looked utterly dejected as he stared moodily into his cocktail glass: his plump shoulders were slumped in despair. John patted him on the back.

'Have another Orange Blossom. You'll feel better.'

'Okay, thanks a lot. . . . Sorry I called you down on the street just now, but I just couldn't stand one more person grinning at me.' He looked up. 'I wish you had some dough though, we could make a fortune.'

'Well, I've told you how much I've got,' said John, 'and incidentally I've got to go out and look for a job this afternoon because I'm going to need some more pretty soon.'

Milton Myers looked at him thoughtfully for a long time.

'English, aren't you?'

'Scottish actually, but I probably sound like an Englishman. . . . I've lived there nearly all my life. . . . Why?'

'Have you ever played squash racquets in England?'

'Yes, I used to play quite a lot.'

'Then if you want a job I can get you one this afternoon.'

'Playing Squash?'

'Playing "Squashette".'

'Squashette?'

Milton Myers wiggled a little on the bar stool.

'Christ, these pants are tight. . . . How the hell do those guys ride horseback when they're inside these goddamn things?'

He composed himself more comfortably within the 'blue jeans' and continued.

'Mr. Hamilton, before we go into the question of Squashette, I'm going to tell you about myself.'

John ordered two more drinks, and Milton Myers continued.

'All my life I've been connected with show business here on the East Coast. . . . I used to be a leg man for a circus, then I became a promoter. In my time I have promoted many things . . . a tortoise race in Miami . . . mole races in Boston . . . boxing matches between men and kangaroos in West Virginia . . . blindfold all in wrestling, two women to one man, on Rhode Island . . . and . . .' he paused, touched his fingers to his lips and blew a kiss to past glories 'my greatest success—falconry! . . . with the spectators in helicopters. . . . That was in Maryland. Now here I am with the best idea of them all.'

'Squashette?' asked John.

'No, no, no,' Milton Myers answered impatiently. 'We'll come to Squashette in a moment. The best idea of all, and the only guy who will even listen to it has only got twenty-five bucks in the world.'

'Twenty-three,' murmured John.

'Let us have another drink,' said Milton Myers.

'Don't forget about Squashette,' said John as he nodded to the barman.

'Squashette,' said Milton Myers with dignity, 'comes later.'

He looked searchingly at John before continuing.

'Of course I'm a mug to tell you this. . . . What's to stop you from going ahead and promoting the idea on your own?' He sipped his drink reflectively still looking at John over the rim of his glass.

John said nothing. At last Milton Myers appeared satisfied.

'Okay, I'll tell you.' He put down his drink and looked over his shoulder to make sure he was not being overheard. Then he leaned forward and, like Guy Fawkes ordering another barrel of gunpowder, whispered the magic words, 'Indoor horse racing.'

John had a momentary vision of the whole of Aintree being covered with a tarpaulin for the Grand National.

'Won't you need a lot of money for that type of thing? I mean covering whole racecourses . . . and quite a lot of people like to watch racing out of doors, in the first place.'

Milton Myers smiled pityingly.

'You haven't got it, have you?'

'No, not exactly,' admitted John.

'The courses, or tracks as we call them in this country, are built already.'

'You mean that you have covered racecourses over here?'

'I mean that there are plenty of covered auditoriums and stadiums in this country large enough to hold a race track. Not a full-size race track, of course. All we need is a quarter of a mile, then instead of horses we use ponies. Now have you got it? The Boston Garden, Madison Square Garden, the Municipal Auditorium in Atlantic City,' he reeled them off on his fingers, 'and many more all over the country. We could make a fortune.'

John rallied slightly.

'But even so, the average race only lasts for about two minutes.'

Milton Myers thumped the top of the bar in his excitement.

'My races are going to last for fifteen minutes!' he announced.

John was out of his depth again.

Milton Myers' voice was that of a patient governess.

'The betting will be on the jockeys, not on the ponies. The stamina of the rider will be the thing that counts. You see,' he paused for dramatic effect, 'there will be four jockeys in each race—fifteen ponies to each jockey and each pony races for only one minute. At the end of each minute the pistol goes off, the jockeys dash to their corners, leap on to the next pony and away they go again.' Milton Myers crouched at the bar and his voice shook with emotion. 'I can see it all . . . the packed audience, tier upon tier all yelling their guts out . . . one of the jockeys, through pure exhaustion, falls from the saddle, and has to be brought round by his seconds . . . the whole place rises to its feet and gives him a big hand as he climbs back into the saddle and starts to catch up . . . lap after lap, lap after lap . . . then the gun goes again . . . he is so weak he can hardly make the change onto the next pony, but the leader is in bad shape too and he makes a bad change . . . and this time they have to change their saddles as well, so his saddle starts slipping off, and the whole house is trying to warn him as he gallops round . . . lap after lap, lap after lap. . . .'

John was beginning to feel the excitement, he was gripping the edge of the bar. Milton Myers was sweating profusely.

'It can't miss, can it?' He grabbed John by the arm. 'You know it can't miss, don't you?'

'No,' said John in a daze, 'I don't believe it can!'

A break came into Milton Myers' voice. 'But it's no use. They just won't listen to me . . . I've been in to see them all, and they all say the same—let's look at it first; then . . . if it's good—we'll buy it. I reckon we could open for twenty grand, and,' he thumped the bar again, 'for Christ's sake, that's nothing! Nothing! When you think that those guys will put five times that amount into a show on Broadway just because they are laying some doll and she wants to be a star.' He shook his head sadly. 'No, I'm afraid I'm washed up this time.'

His shoulders sagged dejectedly within the gay silk shirt: he was like a man who has come to a fancy dress party on the wrong night.

John felt very sorry for him and ordered some more drinks.

That was a fatal mistake. Two hours later he accepted the Presidency of INDOOR HORSE RACING ASSOCIATION, INC.

When Ann heard of the latest development, she was not enthusiastic.

'Oh, Johnny. . . . Couldn't you try an office job just once? Something that will lead somewhere . . . something . . .' she hesitated, 'that would mean security and a chance to settle down sometime.'

He put his arms around her.

'Darling, I'm hopeless. I don't know what it is. . . . I suppose it's the war. I don't think I'll ever be able to settle. I'd go mad in an office. I think I'd go mad if I always knew what to expect the next day, but give me time: I'm only twenty-five and if this pony racing doesn't work, I promise I'll try something more sedate.'

She smiled at him; and being a mere male he only saw the front part of the smile, he did not see the disappointment and the anxiety behind it.

'What are you going to live on while you and Mr. Myers are trying to raise the money?' asked Ann.

'Oh! I forgot to tell you I have a new job—a part time job,' he grinned. 'Every day I go to Stacey's and put on a pair of white shorts and a sweater with "Squashette" written across the chest, then I demonstrate in the window.'

'Squashette?'

'Yes. It's a sort of table squash racquets, the way ping pong is table tennis. They have a notice in the window saying that I am the world's champion, and as I am the only person who has ever played the game I suppose it's true! For the first few days I have to play in the window with a girl from the sporting goods department, but after that,' he said proudly, 'I am going to accept challenges from the spectators. It's only a few hours a day and they are paying me thirty-five dollars a week—in advance.' He hesitated. 'Happy Birthday, darling.' He thrust a small package into her hand.

Ann unwrapped it excitedly and a small brooch fell into her hand: a tiny gold racquet on which reposed a ball . . . a diminutive pearl.

'Oh, Johnny darling, you shouldn't have done that,' she said in a whisper. For a few seconds her head remained bent over the present; and being a mere male he did not see that she was crying.

Patricia Polliniri was the one who really put Indoor Horse Racing Inc. on its feet. John had just come back from his first challenge game of Squashette in Stacey's window and his natural gloom at being soundly defeated by his challenger—a horrid little boy of eleven—was immediately dispelled when he heard the news.

Mr. Armstrong had decided to accept his very generous offer to let him have the last two thousand shares of stock for fifteen hundred dollars. Milton Myers on hearing the news immediately changed into top gear.

'First we must have an office and a secretary,' he announced. And later that day John was horrified to hear his partner addressing the renting agent of a large office building on Park Avenue.

'Sure, we will need a lot of space. A floor: two floors, maybe. But in the meanwhile, to help you out, we could probably fit into just two or three rooms while we are getting ourselves organized. The rest of our staff will be arriving in a week or two, from our California office.'

The renting agent was impressed. 'Well, gentlemen, if you really wouldn't mind letting us fix you up in a small office for the time being, it would give us time to look around and see where we can arrange for the large amount of space you will be requiring later.'

'Okay, fine,' said Milton Myers, 'but of course, we don't want to clutter ourselves up with a lease on the small one, you understand.'

'Why, I should say not,' said the renting agent. 'Just make use of it until you are ready for the big space.'

Miss Fitch arrived the next day. She was twenty-eight, spotty, wore glasses and ate Hershey bars all day long. She fell in love with John at first sight, and brought her own type-writer with her, which was a blessing.

Salesmen for various articles of office equipment started to pour in. John, learning that they were working on a per-centage basis, felt sorry for them, and the rooms were soon filled to capacity with various brands of drinking water, piles of towels, and twenty-five different species of pencil sharpener.

The financing was done surprisingly quickly; Jake Despard decided to put in a thousand dollars and two of his friends enthusiastically came in as well: soon ten thousand dollars were subscribed and John felt tremendously important as he signed his name on the stock issue above the word 'President'.

The services of a moderately reliable horse-coper were next obtained, and the buying of the ponies was put in hand. It was essential, for the spectacular effect of the venture, to collect fast, good-looking animals; but it was equally im-portant to spend the minimum amount of money in so doing. Jarrold, the horse-coper, was therefore given instructions to start buying one hundred and twenty ponies at an average cost per animal of not more than one hundred and fifty dollars.

Shrewdly, Milton Myers had reckoned that a polo pony the right age and sound in wind and limb could not be bought for that low price unless there was something else very wrong with it. He was quite right, and a formidable string of half-witted animals began to accumulate; many were quite mad and could not even be approached by normal human beings.

Normal human beings, however, had little or nothing to do with the enterprise, and the riders were no exception.

Several times a day Miss Fitch stopped her rhythmical mastication of Hershey bars to gape wonderingly at the stream of strange-looking visitors which now flowed through the office: circus riders, ex-jockeys, broncho-busters, and Indians (both turbaned and Red), all came looking for a chance to ride these ferocious beasts. Milton Myers' days with the circus were standing him in good stead.

One day the manager of the building dropped in to say that eleven horse boxes full of horses had arrived outside. 'The driver,' he said, 'shows every sign of unloading on the sidewalk.'

John was slightly shaken, but his partner was more than equal to the occasion. 'The ponies can go to the Gulnare Polo Club at Watch Hill,' he said airily. The manager withdrew and John asked for an explanation.

'The Club, as a Club, has not existed since the crash in 1929,' said Myers, 'but the buildings and stables are all there. An old friend of mine is the caretaker and I have persuaded him to let us use the place till we get moving.' He paused. 'By the way, I promised him a little stock in the Company. Have you any handy?'

'Oh, yes,' said John faintly, 'plenty.'

Milton Myers disappeared for two days to make arrangements for a Grand Opening: when he came back he radiated success.

'Ocean City!' he cried as he trotted into the office. 'It's all set! We've got the auditorium—the biggest in the world . . . holds thirty-two thousand people . . . we can't miss!'

He waved a piece of paper excitedly. 'There it is . . . the contract for six days. Boy! oh boy! oh boy! I knew we'd make it!'

'When is it?' asked John.

'May twenty-six, in three weeks time,' beamed Milton Myers.

'Three weeks time!' cried John in a horrified voice. 'We can never get ready by then, we've got to get saddles and things.'

Milton Myers roared with laughter. 'We've got to get saddles and things, the man says.' He turned in mock appeal to Miss Fitch: her jaws stopped moving for a moment and she stared back in a calf-like way.

'I'll tell you what else we've got to get.' He ticked off the items on his fingers: 'We've got to get another ten G's, and another eighty-seven ponies: we've also got to arrange an advertising campaign and accommodations and stabling at Ocean City. Further to that we've got to arrange to move the whole outfit from Watch Hill two hundred miles to Ocean City: we've got to sell the peanut and popcorn concessions: we've got to fix the local police so that we can have betting, because it's illegal in that state, and we've got to get a uniform for you.'

'A what?' gasped John.

'Oh, didn't I tell you? . . . Each night you are going to lead the Grand Opening Parade—COLONEL JOHN HAMILTON OF THE KING'S OWN MOUNTED MARINES, HERO OF THE BULGE.'

'Oh, my God,' John groaned.

'Well, choose any outfit you like, and we'll dream up a uniform to match it. Now let's get going. . . . We have a lot to do. And don't forget . . . if we have a good "gate" at Ocean City we are all set for Boston, Philly, and probably the Garden itself—everything depends on that first gate!'

Milton Myers unrolled a large poster. 'Now look at this.' It showed a head-on collision at full gallop between two enormous stallions; distended nostrils and flailing hooves were everywhere. Two men were also portrayed. One was being trampled to death by one of the stallions, the other was flying through the window of a blazing house. CHILLS! SPILLS!! AND THRILLS!!! screamed the caption.

'Isn't that great?' cried Milton Myers.

'Wonderful,' said John in awed voice, 'er—what's all that fire business supposed to be?' He pointed to the flaming house.

'Ah, ha! . . . there you are, you see,' chortled Milton Myers. 'You saw it on the poster and you wondered about it . . . so you asked me, didn't you? Now if you'd been in Ocean City you'd have bought a ticket and gone in to find out for yourself, wouldn't you? See? . . . get 'em in there, that's all we have to do! Get 'em in there for those six days— remember everything depends on that "gate". ' He rolled up the poster with a flourish.

The electric enthusiasm of the man was contagious. Miss Fitch was galvanized into action and set about her typewriter like a mad thing. John rushed about doing odd jobs and watched apprehensively as more and more people were added to the payroll; an extra buyer of horseflesh, a stable master, a shoesmith, a couple of advance publicity men, a cashier and a bookkeeper. The whole place began to throb and pulsate.

The next three weeks was a nightmare, but somehow everything was accomplished. Money makes money, and indeed the second ten thousand dollars proved much easier to find than the first. The ponies were bought and the riders somehow brought them to a state of semi-submission; the programmes were arranged; the peanut and popcorn concessions were allocated and the chief of police at Ocean City suggested that he himself should nominate good honest bookies, 'well known to him personally'. John had gone down to handle this part of the preparations and must have shown some measure of surprise at this willing co-operation on the part of the man whose sole responsibility it was to prohibit the making and taking of bets in that part of the world.

'Don't you worry about a thing, kid,' said the chief of police kindly. 'Your customers will get their betting, the bookies will get their bets and I will get . . . er—the gratitude of the bookies.' He spread greedy-looking hands, 'Everybody will be happy.' He leaned forward at his desk. 'One thing I'd like to know, though, is how come you managed to square all this with Lefty?'

'Lefty?'

'Yeah. . . . Lefty Orbach.'

'I've never heard of him.'

'Oh, so you've never heard of Lefty Orbach?' said the chief of police of Ocean City slowly. 'Well now, that's just dandy. That explains everything . . . everything. . . .' He smiled queerly. 'Looks like you should have a most interesting time down here.'

'Now just a minute,' said John. 'Who is this Lefty Orbach?'

The policeman lowered his voice. 'He runs this town, that's all, son. Just runs the whole goddamned town. Why, out of every nickel that goes into a slot machine on the amusement pier two cents go to Lefty. Why, I don't believe that a man could open a shoe shine parlour down here without splitting it up the middle with Lefty, and if anyone operates here without his permission,' he paused, 'well, he just suddenly stops operating.' The chief of police made a loud click with the thumb and second finger of his left hand—'like that. . . .'

'You mean he is a sort of gangster?' asked John.

'Shhhhh,' said the chief of police. 'We don't use that word around these parts. Let us just say . . . he has control of certain business interests here in Ocean City and leave it at that, shall we?'

'All right,' said John. He put out his hand. 'Good-bye, and thanks for all the good news.'

'Good-bye,' said the chief of police.

On his way to the station John pondered deeply over this conversation.

A large advertisement caught his eye:

'CHILLS, SPILLS AND THRILLS'

Although more than ten days were still to elapse before the great opening day, the billboards of the town were already showing signs that the advance publicity men had been earning their salaries.

'CHILLS, SPILLS AND THRILLS'—the posters were everywhere.

John was impressed. As the train pulled out of the station he fell to thinking about the forceful ways of American advertising and how greatly they differed from the placid assertions and the gentle persuasions of England—'OXO PUTS BEEF INTO YOU.' 'GUINNESS IS GOOD FOR YOU'; or that quiet rebuke from Scotland—'DON'T BE VAGUE, ASK FOR HAIG.' He had been brought up with these. As he pondered it seemed to him that the local advertising was based more upon a psychology of fear. He looked again out of the window—'FOUR OUT OF FIVE HAVE IT.' 'IT MAY BE YOUR TURN NEXT.' From the hoardings and the sides of houses came the accusing fingers, the pitying looks of doctors and druggists, dreadful portraits of steaming feet——

DANDRUFF! BAD BREATH! BODY ODOUR! PINK TOOTH-BRUSH! EVEN YOUR BEST FRIEND WON'T TELL YOU! ALWAYS A BRIDESMAID NEVER A BRIDE! IT MAY BE DECEMBER, BUT IT IS AUGUST UNDER YOUR ARMS!

He cringed back in his seat and hoped that the other people on the train would not notice his shortcomings.

Back in New York Milton Myers was bursting with excitement.

'Johnny boy, we are all set up. I have it all figured out. By the time we open on the 25th we will have everything paid for—ponies, saddlery and transportation . . . everything: we will have just enough dough left to pay the boys a week's wages in advance and to buy forage for the animals. Now there's nothing left to arrange except the hospital. . . .'

John was becoming inoculated against surprises. He just waited in silence for the explanation.

'When one of the boys falls off at the turn, which he will do when we give him the signal; and, incidentally, Jim Curtis is the boy for that, he worked for years as a stunt man in Hollywood and he can fall on a dime and bring his horse down with him if we want him to . . . well, when one of the boys falls we must dash out and pick him up on a stretcher and take him to the hospital and patch him up so he can get back into the race.'

'Where is this hospital going to be?' John asked, resignedly.

'Why, out in the middle of the track, under arclights, of course, where the audience can watch him being patched up.' Milton Myers doubled over a little (he always crouched slightly when he got carried away by his own descriptions). 'Then he limps back to his team and mounts again, away he goes, catching up . . . lap after lap, lap after lap. . . . The crowd is on its feet, yelling! Cheering! The bookies are cursing and there's Jim coming round again! . . . blood all over his face!—we can put that on in the hospital . . . and round he goes again! He's fourth! He's third! He's second! He's . . . No! The gun! . . . They have to change ponies!!'

Milton Myers sank back in his chair, and passed the back of his hand across his damp brow before he asked, with the strained voice of an exhausted runner, 'How did you make out with the betting?'

John told him. 'Also,' he added, 'there seems to be a person called Lefty Orbach who runs the whole place. . . . Do you know anything about him?'

Milton Myers did not answer immediately. 'Yeah, that's right . . . I have been expecting to hear from him, but he's got nothing on us and we've got so far along now without any interference that there's nothing much he can do. If we had been getting ready and training down there at Ocean City instead of up here he might have made it plenty tough for us, but I don't think he'll give us any trouble now . . . I hope not anyway.'

John had been so desperately busy that he and Ann had not seen nearly as much of each other as they had before he had smiled by mistake at an uncomfortable cowboy on Fifth Avenue. In the meantime her beautiful face had become better and better known to millions all over the country: she was

135

fast becoming one of the most sought-after cover girls in the advertising world, and the movie moguls of California were already baiting their hooks.

'Johnny darling,' she said one evening, when they were discussing this, 'I don't want to be an actress; in fact I don't really want to go on being a model much longer. It was great fun when it all started, but I hate people staring at me in the streets and they do that all the time now. I'm gradually becoming a different person. I'm not sort of . . . private any more.'

He covered her hands with his.

'I am afraid I have been a poor friend lately, but I really have been up to my neck in this pony business—it's so important to me. It must seem as though I think of nothing but myself and what's going to happen in Ocean City: and that I am not excited and happy about you and all you have been doing—but I am . . . truly I am.'

He paused and kissed a little blonde curl behind her ear. 'Darling, will you promise me one thing?'

'If I can, yes.'

'Promise me that if some good looking fellow with a great big yacht and four Rolls-Royces asks you to marry him, you'll say "No"—very firmly.'

'I promise,' smiled Ann, and her face was bright with happiness.

On the hottest day of the year INDOOR HORSE RACING ASSOCIATION, INC., arrived in Ocean City. Milton Myers, determined that the local inhabitants should be given every opportunity to notice this arrival, arranged for the entire troupe to get lost between the railway station and the Municipal Auditorium on the sea front—a distance of three-quarters of a mile.

A hundred and twenty ponies, controlled intermittently by some forty or fifty cowboys and Indians all in full regalia, took six hours to cover the ground between these points. Not a main street in the city was missed out: traffic throughout the whole area was thrown into hopeless confusion.

Milton Myers was delighted. He and John were following in an open car at the tail end of the procession. 'Good word-of-mouth advertising,' he said. 'How do you feel, Captain?'

John looked down at the uniform which Milton Myers had hired for him—a Broadway costumier's idea of how an officer of the Swiss Guard would have looked at the turn of the eighteenth century. 'If you really want to know,' he said sourly, 'I feel like a commissionaire outside a whore house in Marseilles.'

'Well, don't let that worry you,' said Milton Myers, 'look at me . . . I've been dressed up like a poor girl's Buck Rogers for two months or more. By the way,' he said as they sat sweltering in the traffic jam, 'I've got a great idea if this present setup falls through.'

'What's that?' asked John without much interest: inside the heavily padded red and gold jacket the sweat was trickling down his chest.

'We will take out advertisements in four or five hundred local newspapers all over the country—"Positively last opportunity! Six essential pieces of household equipment for one dollar:" Then all we would have to do would be to buy a paper-knife with which to open the envelopes, and a large suitcase in which to put the money.'

'I see,' said John, 'and what do we send them as the six essential pieces of household equipment?'

'I was toying with the idea,' murmured Milton Myers, 'of sending six sheets of toilet paper. . . . They wouldn't weight much so we would save on postage.'

'Milton,' said John, 'I am not a fussy man, but much as I love your country, I have no wish to gaze out upon the same part of it for years from behind bars. Let us therefore see how we get along with these ponies before we start sprinkling the United States with toilet paper.'

'Okay,' said Milton Myers, hurt. 'Okay. But as you should know, Captain, every good general has an alternative plan.' He leaned toward John solicitously. 'How does the collar feel now?'

'Tight, thank you. How are the blue jeans?'

'Tight!'

They sweltered on in silence.

When at last the caravan reached the auditorium there was great activity. Ponies were being stabled, watered and fed: the equipment was being unpacked and the human element housed. When the hurly burly had died down somewhat, John changed out of the hated uniform and went for a stroll along the sea front by himself. A cool evening breeze was blowing in from the Atlantic. He savoured it gratefully.

His mind was in a whirl. So much had happened in such a short while: in six months to be precise.

He asked himself a searching question. 'Do I really want to marry and settle down? Am I sure?' He stopped and looked out to sea. The sun was setting behind him and the reflection had coloured the sky beyond the horizon into a gentle shell pink. The cool sea air smelled good after the weeks in the crowded noisy city. There was only a gentle ripple of tiny waves at the tide line. 'Yes,' the answer came quite distinctly. 'More than anything else in the world I want to settle and stop moving.' He made a big decision. If the pony races were a success (and according to Milton Myers everything depended on the 'take' at the box office during the next week), he would ask Ann to marry him. Somehow he would find a steady job, maybe back in England, and they would settle down together. She would give up being a model and could feel 'private' again. As he walked back towards the auditorium, in the gathering dusk, his mind was filled. He saw a little house sheltering behind a wall of rose-coloured brick, where a carefully nurtured herbaceous border rose in a gentle slope from the lowly forget-me-nots in front to the giant hollyhocks at the back.

He saw children playing on the lawn and Ann sitting there, calm and lovely in the shade of a great chestnut tree. His pulse quickened. 'Why, oh, why, haven't I asked her before? Maybe she has fallen in love with somebody else in the last few hours. . . . How could I have been such a fool as to take her so much for granted? I shall see her when she comes down the day after tomorrow, but that's a long time and anything can happen between now and then.' Involuntarily he began to walk faster . . . a wave of near-panic swept over him. 'I must telephone her and tell her that I love her and that she mustn't see anybody else until I have had a chance to talk to her.' He began to run.

He put the call through as soon as he got back to the auditorium. Ann was not there. 'She just went out,' said Uncle Don. 'Some fellow called to take her to a show. . . . Is there anything you want me to tell her?'

'No, not really,' said John flatly. 'Just tell her I called to say "hello" and . . . er . . . you might say I am going to buy a yacht and some Rolls-Royces.'

'You been drinking?' asked Uncle Don.

'No, that's just a little sort of joke between us,' said John feeling supremely foolish. 'Good night.'

'Good night, young feller,' came the mystified voice from New York. 'You'd better take it easy!'

The day before the opening was spent in feverish activity. Milton Myers was superb: he rose magnificently to every occasion: no crisis was too great for him to handle, no problem too difficult to solve.

In his office, the Press were received, and left two hours later full of gin and goodwill.

'Incidentally, John,' said Milton Myers, 'in the new edition of the programme you will have a Victoria Cross instead of a Military Cross . . . Okay?'

'Okay,' said John in a small voice.

There was a loud report in the next room. John jumped. 'What's that?' he asked nervously.

'Miss Fitch,' said Milton Myers. 'She has switched to bubble gum. . . . Now about finances: as I told you, Johnny Boy, we have arrived here intact and in the black and everything depends on this next week. However, I made a slight miscalculation and we have not got enough dough left to hire an orchestra, rent the hospital equipment or pay the nurse and doctor to run the joint.' He paused and fiddled with the stubs of some empty cheque books on the desk.

John had an uncomfortable feeling that he was about to hear some disturbing news.

Milton Myers went on. 'I have taken care of the orchestra situation by hiring an organist. This place has the biggest pipe organ outside St. Peter's in Rome and this guy promises to make more noise on it than ten orchestras. . . . So that's all set. Now about the hospital. . . .' He eyed John over the top of the desk. 'This is where you come in.'

'Me?' said John with a sinking heart.

'Sure. As soon as you get back from leading the parade— you become a doctor. All you need is a white coat, one of those little hats like Nehru wears in India, some rubber gloves and a piece of gauze tied over your mouth. . . . We are rigging up some mighty fancy-looking hospital equipment out of some things I've borrowed from an old girl friend of mine; she operates a beauty parlour here in town: so provided no one is badly hurt you will be able to handle them under the hair dryer and so forth.'

John sat down. 'Are you going to be the nurse by any chance?'

'Me? No! I thought perhaps Miss Windsor might help us out. . . . You did say she was coming down for the opening, didn't you?'

John sighed. 'How about that girl friend of yours. . . . Wouldn't she do it?'

'Sure, she'd do it,' said Milton Myers with a minimum of gallantry, 'but she looks so godawful these days that the patients would probably pass out when they saw her.'

The next day Ann arrived from New York.

The box office was due to open one and a half hours before the start of the first race and, before it did so, John took her outside a dozen times so that they could walk nonchalantly past and count the number of people standing in line before the closed windows.

Although a nervous tension permeated the whole company, and even communicated itself to the ponies in their stalls, Milton Myers was as calm as a cucumber. He took Ann and John to have a last look inside the great auditorium.

It was a most impressive sight. Each of the four corners was decked out in a different colour—red, yellow, green and blue —one for each team.

At the moment these corners were empty, but soon the four teams of ponies competing in the first race would make an impressive entrance led by their jockeys and accompanied by their helpers.

The jockeys' silks, the helpers' shirts, the ponies' accoutrements and even the water buckets and feed bags were all picked out in the colours of the teams.

In the centre of the oblong quarter of a mile tanbark track was the hospital: even from the nearest seats it was impossible to realize that its gleaming and efficient-looking equipment was in reality a superb job of camouflaged hair-dryers and manicure tables. The hair curlers looked like life-giving surgical instruments as they stood in their jars of disinfectant.

The popcorn and peanut men in their white caps and coats were setting up their trays and taking up their positions in the aisles; the ushers in the green uniform of the auditorium were gathering at the entrances; the clockers and scoreboard manipulators were moving into their appointed places; and high above the main entrance to the arena, the organist was climbing into his eyrie.

Milton Myers looked round proudly, then gave the signal. The turnstiles clicked out the first welcome news and the seats began to fill up. John excused himself and went off to don his uniform. When he came back Milton Myers and Ann were jubilant. 'It's going to be a full house, Johnny Boy . . . not a seat left in the place. Now all we have got to do is give them a good show.' The ponies were being led out for the Grand Parade; they were in a highly nervous state and a good deal of kicking and plunging was going on: cowboy curses impregnated the air. Finally some semblance of a parade was organized and John went in search of his own mount.

He had ridden Rattlesnake several times in practice at Watch Hill, but it was no good pretending that they had ever seen eye to eye. The animal stood a good sixteen hands—far too big to be a useful polo pony.

Now as he approached the brute's stall John gave a start. In a moment of zeal Milton Myers had ordered Rattlesnake to be specially bedecked for the occasion and there he stood, caparisoned like a war horse of the French cavalry before Agincourt. Unfortunately, Rattlesnake was eminently unsuited to trappings of this sort and the result, combined with his nobbly knees and weak ewe-neck, was a perfect monument to Don Quixote and his attacks upon the windmill.

The shock that John received when he first saw Rattlesnake was as nothing compared to the effect his own appearance produced upon the horse. It took one look at his scarlet tunic and golden epaulettes, his white breeches and fireman's helmet, and a shrill whinny of fear rent the air. As it reared up on its hind legs and pawed the air in terror, the rolling whites of its eyes and the flaming red of its distended nostrils reminded John of a giant rocking horse.

'Steady,' he said hopefully.

Ann clutched his arm. 'Oh, Johnny darling, are you going to ride that awful thing?'

'If I can get anywhere near it I'm supposed to,' he answered grimly.

He took her by the arm and piloted her to a safe place just in case Rattlesnake should make a bolt for the Atlantic Ocean.

'I expect it will get used to me later on,' he muttered.

The horse finally returned to all fours, and stood quivering in the stall; a white foam was playing about its lips.

Milton Myers came up exuding confidence, and John noted with a sudden wave of resentment that he had exchanged his tight blue jeans for a loose-fitting dinner jacket. He had a red carnation in his buttonhole.

'Come on, Johnny Boy, up you hop. We are all ready to

start. . . . Now remember: twice round the ring slowly and a nice salute each time to the mayor in the box with all the flags on it. Then, when you come back, make a real quick change into the doctor's outfit. Miss Windsor will be waiting for you right over there beside the entrance—and good luck, kid.'

'Good luck, darling,' echoed Ann. 'Do be careful please.' And in a desperate attempt to cheer him up, 'I think you look perfectly beautiful in your uniform.'

John smiled the sickly smile of an international spy caught with the plans of the latest submarine protruding from his breast pocket, and advanced upon Rattlesnake.

Several people came to help, and while some anchored the vibrating animal, others picked John up in a sitting position and hoisted him on top. He noted with relief that they placed him facing the same way as the horse, then gingerly he picked up the reins and made a clucking noise with his tongue.

Like a ship hesitantly moving out of dry dock into the unknown of the sea, Rattlesnake edged out of the stall and set an erratic course for the head of the column.

John's progress past the waiting horsemen was punctuated by friendly cat-calls and words of advice.

'Attaboy, Johnny, we'll be right behind you.'

'Sure a snazzy lookin' outfit, Johnny Boy.'

'Good luck, kid,' they called.

It was partly brought on by the uniform, no doubt, but as John took his place at the head of his men, some of the old confidence of the battle-hardened officer returned. He adjusted his gleaming helmet and held his head high.

'Forward march!' he shouted and aimed Rattlesnake in the general direction of the entrance to the arena.

The organist, who had been regaling the packed and expectant auditorium with a few light and popular airs, spotted the gleaming top of John's helmet far below him and also caught a glimpse of the animals and men lined up behind. This was his moment. He pulled out every stop in the organ and brought eight fingers, two thumbs and two feet simultaneously into action—a thunderous chord rent the air. That was all Rattlesnake needed: the animal coiled itself like a spring and leaped forward with the speed of light. John left the saddle and for one awful moment thought he was going to alight in a sitting position on the ground: in point of fact, he landed again on Rattlesnake, but this time behind the saddle instead of on top of it. The reins had left his hands at the same moment that his feet had left the stirrups; the golden helmet had fallen forward over his eyes like the visor of a knight in armour. With the strength of a drowning man he clung limpet-like to the back of the saddle as he slithered about on the sleek and sloping rump of the galloping beast. The crowd roared its delight.

The helmet was bumping about on the bridge of his nose, but by tilting his head far back he could see enough to tell in which direction he was travelling; chiefly because there was no way off the track except through the entrance now jammed with the entering procession, Rattlesnake, having completed one circuit of the track, headed round it again at great speed. The whole 'yipping', galloping horde of horses and men was in full cry behind him, and the thought of what would happen should he slip off gave John a further incentive to hang on. He saw that he was passing the flag-bedecked box occupied by the mayor and, heedful of his instructions, managed to raise one hand in a jerky greeting. Although the crowd gave him a big hand for this piece of courtesy, it was almost his undoing. His other hand worked loose from the saddle and he felt himself gradually slipping off the heaving, rounded, and highly-polished end of the horse. At this point, the tail-end of the column having passed into the arena, Rattlesnake could easily have turned out through the entrance; instead, desiring to be with the other galloping animals, the brute decided to make one more circuit and careered madly after them.

Slowly but surely, John was slipping towards the ground. The crowd was in a fever of excitement. This was a real stunt! . . . What a knockout start to a show!

144

John never knew how he did it. Involuntarily, he put out one hand behind him and there he found Rattlesnake's tail. He grasped the welcome rope of hair and as he slowly slithered off the horse's buttocks he transferred the other hand there as well.

Like a monkey he clung, and by leaning his body far back, he was able to keep his legs up off the ground. The crowd screamed its pleasure. Rattlesnake galloped madly round; but this time as they came once more opposite the entrance, the animal decided it had had enough. To the thunderous applause of the populace it flashed under the archway and out of sight.

Helping hands extricated John. Milton Myers dashed up, his face bathed in perspiration. 'Great stuff! Johnny Boy, great stuff! Just what we needed to start us off. . . . They're all yelling for you. Go out there now, and take a bow.' He propelled John toward the entrance.

John tottered in a dazed way into the arena. From high in the dome of the auditorium the searching finger of a spotlight found him. He stood, a slightly battered figure: the applause was deafening. After a few seconds' acclaim, Milton Myers called him back and Ann rushed into his arms. 'Darling, promise me you will never, *never* do that again. I was sure you were going to be killed.'

John came back to earth as he looked into her eyes. 'From now on,' he said, 'I am grounded.'

Milton Myers bustled up again.

'Quick, get changed, we are just going to announce the first race.'

John dashed away and was back in three minutes quite creditably disguised as a doctor. Ann, already changed, looked adorable in her neat white hospital uniform. Somebody loaded them both with towels and bandages and rolls of cotton wool, and together they marched into the centre of the arena and struck what they hoped were professional attitudes among the camouflaged equipment of the beauty parlour.

Altogether there were six races on the programme and the vast audience loved every minute of it. From where John stood with Ann at the very hub of the wheel, the whole thing seemed like a dream. All around them, bank upon bank, was a white fog of human faces; he was stupefied by the glaring arclights; the thundering hooves; and the blaring loud-speakers. Round and round went the races. The ponies did everything that Milton Myers had hoped they would and more. Some bolted, many bucked and reared, others chased attendants or tried to jump over the barrier into the ring-side seats.

The riders were men of steel. What appeared to be the most appalling falls were taken; and the stretchers came and went like clockwork. No one was seriously hurt and all got the same treatment from Doctor John and Nurse Ann. First, for a few seconds, the patient would be placed at full length under the hair drier. During this time John would question him as to whether he had fallen off on purpose or by mistake; but so well had Jim Curtis and his apprentices learned their trade, that, as the evening wore on, the hospital did not have to treat one unrehearsed accident.

After the hair drier inspection, Ann would pull a large X-ray photograph out of the drawer of the manicure table and John would ostentatiously hold it up to the light. This was the cue for the supposedly injured man to take up an attitude of supplication.

From the point of view of the audience, many of whom had placed bets on this particular rider, here was a moment of acute suspense: the hard-hearted physician was refusing to let the brave jockey remount and carry on despite his fractures. Booing would break out at scattered points only to be drowned by the counter-cheers of those whose money might now stand a better chance.

John and Ann would then confer together, and a decision would be reached. Then Ann would bind up the patient, and John would dispense for him a stiff whisky out of one of the many medicine bottles, all filled in like manner and for the same purpose. The man would stagger gamely back and remount.

The crowd swallowed it and yelled for more. Before the evening was half over Milton Myers, John, Ann and everybody else connected with the INDOOR HORSE RACING ASSOCIATION, INC., knew that they had on their hands a hit of the most satisfactory proportions.

The next morning the Press endorsed their opinion. The sports pages carried glowing headlines: Milton Myers was ecstatic. John began to rehearse in his mind the words he would use when he asked Ann to marry him.

On the morning of the fourth day John was sitting in the little inner office of the great building. He had been busily and happily checking the accounts, but now he was discoursing at length with a Mr. Henshaw—Mr. Henshaw was a reporter from one of the leading New York dailies who, having read in the sports pages of the great success of INDOOR HORSE RACING ASSOCIATION, INC., had flown down, like the good newshound he was, to ferret out some interesting personal facts about the people who had promoted it.

John had answered all the questions about himself and now Mr. Henshaw was waiting for Milton Myers to appear so that he might delve into the lucky dip of his past too.

The door was opened by Miss Fitch. She turned her lovesick eyes upon John. 'Some gentlemen to see you, Mr. Hamilton.'

The gentlemen, six in number, then filed silently into the room. Two came round the desk and stood behind John's chair: two stayed by the door: one took up a position close to Mr. Henshaw by the window, from where the main entrance in the street below was clearly visible; and the sixth, who appeared to be the leader, and who was short and fat and smiling, sat down on the opposite side of the desk and helped himself to one of Milton Myers' cigars.

John, for lack of something better to do, pushed a box of matches towards the man and waited for the conversation to open. After a while it did. 'Good morning,' said the man.

'Good morning,' said John.

There was a long pause after this unusual piece of dialogue. John filled in the time by examining more closely the grim men who were sprinkled about the room. They stared back at him with hard belligerent eyes. Each had one hand in a pocket—the pockets appeared to sag heavily.

John shifted his gaze once more to the small fat man before him, now enveloped in the first blue exhalations from the Corona Corona. The man smiled back affably.

'You Hamilton?'

'Yes,' said John.

The fat little man mopped his neck with a large green silk handkerchief and nodded in the direction of Mr. Henshaw. 'Who's this bird?'

'He has an interest in our company,' said John stiffly.

Mr. Henshaw remained seated in a chair by the window and said nothing. The fat little man contemplated Mr. Henshaw for a minute. 'Okay, he can stay.' He turned once more toward John and smiled again. 'My name is Lefty Orbach,' he announced. 'I was in the house last night. . . . That's a great show you have, Mr. Hamilton, a great show. . . . One of the best I ever saw in Ocean City.'

'Thank you,' said John.

'Don't mention it,' said Lefty Orbach genially. 'It's such a great show that I'm going to be especially generous—I'm going to let it run here for the rest of the week. After all, we don't want to disappoint the public, do we?'

John did not feel any too sure of his ground. He did not answer.

Lefty Orbach took another pull at his cigar and continued.

'So, Mr. Hamilton, I have a very fair and equitable proposition to put before you. If I allow the show to continue, then I should become a partner, shouldn't I?—So I'll tell you what I'll do . . . I'll take forty per cent of the gate money and I shall want to know the result of four out of the six races every night before they start. Got it?'

John thought for a long time, then he spoke very slowly and

distinctly. 'I'll tell you something else you can do. You can have your proposition written out on a piece of paper. Then you can run out and buy a large pineapple, a Hawaiian one would be best. Cut the top off it . . . place the paper carefully inside. . . . Then stuff the pineapple up your arse.'

There was dreadful silence in the room. Mr. Henshaw stiffened in his chair. Two of the henchmen took a step towards John. Lefty Orbach waved them back: then he burst into a guffaw of laughter. 'Gee, that's a great gag. Buy a pineapple . . . ha, ha, ha.' He laughed till the tears rolled down his cheeks. 'Isn't that a great gag, fellers?' He wiped his eyes and turned to the grim men round the room.

'Sure is, Left,' they chorused, and joined rather half-heartedly in the mirth of their chief. The room was full of laughter. John joined in.

As soon as he did so, Orbach's face closed like a handbag, biting the laugh off his tongue. The others stopped, too.

John laughed on alone.

Orbach watched him through eyes that had become slits. He stood up. 'Can it,' he snapped.

John cut his laugh down to a smile and listened.

'Forty per cent of the gate money, and four out of six results before the start,' said Orbach, punctuating his words by banging a pudgy fist on the desk. 'Have you got that straight? And take a little advice from me, stranger: don't try any funny business in this town. Tell that schmuck Myers to contact me—he knows how to do it.' He looked at his henchmen and jerked his head towards the door. They filed out behind their leader.

When they had gone John felt suddenly weak at the knees: he pressed the buzzer on his desk. The spotty face of Miss Fitch bobbed round the door.

'Where is Mr. Myers?' he asked.

'He said something about having to go and make a down payment on the beauty parlour equipment,' said Miss Fitch, 'but I think he was intending to do that last night.'

John bit his lip.

At this point Mr. Henshaw, who so far had not spoken,

looked at his watch. 'Good-bye,' he said, 'I must be going now. It's been a most interesting morning—most interesting.' He shook hands and left, his face shining like a longbowman in the Third Crusade.

Miss Fitch stared at John.

'You look awfully white. . . . Is there anything I can get for you?'

'Yes, thank you. Would you run down to the hospital store and bring up one of those medicine bottles. . . . Any one of them will do.'

'Certainly,' said Miss Fitch. She fluttered her sparse eyelashes. 'It certainly is a pleasure to work for people like Mr. Myers and,' she paused and giggled nervously, 'and you.'

While she was gone Milton Myers burst into the office. He was in high good humour. 'Great news, Johnny Boy. . . . The man from the Boston Garden was in front last night and he definitely wants the show . . . maybe they will even give us a four-week guarantee. He's going to call us when he gets back and talks to his people. He also . . .'

John cut him short. 'He was not the only person who was in front last night. . . . Lefty Orbach was there, too.'

Milton Myers came over to the desk and sat down. 'How do you know?'

'He's been in here telling me so himself . . . he only left a couple of minutes ago. You must have just missed him.'

Milton Myers looked at John for a few seconds. Then he took a cigar from the box on the desk and lit it.

'How much does he want?'

'Forty per cent of the "gate" and the result of four out of six races every night before they start.'

Milton Myers removed the cigar from his mouth and emitted a long, low whistle. 'The sonofabitch,' he said softly. 'I thought it was too good to be true that we hadn't heard from him before. . . . What did you tell him?'

'I told him,' said John, 'to put his suggestion inside a pineapple and then stuff it up his arse.'

Milton Myers sat bolt upright. 'Holy Christ! Johnny Boy, are you crazy? You tired of life or something?'

There was a knock at the door, and Miss Fitch came in with the medicine bottle. They each poured out a stiff whisky.

'Now tell me honestly, Milt,' said John. 'It can't be true in this day and age that this can happen—that a man can walk in like he did and demand part of somebody else's business? Surely all that died with prohibition and bootlegging, didn't it?'

Milton Myers sighed. 'This country grew up fast, kid, so fast that we left undone a hell of a lot of things that we ought to have done. We still have one or two, what we like to call—backward States. Well, the one we are in right now is so backward it seems like it never even got started. . . . Yes, I'm afraid it can happen, and it does happen. It's not going on much longer, believe me, but right now there is not a goddamn thing we can do about it, here at any rate.'

'Do you mean to tell me,' said John, 'that we have either got to do what this bastard says or fold up, just when we have really got going?'

Milton Myers thought for a long time. 'Yes,' he answered at length. 'I guess that's just about the size of it.'

John felt himself becoming angry. 'Well, I'm not bloody well going to stand for it. . . . Are you?'

Milton Myers walked up and down the room before he answered, then he came over and stood in front of John. 'Johnny Boy, I hope you will understand what I am going to tell you because I like you one hell of a lot. You're one hell of a swell guy . . . in fact, I don't know when I've met a guy I've liked more. You see, this sort of game is my racket. . . it isn't really yours. Yes, I'll make a deal with Mr. goddamn Orbach because I can do it without letting it get me. . . .'

John was about to interrupt, but Milton Myers stopped him with a gesture. 'Look at it their way. I'm in a corner so I must play ball: they know that. If I blow my top now, the show will fold,' Myers caught John's incredulous expression. 'Oh, yes, Orbach can close us. . . . He's done that before now. If the show folds we'd be in the red, and we wouldn't be able to hold on till we got to Boston. If we play here the full six days even with only half the take, we've still done pretty good, and, what is much more important for getting other cities interested in the show, we will have gone the full distance with packed houses. Believe me, Johnny Boy, you can't sell a show that's folded, no matter what the real reason was. Lefty waited till the psychological moment to pull this—his timing was always good.'

John knew Milton Myers was talking sense. He was deeply fond of this strange eccentric character, but he knew he could never look himself in the eye again if he knuckled under to the sort of treatment dispensed by Lefty Orbach.

'Yes, Milton, I do understand perfectly. But will you understand if I say I don't want any part of it? I just couldn't go on under those conditions.'

Milton Myers put his hand on John's shoulder. 'Look kid, if it hadn't been for you I could never have got this show started. Most of the money came from people you brought along, and,' he laughed, 'you got us off to a good start that first night; so I reckon a good half the credit for the whole show is yours.

'We hold a quarter of the stock between us, you and I, but we need a couple or more good bookings before we can show a profit and start paying dividends. Boston is definite, and I'm pretty sure of Chicago, too, so you would be due for a salary as president pretty soon. I'd sure hate to see you go, but if you want to quit I think the company should pay you a thousand dollars for your past work. Maybe we could even make it a bit more. What d'you say, Johnny Boy?'

'Good God,' said John. 'I haven't earned anything like that.'

Milton Myers ignored this. 'Maybe you'd like to come back later on. If ever you do . . . well . . . you know how I'd feel about that; but as I said before . . . this is not really your racket. And remember, so long as the company is in the black we are always good for a touch if the ex-president finds himself in the red. . . . Think it over.'

John's heart warmed towards his friend. He would be truly sorry to leave, but his mind was already made up, and he said so.

Milton Myers unlocked the safe and counted out a thousand dollars from the takings of the day before. 'There you are, Johnny Boy. Now you have a thousand bucks, as well as a clear conscience. . . . If I wasn't forty-five years old and completely unscrupulous, I believe I'd envy you!'

They both laughed. John experienced a wave of regret that he had been so hasty, but his reaction against Orbach had been instinctive and instantaneous—the way he usually made decisions.

'Oh by the way,' he said, 'Orbach wants you to call him.'

Milton Myers nodded grimly, 'Okay, I'll get around to it later. By the way, kid, leave town. . . . Don't hang around and give the bastard time to have second thoughts about that pineapple.' He laughed again. 'Christ! I wish I'd heard that one.'

They shook hands. 'Good-bye, Milt . . . I'm really glad I met you. It's been great fun. Good luck.'

'So long, Johnny Boy. It's been great, and I have a funny hunch we'll meet up again somewhere along the line. My love to the dream girl. . . . She's the right one for you.'

'Yes,' said John, 'I know. Good-bye. . . .' He walked out of the office.

Miss Fitch, who had been listening at the keyhole, burst into tears.

Once outside the building John spent the first hundred and twenty dollars of his newly acquired wealth. He ordered a big box of chocolates to be sent to Miss Fitch, a huge box of cigars to Milton Myers and a case of whisky to the pony riders of the troupe: then, armed with two dozen red roses, he headed for the small hotel on the sea front where Ann was finishing a late breakfast.

He took her down to the beach, and they put an old tin can on a stick and threw stones at it. Ann was bubbling with enthusiasm over the success of INDOOR HORSE RACING ASSOCIA-TION, INC.

'Oh Johnny, it is wonderful! really wonderful! . . . I never thought it could be such a success, did you? I suppose there is no end to it now . . . the show will just go from city to city and you and Milton will drive about in great big Rolls-Royces.'

At the mention of the Rolls-Royces John looked at her.

She was looking up at him in the sunny, smiling way she had: her hair was blowing in the sea breeze and a little wisp of it caught for a second in the corner of her mouth: she brushed it away with a slender hand. John's heart contracted: he hated having to tell her.

'Darling, I am afraid I don't belong to the show any more. I . . .' he hesitated and smiled ruefully. 'I am looking for a job again, but this time I have a thousand dollars. . . . Well, nearly a thousand dollars, to start with.'

Her eyes, the lovely eyes that were neither green nor brown, clouded with disappointment. 'Tell me what happened,' she asked quietly.

He told her. He did not look at her while he was talking, but stared out to sea, and threw stones at the tin can in a desultory sort of way as he talked. The pineapple part of the story he managed to handle with a certain delicacy, but the interview with Lefty Orbach, as he told it, was no less interesting for that.

When he had finished, he turned towards her. Her eyes were shining, and her lips were slightly parted. 'Oh Johnny,' she breathed, 'I am so glad! . . . So glad!' She held his hand tight. 'Of course Milton was right. You were never cut out to be a circus man, darling, and of course, you couldn't be mixed up with people like this dreadful gangster person. . . . I think it's wonderful.'

John kissed her then. 'You are so sweet,' he said softly. 'I could eat you with a spoon. I thought you would be terribly disappointed to hear that I had got to take to the high road again.'

Ann said quietly, 'Yes, of course, I am disappointed, in a way, but one day you will find the right spot and then . . .' her voice trailed off.

John took both her hands in his, this was to be the moment. . . . Although he had less than nine hundred dollars in the world they could manage somehow. Something would turn up. It always did. . . .

'Ann . . . darling . . .' He looked deep into her eyes. 'I was wondering. . . .'

There was a loud shout behind them. 'Johnny—for God's sake, we've been looking for you all over town.'

John spun round. Standing on the sand at the top of the beach was Jim Curtis, the ex-Hollywood stunt rider, and six or seven of the cowboys.

'What's the matter?' he asked.

'Only this,' said Curtis as they hurried down the beach. 'Orbach's mob is looking for you and you're leaving town.'

One of the other men spoke up, his rugged face a study of consternation. 'It seems some big New York newspaper guy got hold of a story about where you told Orbach to get it stuffed . . . er . . . pardon me, lady,' he said to Ann, 'and Orbach is fit to be tied. . . .' 'Yeah, they say it's all over the front page in New York,' said a third man, 'and boy! is Orbach mad now.'

Ann clutched John's arm. They both stood up.

'What am I supposed to do?' he pointed out to sea, 'Swim to Europe or something?'

Jim Curtis spoke up. 'That's just about it, feller. Milt says you must skip the country for a while. Take off for Canada or some place. He says this guy is not kidding, and if he catches up with you you'll get yours. Milt is over at your hotel now with some more of the boys. . . . Everyone is out looking for you.'

John looked down at Ann. 'Do you think it really is this serious?'

'Yes, I do. I think Milton is quite right.' She looked at Jim Curtis. 'It wouldn't be for long, would it?'

155

Curtis scratched his cheek with a horny forefinger. 'Well, ma'am, the way Milt figgered, it was like this. . . . This guy Orbach knows that he's about washed up anyway, and this story about Johnny here might be the thing that finished him but good. That's why he's so darn mad. . . . Milt figgers that Johnny ought to get clear away for a while to let the thing settle itself one way or t'other.'

A fourth man spoke up. 'Let's get goin', Johnny, whatya' say?'

The cowboys shepherded John and Ann over to John's hotel. Milton Myers was there with a dozen others. He left no doubt in John's mind that the situation was serious—more than that—really dangerous.

'They're out gunning for you, Johnny Boy. We've got to get you out of the way, but fast. . . . Got any suggestions where you could go?'

John thought for a minute then he had a brainwave.

'How does one get to Bermuda?' he asked.

Ann knew the answer to that. 'Uncle Don nearly went last summer, and I made all the arrangements for him. You can fly from New York or Cootesville . . . I believe there are two planes a day.'

'Cootesville,' cried Milton Myers. 'Why, that's great. That's only an hour or more from here. We could take you over there ourselves to make sure nothing happened to you on the way, couldn't we, fellers?'

'Sure could. . . . You're damn right,' came the lusty chorus.

John felt a catch in his throat as he looked at the circle of tough friendly faces, and his mind jumped back to a similar group that had been gathered around him as he had stood on top of 'Mae West' at cross-roads X236410, deep in the heart of Germany, not so long ago.

'Miss Ann,' said Milton Myers, with a twinkle in his eye. 'Would you mind going on the plane with our boy? . . . We want to make sure that he arrives there safely, don't we fellers?' The anxious expressions dissolved into smiles and winks.

'Sure do, Miss Ann,' they chorused.

Ann coloured slightly.

'Please,' begged John, 'you could always come back on the next plane if you didn't like it.'

Ann thought for a moment. 'No, I can't possibly go without seeing Uncle Don, or he'd think the worst. Also, I haven't got any clothes. . . . No. I'll see you off, then I'll go back to New York. If I can fix my boss and if Uncle Don doesn't mind, then I'll fly down tomorrow or the next day and join you. How's that?'

'Wonderful!' said John. 'Absolutely wonderful.'

'Let's get going then,' said Milton Myers. 'There'll be a nasty accident if you hang around this joint much longer.'

Milton Myers would not allow John to send a cable to Oglethorpe giving warning of his impending arrival. 'We don't want that sonofabitch Orbach to have any idea where you've gone. . . . You've just got to get lost, that's all.'

Three large cars arrived and the bodyguard swarmed aboard. John and Ann were put in the middle one and the whole caravan set out for the Cootesville airport.

Outside Ocean City on a long country road a sinister-looking black limousine joined on behind the others. Milton Myers had expected this, and the driver of the last car had been carefully rehearsed in how to act in just such an event. Very gradually he slowed down, and each time the newcomer tried to pass him he thwarted him.

The drivers of the other two cars, seeing what was happening behind them, put on all speed, and soon were so far ahead that there was ample time to make a sharp turn up a side road and so proceed unmolested by devious routes to Cootesville.

Once at the airport, so that a sudden influx of cowboys into an urban travel centre would not cause comment, the bodyguard remained as inconspicuously as possible near the gate. John waved his thanks to them and, accompanied only by Milton Myers and Ann, went into the booking office and purchased a ticket to Bermuda in the unimaginative name of Jack Smith.

A handshake from Milton Myers and a kiss and a hug from Ann ended an anxious two-hour wait for the plane. Then John settled comfortably back in his seat as the powerful DC6 roared off the end of the runway and headed south-east towards the Gulf Stream.

CHAPTER SEVEN

THE COCKNEY VOICE of the steward came as something of a shock to John. In the hustle and bustle of his precipitous exit from the United States he had overlooked the fact that he was heading once more for British territory. He settled back and proceeded to enjoy the flight over the ocean.

Two and a half hours later, after a practically motionless trip, a slight deafness and discomfort in the eardrums told John that the great plane was sliding gently down the sky. The mysteries of navigation had always been profound for him. During the war, with the aid of the most up-to-date maps, signposts and the helpful gesticulations of half-witted locals, he had still encountered the greatest difficulties in finding his way about: it was therefore with deep admiration that he now thought of the men in the nose of the plane who had brought him, safely and surely, six hundred miles through trackless space to a tiny island in the middle of several million square miles of water.

They came down to five or six hundred feet and the craning necks in the seats in front told John that Bermuda was close ahead. Soon he saw it. The plane tipped over obligingly and he looked down on the rash of green islands, each dotted with white, pink or blue houses, the whole being set in the azure of the water above the coral depths. It looked good to John.

The plane touched down, and ten minutes later he was telephoning to Butterfield's Bank.

Yes, Mr. Oglethorpe was known to them and he lived at Devonshire Bay. They gave John the telephone number and in a minute or two he heard the voice of his old friend at the other end of the wire.

'Hello, who is that?' John could not repress a surge of fun as he thought of the surprise he was about to spring.

'John Hamilton.'

There was an almost imperceptible pause.

'John Hamilton, the seducer of colonels' wives?'

'Yes,' laughed John, 'the same.'

'John Hamilton, the goat with the awful udders? . . . Are you in New York?'

'No, I'm at the airport here in Bermuda.'

Oglethorpe was unmoved, he took it all in his stride.

'Well hurry up, old man. I've been expecting you for weeks. Take a taxi and tell the fellow to go to the Pink House, Devonshire Bay. He'll find it. . . . Good-bye.' The telephone clicked. John grinned with anticipation.

A quarter of an hour later, the first greetings over, John and Oglethorpe were reclining in two long chairs, each sipping a Planter's Punch and watching the fantastic colours of the sunset over the ocean. They had much to discuss; many gaps to fill; and as they talked, the brilliant flowers of the hibiscus folded themselves in sleep, the full orchestra of tree frogs struck up for the evening performance, and the sky at the horizon turned from orange to pink, from pink to purple, and finally from purple to the black velvet of night. The stars winked out above them and the twin points of their cigarettes glowed in the scented darkness of Devonshire Bay.

The next day Oglethorpe took John on a tour of his orchid plants. This he did with a considerable flourish and John was suitably impressed at the nonchalant bandying about of such names as Cyprepedium and Laeliocattleya.

Oglethorpe's establishment was impressive. The house itself was made of coral; so was the roof, which was designed to catch the rain—the island's only water supply. The colour of the house matched its name, and made a most attractive background for the bright blue hurricane shutters.

The lawn in front of the house, gracefully shaded by the tall hibiscus and the gently waving palm trees, ended with a white wooden picket fence thirty feet below which, fringing the emerald green waters of the lagoon, stretched the pink coral sand beach of the bay.

As John stood looking out across the lagoon the great Atlantic rollers were pounding the distant coral reef: a long-tailed sea gull flew lazily by. He sighed and turned to his host.

'You seem to be pretty well set up here.'

'Yes, it's wonderful,' the tall man agreed. 'I have never been happier; and provided a large number of males continue to be optimistic enough to believe that the quickest way into a warm bed is by producing a frozen orchid out of the icebox . . . I should be able to stay here for years.'

Three halcyon days passed, then Ann arrived. She was bubbling over with excitement and bursting with information. Her words came with a rush.

'Oh, Johnny darling, such an exciting thing has happened . . . at least I think it is going to be exciting. When I got home Uncle Don had been trying to contact me in Ocean City. There was a long distance call from California, you see. Meadowbrook, that's one of the better film companies in Hollywood, wanted to talk to me urgently. Well, I called the operator and pretty soon I was talking to Mr. Ingersoll, he is the . . . oh, I don't know what he is . . . I couldn't quite hear what he said, but anyway, he wants to put me under contract to the studio, and they want me to make a test and if it's good I'm to play the leading part opposite Ralph Ridgway in his next picture, a great big technicolour thing called "Backwash" . . . all about Ruritania . . . wonderful costumes and duels and things. You see, according to Mr. Ingersoll, if I get this part then the studio will give me all sorts of other parts, one after the other, and in five years or so,

I will be able to save quite a lot of money, in spite of all the taxes and things. . . . But if I don't get the part, then in three months the studio will release me anyway, and the worst that will happen will be a lovely trip to California. . . .'

John felt his knees turning to water, but as he looked at her flushed, excited face he knew he must not fail her now. He forced a cheerful smile.

'I think it's wonderful, and I know you will be terrific, darling.'

She looked up at him in that way he loved so much. 'Don't be too disappointed in me, Johnny. I am not the oldest woman in the world yet, and it is a wonderful opportunity, and it could be great fun. . . . Whatever happens.' She paused. 'I know what you are thinking. You are remembering what I said a little while back about modelling . . . that I hated people staring at me, and that I didn't want to do it much longer because now that everyone was getting to know my face I didn't feel private any more. . . . Isn't that it?'

John smiled down at her. 'Yes, that's what I was thinking all right, and you also said, though god knows you can change your mind if you want to, that you didn't want to become an actress. . . . Remember?'

Ann's eyes clouded for a moment.

'Yes, that's true,' she said slowly, 'but when I said that I didn't realize how much . . . I wanted . . .' she looked away across the lagoon '. . . how much I wanted . . . something else . . . and this seemed like a chance to . . . I thought it might make it a little easier, that's all.' She still looked away from him, and her lower lip trembled. 'See?'

John felt a great happiness surge up within him, almost choking him: he put his hands on her shoulders and slowly turned her round to face him: he held her very close and kissed her very gently before he spoke.

'I wonder where in Bermuda one can find a good serviceable engagement ring. . . .'

Several minutes later Oglethorpe appeared from inside the house: he found his two guests still clasped in each other's arms, and no amount of discreet coughings and disinterested whistlings produced any effect whatever.

He regarded the scene for quite a while before he spoke. 'Is there anything I can do to make you two more comfortable?'

John turned his head a little.

'You can kiss Ann on the cheek and you can shake my hand.'

Oglethorpe advanced. 'You mean I can congratulate you both—is that the form?'

'That is the form,' said John.

Ann was only able to stay a few days at the Pink House, and most of that time was spent in the making of plans for the future: Oglethorpe was part of the planning committee, but it cannot be recorded that he helped a great deal.

It was decided, in the broad outline, that Ann should proceed with the Hollywood idea; make her screen test and, as a result of it, become either Ralph Ridgway's leading lady, or just another drop in the stream of beautiful girls that has passed unnoticed through the watermill of Meadowbrook Pictures, Inc.

It was further decided that John's future movements would depend upon the success or failure of this test. He would remain at the Oglethorpe sanctuary until a cable arrived announcing the result: if it were successful then he would follow Ann to Hollywood; if unsuccessful she would be returning straightaway to New York and John would join her there.

Lefty Orbach was marked down as a 'calculated risk', and in view of the latest reports which Ann had brought with her, it was felt that he was now so blatantly exposed by the New York papers that it was unlikely that he would dare to leave the backward State in which he enjoyed so much protection.

The days in Bermuda passed all too quickly for Ann and John. They were ecstatically happy, and the future seemed to be the most uncomplicated thing upon which their thoughts had ever dwelled.

On the last day of Ann's visit, John and Oglethorpe took her spear-fishing on Big Reef—eight miles out in the ocean. Ann could swim well enough, but she viewed with disquiet the prospect of doing so in water well known to be infested by barracuda, moray eels and sharks.

Besides John and Oglethorpe there were others in the party that set out in the large motor boat—three officers from H.M. cruiser *Falmouth*—a lieutenant commander and two lieutenants, all reputed to be experts in the art of spear-fishing. As the mainland slipped farther and farther astern John, who had hitherto only poked about among the small fish in the enclosed waters of Devonshire Bay, began to share Ann's misgivings.

He addressed the largest lieutenant. 'What is the drill when we get to the reef?'

'The great trick is to keep together,' said the bronzed and smiling giant as he produced a large file and started working on the point of one of the spears. 'It's really pretty safe as long as you do that. And of course, never turn your back to the blue water.'

John peered over the side of the boat into the azure depths below.

'It all looks rather blue to me,' he said. 'How do you manage to keep your back out of it?'

'When we get to the reef itself, you'll see what he means,' interposed the lieutenant commander. 'The blue water is the deep water. It really is deep too, round here it's several hundred fathoms. The reef is about two miles long and half a mile across, but the sides drop off like a cliff down to the ocean bottom, so if you happen to be at the edge of the reef, don't turn your back to the deep water because that's where the trouble generally comes from.'

'The trouble?' said John, glancing nervously at Ann.

'Yes,' said the youngest lieutenant casually. 'The sharks—they fairly whiz up from below.'

John gulped, Ann paled visibly, and Oglethorpe inquired after the brandy stocks on board.

The large lieutenant, named Jack, had not taken his eyes off Ann since she came on board. He addressed her now. 'Really you don't have anything to worry about. . . . We'll look after you. The sharks only go for the fish you have speared —they hardly ever go for people. Just don't get left behind, that's all, because the barracuda sometimes gang up on you. They can be quite a nuisance.'

By way of changing the subject Oglethorpe pointed to the spear which the large lieutenant was sharpening. It was of stainless steel, about twelve feet long and half an inch in diameter. 'I notice there is no barb on the end,' he said. 'Why is that?'

'Well, we've tried everything. All those underwater guns and elastic belt propulsion outfits and all that stuff, but we have decided that this is by far the best. You just stick it through the fish—right through on to a rock or something, so that the fish is properly skewered. Then you dive down and get a hand underneath him and bring him up, sort of on the spit.'

He tested the needle-point carefully with his thumb. 'We had to give up having barbs at the end because you never know when you are going to need your spear in a hurry. . . . Incidentally, when you spear a fish, yell for the dinghy. One of these blokes is with us all the time and he takes the fish as we catch them. If you get tired you can hang on to it too. . . . Oh yes,' he added as an afterthought, 'one thing . . . you'll see lots of parrot fish. Don't spear them because they bleed like mad and that's just asking for trouble.'

He pointed ahead. 'We are nearly there now.'

John, Ann and Oglethorpe looked nervously in the direction he was indicating. All that was visible to the eye was several acres of what appeared to be brown water in the middle of the deep blue of the Gulf Stream. As the boat drew nearer it became apparent that this brown discoloration was, in fact, the great expanse of submerged coral lying, as the sailor had described, just a few feet below the surface. The helmsman steered the boat to where he judged he could throw his light anchor onto the rocks and leave the boat floating safely at rope's end in the deep blue water.

The youngest lieutenant handed out rubber 'frogmen' flippers for their feet and presented each of the newcomers with a rubber mask that covered eyes and nose. This contained a circular glass panel. 'The best way is to spit on the inside of the glass, then rinse it out with water . . . that stops it from fogging up.'

They thanked him and waited apprehensively for the next instruction.

'All ready?' asked the lieutenant commander.

They struggled into their flippers and dutifully spat into their masks. 'All ready,' they answered in a shaky chorus.

He looked them over. 'It's quite a short swim to the reef, and remember, whatever happens, stay close together. Now then . . . . Who is first?'

There was a pause. John glanced through his face piece at Oglethorpe. The enormous moustaches stuck out stiffly beneath the mask; the long lanky frame was adorned with a pair of shocking-pink bathing trunks: the giant feet were squeezed into bright green rubber flippers, a twelve-foot spear was gleaming in his hand. He looked like something straight out of the pages of Alice in Wonderland. Oglethorpe bowed slightly. 'After you, old man.'

John lowered himself over the side into the blue water.

'We'll be right behind you,' said the lieutenant commander cheerfully.

John took a deep breath and submerged his head. Through the glass frontpiece the water below and around him was a beautiful peacock blue. The shafts of sunlight reflected from the ripples above his head flickered downward into the hazy deeps below. Looking ahead he could clearly see the cliffside of the coral reef some twenty yards away—it looked much farther. His spear, which had weighed a pound and a half in the air, was now of inconsiderable weight in the buoyant salt water: the flippers on his feet doubled his speed of swimming. He made for the reef, looking below all the time and fully expecting to see the ugly black shape of a shark sliding toward him.

Once at the reef he found a convenient rock and stood up, with his head and shoulders above water. The islands of

Bermuda were out of sight and none of the rocks of the reef were visible above the surface, so, to all intents and purposes, he was standing alone in the middle of the Atlantic—he rather liked the feeling. Ann and the others soon splashed toward him. The dinghy was lowered from the motor boat and, with one final reminder from the lieutenant commander not to be left behind, the hunt was on.

John found that his progress over the reef was far easier than he had anticipated; there was nearly always something he could get a foothold on; and when there was not, or when he wanted to swim fast, he perfected a method of punting himself along with his twelve foot spear.

As he moved over the face of the reef with his head more or less continually submerged, he found beneath him a whole new world—a world of breathtaking beauty.

The rocks, themselves of coral, were covered with a dense vegetation of brightly coloured weed, and everywhere, like miniature trees swaying gently in the breeze, the great coral fans, pink, blue, purple and yellow, moved lazily with the swell. Sometimes these fans grew in miniature forests, the forest clearings being the pools between the clusters of rocks. The sand at the bottom of these pools was pink or white and of extraordinary brightness. The water was crystal clear.

So fascinated was John by the beauty of his surroundings that he was not prepared for his first contact with the under-water inhabitants. He had just punted himself round the corner of a large rock and into a clear deep pool when he saw it. A huge fish was immediately below him and staring upwards: black and evil-looking and seemingly as long as the *Queen Elizabeth*.

John's stomach tightened with fear and he tried to yell a warning to the others. As his head was still underwater, this proved to be an elementary mistake, and with much coughing and spluttering, he surfaced. Ann, he saw, was half-submerged a few yards away on his right. The youngest lieutenant providently had his head above water on his other flank. He tried to keep calm as he addressed him.

'Er . . . if you are not too busy. . . . I think there is a large shark in this pool with me.'

The young man immediately submerged and swam toward him. John, too, went under again, expecting at any moment to feel the dreadful teeth ripping at his entrails.

The huge fish did not seem to have changed position very much while he had been away. It was still staring up at him. John returned the stare.

A sudden turmoil in the water on his left caused John to turn his head sharply in alarm. With great relief he saw it was the young lieutenant shooting out from behind a rock, his spear held like a lance: with flippers twinkling he was launching himself downwards, straight at the fish, then with the grace of a fencer and with much the same thrust of arm, he plunged his spear into its flank.

The point went right through its body. A tremendous upheaval took place. John watched spellbound, as the huge fish thrashed about in convulsive twists and turns, its maddened writhings raising the sand from the bottom of the pool in billowing, obscuring clouds. Still the swimmer held fast to the end of his spear, bearing down all the time in an effort to pin his prey to the ocean floor.

John came up for air and found himself yelling, in his excitement, incoherent shouts that had no effect whatever on his semi-submerged neighbours all intent on their own under-water pursuits.

He submerged again. Ten feet below him the lieutenant and the fish were still engaged in their desperate struggle.

Visibility in the pool was bad now, but John got the impression that the lieutenant was signalling up at him, and certainly it seemed high time that he did something to help. He swam downward into the battle arena and in the murk made a vague thrust in the direction of the fish. To his great sur-prise, his spear passed through its body somewhere near the tail; he felt it strike the hard sandy bottom below. The lieutenant then left his spear in the quarry and shot to the surface for air. John was alone on the floor of the Atlantic with the fish.

As though sensing a lowering in the quality of its attacker, the great black monster redoubled its efforts to escape. With bursting eardrums, John held fast to his spear: he was buffeted, tossed about and prodded continually by the lieutenant's spear, which was flailing around at the other end of the fish. Suddenly, with a particularly violent contortion, the fish tore the spear out of John's hands, but by some miracle, he managed to grab hold of the one lately vacated by the lieutenant: he now sustained further and more violent batterings from his own, which remained fast through the threshing tail. His lungs were a torture and his whole head was palpitating, but somehow John hung on till the lieutenant came down again.

When this worthy arrived, John shot gratefully to the surface. He gasped for breath for several seconds before he looked down again. When he did, the battle was won—the great fish had rolled over on its side.

The lieutenant surfaced, apparently untroubled by his exertions, and slipped his mask up onto his forehead. 'That's a good fish,' he grinned. 'We must get it up before the sharks come.'

'Well, what the hell is that then?' panted John.

'Oh, just a small rock fish. We'll get plenty of those.'

The lieutenant yelled for the dinghy and went below to bring up the catch. This proved quite a business and by the time the dinghy man had hauled the eighty pound fish aboard, John and the lieutenant were some distance behind the rest of the party.

'Come along. . . . We'd better catch up,' said the lieutenant.

As they swam and punted themselves over the surface of the reef John saw all manner of life below him. The lieutenant pointed out the brilliant green, red and blue parrot fish with sad round eyes and large protruding front teeth.

He saw the big white hogfish that looked like huge Dover soles swimming on their sides; these, the lieutenant told him, made the finest eating and certainly, in view of their shape, they were the easiest target for the spearfisherman. John learned to identify the yellow grunts, the red squirrel fish, the groupers, the square box-fish, and the myriad little black and yellow 'sergeant-majors': it was with an underwater gasp of pure delight that he saw for the first time the beautiful pale blue body and whispy yellow tail of an angel fish.

They were almost abreast of the rest of the party when the lieutenant said quite casually, 'I think you are being followed.'

John looked over his shoulder and beheld four large fish some five feet in length immediately behind him. He was not so much struck by their colour—a yellow and black ensemble— as by their general demeanour. They had long thin faces above huge fang-pointed, undershot jaws. They were watching him intently. He kicked his foot at the nearest one. The fish reacted to this as a good watch dog should toward a suspicious stranger—it snapped at his heel.

John felt less confident than he had before, and was considering what his next move should be when the lieutenant speared the nearest of his four followers: he did not spear it in the same way as he had dealt with the rockfish; he just punctured it, pushed his spear through it, and pulled it out again.

For a split second the fish looked surprised, then it made a slow full turn and went away, leaving a muddy discoloration in the water behind it.

The other three fish glanced meaningly at each other, then, as if by common consent, they too turned and followed hungrily after their friend.

John surfaced and asked the lieutenant what they were.

'Barracuda,' he replied ' . . . it's bad to get too far behind.'

When they rejoined the other swimmers, John's confidence returned. He swam over to Ann and they rested with their feet on a rock for a while and watched Oglethorpe vainly trying to come to grips with a huge lobster.

Ann was bubbling with excitement. 'Isn't it beautiful? I've never seen anything like it, and I've speared a fish! I don't know what it was, but anyway I touched it and then chased it round a rock and lost it. . . . Please collect some of these coral fans to take home. . . .'

During two hours in the water, everybody speared fish and the dinghy was loaded with a most impressive catch.

They had been moving over the reef in a big circle, and were almost back at the motor boat when the main event of the day took place. The entire party was gathered at the edge of the reef taking a short breather before the final swim across the deep water to the boat. The biggest lieutenant, who was a magnificent swimmer, and who seemed able to stay at the bottom of the deepest pools for frighteningly long periods, had taken one last poke at a grey snapper—a fair-sized fish of about twenty pounds, which he had had difficulty in cornering for his final thrust. Ann and John and the rest were standing in about five feet of water with their face pieces below the surface watching the exhibition in the pool below. The snapper was lying on its side in about fifteen feet of water with the spear through it, and the big lieutenant was on his way up for air before diving once more to bring up his catch. They watched as his lithe brown body shot through the crystal-clear water to the surface.

'Better get a move on, Jack,' said the lieutenant commander. 'We are pretty close to the edge here.'

'Okay,' said the big lieutenant. 'Won't be a second.'

He filled his lungs with fresh air and his bright green flippers propelled him downward once more to the pink sand at the bottom of the pool.

Oglethorpe saw it first. He raised his head from the water. 'Look out!' he yelled. 'Shark!'

The others, if their heads at that moment were not actually out of the water, had their ears near enough to the surface to hear the dreaded cry; instinctively they all plunged their heads under so that they might see the enemy, and know from which direction the attack was to be expected.

It was a shark right enough, and even those of the party who had never seen one before knew with dreadful certainty that there was no mistaking the great brute with its white underbelly, its sharp pointed nose and cruel crescent-shaped mouth.

It was cruising along in the blue water just over the edge of the reef. They all watched it, fascinated: all, that is, except Jack, the large lieutenant, who, at that moment, was in the pool fifteen feet below the surface adjusting a bleeding fish to his spear.

Suddenly the shark became excited: its movements quickened, and with a flick of its great tail, it flashed forward: twice it turned and doubled back again on its tracks as though trying to trace a scent: then, to the frozen horror of the on-lookers, it shot up over the edge of the reef, turned its white belly to the sun and catapulted itself down into the pool.

What happened next was never quite clear to John. He remembered seeing the other two naval officers, their gleaming spears in their hands, launch themselves downwards like two avenging angels: he heard Ann scream, and Oglethorpe swear, and saw the shark flash upwards again, out of the far side of the pool: half a grey snapper with a streamer of en-trails was hanging from its jaws.

The three sailors shot to the surface. The large one, Jack, was minus a large patch of skin from his left shoulder: it was just starting to bleed.

He grinned. 'That old boy must have been very hungry. . . . He took the snapper right off the end of my spear.'

'Did he bite you, too?' asked Ann in a small voice, pointing to the injured shoulder.

'No, they don't bite people,' he said, 'he just nudged me out of the way—they have an awfully rough skin.'

'I see,' said Ann.

'I think we'd better get aboard now,' said the lieutenant commander. He glanced at the bleeding shoulder. 'Jack's pretty good bait himself at the moment and we don't want to lose him yet—he hasn't paid his mess bill.'

John and Oglethorpe gave sickly grins and swam on either side of Ann on the way to the motorboat; they tried, all three of them, to look as though they were in no hurry. Once aboard, the navy produced a bottle of rum.

'You must come with us at night,' said the smallest lieutenant. 'That's really much more fun.'

'I'd love to,' said John. With a shaky hand he held out his glass for a re-fill.

The sailors came back to the pink house and that evening, Ann's last on the island, Oglethorpe was host to a small outdoor dinner party: the lobsters caught during the day were eaten: and the engagement between Ann and John was officially announced.

After the last good night had been said, and the last pulsating throb of the departing calypso players had been borne to them on the warm scented breeze, John took Ann into his arms. No cloud appeared on the horizon of their happiness.

The next morning Ann soared away and headed westward for New York, leaving John, a disconsolate figure, to help Oglethorpe with the orchids and to await the fateful cable from Hollywood.

Within the week it came. 'DARLING THEY LIKE THE TEST. . . . I THINK IT IS GHASTLY. STARTING RIDGWAY PICTURE IMMEDIATELY. HE IS GHASTLY, TOO. MISS YOU DREADFULLY. PLEASE HURRY DARLING. ALL MY LOVE. ANN.'

CHAPTER EIGHT

LESS THAN THREE WEEKS after the receipt of Ann's cable, John stepped ashore in California. His trip had been uneventful in all respects except in the actual mode of his locomotion. The lieutenant commander, his friend of the spear fishing trip, had suggested and arranged it—he travelled the whole way from Hamilton Harbour, Bermuda, to San Pedro Harbour, Los Angeles, in one of His Majesty's warships.

H.M.S. *Falmouth*, as flagship of the West Indies Station, had been due to take the annual Goodwill Cruise through the Panama Canal, up the west coast of Mexico, California, Oregon, Washington and Canada; and a few civilians, as guests of the officers, and provided accommodations were available, were permitted to take passage.

Few naval dockyards are beautiful. The one at San Pedro is no exception: on the day John landed it also smelled badly of mercaptans: John learned this word from the truck driver who stopped in answer to his appeal for a lift on the great 101 Highway.

'That's the name those guys at City Hall gave it—mercaptans, it's a pretty crappy stink and it comes from all these goddamned oil refineries around here. Why, a while back it got so bad, one night, that the stink carried clear up through the city of Los Angeles and out into the San Fernando Valley. . . . Then a lot of people out there called up the sheriff's office and said that the Russians had started a poison gas attack. When everything settled down again the county appointed a "polluted air control office."

'Of course that's just another way of spending the taxpayer's dough. Anyway, they had to justify themselves so they dreamed up this word—mercaptans, and that goes now for this crappy stink around here today—mercaptans, my foot.' He spat out of the window.

The giant fruit truck thundered north with its load of oranges.

'Are you a California man?' asked John.

'Marion, Ohio, is my home town, but I came out here after the war. I used to work in a garage back home before that, but I got to driving trucks in the army overseas and kinda liked it. If you're going to drive, there is no place like California. Good roads, good weather and good wages. No, sir . . . there's no place like California.'

He applied the air brakes. 'Well, so long, feller, this is as far as I go along this route. You'll find it easy enough from here on.'

John thanked him and waved good-bye as the diesel motor roared away down a side road. He sat for a while on his holdall by the roadside, and watched the stream of cars go past. He was in no hurry. Ann, he knew, did not get home from the studio before seven o'clock, so he had plenty of time. Ann knew he had left Bermuda in a battleship headed for California, but official naval matters being the only messages transmitted by His Majesty's ships at sea, there had been no further communication between them. She didn't even expect him today. He had not telephoned her on landing, because, in a childish way, he loved to give people surprises. He promised himself just such a treat now, and thought with great happiness of the nonchalant expression he would arrange upon his face when Ann opened the door and found him standing there.

'Hey, bud, want a ride?' said a voice.

John looked up. A small Chevrolet had stopped and a friendly red face was looking down at him.

'Thanks very much,' said John. 'I'm trying to get to Beverly Hills.'

'Hop in, then. I'm going to Santa Monica. It's easy from where I turn off.'

His benefactor, it transpired, worked for a company that made bathing suits. He did a great deal of travelling. As details of personal information flowed from his lips, the broad highway poured beneath the wheels of the little car. Like so many of his race, this kindly man enjoyed opening up the pages of his private life for the benefit of a total stranger: and he, in his turn, had every intention of finding out all he could about this young man he had seen sitting on a battered piece of luggage by the side of the highway.

John had grown accustomed to this side of the American character and took it for what it was meant to be—a gesture of open friendliness; but every time it happened he thought with a certain wonder of his own countrymen who, when taking a long train journey, inevitably would look for an empty compartment, take up a strong position in a corner, space

174

out an umbrella and a hat on the seat adjacent; distribute a newspaper, an attache case, and a brown paper bag along the one opposite: then, if any fellow traveller should be brazen enough to see through this piece of bluff, would sit in stony silence for the entire trip, bursting with righteous indignation that privacy should thus have been invaded.

'Perhaps it's something to do with the comparative size of the two countries,' mused John as the bathing suit man prattled on. 'Millions of British people have been cooped up on a little island for centuries, so minding one's own business has developed into a necessary national art; over here, for a long time, there were hardly enough people to go round, so, when one inhabitant suddenly stumbled across another the natural tendency was to exchange life histories while the going was good.'

However, he was definitely in the bathing suit man's debt, and politeness demanded a more attentive ear.

' . . . well, sir, Mr. Fromkess, he's the boss, he took this trip to Europe, and over there he saw those French girls running around those beaches in those little French swim suits. Now I don't know what got into Mr. Fromkess, but the next thing I know I'm on the road trying to sell about eleven square inches of material to cover up several square feet of American womanhood. Now I reckon it all boils down to the navel.'

'How's that?' inquired John.

'Well over there in Europe it's perfectly okay to show the navel, see? . . . And once that's been decided, then you don't have to draw the line for about three . . . maybe four inches on the average dame. You can get that nice curve of the hip exposed.'

'Well there's nothing wrong with that.'

'Nothing wrong with it at all, once the public has been educated to it, but over here we have the Legion of Decency and all those women's clubs, too, and so far we haven't been able to sell them the navel.'

'Too bad,' said John.

He thought for a moment. 'I wonder if you could persuade the women's clubs that it is good for health to expose the navel to the sun or something like that?'

'Oh, we're trying everything.' The bathing suit man shook his head gloomily. 'Yes, sir, it sure is tough sledding, and more so since that dumb Miss America had her photo on the front page every morning giving an interview on the beach some place in Europe saying that no hundred per cent American girl shows her navel or wears falsies.'

'What do you sell in the winter?' asked John.

'Oh, it's much easier then. . . . I sell space for a big burial ground concern.'

'Do more people die in wintertime in California?'

'Well, I guess they must. At least this organization takes on twenty extra salesmen each year between October and April. Mostly traffic accidents, of course. . . . Seems the tyres get smooth on those long vacation trips during the summer and then when the rain comes the skidding starts.'

'I see.'

They drove for an hour through forests of oil derricks, past nauseous refineries, over brown hills scorched by the California sun. They flashed by the vast municipal airport and ran between acres of celery beds. The great billboards advertising hotels, cigarettes, cooling drinks and undertakers were packed together along either side of the highway and at some points of particular vantage, and effectively screening the view, they were staggered, each one peeping out from behind the next, like the medals on the chest of a field marshal.

The bathing suit man slowed down. 'This is as near as I go.'

John looked out of the window, and beheld, at the intersection, a thin, sallow-faced individual sitting beneath a bright yellow umbrella. He was wearing a huge Mexican hat and horn-rimmed spectacles: behind him was a large sign, 'This Way to Hollywood. Buy Your Map Here. Guide to the Movie Stars' Homes.'

John climbed out of the car and thanked his navel-conscious benefactor for his kindness.

'Not at all. Glad of the company,' the man replied.

'Good luck with the swim suits,' John shouted as the car pulled away, 'and . . . er . . . the other things, too.'

The man smiled, waved good-bye, and disappeared towards Santa Monica with its beach clubs and prospective customers. John crossed the road to the yellow umbrella.

'Guide to the movie stars' homes?' asked the man under the Mexican hat.

'No thanks,' said John.

'Aren't you interested in the movies?'

'Not particularly.'

'That makes two of us . . .' said the man.

John laughed outright. 'Looks as if you have the wrong job.'

'Oh heck, I'm not complaining about the job, but most of my customers are real drips . . . they come from all over like the goddamned pilgrims going to Mecca—they hardly ever see a movie star when they get there.'

John indicated the pile of maps the man had for sale. 'Well, at least they can have a look at the outside of their houses.'

The sallow face cracked into a toothless grin. 'That's what they think.' He spat on the ground. 'Drips!'

In another hour his sixth benefactor of the day deposited him at the end of South Morton Drive. John picked up his solitary piece of baggage and set forth in search of number 1059½.

John looked up at the pleasant sundrenched house standing back in the shade of a giant jacaranda tree; an elderly man in his shirtsleeves was swishing water from a hose on to a patch of bright green lawn, and a large nightblooming jasmine and a bed of pink petunias already dripped with moisture beneath the downstairs windows. The man paused in the middle of his watering and initiated John into the intricacies of the numbering.

With a pounding heart, he mounted the outside stairs and knocked on the door of the top apartment. Just above the door-knocker there was a little circular aperture edged with brass: after a short pause a large brown eye filled this hole and stared out at him suspiciously.

'Who is it, please?' came the unmistakable accents of an American negress.

'John Hamilton, I've come to see Miss Ann Windsor.'

'Well, Miss Windsor is still at the studio and I don't expect her back for an hour or more.'

'I see. Well, I am a very old friend of hers: I wonder if I could come inside and wait?'

'Miss Ann expecting you?'

'In a way she is, but I've just come off a ship and I didn't call her to warn her I was coming.'

'Well, you just wait out there a minute and I'll call Miss Ann at the studio and ask her if it's okay to let you in. . . . What name did you say again?'

'Mr. Hamilton,' said John.

The brown eye disappeared from the peephole and some sort of inner shutter was replaced: Two seconds later it was back.

'Mr. *Hamilton* did you say?'

'Yes.'

'Mr. John Hamilton?'

'Yes.'

'Mr. John Hamilton what is going to marry Miss Ann?'

'That's right.'

A shriek of delight. 'Why, I declare, I didn't hear aright the first time. . . . Come right in, Mr. John, we've been expectin' you right along.'

The door flew open and he found himself enveloped in a warm bearlike hug.

'Man! is this exciting! . . . Miss Ann will be fit to be tied she wasn't here when you arrived. . . . Now let me look at you, Mr. John.'

John was held at arm's length and although he still only just cleared the enormous bosom, he was inspected, shaken, patted, and hugged again.

'Well my Lord! is this a ball! . . . Mr. John, I'm Clarabel, and I sure am glad you got here. . . . Miss Ann has been so lonesome, and she's been looking forward so much to your getting here. She'll like to faint when she sees you.'

John was given one more squeeze and released.

Then Clarabel started bustling about the room. Did Mr. John want anything to eat? Coffee? . . . a drink maybe? He was forced into a chair and plied with cookies. At last the excitement began to die down somewhat and the storm centre moved out into the kitchen. John looked round the room. It was small, comfortable, gay, feminine and lived-in: he got up and peeked round the door into the minute, cool, green bedroom: a snapshot of himself stood beside the bed, and he shuddered at the sight of the rather self-conscious face that smiled out from the little silver frame. The picture had been taken outside Buckingham Palace at the Investiture on the occasion of his receiving his Military Cross. One of the Aunts had bought five copies from the news agency. He made a mental note to replace it as soon as possible, and turned back into the living-room, then his heart leaped.

Ann was standing there open-eyed, staring at him: for a split second they stood thus, and then in a flurry they were in each other's arms.

Later that evening when Clarabel produced an enormous dinner, they sat side by side on the floor and stared at the spread on the coffee table—they were much too excited to eat.

Every now and then Clarabel's shining face would appear round the kitchen door: she was determined that not a scrap should be left uneaten; and much care had to be taken to safeguard her feelings. Selected morsels were surreptitiously wrapped up and hidden under the sofa to be taken to Meadowbrook Studios on the morrow and distributed among several dogs of Ann's acquaintance; the rest was sneaked into the bathroom and flushed into obscurity.

John noticed the little black smudges of tiredness beneath Ann's eyes and he was not surprised when she told him that she got up every morning at four-thirty, drove herself to the studio, spent two and a half hours or more with the hairdresser, another hour with the makeup man, gulped some breakfast, and dashed on to the sound stage at nine o'clock— there to remain under the blazing arc lights until six o'clock in the evening.

'It's tremendous fun though, Johnny darling, and all the crew are absolutely sweet. I think I am rotten in the part, but the director, Mark Roseleaf, is divine and helps me so much.'

'What's Ridgway like?' asked John.

Ann made a little face. 'Oh, he's all right I guess, but he's not my type.' She snuggled up to him, 'practically nobody is.'

Breathlessly Ann told John about the film she was making: she told him the story down to the smallest detail; she described the sets, the camera work and her dressing-room: she was very keyed up and over-excited. He was quite relieved when Clarabel appeared in her street clothes.

'I'm off home now, honey, and you should be in bed anyway. . . . It's way after nine o'clock.'

'Off you go, darling,' said John, 'if you are going to look your best at four o'clock in the morning, you'd better get some sleep.'

'You said it, Mr. John . . . but Miss Ann will stay up with you all night unless you watch it.'

'I will, Clarabel,' said John, 'don't you worry. . . . Good night.'

'Good night, folks. . . .' The lazy, happy voice floated up from below as Clarabel went singing down the street; singing the songs of the cottonfields as she walked towards the street-car terminus, and stoically faced the clanking, jolting eight-mile journey to Main Street, where she would spend a hot, restless night in the overcrowded tenement room that would rattle and shake as the great streamlined trains, in a blue haze of diesel oil, thundered past her window.

Ann made little bird noises of denial, but it was obvious to John that she was utterly exhausted. She gave him a wan smile.

'I'll go and have a hot bath and smother my face with cold

cream: you have a drink in the meanwhile and pop in and say good night before you go.'

John helped himself to a whisky and soda and ruffled through the pages of *Harper's Bazaar*. After a while the splashing and soaping sounds that came to his ears were replaced by tiny grunts which accompanied the brisk use of a towel; the egg-beating noise of toothbrush against a tooth glass was followed by the 'klop' of a replaced jar top: another few seconds of busy little movements denoted a general tidying up; then, the click of a light switch, the closing of a door and the squeak of a bedspring made it quite clear that the day, for Ann, was over.

John put down the magazine and crossed quietly to the bedroom door. 'Good night, my angel,' he said.

She looked up—very small, very tired, very greasy and very beautiful: she raised her two arms to him. John moved to the side of the bed and kneeled down: the arms closed round his neck and her face was beside his.

'I love you, little one,' he whispered.

'So do I,' she whispered back, 'with all my heart.'

John stayed there kneeling beside the bed till Ann's breathing became steady and deep against his cheek: then gently disengaging himself, he covered her up like a small child, switched off the bedside light and tiptoed from the room.

Ann's landlady had found John a room in the next street. He let himself out of the apartment and carried his bag through the scented evening—his heart was singing. Ann and he were right—so completely right. He felt he could burst with happiness.

It had been arranged that the following day John would go to the Meadowbrook Studios and have lunch with Ann.

When he arrived there, he thought at first that he had come to an aircraft factory. The huge sound stages looked like hangars, and the heavily-armed police at the gate seemed far better suited to the guarding of the latest jet-propelled bomber, than to the protection of blonde movie actresses from the occasional sex-maniac who might suggest that they do strange things together in a diving bell off Catalina Island.

John stated his business. 'I have come to have lunch with Miss Ann Windsor.' He was directed to another entrance. There, after searching interrogation, he was passed through into a large ante-room, at the far end of which a policeman was seated behind a desk: the policeman was chewing. 'I wonder if you can help me?' said John. 'I have come to have lunch with Miss Ann Windsor.'

The policeman did not look up: he went on chewing. John, thinking the man was deaf, repeated his statement with a greater volume of sound.

'I have come to have lunch with Miss Ann Windsor,' he roared.

The policeman looked up and stared fully at John for several seconds: his jaws still moved rhythmically. At last he switched his gum to another part of his mouth and leaned forward. 'Well now,' he said, 'ain't that just dandy for Miss Windsor.'

John, though slightly taken aback, would have entered happily into this verbal give and take if he had not at that moment become aware that at least twenty people were listening—they were seated round the walls of the ante-room on very uncomfortable wooden chairs.

In addition to several leggy, peroxide blondes accompanied by blue-jowled men with briefcases, there was a man with no hair at all whose head was polished like a billiard ball; a distinguished-looking man with a white moustache and a monocle; a wild-eyed old man with a mane of untidy grey hair who balanced a trombone on his knees, and a doting mother with a dreadful little girl of six who had her hair permanently waved and lipstick on her tiny spoiled mouth.

'Take a seat Bud, and wait your turn,' said the policeman curtly.

John obeyed. He felt no resentment, only the wondering curiosity of an explorer coming suddenly upon a lost civilization in the depths of the jungle.

One of the blue-jowled men leaned toward him with a

conspiratorial air. 'That sonofabitch is terrible: he keeps people waiting just for the fun of it: he's been here for years. . . . Who are you trying to see?'

'I am supposed to be having lunch with a friend of mine. She's working in a picture here.'

The man looked incredulous.

'She's working in a picture! Who is the producer?'

'er . . . Ingersoll, I believe.'

'Mr. Ingersoll!' the man's tone was reverent and hushed; he moved a little on his chair to make sure John had plenty of room.

Ten minutes later the telephone rang at the policeman's elbow. He listened for a moment; then spoke in an ingratiating manner, 'Yes, Miss Fenchurch. . . . I'll just see, Miss Fenchurch. . . . One moment, please, Miss Fenchurch.' He clapped his hand over the mouthpiece. 'Any of you characters named Hamilton? . . . John Hamilton?'

John admitted to this. All eyes turned upon him with renewed interest.

The policeman glowered for a moment, then took his hand off the mouthpiece. 'Yes, Mr. Hamilton is here, Miss Fenchurch, he just this moment walked in . . . certainly Miss Fenchurch . . . I'll have him wait for you . . . thank you, Miss Fenchurch.' He hung up and crooked his finger in John's direction.

John sauntered over to the desk. The policeman leaned toward him and whispered confidentially, 'Mr. Ingersoll's secretary is coming down to fetch you.'

'Thanks,' said John.

Miss Fenchurch was full of apologies. 'Mr. Ingersoll is most upset, Mr. Hamilton . . . he quite forgot to tell me to arrange to have a pass here at the desk for you. . . . I do hope you haven't been waiting long?'

John followed Miss Fenchurch down a maze of passages and out into the brilliant sunlight of a street: the glare from the white walls of the towering sound stages was overwhelming: the heat rose in hot waves from the pavement.

Miss Fenchurch was incredulous that this should be the first time John had ever been inside a film studio. She took a verbose delight in explaining everything as they hurried along; she also told him that Mr. Ingersoll was expecting him to lunch and that Ann would, of course, be there; for good measure she added that Mr. Ingersoll and the other high executives of Meadowbrook Pictures, Inc., regarded Ann as the greatest discovery since Mabel Norman. 'She is going to be a sensation in "Backwash" and they have great plans for her after that.'

The various production companies presently at work within the huge confines of Meadowbrook Pictures, Inc., were just breaking up for the one hour luncheon interval. Hungry employees were being disgorged from the maws of the vast sound stages: the stars were sauntering towards their bungalow dressing-rooms, the executives were bustling in the direction of one of the three private dining-rooms (each one graded in customer importance), while the small-part actors, the extras and the hundred and one technicians connected with the making of pictures were all hurrying toward the giant commissary in the middle of the studio.

'Look,' cried Miss Fenchurch, clutching John's arm in a vice-like grip, 'over there . . . just going past the fire hydrant, over there . . . Jason MacDougal! and look, Maria Maxton—over there talking to William Wolfgang.'

John, who regarded a film as something you occasionally went to see on a wet afternoon, glanced disinterestedly at these bearers of fabulous household names: he was far more interested in the swirling mass eddying round him headed for the commissary.

Cowboys and Southern colonels, cancan dancers and French sailors, a giant negro with a leopard-skin loincloth, midgets, bevies of tall and incredibly beautiful girls, sudden spates of elderly people in full evening dress—all these he found fascinating.

Miss Fenchurch steered him through the mob and towards a white bungalow set a little apart. It was surrounded by a picket fence: a small bed of asters was on either side of the door, and above was a sign which read 'Isaac Ingersoll.' They passed beneath the sign and into an ante-room. The only difference between this ante-room and the one over which the obstructionist policeman had presided was that it was smaller and here a flashing redhead with a disillusioned face was at the receipt of custom: the uncomfortable wooden chairs were occupied by the mixture as before—leggy blondes accompanied by blue-jowled men holding briefcases, bald men, hairy men and musicians with instruments. Several stood up as Miss Fenchurch swept disdainfully through the room.

Past the eye-filling receptionist and through a door was another and more comfortable waiting-room: here green leather chairs were dotted about; magazines were at hand and this time, at the sight of Miss Fenchurch, all the occupants of the chairs stood up. John remembered a toy he had particularly disliked as a child—a large brightly-coloured box with a smaller one inside, inside that had been a third which in turn had contained a fourth; there had been seven or eight of these until finally a minute box with a lid had been unveiled: John vividly remembered his disappointment when he had lifted the top of this inner receptacle—the little box had been empty. A wave of pity swept over him. There had been a look of desperation on many of the faces he had seen on his journey through the waiting-rooms.

Miss Fenchurch knocked on the door of the inner sanctum and bustled in. 'Mr. Hamilton is here, Mr. Ingersoll.'

John followed her into the holy of holies.

The first shock he received was when he saw the furniture. A beautiful Sheraton bookcase stood in one corner; Chinese Chippendale armchairs stood near a fine drum-top table, a delicious Aubusson was on the floor, and the walls sang with three sumptuous seascapes by Van der Velde the Younger.

The desk, small and beautifully made, topped with fine old red leather, was veneered with the rarest Caramandel wood.

From behind it Isaac Ingersoll now rose, and John received his second shock.

On the few occasions upon which he had given any thought to big movie moguls it had been in the diffused light shed upon them by newspaper cartoonists—gross cigar-smoking elderly Jews, with jewelled fingers and lascivious lips: he had taken it for granted that Isaac Ingersoll would conform to this type. The man who now advanced toward him with outstretched hand was very different: tall and fit-looking with fine dark eyes. A charming smile lit up his deeply tanned face.

'Very glad to meet you, Mr. Hamilton. . . . Ann has talked so much about you I feel I almost know you. . . . Please sit down. She'll be here any minute.'

He apologized most handsomely for forgetting to send a pass down to the reception desk. 'I was sent for by Bengy early this morning and when that happens everything goes out of your mind.' He laughed. 'Would you like a martini?'

While Ingersoll was mixing the drinks at a small alcove bar, John broached the subject of fine old English furniture reposing in a Hollywood executive's office.

'I've been collecting it for years,' explained his host. 'I have a lot at home, but I hardly ever get a chance to see it there, so I move my favourite pieces down here to my office from time to time, then at least I get some pleasure out of my collection. . . . Bengy has us working around twelve to fourteen hours a day right now.'

'You seem to have travelled around quite a bit,' said John, as he lifted his cocktail glass.

'Isn't that what is expected of the wandering race?' smiled Isaac Ingersoll.

They sipped their drinks in silence for a moment.

John spoke first. 'Is Ann really good in your picture?'

'She is absolutely wonderful. I honestly believe within two or three years she will be one of the biggest names in the industry: she has a great natural talent—great. She's a wonderful girl, too, but I don't need to tell *you* that. You are a very lucky man. Ann told me as a secret . . . I am very happy for you both.'

'Thanks,' said John. 'Yes, God knows I am lucky.' But the words 'in two or three years one of the biggest names in the industry' sounded the first tiny note of alarm in his heart.

Ann burst into the room.

She was heavily made up with a yellowish greasepaint and wearing a thin silk dressing-gown: her carefully dressed hair had been equally carefully shrouded in a pink hair-net. John also noticed, with some alarm, that she sported long false eye-lashes and that her mouth was no longer the same shape as the one which God had given her.

She kissed him on the cheek. 'Oh darling, don't look so shocked! . . . I know I look awful, but they say it photographs all right.'

'It certainly does, Ann,' said Isaac Ingersoll.

John noticed that a tall, broadshouldered young man with thick wavy hair and a weak, too goodlooking face had entered the room behind Ann. He, too, was painted yellow. He wore a dressing-gown of the MacKenzie tartan.

Ingersoll introduced him to John—'Ralph Ridgway, the star of our picture.'

Was there just the tiniest hint of distaste in Ingersoll's voice?

'How do you do,' said John.

'Pleased to meet you,' said Ridgway. There was more than the tiniest hint of cockney in his.

'I don't offer drinks to my cast at lunch'time,' laughed Ingersoll. 'Let's get some food right away: if anyone is late on the set I don't want Bengy to blame me.'

Polite general laughter followed this sally, and they all filed into the next room.

A Filipino waiter in a white jacket helped Ann to her chair. The table was set with cold consommé, an assortment of cold meats, a large salad, and iced coffee.

'How is poor old England?' asked Ridgway when they were seated. 'Pretty well on her last legs, eh?'

'I expect she'll pull through,' said John quietly. 'She generally does.'

'Doesn't look as though your government knows which side its bread is buttered. . . . After all, here we are in America, taxed out of existence just so that England can keep on her feet, and all they do over there is spend it on a lot of nonsense . . . giving away false teeth and wigs and that sort of rot.' Ridgway laughed a carefully-rehearsed laugh, and John, dwelling momentarily on the subject of teeth, noticed that Ridgway's had been filed into a straight line. He looked like a piano.

'We will take you on the set after lunch,' said Ingersoll, changing the subject, 'or will that make you nervous, Ann?'

Ann smiled. 'I'm always nervous, but Mr. Roseleaf is such a darling that I hardly notice it once I get started.'

'Mark Roseleaf is the director,' explained Ingersoll.

'I see,' said John. 'Please forgive me for being so ignorant, but what is the difference between a producer and a director?'

Ingersoll pushed his plate on one side and grinned. 'Let me see how I can make it simple for you.'

While Ingersoll initiated John into some of the intricacies of film making, Ridgway worked diligently with a tooth pick. When the producer stopped talking he said reflectively . . . 'one would think that they would tighten their belts over there in England and try to stand on their own feet for a change. After all . . .'

Ann broke in. 'Mr. Ingersoll, I think I'd better run back to the set . . . I have to have my makeup fixed and it's almost time. . . . Thanks so much for lunch.'

Ingersoll stood up. 'All right, Ann dear, run along then. I'll bring your young man over to the set in a little while.'

'I'll come with you, Ann,' said Ridgway. He turned at the door and linked his arm familiarly through hers. 'You won't see much. . . . It's a pretty dreary scene, but I am doing my best with it . . . see you later.'

Ann looked a little lost. She blew John a kiss. 'Bye now.'

'Let's have a little brandy, shall we?' said Ingersoll when the others had left.

They sat down again at the table.

'What do you think of the great Ralph Ridgway, idol of millions?'

'He's English, isn't he?' asked John.

'He *was* English. He came out here in thirty-eight; but when the war in Europe broke out a year later he took out his naturalization papers to become an American citizen—he was about twenty-four then.'

'What happened after Pearl Harbour? . . . Wasn't he drafted into the American Army?'

Ingersoll savoured the bouquet of the Courvoisier.

'Bengy got him deferred for a year or so, but when they finally caught up with him the sonofabitch signed a statement at the draft board saying he was a fairy.'

'Is he?' asked John.

'I've never had any desire to find out, but he certainly doesn't behave like one.'

'Is he very popular?'

'Oh sure, he's up in the first ten at the box office . . . but don't forget there were no leading men here for four years or so, he just had to get popular, in spite of himself.'

Ingersoll blew out a heavy cloud of cigar smoke. 'He's unbearable now: Bengy thinks the world of him, but he can't act his way out of a paper bag.' He twirled his cigar and studied it. 'I give him a couple of years more at the most—he's like a lot of them—just couldn't take prosperity I guess. . . . Like to walk over to the set?'

'Love to.'

John followed Ingersoll back into his beautifully furnished office and heard him give his instructions.

'Miss Fenchurch, I'm just going over to Stage 6. I'll be there a short while only. . . . What time is my appointment at Twentieth? . . . Okay. . . . Anybody waiting to see me? . . . Well, get rid of them . . . and say . . . that story conference will probably go on forever, so have Dominic get some food in. . . . We'll have dinner here . . . and call Mrs. Ingersoll and tell her I'll be home late again . . . after dinner.'

Ingersoll opened a door that led directly from his office into the street behind the bungalow. 'This is my escape hatch,' he explained. 'If we go this way we can avoid all those people waiting around out there.'

The desperate faces in the ante-rooms had been bothering John ever since he had crossed the threshold of Meadowbrook Pictures, Inc.: they had been at the back of his mind all the while; something left undone that ought to have been done; a draught had been playing on his heart as though someone had left a door open.

'What about all those people?' he asked, as they slipped out into the brilliant sunlight.

With surprising sharpness Ingersoll turned to him. 'Four-fifths of them ought never to have got into this racket. They ought to have stayed home—every extrovert alive can dream up an urge to take the world by storm from behind the footlights. . . . Half the people who go to the movies are quite convinced that they can do it better than the actors they are watching on the screen.' He quickened his pace to match his impatience.

'Sure it's pathetic, sure you can feel sorry for them. There is ghastly suffering in this town, but they should have stayed home in the first place. When they find that out—it's too late. . . .

'So some kid wins a beauty contest in some jerk town some place, so she gets all her savings together, borrows the dough maybe, and hops a train for Hollywood. . . . No talent—nothing. . . . Just long legs and a couple of big jugs. . . . She's so dumb she only gets a one-way ticket, never a round trip. O, no! Then it starts . . . casting offices, agents' offices, directors' offices, producers' offices; the money goes. . . . Sooner or later she's desperate. Sometimes she earns enough at something else to get back on that train and go home. . . . Most times she is too proud to go home and tell the folks she couldn't make it . . . she just sticks around and hopes. She becomes a waitress, a car hop, a whore, maybe. Anything—but she sticks around.' Ingersoll's voice dropped and he shook his head. 'Why don't they stay home?' he asked, addressing no one in particular.

They walked for a while in silence: then they passed a giant generator plant. Ingersoll said, 'We make enough electricity here to light a city of five hundred thousand.'

John felt that he ought to be impressed by these statistics. 'That's terrific,' he said, and Ingersoll agreed.

Ingersoll told him that there were also two hundred acres of back lot which included the permanent sets such as the Mexican Village, the New York Street, the Western Town, the Opera House, the big tank for the sea pictures, the theatre entrance, the prison wall, the French Village Square (with guillotine). The waterfront, the English village green surrounded by thatched cottages, and a complete replica of the White House.

'That's terrific,' said John again, and Ingersoll agreed once more.

They reached a small door in the vast side of one of the Stages.

For a moment John thought they had come to the wrong stage—it seemed empty. Then from the gloom at the far end of the cavernous building, more like an airplane hangar than ever now, came a shout.

'Lock 'em up.'

An electric bell rang out and the door through which they had just passed sealed itself behind them with a loud click.

'They are just going to shoot,' whispered Ingersoll. John followed nervously as they headed for a glow of light in the far corner of the sound stage. They tiptoed like a couple of burglars across thirty yards of open space.

'Ready Ann? . . . Ralph?' asked a quiet voice from behind a canvas wall in the distance.

'All right then, turn them over.' A pause: the quiet voice spoke again. 'Action!'

Upon the instant and as though someone had turned on a tap there arose from behind the canvas wall all the clamour of a successful dinner party. Heading for this sound, Ingersoll led the way and John found himself behind a huge wheeled crane which was reposing upon a small railway track.

'Start the crane,' yelled a voice from somewhere far above him: peering upward into the gloom, he perceived several men perched precariously on the end of the arm: they were crouched behind a large camera: the crane, which was steered along the tracks by a man manipulating an electric motor, now started forward in the direction of the party noises. John followed.

Gigantic doors in the path of the crane swung open: it passed majestically through and there, in the glare of a hundred arc lights, was a banquet in full swing. Dazzling women smiled archly upon resplendent officers and diplomats; toasts were offered and received; hands were kissed; glasses were clinked; the merry quip was on every lip: medals, monocles and molars flashed brightly on every side: a babel of voices beat upon the dusty air.

At the sight of so much gaiety, the crane, like an inquisitive brontosaurus, lowered its head and the camera came on a level with the end of the long banquet table.

'Cut the dialogue,' came a curt command from somewhere outside the brilliant scene: the tap was turned off. The babel, as if by magic, ceased as quickly as it had begun. Miraculously, the noise was all that stopped completely; in pantomime the party still went on as gaily as before: only a lip reader could tell what nonsense was now being mouthed between diplomat and duchess; the smiles and raised glasses were still there and a large man, wearing the Order of the Garter, even threw back his head and indulged in a silent guffaw.

Slowly, inexorably, the crane moved forward, its head, with the camera and camera crew upon it, now skimming slowy along just above the top of the table. The silver candlesticks and the great dishes of fruit passed unheeded beneath it; on either side, and as though in review, the faces of the guests slipped smoothly by. However, once safely behind the all-seeing camera, instead of in front of it, the actors no longer acted—the happy faces of the beautifully dressed nobility no longer mouthed and smiled; hard lines of tiredness and boredom settled upon them; yawns were stifled, spectacles were wiped, teeth were picked; thus, slowly but surely, as the shadow of a summer cloud will darken and change the face of a sun-drenched meadow, the camera headed down the line toward its ultimate goal—Ann and Ridgway—side by side at the far end of the table.

The crane came to the end of its journey, bringing the camera directly in front of the two principals, and their voices sounded unnaturally loud as they started to play their scene.

Ann, looking exquisitely lovely in a white dress and small diamond tiara, was the first to speak. She smiled as she said her lines.

'Tell me, Ezio, have we made you comfortable here?'

'Oh, yes, Maria, very comfortable, I thank you.'

'Do you have a good view from your windows?'

'Oh, yes, Maria, very good, I thank you.'

'What do you see from there, Ezio?'

'It's all walls. . . .' Ridgway stopped, thumped the table so that his plate and glasses jumped, 'Christ!' he said very loud indeed.

'Cut!' said the quiet voice of the director.

'Save your arcs,' said the head electrician.

'Pull the crane back,' said the assistant director.

'Open the doors,' said the second assistant director.

'What happend this time?' asked the director, who, John now saw for the first time, was one of those crouching beside the camera.

'I don't know who wrote this crappy dialogue, but it just doesn't play,' said Ridgway, 'also, a lot of people seem to be moving about back there,' he waved his arm vaguely in the direction of a corner of the sound stage where no one was standing.

The director caught Isaac Ingersoll's enquiring glance, shrugged his shoulders and rolled his eyes upward in an eloquent expression of bored disgust.

'Okay, let's try it again,' he said.

'Close the doors,' said the second assistant director.

'Light your arcs,' said the head electrician.

'Stand by with the crane,' said the assistant director.

When all was once more in readiness, the patient voice of the director came from the heights whither he had been returned for the eighth time. 'Ready Ann? Ralph? . . . All right, then, turn them over. . . . Quiet please.' A pause. 'Action!'

Five more times on one pretext or another was the patient director wafted aloft before Mr. Ridgway managed to remember the whole of the two minutes of dialogue required by the scene. Ann became increasingly nervous, but she did not falter. Isaac Ingersoll was not so patient.

'If that jerk would take the trouble to work,' he muttered, 'we might get this picture finished before Christmas.'

Once this particular scene had been satisfactorily dealt with there was a lull in the proceedings as far as Ann was concerned.

She was able to sit down and talk to John while the crew swarmed busily about preparing for the next phase of the operation.

Ann introduced John to everyone and in spite of the smooth speed with which their mysterious work was proceeding, all found time to be friendly and instructive; it was obvious that they adored Ann. No queen ever received such unflagging and loving attention from her handmaidens as that bestowed upon Ann by her hairdresser, makeup girl, wardrobe mistress, and stand-in. Mark Roseleaf, the director, was lyrical in his praises:

'Not only is she a wonderful natural actress, but she is one of the sweetest people I have ever worked with: there's not one member of this crew who wouldn't walk from here to Warners on hands and knees if Ann asked him to, and that,' he added with a wink in the direction of Ralph Ridgway's back, 'is more than they would do for *some* people around here. . . .'

'Oh-oh! let me out of here,' he said suddenly, 'here comes Annie.'

John followed the man's startled gaze and beheld a

diminutive, elderly woman dressed from head to foot in black satin: she was smiling benevolently through pince-nez which were attached to a chain, the end of which disappeared into a large, round button, pinned high upon her tightly corseted bosom.

At first John thought that she must be somebody's well-meaning aunt: but when he noticed the fawning attention she was receiving from a group of important-looking men (which included Isaac Ingersoll), he further deduced that she must also be very rich, have no heirs, and be about to collapse from some strange and incurable tropical disease.

He grabbed the coat tail of the fleeing director. 'Annie who?' he whispered.

The man turned. 'Why Annie Argus, of course—and brother! is she syndicated! . . . Over six hundred newspapers print her lousy column . . . and me trying to get a quiet divorce! . . . Let me out of here . . . I'm going into the can for a breath of fresh air.'

Ann, too, had deserted John. She was in a corner where some slight adjustments were being made to the shoulder of her dress. John stood alone, a solitary stationary figure with the tide of activity swirling about him.

Out of the corner of his eye, he saw that he was becoming a subject of interest within the Annie Argus group; heads were turned in his direction, voices were lowered. Finally Annie Argus and Ingersoll detached themselves from the others and advanced upon him—he was formally introduced.

Annie Argus seated herself in a chair and patted a vacant one beside her: she then dismissed Ingersoll with a slight backward inclination of her head.

'I understand you have just arrived in Hollywood, Mr. Hamilton,' said the little woman.

She had a quiet, rather musical voice. She seemed very harmless.

'Yes,' said John. 'I got in last night.'

'Is Bengy going to put you into pictures? . . . You are very good-looking.'

'Good heavens, no. I just came out to see a friend.'

'Did you fly out?'

He told her all about the trip in H.M.S. *Falmouth* and she was most interested—'a good listener,' thought John.

'Who are the friends you are visiting?' she asked him in an offhand way. 'I wonder if I know them.'

John began to feel slightly trapped. Ann and he were going to be married soon; they had not yet had a chance to decide on the time or the place, and he most certainly did not want to discuss it with a total stranger. John knew nothing of publicists or columnists . . . being a firm believer in minding his own business, he became profoundly embarrassed when others did not do the same.

'. . . oh, I don't expect you'd know them. . . . They only just arrived . . . er . . . actually . . .' The eyes behind the pince-nez were not as benevolent as they had been before: they had become brighter, more intelligent. They seemed to have sharpened. Annie Argus said nothing.

The ensuing silence seemed to John to be his responsibility, '. . . he keeps bees,' he added vaguely.

'Who keeps bees?'

'Oh the husband . . . the wife doesn't keep anything much . . .'

He faltered: another pregnant silence was the result.

Annie Argus allowed a flicker of a smile to disturb the tranquillity of her expression: she was used to searching for chinks in the armour of the publicity-wise—this was like taking candy from a baby.

'You are English, aren't you?'

'Scots, actually.'

'You don't have a burr. . . . What happened to that?'

'I expect it got rubbed off at school. . . . I went to school in England before I went into the Army.'

'In the war?'

'Yes, that's right.'

'I heard a rumour just now that you were very highly decorated.'

'Oh, Lord, no! My colonel lost his head and got me an M.C. for not being caught running away—that's all.'

'An M.C.?'

'Military Cross.'

'What is the difference between a Military Cross and a Victoria Cross?'

John laughed. 'Well, to get a Victoria Cross you have to do something fantastic, like capturing the whole of the German General Staff, armed with an umbrella. . . . They only awarded about thirty of those in the whole war.'

'Like the Congressional Medal of Honor?'

'Yes, that's it—it's the same sort of idea.'

'Why didn't they give you a Victoria Cross?'

John felt on safe ground: this was stuff he knew. He laughed. 'Just a small technical hitch—I didn't deserve it.'

Annie Argus smiled charmingly.

'Just a small technical hitch? That is very modest of you. . . . Tell me about Ann Windsor.'

The question came so suddenly, so unexpectedly, that it caught John completely off balance and his mental reflex was unchecked.

'She's wonderful,' he said fervently.

Annie Argus leaned towards him, and the rustle of her black satin dress sounded like a snake moving over dead leaves.

'I hear she is completely stuck on you. When are you going to be married?'

John looked round helplessly, and thought with longing of the sanctuary to which Mark Roseleaf had but lately repaired.

'Please don't think me rude,' he said, 'but there are some questions one just can't answer.'

Annie Argus removed her pince-nez: the spring inside the black button on her bosom made a little 'zipp' as the thin chain curled away out of sight: she patted his knee.

'My dear boy, forgive me. . . . I am an inquisitive old woman. . . . You should have told me to mind my own business.'

John did not notice the imperious nod of the small, intelligent head. Isaac Ingersoll saw it from behind, in fact he had been watching for it; he hurried forward.

'Annie darling,' he enquired solicitously, 'anyone else you want to see?'

She rose from her chair. 'Not really, unless . . . unless Mark Roseleaf is anywhere about? But please don't bother him. . . . He must have *so* much on his mind—'

Isaac Ingersoll was galvanized into action. He summoned the assistant director. Annie Argus turned to John and smiled with infinite sweetness. She put out her hand: 'Goodbye, Mr. Hamilton, it was so nice meeting you . . . the trip in the battleship sounded just wonderful, how I envy you.'

'Good-bye,' said John, taking the small white hand.

'My love to the beekeeper,' said Annie Argus; and John, caught, like many a good man before him, in the net of his own fabrication, for one fatal second faltered.

'Beekeeper?'

'Good-bye,' smiled Annie Argus. She turned away.

A couple of minutes later Ann came back to him. 'I saw you were cornered by the Gestapo—so I kept away. . . . If she finds out about us we will never have a moment's peace. . . . What did you think of her?'

John had not yet had time to form a strong opinion. 'She seemed very sweet really, but I expect one has to watch one's step with her. I don't think I gave anything away . . .' a thought smote him; he felt a surge of righteous indignation.

'What the hell has it got to do with her anyway?"

Ann put her hand on his arm.

'Darling, it seems I have got myself into a strange business. . . . Remember I used to worry that being a face on a magazine cover was going to interfere with my private life? Well, unless I'm very lucky, being a movie queen is going to mean having no private life left to be interfered with. I'm public property now . . . at least that's what the publicity department informs me several times a day, and people like Annie

Argus are here to see that I don't ever become anything else.'

Ingersoll joined them.

'I have to go over to Twentieth for a conference. Stick around here as long as you want to, of course, but if you want a ride back to Beverly, I can drop you off. . . . What'd you say?'

'Johnny darling,' said Ann, 'I'd love you to stay, but it's pretty dull for you, so please don't be gallant about it.' She smiled up at him. 'I'll soon be home anyway.'

He bent down and gave her a peck on the cheek. 'All right, my darling, I'll press on then. Hurry home . . . I love you,' he added in a whisper.

'I love you,' Ann whispered back.

As John straightened up he saw Annie Argus watching them closely from the shadows in the corner of the sound stage: she smiled at him and turned back to give her undivided attention to the harassed and ineffectual answers of a mild man whose future happiness depended on a quiet divorce.

'Let's go,' said Isaac Ingersoll.

As the film producer's light green Cadillac convertible slipped in and out of the traffic, John looked about him. Not even the Chamber of Commerce could seriously use the adjective 'beautiful' when describing Los Angeles. Huge?— yes: Sprawling?—yes: Interesting?—most definitely: but 'beautiful'?—unfortunately no. Like a garden occasionally tended with bursts of fanatical zeal, but left for the most part to its own devices, the great city has patches of beauty and patterns of careful planning, but the tardy building restrictions allowed the weeds to choke and spread, and in consequence large tracts of the city are disfigured by houses and shops of breathtaking ugliness. It was through one of these areas that they were now passing. With a sudden sense of guilt John remembered the patient desperate faces in Ingersoll's waiting-room. Tentatively he mentioned them again to the producer and as it was patently none of his business he excused himself by adding 'I am afraid they were rather a blow to me. . . .

I always imagined that the entertainment world was a happy, gay, bubbling thing and that everyone connected with it spent twenty-four hours a day having a wonderful time.'

Ingersoll glanced at his watch. 'I have plenty of time; I'm going to show you something now which will cure you of that idea once and for all; it's only a couple of blocks from here.' He swung the Cadillac off the main thoroughfare and in a minute or two they parked outside a very modern white building. John looked up at the sign above the door— METROPOLITAN CASTING OFFICE, he read.

Ingersoll got out of the car and John followed him through the door marked 'Entrance'. Once again he saw the inevitable waiting-room, though this one was so large it would have done credit to a railway terminus: the now-familiar figures were seated on the same uncomfortable chairs, unmoved, apparently, by the fact that the walls above their heads were plastered with large posters which could offer them but little encouragement.

'DON'T TRY TO BECOME AN ACTOR'—'THIS IS THE MOST OVERCROWDED PROFESSION IN THE WORLD'—'GO HOME'— 'THE ODDS AGAINST YOUR BECOMING A STAR ARE TWO THOUSAND TO ONE.'

As Ingersoll and John passed through the room, expectant faces were lifted towards them. 'You must be important,' pleaded the eyes. . . . 'Give me a break, mister . . . All I need is a chance to show what I can do. . . .' 'Give me a break . . .' 'Please God, give me a break.'

Inside the private office John was introduced to the manager of the Metropolitan Casting Office—a charming little man with a kindly worn face.

'We are the servants of the studios, Mr. Hamilton. . . . All our operating costs are carried by them. It's a heart-breaking business, really. . . . We do all we can to discourage the ones who shouldn't be here. Did you see our posters out there? You did?' He sighed. 'It makes no difference. . . . Every day they come here. . . . It's endless.'

Encouraged by Ingersoll the manager explained the

function of his organization. 'We classify them according to their types. Of course the biggest classifications are the racial ones.' He looked at John. 'You, for instance, with your colouring and the structure of your face, would be classified as Anglo-Saxon type, Scandinavian type, or possibly even as Germanic type, but never as Latin type.

'Within the major classifications come the minor ones—age, height, weight, ability to ride horseback, swim, ski, dance and so on. All these qualifications are cross-filed so that we can provide the studios with their requirements with the minimum of delay. Now; say I get a call from M-G-M for three fat, Argentinian-type men over six feet tall who can swim; they would come under . . . let me see,' he looked at a printed index on his office wall. 'They would be P40's. . . . So I phone through to the switchboard and the order for three P40's is flashed up at once: after that the first three P40's to call in get the job and are told to report to M-G-M at seven o'clock tomorrow morning. . . . The studios always let us have their orders a day in advance, unless of course, there is an emergency. . . .

'Would you care to see the switchboard?' They moved after him.

Twenty-five or thirty operators were seated before the board, their hands plucking and poking in endless rhythm. On the far wall high above the switchboard was the 'Requirement Statement.' This was electrically controlled on the system of the totalisator; at the moment the only requirements being stated were 120 R34 and 28 D1. The manager translated this as one hundred and twenty Red Indian types and twenty-eight American types who could produce their own evening dress clothes. As they watched, the number twenty-eight winked down to twenty-seven, then to twenty-six.

'The calls start coming in very fast at this time of day,' explained the manager. 'We handle several thousand in each twenty-four hour period.'

Throughout this conversation John had become aware of a strange humming sound. He now located it. It was a low continuous murmur from the long line of switchboard operators. They were answering the anxious or desperate voices coming into their earphones. John could not hear the requests that were pouring into the ears of these girls, but he could guess what they were like.

'Anything for me honey? Type H28?'

'Type R26. . . . Any call?'

'Any chance for X11?' The operators glanced at the Requirement Statement and except for 'Red Indian type' and 'American type with full evening dress' it was the same answer over and over again.

'Sorry, call later.'—'Sorry, call later.'—'Sorry, call later' that was the hum John heard—the dreadful hum of disillusionment, and it filled the room.

Ingersoll caught John's eye. 'Seen enough?'

John nodded. They thanked the little manager and left. As they walked out once more through the ante-room John could not bear to look at the occupants of the hard uncomfortable chairs: he could feel their expectant eyes following him down the long room.

'You must be important.' 'Give me a break, mister. . . . All I need is a chance to show what I can do.' 'Give me a break.' 'Please God, give me a break.'

Outside in the strong sunlight the glare from the white building beat upon them. John shaded his eyes and turned to Ingersoll.

'My God, how awful,' he said.

Ingersoll smiled gently, and took John by the arm. 'Forgive me for blowing my top after lunch,' he said.

John did not go any further with Ingersoll: he wanted to be alone: he wanted to consider his own situation for a little while.

Ingersoll drove away in the green Cadillac to keep his appointment and John started walking. It was no later than three o'clock: Ann would not be home for another four hours: he had plenty of time.

He started walking in the warm sun, and the exercise felt

good; he had been cooped up too long in the battleship and he welcomed this chance to stretch his legs. He took off his coat and slung it over his shoulder, then he lengthened his stride and headed for the high hills behind Hollywood.

Soon he came to an important main thoroughfare; he glanced up at the name—Hollywood Boulevard. He crossed over and took a road that led up beyond the town. The way was steep; the muscles in his thighs and calves came into play. He flattened his belly and climbed steadily.

Soon there were no more houses: sweat was streaming down his face: he switched his coat over to his other shoulder. Overhead in the brassy sky, two buzzards circled lazily, soaring with the air currents: John watched them; although he had not taken much exercise lately, he felt they were showing an indecent interest in his well-being. As he walked he pondered, and by the time he had reached the top, he had arrived at a decision—it was perfectly simple, and certainly nothing new: he must find a job. He turned and looked back whence he had come. A great sight met his eyes. The whole city of Los Angeles lay at his feet, white and shimmering in the hot afternoon: as far as the eye could see, like a thin layer of white painted upon the brown undulations of California, it seemed that it could easily be scraped off and the desert, scorching and sinister, would surely be beneath the surface—it was the very thinnest veneer of civilization. To his left, as he looked down, were the tall buildings of the business section of downtown Los Angeles: at his feet lay the suburb of Hollywood itself: and to the right, the greener residential sections of Beverly and Holmby Hills stretched their luxurious arms to the distant, sparkling ocean. Catalina Island, long and dark and whale-shaped, lay thirty miles off shore.

John sat on a rock and gazed for a long while upon the scene. From below the faint hum of traffic rose from the busy thoroughfares, cut like asphalt scars straight and deep across the face of the city: in the far distance the black smoke from a burning oil well smudged the sky.

He shivered; the warmth was going out of the day: already

the white face of the city was changing to pink and gold beneath him. He put on his coat and, standing, watched the flaming sun plunge into the golden Pacific. A million lights winked up at him from below. He started down from the hills. It was dark.

By the time he had arrived once more at the bottom of the road, he had decided that his first essential need was some form of conveyance. The city had looked so vast and so sprawling from the hills that the thought of tramping about it job-hunting appalled John: so for ninety-eight dollars he bought a car from a man on Melrose Avenue. When Ann came home an hour later she found a very excited young man waiting for her outside the building.

'What's it supposed to be?' she asked.

'It's a mongrel, actually. It's part Ford and part Auburn, part Chevy and I think it looks like a Viking. I'm going to call it Hengist. It does ninety-five. The chap at the place gave me a guarantee with it for three months because it was put together by his son—it's called a hot rod, apparently.'

Ann walked over and inspected the wheeled monstrosity. 'Don't you think Hengist would look better if he had some mudguards and his engine covered over?'

'Oh, I don't know. I rather like to be able to see all the works when I'm going along. Look, Darling, it's got two exhaust pipes. . . . Come on, hop in, let's go for a drive.'

The evening was made hideous as Hengist roared away.

The next morning, as usual, Ann went to the studio at five o'clock, and at eight-thirty John climbed on to a stool at a drugstore counter and ordered his breakfast. He felt very well and very pleased with himself; looking for and finding new jobs was always an excitement. Hengist stood expectantly at the kerbside.

He opened his newspaper, and searched amid the unfamiliar pages for the '*Situations Vacant*'. Suddenly he shied like a startled mustang. In letters of fire across the top of a page was a headline,

ANN WINDSOR TO WED WAR HERO?

John felt dizzy. Hardly daring to trust himself, he read the rest.

'Bacon and eggs, sunny side up,' said the girl behind the counter. Had she been a keen student of embarrassment she would have noticed, at this point, that a dull flush was spreading slowly upwards from her customer's collar.

'Beautiful Ann Windsor,' read John, *'the new white hope of Meadowbrook, was dewy-eyed when I visited her on the "Backwash" set and not because I was there, either! Handsome John Hamilton, the British war hero, was the reason! And I met him, too! Lucky me! Brought out here all the way in the GREATEST SECRECY by the British Royal Navy, John told me that he had come to "visit some friends," but a little bird has since told me that he has rented an apartment only a few yards away from the gorgeous Ann. Romance! Romance! Romance! John, in recognition of his brave war-time deeds of valour, was decorated by His Majesty the King with the SIGN OF THE MILITARY CROSS. When I asked him why he had not been given the Victoria Cross, which, in case you don't know, rates with our Congressional Medal of Honor, he replied in his clipped British accent, "just a small technical hitch". . . . HOW MODEST CAN YOU GET?'*

John sat for a long time after he had finished reading this. His food remained untouched: slowly the yolk of one of the eggs which had been broken in the frying pan congealed against the side of his plate. He paid his bill and walked out of the drugstore feeling rather sick.

All day long he searched for a job. He followed up a score of advertised possibilities that would have led to a healthy open-air existence—park keeper in Pasadena, beach-club attendant in Long Beach, children's fun fair operator in Inglewood, but each time he had been too late and the position had been filled by the time he had found his way to the correct address.

Late in the afternoon, however, he struck lucky. He was employed by one Jack Morgan, a smiling giant of an ex-marine, as deckhand on a fishing boat operating daily from Malibu Pier.

The arrangement had been arrived at over several cans of beer, in the *Chowder Keg*—Jack Morgan's favourite seaside resort.

John was told he would have to be aboard by six o'clock each morning. The boat, which could accommodate up to thirty ardent fishermen, carried a live bait tank aft. At seven o'clock they would purchase sufficient live sardines from the bait boat when it called at the pier and at seven-thirty they would shove off with the customers. Jack Morgan said that he charged them two dollars a head and kept them out till around three-thirty if it didn't get too rough.

Besides keeping the boat clean and the gear in good condition, John's main jobs would be dropping and raising the anchor at the fishing grounds; 'chumming,' which Morgan explained was throwing scoopfuls of sardines into the water to encourage the fish to feed thoughtlessly; gaffing the big ones, and 'cleaning' the customers' catch on the way home.

Morgan told him that yesterday the yellowtail and skipjack had been running in huge schools and that everyone on board had taken home a sackful of fish. When he told John he would pay him thirty-five dollars a week he little knew that his new deckhand viewed the whole prospect with such pleasure that he would gladly have worked for nothing.

Clarabel was cooking dinner when John arrived back at Ann's apartment.

'Mis' John that sure was one beautiful write-up in Miss Argus' column this morning. . . . I never thought you was no war hero. . . . You just don't look like one.'

John was framing a tart reply when he caught sight of the honest admiration in the smiling black face.

'Tell me, Clarabel, do you believe everything you read in that column?'

'Yes, sir, Mis' John . . . I jus' love that Annie Argus. . . . She gives me so much news of all the studio folk. . . . I never miss a word of what she writes.'

While John was pondering over the full horror of this statement there was a sound behind him.

'Hello, you great, big, beautiful war hero, you,' laughed Ann from the doorway. John turned and kissed her.

'Oh, darling, I've never been so embarrassed in all my life. I hope to God she isn't syndicated in Buckingham Palace or the War Office or the Admiralty.'

Ann kissed the tip of his nose.

'Don't worry. We're in the movie business now, and they have a saying out here that it doesn't matter what anybody writes about you, just so long as they spell your name correctly.'

John was somewhat mollified.

'Anyway she scared me right back out to sea again—to-morrow at six o'clock in the morning I start fishing for a living.'

Ann's feelings when she heard about this latest project were mixed but she listened attentively while John described his new job.

'I must say I never expected to marry a fisherman, but I guess I shall just have to take you as I find you . . . and at the moment'—she kissed the tip of his nose again—'I'm not complaining.'

CHAPTER NINE

ANN AND JOHN were married very quietly in a little church in Santa Monica. Uncle Don flew out from New York for the wedding and did all he could to compensate for the fact that Ann's mother was in bed with a touch of bronchitis and her father would not leave without her.

'Glad you made it, young feller,' he said to John. 'Always thought you would.' He was not in the least disturbed by the fact that Ann had married a man who, to say the least of it, was not financially stable.

'He'll find his level,' he confided to Ann. 'Right now he is still thrown off balance by the war . . . he'll settle down and you'll have a fine life together; have a baby real quick, that'll steady him up.'

Ann and John never told anybody else that they were married. It was not so much that they wanted to disguise the fact, it was just because nobody ever asked them. Their hours of work gave them so little time together anyway, and, truth to tell, they rather enjoyed hugging their secret to themselves; even occasionally drawing a red herring across their tracks.

For the first two months of their married life, they stayed in Ann's apartment; the devoted Clarabel stayed with them.

Sunday was the one day of the week on which they did not have to get up early, or have to do anything unless they wanted to do it; then they indulged in their favourite luxury— breakfast in bed. Oft-times on Sundays they would hire horses and ride miles over the hills into the San Fernando Valley, where they would consume vast quantities of hot dogs and hamburgers, thereby making it practically impossible to ride home again. On the warmer days they would drive Hengist to the beach at Zuma and spend golden hours just in or just out of the blue Pacific Ocean.

When 'Backwash,' Ann's first film, was shown in the theatres, as Meadowbrook Pictures, Inc., had prophesied, she made an instantaneous hit with critics and public alike.

Fan magazines and film correspondents from all over the world clamoured to interview her. The publicity department turned on its big white spotlight, and whenever she was not needed before the moving picture cameras she was whisked away to the tender mercies of the temperamental André, the chief portrait artist of Meadowbrook Pictures, Inc. Her likeness appeared all over the globe, dressed in leopard skins, or tennis clothes, draped in fish nets, holding a golf club, a baseball bat, a dog, or a bow and arrow: she was shown eating, sleeping, sucking straws, laughing or reading: she was displayed on a bicycle, in a car, on a horse, even on one dreadful occasion, on an emu: she was flown to the mountains to be photographed in the snow, and to the desert to be photographed in the sand. Her cheeks ached from smiling.

'*This glowing unspoiled child,*' Annie Argus cooed, '*this apple of the great Bengy's eye, is also an enigma. She never goes to parties and has no beaux that I can see. If she has a secret passion it certainly isn't for the bemedalled war hero, John Hamilton. She brushed him off many weeks ago and IS HE CARRYING A TORCH! Ann's studio is vetting all her dates now, but a little bird told me that gallant Ralph Ridgway has the inside track. Anyway the announcement has just been made by Meadowbrook that they will be co-starred together in "Commando" as soon as Ann has completed her present assignment in "Downbeat". Then we shall see what we shall see!!!*'

Ann and John had read this together one Sunday morning and had laughed till the tears ran down their cheeks.

'Poor little woman,' said Ann. 'She's going to be awfully disappointed when she finds out. . . . Do you think we ought to tell her?'

John was not so softhearted about the 'poor little woman.' 'No, let her find out for herself. . . . Let's go on behaving perfectly normally and if anyone ever asks us if we are married, then we just say "why yes, of course". . . . I'm sure it will gradually become known. She'll hear about it sooner or later.'

He picked the paper up again. 'I wish she'd stop this bemedalled war-hero stuff. Oglethorpe or someone might read it. . . . I dread to think what he would say. Or Blossom—'

John sat up in bed. 'I'm terribly worried!'

'What about, darling—Blossom?'

'No, Hengist. . . . He's been getting awfully temperamental lately. Since you became a great big glamorous star, he hasn't been himself at all—'

'Perhaps he's ashamed of me.'

'I don't know what it is, but even with the handle he's getting more and more difficult to start. . . . I'd hate to put him in a garage. . . . He would seem so out of place somehow.'

Ann reflected for a moment. 'I wish he was a little less bumpy,' she said slowly.

'You've never said that before.'

209

Ann smiled a secret smile. 'I've never had to worry about it . . . before.'

John turned round and looked at her with widening eyes. 'I don't believe it,' he said in a half whisper, 'I just don't believe it.'

Ann flung her arms around his neck and pressed her face against his.

'Yes! Yes! I am, darling! . . . Oh, I've been longing to tell you, but I wasn't absolutely sure.' She was laughing and half crying.

Very gently John laid her head down on the pillow beside him.

'You are clever,' he whispered softly. 'You are clever.'

Apart from royalty, few unborn babies have caused so great an upheaval as did Christopher Peter Hamilton. Annie Argus, of course, was furious; she took the whole affair as a personal affront.

'I just don't know how that girl had the nerve to do this to me,' she squealed down the telephone to the head of publicity at Meadowbrook Pictures, Inc. 'After all I've done for her, too. . . . And a lot of it is your fault, and don't think I'm going to forget it. . . . Why, only yesterday morning *you* called *me* and told me that it looked as though Windsor and Ridgway were going steady.'

The head of publicity, a tired, embittered man, who knew on which side his weekly pay-cheque was signed, mumbled an explanation, but his words were forced back down the wire by the spate of verbiage from the irate columnist at the other end. He held the instrument away from his ear and grimaced at an assistant, 'Jesus, can this dame talk. . . . She must have been vaccinated with a phonograph needle.' The voice of Annie Argus, sounding tinny in the room, still poured unchecked from the earpiece:

'. . . So I go ahead and print what you tell me; then last evening, a contact of mine who works in a medical building in Beverly Hills calls to say that Windsor is going to have a BABY. . . . Can I get anyone from your department on the goddamned phone after seven o'clock? Hell no! . . . So I take a chance, I have a deadline goddamnit, and I let the story you gave me go out; but this morning to check up on the one from my contact, I call Windsor and I say, "I think you ought to know there is a very nasty rumour going around town about you." . . . She asks me what it is and I say, "Well, honey, it's about a baby": and Windsor says, "I wonder how they found out so quick . . . I only knew the day before yesterday myself!" . . . Of course I cover up and ask a few routine questions and then she has the goddamned gall to tell me that she's MARRIED TOO! and to make it worse to that jerk Englishman or Scotchman, or whatever the hell he is, who is supposed to have gone away weeks ago.'

The head of publicity came back more strongly this time. 'Well, Annie honey, I never told you *that*, now did I . . . I mean about him going away?'

'No, that cheesy little starlet of yours did though. I asked her where he was and she said, "Oh, on a boat some place, miles away." But just let me tell you this . . . no one is going to do that to *me* and get away with it. . . . I have my readers to consider.' The phone clicked into silence. It was followed immediately by the far more sinister sound of the buzzer which heralded the fact that the Great Man himself was about to speak over the inter-office communication system. The head of publicity paled when he heard the sound, and whispered to his assistant, 'I hope to Christ Bengy hasn't heard . . . he won't like this at all.' There was a hissing noise and then came the dreaded voice—'What's this I hear about Ann Windsor being married?'

'I'm afraid that's what happened, sir,' said the head of publicity.

'Well, how do you account for that? . . . Why in hell didn't you arrange a proper marriage ceremony? You know I'm trying to build her up . . . and I never heard a goddamn thing about it until my Secretary shows me a clipping today from a San Diego fishermen's paper. . . . For Christ's sake where did *they* get it from?'

'I understand the man she has married is a professional fisherman, sir.'

'Holy God! Here am I trying to give the girl a background . . . . trying to get her some class and she goes off and hitches up to a goddamned fisherman! Now you know what I hire you for. . . . Go ahead and build this marriage up . . . make him out to be a deep sea research expert, some angle like that . . . . He's not to be just a lousy fisherman, understand?'

'Yes, sir—er,' the head of publicity crossed his fingers and looked prayerfully at his assistant before he took the plunge. 'There is something else to the thing—I'm afraid, sir—'

'Something else! What the hell else *could* there be? Isn't this bad enough?'

'I'm afraid she is pregnant, sir.'

'What do you mean, she's pregnant?' came a shout from the other end. 'You mean she is going to have a *baby*?'

'I'm afraid that's the gist of it. Yes, sir.'

The voice rose still higher over the inter-communication system. 'For Christ's sake, she can't do that. . . . She's got to start another picture as soon as she gets through with this one. . . . We've got to milk her while she's hot. . . . When is the little bastard due?'

'In six or seven months.'

'Jesus Christ! That means she'll be half-way through "Commando?" . . . She can't have it. . . . Do you hear me? . . . Stop it!'

'Yes, sir.'

'Call her doctor and tell him to do something.'

'Yes, sir, right away.'

The machine went dead. The conversation was at an end. The chief of publicity for Meadowbrook Pictures, Inc., rose heavily from his chair and crossed to an early American cabinet which stood against the wall. He addressed his assistant: 'Care for some bicarbonate?'

The assistant nodded gratefully.

John forced Ann to take elaborate care of herself. He told her she was not allowed to lift or push, to climb or descend.

'But, darling, it's not going to happen for months,' she laughed.

'You mind your own business,' he retorted. 'This is MY baby.'

He hated her working such long hours and his heart contracted when she came home day after day from the studio with tiredness under her eyes: she told him that she would have been tired out anyway, and that, at this early stage, it couldn't be anything to do with the baby. But John broke his unvarying rule and went one day to her studio. He marched into Isaac Ingersoll's office and told the producer how worried he was about Ann overworking.

Ingersoll was reassuring. 'I've talked to her doctor, John, and he says there is absolutely no danger in her finishing off this one picture. If she doesn't feel well enough to work at any time, she has promised to tell me, and I promise you I will send her right home. . . . And don't forget this, she is playing a virgin, so from a photogaphic standpoint she can't work *much* longer.' John saw the logic of this. 'All right, then,' he smiled, 'just mark me down as a nervous husband. . . . Don't tell her I was here, will you?'

Ann's doctor, too, was soothing.

'She's fine, Mr. Hamilton . . . she is a strong healthy girl and it will do her good to keep working as long as she can, or as long as she wants to. She won't want to much, however, after another month or so, but I understand her picture will be finished by then. You'd better keep an eye on Bengy though. . . . He'll be trying to get her to work in some costume piece where it won't show. . . . He's done that before. He had Jayne Maxwell playing Nell Gwynne 'til she was eight months gone, poor girl. She was carrying that basket of oranges around in every scene; the camera crew called it the Battle of the Bulge.'

'If he tries that on Ann,' said John, 'I'll put a match to his bloody studio.'

'I wouldn't blame you,' said the doctor.

Twelve weeks later Ann finished 'Downbeat,' her second picture. The crew who had worked on it gave a party for her on the day she was to leave the studio. John attended, and as the evening progressed, he was accosted with great regularity by unsteady electricians and carpenters who thrust flushed faces into his and shook huge fists beneath his nose while they told him what they would do to him if he did not make 'their Ann' the happiest little mother in all Hollywood. John swelled with pride.

Autumn in the vicinity of Los Angeles arrives late and slips almost unnoticed into the garments of winter; a few trees shed their leaves, just a few, not many, and it becomes slightly less warm; otherwise, until the rains start and some children get washed down the storm drains, it is difficult to realize that the change has come. This year was no exception. In late November, Ann and John moved into a small house on a hill above Brentwood. From their little garden, then ablaze with chrysanthemums, they could look up at the Santa Monica Mountains. These good sturdy hills, mantled in the dark green of scrub oak and beautiful when caressed by the golden light of the sunset, flanked the house on one side; on the other, through the tall graceful eucalyptus trees, the silvery glint of the ocean could be seen. On the hillside above their house was a large orange grove and the sweet smell of the autumn blossom lay heavy on the air. Clarabel, of course, was in attendance. Ann's little Ford was in the garage while Hengist, as usual, slept in the open. Hengist had become a problem. He had arrived at the new house in a series of short sharp rushes, but once there, had refused to move again, and no amount of cranking with the starting-handle, kicks, or oaths were of any avail. True, he gave one great cough when John, as a last resort, had poured some whisky into his carburettor, but otherwise he lay there, immobile, and apparently moribund—he was badly in the way.

It was decided to give him a Viking's funeral. Ann had read some of the sagas and was fascinated by the idea of those ancient heroes sailing out to sea, alone on their funeral pyre.

'Let's fill him with straw and gasoline and things, then light it and push him over the cliff some place,' she suggested.

John had thought this a wonderful idea, so one day Hengist had been towed twenty miles behind Ann's Ford to the brink of a sheer drop of two hundred feet. Straw and newspaper, and old boxes were piled inside him and a runway was cleared so that all that was necessary was to soak him in fuel, light him and snatch away a rock from beneath his back wheel.

'There is at least a hundred feet of water for him to fall into,' said John as he produced a box of matches. 'Will you light him, Ann?'

'I hate to see him go like this . . . you do it, Johnny.'

John had stalled for time: the strange-looking conveyance had looked so forlorn and defenceless perched there on the edge of the cliff.

'I'm going to give him one last chance.' He seized the starting handle and gave it a sharp turn. Hengist's engine roared into life. That was the reprieve. Hengist was towed home (he was far too smelly to be driven), but he never started up again; he slept the rest of his days outside the little house in Brentwood, badly in the way.

The great Bengy suspended Ann's contract till she should report back to work. 'I don't pay my artists to have babies, goddammit. . . . You tell her to get her can back in the studio if she wants a pay-check.' Annie Argus printed a short announcement. '*Ann Windsor, who I hear has been getting very hard to handle lately, has been suspended by Meadowbrook.*' There was no mention of the reason and Ann had laughed gaily as she put down the paper.

'The least I can do for her is to have a miscarriage . . . but I must remember to call her up and tell her about it before I have it, then she can have a scoop.'

One day Isaac Ingersoll telephoned from the studio.

'John, can you help us out? . . . We are in trouble with this picture we have just started—the one about the commandos. Confidentially, the technical adviser Bengy gave us doesn't seem to know much about the subject, and I wondered if you could come out and give us some advice as we go along. We would want you here all the time, of course, for at least three months, and there's a hundred bucks a week in it for you if you can do it. What d'you say?' And John said, with alacrity, 'Yes.' The fishing season was about over anyway, and Jack Morgan would soon be laying up the boat.

Although a hundred dollars a week was a lot of money, John considered that he earned every cent of it, for apart from the almost insurmountable task of making 'gallant Ralph Ridgway' look, talk and move like a commando, there was also the permanent hazard of Major Hodgkinson, Bengy's choice as a technical adviser. The 'major' who had a brushed-up moustache, a monocle, a very 'refained' accent and several books of reference, had never, it was quite apparent to John after five minutes' conversation, been in the British or any other army. Furthermore, he deeply resented what he considered to be John's interference and sat in a corner all day long wearing an injured expression.

Quite early in the proceedings, they came to a scene in the film which was supposed to take place on the French coast at night. Ridgway having gallantly landed at the head of his men was meeting the leader of the French Resistance Movement in a deserted windmill.

'Major Hodgkinson,' the director called out, 'is Mr. Ridgway's outfit okay?'

'Yes, rather, dressed him myself . . . checked every item personally, don't you know?'

'How does it look to you, John?' asked the director, who shared Ingersoll's views with regard to the great Bengy's friend.

John looked at Ridgway. He was upholstered in an immaculate battle dress uniform, made for the occasion by the La Brea Costume Company, his boots were highly polished and his eyes shone expectantly from beneath mascaraed lashes. Perched on his head at a jaunty angle was a steel helmet.

'Well, to begin with, he'd better get wet up to the waist,'

said John. 'That is, if he has just waded ashore from a landing craft . . . he's probably done some crawling on his belly on the wet sand too . . . and that tin hat should come off . . . a stocking cap was the usual form, and of course, he'd have a black face—burnt cork was pretty good.'

There was a bleat of disgust from Ralph Ridgway. 'A black face!'

'That is absolute nonsense,' interposed 'the Major' striding up. 'In all my service I never had a black face. . . . What a ridiculous boy-scout idea.'

Ridgway appealed to the director, 'I can't play that scene in blackface. . . . The audience would laugh.'

The director scratched his head. 'Are you quite sure a black face would be correct, John? . . . Isn't it just possible that he could have forgotten to put it on, or something like that?'

John was adamant. 'If Ridgway is supposed to be leading a commando raid at night he would have a black face.'

The director sighed, and, as everyone knew he would, he phoned through and asked for instructions.

In three minutes he was back. 'Bengy says no black face.'

For the rest of the day Ralph Ridgway looked aggrieved, and Major Hodgkinson wore a maddening air of superiority.

'Don't worry about it, John,' grinned a man from the publicity department. 'That always happens to technical advisers—nobody ever takes any technical advice from them.'

A few days later another argument arose. The leader of the French Resistance Movement had turned out to be a colonel in the Gestapo and Ralph Ridgway was now a prisoner in the windmill. In this scene he was waiting tensely for the first intimation that his rescue was at hand—that the commandos were coming once more! According to the script Ridgway was to be 'thrilled by the distant sound of bagpipes.'

John suggested that as several gruelling months of training were undergone by all commandos to ensure that they would arrive at their objectives with the maximum of surprise to the enemy, it might, in his opinion, prove too great a surprise for the enemy if their approach was heralded by the sound of bagpipe music drifting across the Channel.

Major Hodgkinson entered the lists and argued that Highland music was good for morale. 'Also, the piece I have selected as appropriate to the occasion is the "Skye Boat Song" and that,' he added, with the air of a man laying down a whole fistful of aces, 'has been approved by the front office.'

Somewhere, in a gloomy corner of the sound stage, a telephone rang—the director was called away. When he returned he said, 'Bengy has just rung through—the bagpipes are in.'

'But nobody even asked him, did they?' asked John, exasperated. 'How did he know we were even discussing it?'

The director put his fingers to his lips and led John away from the others. He spoke in a whisper.

'Bengy has a special device in his office, if he wants to know what is going on on any of the sound stages he just connects himself up with the microphones and finds out. . . . He says it's so that he can listen to the way the scenes are being played, but—' he shrugged his shoulders, 'what the hell, we get paid every Wednesday, don't we?'

For six or seven weeks the film about the commandos went more or less smoothly along. On some days Ann brought her sewing to the studio and sat with John while he and 'The Major' (with whom he had made an armistice) played endless games of Canasta and between them cooked up answers to any technical questions that might arise.

John watched Ann's lovely face, radiant now with a calm inner happiness; he had never seen her so beautiful.

One day, when John, covered with goose pimples of embarrassment, was standing near the camera watching Ralph Ridgway issuing his orders for an attack, he became aware that he, in his turn, was being carefully scrutinized. Two dark young men wearing loud tweed coats and open shirts were standing a little apart from the usual knot of people in the vicinity. John noticed them chiefly because he did not recognize them as being permanently connected with the

218

production. The young men stared long and thoughtfully at John, then turned their backs upon him and talked earnestly together. From time to time one or other of them would sneak a further unobtrusive look in his direction, and finally after a last lengthy inspection, they hurried away.

John became engrossed once more in the military horror being perpetrated by Ralph Ridgway, and would have dismissed this strange interlude from his mind if, ten minutes later, the two dark young men had not returned—this time reinforced by another, wearing a large brilliantly-coloured necktie arranged carefully in what, for some strange anachronistic reason, is called in Hollywood—The Prince of Wales knot.

As the three men stared at him, John became a trifle uneasy. Finally after a long spate of sibilant discussion, the latest arrival detached himself from the group and sauntered too casually across the sound stage.

'Mr. Hamilton, my name is Bobby Spicer. I'm the head casting director here at Meadowbrook.'

'How do you do,' said John.

'How do you do,' said Mr. Spicer.

They shook hands, and as they did so, John noticed with a start that the man was wearing a toupee—beautifully made with a few strands of grey over the temples. It would have been hard to detect if it had not been for the fact that it was particularly hot on the sound stage that afternoon, and it had in consequence come unstuck in front. This meant that when Mr. Spicer wrinkled his forehead (which he did a great deal for he possessed an animated face), the hair above it stayed perfectly still, thereby drawing instant attention to itself.

John's interest was riveted upon Mr. Spicer's hairpiece, and it was a delight for him to discover, as he did in later weeks, that the good man wore a windblown one on the golf course and a rumpled one when worried in his office.

With difficulty he tore his eyes away. 'What can I do for you, Mr. Spicer?'

'You can play Curtis, that's what you can do,' said Mr.

Spicer, in the tones of a man presenting someone with the freedom of a large city. 'Can't he, boys?' he asked, turning to the two young men, who by now had also sauntered casually over and had taken up station astern of him.

'On his head, Mr. Spicer,' said the first young man.

The second said nothing—just raised his eyes to heaven and blew a kiss with his fingers.

'What is Curtis?' asked John, wondering if it could be an offspring of Canasta.

The three laughed goodnaturedly, and one of them said: 'That's a great gag.'

'You'd be sensational—wouldn't he, Jack?' said Mr. Spicer, turning to the first young man.

'He certainly would, Mr. Spicer,' said the first young man. The second blew again on his fingers.

Mr. Spicer gave his reasons.

'You're the right height . . . right build . . . you've done it before in real life and . . . you've got an English accent.'

The part of Curtis was one of those small cameos, which, because of their sympathetic relationship to the construction of the stories in which they appear, and because of their sudden and unexpected freshness compared to the general mood of the pictures which contain them, can, if well played, be remembered by audiences long after the leading players and the main situations of a film are forgotten.

The part of Curtis, though it would be completed in three days of shooting and would appear only in three short sequences, might, in fact, make an unknown actor famous overnight. John understood nothing of this. He roared with laughter when he told Ann that he had accepted; and a week later breezed through the part, which came perfectly naturally to him, without ever giving the whole thing a serious thought.

The result, to everyone but John, was a foregone conclusion; before he had finished his first scene on the first day, it was obvious that he would 'steal' the picture from Ralph Ridgway.

On the second day, when he was invited to lunch by the great Bengy himself, John still failed to grasp the full import of what was happening. Ann knew. She had been around the studio long enough to sense an atmosphere, and when, on the third day, John begged her to come down and 'watch me make a damn fool of myself', it took her less than a minute on the sound stage to realize the fact that she had married a man who, if he so desired, could climb the dizziest of the Hollywood heights. She did not have long to ponder upon this, for that night her baby was born.

Ann opened her eyes in a room so full of flowers that at first she thought she was in a garden, then she turned her head, still weighted with the anæsthetic, and saw John sitting by her bedside. Seeing her movement and her open eyes, John laid his head on the pillow beside her and kissed her damp forehead.

'Well done, my darling,' he whispered, 'it's Christopher Peter all right—it's a little man.'

Ann raised an arm with difficulty and felt his cheek. Then with a smile of pure happiness, she slept again.

John's refusal to sign a contract with Meadowbrook Pictures, Inc., until Ann was well enough for him to discuss the suggestion with her, was taken by the highly-paid executives of that company to be the normal manœuvre of a sought-after actor, well briefed in the art of being 'hard to get'; they were not paid their high salaries for nothing, however, so they congratulated themselves on having made their original bid far below the sum they were in fact authorized to pay, and doubled their offer.

John was far too happy and excited over Christopher Peter to consider this and even left a message to say that he was too busy to talk nonsense.

The highly-paid executives of Meadowbrook Pictures, Inc., shook their heads when they received this information and raised their offer to six hundred and fifty dollars a week—they did not like the turn events were taking: they were getting perilously close to the eight hundred and fifty dollars ceiling beyond which they were not allowed to go.

'Bengy won't like this,' said one. 'He'll cut our hearts out if we have to go the full amount,' said a second.

'My ulcer is coming back,' said a third.

But they need not have worried, because a few days later John agreed with Ann that it would be worth a trial. 'Anyway, darling,' she said, 'if one of us is going to earn a living in pictures, it had much better be you . . . I am going to have my hands full with your son.'

So John signed his contract with Meadowbrook Pictures, Inc., and Ann asked for hers to be cancelled.

In the great front office, festooned with fake Impressionists, the reaction was immediate; to those who knew the inmate, they were typical; a memorandum was dictated—

1. Send the usual telegram of welcome to John Hamilton and give him the usual build-up, allowing him to choose furniture and wallpaper for dressing-room, etc., etc.

2. Inform Ann Windsor that her contract with this studio is *not* cancelled; it is *suspended*, and should she at any time attempt to work for any other company in any field of entertainment, she will be sued, and if necessary, her case will be taken to the Supreme Court.

The secretary waited with pencil poised above notebook for further instructions. They were given verbally. 'Now, take that picture of Windsor off the wall and put one of Hamilton there instead . . . that is all.'

Silently the secretary did as she was bid.

At lunchtime in the commissary she leaned across the table and spoke to her friend; she leaned so far across, that some tunafish salad attached itself to her blouse.

'Bengy is in wonderful spirits today,' she whispered, 'just wonderful.'

Annie Argus blazoned forth with a glaring headline

announcing a 'sensational new discovery,' but she could not resist her thimbleful of venom. '*Apparently Meadowbrook feels that one member of the Hamilton family should be on their payroll; John goes on where his wife Ann Windsor left off. Her brief career was described to me today as "the Light that Failed."* '

John was made to feel that Meadowbrook was his oyster; he was taken around by the head of publicity and introduced to the various dignitaries. A syrupy wave of flattery closed over his head. The head of publicity, looking tired and disillusioned, took him to lunch in the commissary. As they entered there arose a buzz of interest. Many heads were turned in their direction and many a heavily laden fork was halted on its journey mouthward. 'That's John Hamilton,' came the whisper from every corner. Nor, it must be recorded, did the object of all this attention fail to notice the stir of which he was the cause. He found himself rather liking it.

'You'll soon get used to being stared at,' said the head of publicity, 'but this is what happens when you dive headfirst into a goldfish bowl.' He was a talkative man, and a caustic one. John was given thumbnail descriptions of every person of importance within the confines of the studio.

'Bengy is thinking of starting you off with Marie Davenport in your first picture. . . . Well, that ought to be fun for you. Marie is a sort of sexual terminus—everyone gets there in the end.'

John smiled. 'I happen to be a very happily married man.'

'Oh, sure, but don't let that bother you.'

The coffee came. The head of publicity stirred his thoughtfully, then produced a notebook. 'Now then, I have got to make you palatable to the American public—you are British, aren't you?'

'Yes, born in Scotland.'

'I see. Well, we ought to be able to cover that up.' He wrote the words 'Scottish descent' in his notebook. 'What about your parents?'

'They are both dead.'

The head of publicity looked up quickly. 'Anything interesting?'

'I beg your pardon?'

'How did they die?'

'Well, if you must know, they were drowned . . . out fishing when I was very young.'

'Jees, that's wonderful!'

John watched fascinated as the words 'major maritime disaster' were added in the notebook. He wondered whether the time had come to take a stand. Should he tell the true facts? . . . That the cork had come out of the bottom of a rowing dinghy two miles off Frinton and that somehow or other his father had omitted to put it back in again? No. . . . With a twinge of shame, he realized he rather liked the sound of 'major maritime disaster.'

After lunch the head of publicity took John over to his office and told him that he had been assigned a personal publicity man.

'This man,' said the head of publicity, 'is one of the best in the business. . . . He is new here at Meadowbrook, but he has the highest recommendations: he was the head of publicity of the old UFA studios in Berlin before the war and he's worked with several continental companies since then. I'm sure you will like him.'

He led John down a passage and paused outside a glass door at the far end. 'Entrez,' said a voice that sounded to John vaguely familiar. In another moment he knew the reason, for there at a desk, thinly disguised by a sharply-pointed black beard, sat—Milton Myers.

That the erstwhile cowboy and ex-pony racing promoter was better prepared for this sudden encounter than John was obvious; Milton Myers stood up, flashed a suspicion of a wink and clicking his heels together, bowed low over John's hand. Then, in an accent that would never have deceived one of the ponies at Ocean City, he bade John welcome and told him how pleased he was to make his acquaintance.

'My name,' he announced, 'is Paul Reuter, a relative of the news service people, you understand.'

The pain of trying not to laugh was so great that John closed his eyes for a second before turning to the head of publicity.

'I think it would be a good plan if Mr. Reuter and I had a little chat, don't you?'

'Yes, that will be fine,' said the head of publicity. 'I'll be in touch with you in a day or two when we have mapped out our campaign on you.'

Half an hour later, back in the little house in Brentwood, John was being brought up to date on what had happened to his old friend since the day he had left him to the tender mercies of Lefty Orbach.

In Ann's bedroom, Milton Myers told them that he had run the ponies at several places after John left—Boston, Cleveland, Minneapolis, places beyond the sphere of Lefty Orbach, but the overhead had been so enormous and the labour problems in the various cities so complicated, that he had jumped at an offer in Seattle to sell the whole outfit, goodwill, stock and all. This he had done, but had managed to keep the twenty-five best ponies for himself. Of these, he had sold half to polo players in Burlingame and the others he had brought down and disposed of most profitably among the polo players of Los Angeles. That had been a week ago. Then he had hit upon the idea of working in one of the film studios and had invented the character of Paul Reuter.

'This morning when I was called in and offered the job of being personal publicity man to one John Hamilton, I nearly passed out. Until that moment, I didn't have the faintest idea that either of you were in town, much less married, and,' he smiled at Ann, 'in production.'

'When is it going to be safe for me to go back to Ocean City?' asked John.

Milton Myers grinned. 'Hell, you can go back now and they'll make you mayor of the joint . . . You, with your pineapple and that little guy with his New York newspaper stirred up such a scandal between you that they pinned a Federal rap on Lefty and he looks like doing about twenty years in Leavenworth for tax evasion.'

Ann was carried downstairs and lay on the sofa in front of the fire: Christopher Peter lay fast asleep in his crib beside her: Clarabel excelled herself in the kitchen: and as John looked round at the glowing faces he knew that he had reached a pinnacle of happiness.

CHAPTER TEN

JOHN, AS THE head of publicity had prophesied, was being considered for the leading part in Marie Davenport's forthcoming picture, and one day he was called down to the studio so that Meadowbrook's biggest money earner might look him over.

She was very beautiful indeed. She also had that quality which, when she entered a crowded room, made every man present feel that she was physically aware of him and him alone, and that all he had to do was to stretch out a hand and take her. John felt it as soon as she walked into his dressing-room. He was alone at the time—the only man in a crowd of one.

He had been waiting for some time for someone to tell him where in fact Miss Davenport was: he was supposed to meet her but she was reportedly very busy posing for portraits with M. André.

For a long time he had sat in his dressing-room smoking cigarette after cigarette, not caring whether he ever saw Miss Davenport and completely disinterested in playing a part in her forthcoming picture. He was, when he was interrupted, thinking happily about a forty pound fresh-run salmon he had once caught on the Spey.

'I live next door in dressing-room No. 4,' said a husky voice behind him, 'so I thought I'd call on you.'

John stood up.

'I was on my way to change costume,' she went on. 'I thought I'd save you the trouble of chasing me all over the lot. . . . Besides, I wanted to see your wallpaper. . . . How do you do. . . . I'm Marie Davenport.'

She flashed her famous smile at him, and her thin peach-coloured silk dressing-gown fell slightly apart as she sat down. The inside of a satiny thigh gleamed invitingly until, with an exaggerated flourish, she covered it up again.

'Pardon me, I'm practically naked, but André likes me that way—it's a pity he's a queer—he's very attractive.'

As John offered her a cigarette she held his wrist.

'What a stunning case. . . . I wonder what you did to some poor girl to deserve that?'

It had, as a matter of fact, been a present from Carole in the almost forgotten days of Blagthorpe. With a start, John realized that this girl reminded him most strongly of Carole. It was not so much her looks, but her walk and the thrust of her breasts. It was the provocative tilt of her head, and, he realized with a sudden quickening of his pulse, the unmistakable fact that he had only to stretch out a hand and take her.

'It's lovely and cool in here,' she said, and his hand was unsteady as he lit her cigarette.

'I'm afraid I can't offer you anything,' he said, 'I haven't really moved in yet.'

'Can't you?' she smiled back, 'What a pity.'

There was a long pause during which John became more than a little disconcerted by the direct gaze of the bright blue eyes.

'Well,' she said at length, 'do you want to be in the picture with me?'

John laughed. 'I think you ought to know about me . . . I'm not an actor at all. . . . I was just advising them on that commando picture. . . . Then one day somebody dropped dead or something, because the next thing I knew I was playing a part in it. . . . I've never acted in my life.'

Marie Davenport blew three large smoke rings.

'I saw that picture yesterday. . . . They ran it for me.

. . . In case you're interested, you *are* an actor—a hell of a good actor, and among other things, you stole the show from that heel Ridgway.' She paused. 'Bengy thinks you ought to have more experience before you play a big part, but this picture of mine won't start for several weeks and we could work together in the meantime, that is . . .' she lowered her eyes in mock demureness, 'if you want to work with me.'

John laughed again. 'Of course I'd love to. . . . I'm terribly flattered that you should think of it . . . but I can't help feeling. . . .'

Marie Davenport stubbed out her cigarette and stood up, her flimsy dressing-gown clung to her superb figure. 'Come here. . . . Let me see how tall you are.'

John walked across the room and stood in front of her. She moved close up against him. He could feel the firm curve of her thighs against his, the swell of her breasts warm and hard against his chest. Her skin was flawless, smooth and sun-kissed. She looked up into his face and he saw that her eyes were shining unnaturally. He made no move, but his heart was thumping against his ribs.

At length with an almost imperceptible toss of her blonde head she moved away from him and spoke over her shoulder, 'Yes, I think we would do very well together.'

She walked across the room and peered at the wall. 'My God! Is this the stuff they gave you?'

John, relieved that the tension in the room had somewhat lessened, poured forth information about the wallpaper.

'Well, they were very kind and told me I could have any I wanted, but I didn't see anything wrong with this stuff, so I asked them to leave it. . . . After all, I don't suppose I shall spend much time in here, and I don't know much about wallpaper anyway, so I thought I'd wait. . . . If I grow to hate it, I can probably get it changed later. . . . It seems pretty inoffensive, though.'

'Yes, but it's somebody else's—you must have your *own*. And if you won't do it yourself, then I am going to choose it for you.'

'No, please . . . I really. . . .'

Marie Davenport put a finger on his mouth. 'That's settled, I have all sorts of odd chairs and things too I can lend you, which would make you more comfy. . . . You won't know the place when I finish with it.

'Now I must fly or poor André will have a stroke. . . . It's been wonderful meeting you.'

John opened the door for her.

'We'd better not leave together,' said Marie Davenport in a conspiratorial whisper. 'It looks so bad in the middle of the afternoon. . . . Give me a couple of minutes to get round the corner, in case anyone is looking.' She blew him a kiss and disappeared.

John sat for a minute or two before he lit a cigarette. His knees felt peculiar and he also felt guilty: extremely guilty; and it annoyed him that he should have this reaction, because he would have much preferred to be able to congratulate himself on his steadfastness and his resistance to temptation. But he could not, and his heart pounded afresh at the recollection of the firm rounded scented body that had been pressed against his.

There was a knock at the door. Half expecting to see the voluptuous figure in the flimsy dressing-gown standing there again, John turned round. 'Come in. . . .'

'How are you today, Mr. Hamilton?' asked Annie Argus sweetly as she walked into the cool room. 'I was looking for Marie, really, I just caught a glimpse of her as she darted out of here. . . . She seemed in a great hurry!'

'Yes, I think she was,' said John uneasily. . . . 'She is doing portraits with Mr. André, and I believe he doesn't like to be kept waiting long.'

'Not *too* long, anyway,' said Annie Argus, and her eyes twinkled benevolently behind her pince-nez.

John was subjected to a barrage of kindly and searching questions about his private life . . . about Ann . . . about Christopher Peter . . . and about his future career as a film actor. At length a worried official from the publicity department appeared at the door.

'Oh, there you are, Annie honey . . . you gave me the slip. . . . I've been looking all over for you.' Annie Argus smiled benignly.

The next morning Ann showed John the result of his impromptu interview with the newspaper woman; it was quite short. '*John Hamilton is spending his spare time at Meadowbrook entertaining the luscious Marie Davenport; a little bird told me that he may be her next leading man.*'

John read it and avoided Ann's eye. 'What nonsense. . . . I've never set eyes on Marie Davenport.'

Just why he lied to Ann he never knew. Even as he did so his heart gave a sickening lurch. It seemed easier at the time than telling the truth.

Milton Myers was full of bright ideas all designed to bring John's name before the public in the most favourable light; and John gave in good-naturedly to the wildest suggestions. He allowed himself to be towed on water skis behind an autogyro at Lake Arrowhead: he posed with a lioness and her cubs when the circus came to town, and he even acquiesced when his old friend suggested that he should play polo in a charity match at the Redwood Country Club: the Tomahawks versus the Thunderclaps.

'I've never played in my life,' he said.

'Don't give it a thought,' Milton Myers replied cheerfully. 'Just gallop around looking good, it doesn't matter if you never hit the ball. . . . I'll have four cameramen handle it. I reckon we'll get you on the cover of *Life* magazine with this.'

John allowed himself to be outfitted for the occasion by the studio: his helmet was a size too small and sat perched upon his head: his boots were several sizes too large and squeaked protestingly when he walked: his breeches resembled Victorian cycling bloomers.

'You look great, kid,' said Milton Myers approvingly when he saw him.

At the stables of the Redwood Country Club, John was introduced to J. Vandenburg Hill, the president of the club and captain of the Thunderclaps.

'Very good of you to turn out today, Hamilton, otherwise the Tomahawks would have been one short.' He nodded towards Milton Myers. 'Reuter here told me you played in the British army team before the war, so we put that in the programme: we've got a big crowd today, too, I'm glad to say.'

John paled. Milton Myers was busy with his shoe-laces.

They walked into the dressing-room and in a dream John found himself being introduced to various half-naked giants —members of the Thunderclap and Tomahawk teams. The Thunderclaps donned green numbered vests, and he and the other three Tomahawks were handed red ones.

'Aha, Hamilton,' said J. Vandenburg Hill, 'so we shall be marking each other, eh?'

'Yes, indeed,' John answered vaguely, and tried to smile, but he was so nervous, and his mouth was so dry, that his top lip became stuck above his teeth: he caught sight of himself in the dressing-room mirror—he looked like a Japanese general.

'Don't worry, Johnny Boy,' whispered Milton Myers. 'Remember the opening night in Ocean City? . . . You can make it.' He thumped John hard in the region of his kidneys.

'Incidentally, I have told the groom who is looking after your ponies that you've never played before and slipped him ten bucks. . . . He'll take care of you.'

Somewhere a whistle went and John remembered being helped up on to a pony; the reins and a whip were put into his left hand and his right wrist was slipped through the leather loop attached to the handle of a polo stick.

'Now you're foin, me buoy,' a whisky-laden Irish voice whispered up at him. 'Just stick loike glue to Mr. Hill and nivver let him touch the ball atall, atall.'

A crowd of two or three thousand had come to watch the

game: they gave a great welcome to the two teams as they cantered on to the field.

The first period was a nightmare for John; he galloped madly about the field vainly chasing the ball and bumping into anybody wearing a green vest and trying to avoid those wearing red ones. Several times he charged into J. Vandenburg Hill, and once, when taking a great swing at the ball, he missed it, and knocked the unfortunate man's helmet over his eyes. The purple-faced captain of the Thunderclaps roared with indignation. 'Just because this match is in aid of a hospital, there's no need to be so goddamned rough, Hamilton.'

John pretended he did not hear and careered off again after the ball, which had once more been hit up to him by someone on his own side. It had stopped in the very mouth of the goal and all he had to do was knock it forward a few feet to score. He began to enjoy himself. . . . It looked so simple. He could see the photographers lined up behind the goal, the crowd was cheering: he spurred his pony forward at full gallop and waved his polo-stick above his head. He even yelled an unintelligible war-cry as he bore down upon the ball.

Unfortunately, his steering was at fault, and instead of coming alongside the ball and tapping it gently between the posts, he galloped straight over the top of it and the pony trod it into the ground. The ball disappeared completely from view beneath the turf and John scattered the cameramen in all directions as he charged through the goal mouth.

The first period over, 'Whisky Breath' informed him that he would now be riding St. George.

St. George was not so fast as J. Vandenburg Hill's mount and when he and John were galloping neck and neck after the ball, St. George started to fall resentfully back. When his head was level with the middle of the other pony St. George, noticing that J. Vandenburg Hill was bending over preparatory to striking the ball, turned and sank his teeth into the fabric of his breeches. There was a yell of pain. John caught a momentary glimpse of the ball passing somewhere below him, and in an effort to remain aloof from what was going on between his mount and the captain of the opposing team, he took a nonchalant swing at it. He missed, of course, and his stick passed underneath J. Vandenburg Hill's pony's tail. This pony, being particularly touchy about that kind of approach, clamped its tail against its buttocks, and there imprisoned the head of John's stick.

St. George's teeth were still attached to the quiet end of the now roaring captain of the Thunderclaps, and John, whose stick was looped round his wrist, was, in turn, firmly attached to the rump of the captain's pony. To the thunderous applause of the crowd, this odd triangle galloped down the middle of the field. John was wondering vaguely how the end would come, but he did not have long to wait. . . . Seeing that they were headed straight for one of the goal-posts, St. George relinquished his hold on J. Vandenburg Hill and swerved sharply to the left. The other pony omitted to relinquish its tail grip on John's polo-stick and swerved equally sharply to the right.

John flew through the air and hit the goal-post alone. He was not really hurt at all, but Milton Myers, who was first upon the scene, forced him to lie still. . . .

'Pretend you're unconscious, you dope,' he hissed, 'it's your only possible exit.'

The next day, while John and Ann were having breakfast, Milton Myers burst into the house waving the morning paper. 'What did I tell you, Johnny Boy! . . . When you hit that goal-post you hit the front page. . . . Look at this.'

John studied a large picture of himself zooming through the air, clutching a polo stick. . . . There was no sign of a horse, and above was the caption. . . . SHOOTING STAR.

Whether helped or hindered by Milton Myers, the publicity department at Meadowbrook Pictures proceeded apace with the planned build-up of their latest discovery. The countless articles that appeared about John in fan magazines and daily papers began to reap their strange harvest.

Letters by the hundreds poured in. Homely women wanted to marry him: and lonely women to do worse. Some sent him recipes for making angel-food cake, and one sent him her knickers. Ann dealt with all this correspondence.

One day John came home from the studio: where, at the request of a Meadowbrook producer who said he was considering him for the part of Alexander Hamilton in a film dealing with the life of Aaron Burr, he was now taking fencing lessons.

'There will be a great duel sequence,' the producer had told John, 'and of course you get bumped off—very sympathetic role.'

John, whose slight knowledge of American history led him to believe that Aaron Burr had, in fact, shot Alexander Hamilton with a pistol, said nothing, and started to learn how to handle foil and épée.

When he walked into the house, Ann was sitting at the writing table. The floor was covered with postcard size photographs of himself and a large pile of clean, stamped and addressed envelopes bore mute testimony to the length of time she had been working. She lifted up her face to be kissed.

John brushed her forehead with his lips and crossed to the crib where Christopher Peter lay gurgling happily at the ceiling. He put his forefinger out for his son to play with: the little boy took hold with his tiny hands.

'Gosh, he's getting strong,' said John, and then, after a pause, he added casually, 'Oh by the way, I took on a secretary today to do all that stuff.'

'A secretary?' said Ann, puzzled. 'Why, for heaven's sakes?'

'Oh, I don't know—it's an awful bore for you, isn't it?'

'No, darling, of course it isn't, and anyway, there isn't enough for a secretary to do.'

John bridled. 'Well, there's quite a lot, considering I've only just started.'

Ann crossed over to him. 'Oh, Johnny, don't misunderstand! I think it's perfectly wonderful that all those people write to you. . . . It's very very exciting, but I can do it easily. . . . I love to do it, and oh, I don't know—a secretary! . . . It sort of isn't . . . us . . . is it?'

John turned back to the crib. 'Well anyway, she is only going to come two days a week to start with. . . . She works for someone else, really, but she can manage it as a special favour.'

'I see,' said Ann. 'Who else does she work for?'

'Oh, a girl at the studios—Marie Davenport. . . . You haven't met her, have you?'

'No,' said Ann, in a small voice. 'No, I haven't.'

So the secretary came twice a week. More often than not her visits coincided with the days John spent at the studio, learning how to fence; and on these occasions Ann would tuck Christopher Peter into his little carriage and take him for a long walk among the hills behind her house: she found him a sympathetic audience.

'Oh, Christopher Peter,' she said one day, 'I have a dreadful lost feeling in my tummy.'

And when Christopher Peter had bubbled happily in reply, Ann's eyes filled with tears and the hills swam mistily around her.

John produced a large red leather scrap book with 'J.H. from M.D.' embossed in gold letters upon the outside, and Miss Seago, the newly acquired secretary, spent much of her time clipping pieces out of newspapers and magazines and sticking them between its heavy covers. When Miss Seago left at the end of the day, no matter how cold it was, Ann would open wide all the windows, and John would come home to find her upstairs curled up like a kitten in the big armchair beside Christopher Peter's crib.

'We must go out more, darling,' he said one day. 'You never want to go anywhere any more, and we are always being invited. . . . Besides, I believe it would do me good to be seen at some of these parties—at least that's what I am told.'

So Clarabel would look after Christopher Peter and John,

in his new Buick convertible, would drive Ann to one gay, noisy party after another. A famous actor gave a big party; and, misguidedly confident in the belief that all he had to do was to include a few film producers among his guests to enable himself to deduct the cost of the evening from his income tax as a 'business expense', he had been lavish in his arrangements.

The host was about to make a film entitled 'The Monarch of the Glen'. The waiters wore kilts and among other horrors some live goldfish swam about for a short while in a small pond with sides of aspic. They were the centre piece of the buffet. They died about midnight but nobody noticed.

That night Ann met Marie Davenport. The Meadowbrook Studio's top money-maker looked dazzlingly beautiful in skin-tight white satin. Fabulous brooches, clips and necklaces flashed all over her, the brilliance of each one tending to cancel out the effect of the next, thereby producing that sumptuous monotony so often noticeable in art galleries. She swooped upon Ann.

'Why, Mrs. Hamilton! . . . John has told me *so* much about you. I've been just *longing* to meet you. . . . And how is the baby? . . . Your husband is *so* popular at the studio—everyone just *adores* him. . . .'

Ann found herself being kissed on the cheek.

'Isn't this a wonderful party? You look absolutely stunning, Ann. May I call you Ann? . . . Now wherever did you get that dress? . . or is it a secret? . . . And how clever of you not to wear *any* jewellery with it. Come along . . . let's all sit together, otherwise we will get cornered by some of the godawful bores I see around here, and everyone will start telling me about their scripts and their operations.' She laughed gaily, 'Come along, let's find a table.'

Marie Davenport took Ann's hand in hers and led her through the crowd: John followed behind, hailing acquaintances to right and left. Annie Argus planted herself firmly in their path.

'Why hello there, Marie darling . . . Hello Ann. . . .

Hello John. . . . Well! You all look mighty happy together I must say,' and as she spoke, the shrewd eyes gleamed with pleasure at the thought of what she would write about them on the morrow.

'*I saw Marie Davenport and Ann Windsor together—those two really have something in common!* '

Several old friends from Ann's studio days were there, and she was flattered and pleased when they said how much they had missed her. While John was dancing with Marie, the head of publicity of Meadowbrook, looking more disillusioned and ulcerated than ever, sat with her, chain-drinking large mahogany-coloured whiskies and regaling her with his benevolence.

'Look at him,' he said, pointing to a popular leading man. 'Jesus, what a ham! . . . The sonofabitch is still playing juveniles, and he's old enough to have been a waiter at the Last Supper.'

A famous actress caught his jaundiced eye. 'She's such a bore that if you ask her the time, she'll tell you how a watch works . . . and Jesus! . . . those teeth! . . . Why doesn't she have 'em fixed! Right now she's the only woman alive who could eat an apple through a tennis racquet . . . and that jerk she's dancing with—he thinks he's a Greek God—the goddamned Greek! . . . he's a fag too . . . one day someone is going to toss him a poisoned choir boy.' He went on and on, but Ann was grateful to him and his verbal vitriol because John seemed always to be dancing down the far end of the room.

'Ann darling!' a voice interrupted. 'You look more beautiful than ever.' It was Isaac Ingersoll.

'How lovely to see you again,' said Ann warmly. 'Come and sit down!'

'Where's John?' he asked. 'Is he here?'

'Oh, he's dancing somewhere,' Ann answered lightly.

Ingersoll glanced at her with dark thoughtful eyes, then turned and looked over the heads of the dancers. 'I expect he's gone to the bar.'

'Yes, I expect so,' said Ann.

237

John was not at all enthusiastic when Ann said, soon after midnight, that she was tired and wanted to go home; and later they found it difficult to talk of the party the way they generally did. 'The post mortem,' they had always called those discussions. They undressed in silence.

When they were at last in bed and just before he kissed her good-night, John stifled a yawn. 'Marie tells me she knows some wonderful exercises that will help you get your figure back quicker.'

Ann turned over on her side, and in the darkness her tears made no sound as they fell upon her pillow.

One damp winter's day Miss Seago came bouncing into the house. 'Good morning, Mrs. Hamilton, have you seen Annie Argus' column today?'

'No,' said Ann. 'I never read it—I think it's dreadful.'

Miss Seago sniffed. 'Well, I wouldn't know about that. . . . Anyway, she has given Mr. Hamilton a very nice write-up this morning.' She thrust out the paper.

JOHN HAMILTON TO PLAY OPPOSITE MARIE DAVENPORT

Ann glanced at the smaller type below.

'. . . *John Hamilton, who made such a sensational hit in his first picture, "Commando," has now been given his second assignment by Meadowbrook. He will play the Canadian lumberjack in "Loggerheads" opposite Marie Davenport! Young Hamilton thus collects one of the acting plums of the year and a little bird told me that La Davenport threatened that she would walk out of the picture unless Meadowbrook handed her John for her leading man. Much of the picture will be filmed on location far from civilization—some people get all the breaks!* '

As Ann read this, she felt as though a hand were slowly closing into a fist around her insides. Miss Seago was watching her closely.

Ann handed back the paper. She forced a smile to her lips. 'Isn't that wonderful! . . . he wanted that part so badly.'

During the weeks before 'Loggerheads' went into production, it seemed to Ann as if there were a leak in the pipe-line of her happiness. John seemed to be half-hearted in the way he enjoyed the things they did together, and when one day Jack Morgan came to see the baby, John was almost condescending when he enquired after the fishing boat and faintly patronizing about the new deck-hand, who had replaced him on board.

Jack Morgan raised his eyebrows as he listened, then glancing at the large red scrapbook and the piles of clippings surrounding it, he winked at Ann. 'What's got into this guy— he going Hollywood or something?'

John had not laughed and the subject had been dropped, but Jack Morgan's visits to the little house in Brentwood became less frequent after that.

Milton Myers noticed the change, too.

'Say, I hear you've taken on an agent.'

'Yes,' said John, smoothing down a new Sulka tie. 'I feel that any minute now I may need to have a little argument with Bengy over salary, so I want to be sure of making the best deal I can.'

Milton Myers, too, had winked at Ann. 'I suppose you'll be taking on a business manager soon to help you spend the raise?' Again John had not laughed.

'Funny you should mention that, because only today I was discussing it with someone at the studio, they have a very good man. . . . They say he saves them a packet every year, fiddling the expense account and tax returns and so on, and making good investments in apartment buildings and things like that. . . . They're going to send him round to me so that I can have a look at him.'

Milton Myers noticed Ann's worried and unhappy eyes.

'For Christ's sake,' he burst out, 'all you need out here is a good attorney.'

John looked at him unsmiling. 'Yes, I shall probably need that too, in due course.'

Milton Myers groaned. 'Say, where in hell do you get

that "in due course" routine? Have you got somebody writing your dialogue for you as well now?'

John smiled thinly. 'Yes, that was rather pompous, wasn't it?'

Milton Myers relaxed a little and helped himself to a drink. 'You're damned right it was, Johnny Boy. . . . Anyway, if you ever need a good lawyer, I know just the guy for you—Al Bernie—he's so smart he could find legal holes in the Ten Commandments.'

Gradually, relentlessly, the wall was built in front of Ann: piece by piece, with minute particles of hurt. She longed to face John; to accuse him even; but the wall was too subtle in texture to be taken by frontal assault—it would just give ground and retain its substance. Ann looked back miserably on their former happiness; it seemed so cruel that this was happening, that the light was being almost imperceptibly taken away. She felt quite powerless to stop the process, and then one afternoon John hurried into the sitting-room; he had been telephoning in the kitchen. 'Darling, terribly sorry I can't take you and Christopher Peter for a drive after all: the studio has just called and I have to go over right away to do some fittings.'

That had been at two o'clock. At four o'clock the studio telephoned. . . . 'This is the wardrobe department. . . . Would you tell Mr. Hamilton that we will be ready for his fittings tomorrow afternoon at three?'

'But he's down there now,' said Ann with a sickening feeling inside. 'He's doing a fitting now.'

'Hold the line, please,' said an impersonal voice. 'I'll just check,' and then a moment later, 'No, Mr. Hamilton has not been inside the studio at all today. There is nothing ready for him to try on yet. Would you please see that he gets the message—wardrobe tomorrow at three?'

'Yes, I'll give it to him,' said Ann, tonelessly. She hung up the receiver, and because her legs felt as though they were giving way, she sat down. How long she sat, she did not know. She felt cold and empty inside: she tried to tell herself that she must not behave like a jealous, stupid wife, that there must be some perfectly good explanation. He had probably got the wrong message, or the people in the wardrobe department had made a mistake—of course it would all be perfectly clear when Johnny came home—he had been playing golf or something. 'Maybe he's had an accident,' she thought, almost hopefully. But deep down in her heart, she knew there had been no mistake, no accident, and another cold wave of misery swept over her.

At last she stood up, and dully put Christopher Peter into a warm coat and carried him out to his carriage. As she walked along, she talked to her little son, automatically using intimate mother sounds as she went. If Christopher Peter sensed anything of his mother's unhappiness, he gave no sign. He smiled up at her, burbled and bubbled and kicked his feet with stabs of delight; and Ann hardly saw him through her swimming eyes.

When John came home he was just in time for dinner. Ann bit back the question she wanted so desperately to ask, and John vouchsafed no information on his own. All through the meal he talked about the fact that they ought to move to a bigger house. One-half of Ann's mind was forming the phrases she was using in trying to persuade him that a swimming pool was not really a necessity and in trying to disenchant him of the idea of borrowing a large sum of money so that he could order one; the other half was filled with a single cold, clear question. But she dare not ask it: she dare not hear him say: 'Yes, I was with Marie Davenport,' so she listened, and talked with the first half of her mind, and wished with all her heart she had never heard of Meadowbrook Pictures, or Isaac Ingersoll, or Bengy, or Annie Argus, or . . . of Hollywood, itself.

As they were going up to bed, Ann realized with a start that she still had not delivered the message from the wardrobe department. Now it was inescapable: now she was forced to face the issue.

Trying to sound casual, as she was seated at her dressing-table smearing cold cream on her face, she spoke over her shoulder: she tried to keep her voice steady.

'Oh, by the way, Johnny, the studio called up just after you left—they want you for a fitting tomorrow at three.'

She could not see the reflection of his face in her mirror, but the pause before he answered was just a shade too long.

'That's funny, they never said anything about it when I was down there this afternoon. . . .'

So, the torture was to continue: Ann heard the words and knew she must join battle once again with her thoughts, with the heart-numbing, nagging uncertainty.

Soon John started work on his picture, and Ann made it a habit to get up at seven and have her breakfast with him before he left; she would be waiting with his supper ready when he came home after work.

She knew that he finished before the cameras at six o'clock—everyone did; it was a studio rule. She also knew that from Meadowbrook Studio to Brentwood, at the very most, was a twenty-minute drive; no man needed more than ten minutes for removing make-up and changing his clothes; so seven o'clock became for her a dreaded deadline beyond which every minute was unendurable.

Several times John phoned her with excuses . . . he 'had to stay late at the studio to see some of the film that they had shot,' or to have 'a meeting with the producer,' and on these occasions Ann was too proud, or too frightened of what she might discover, to make any one of a number of simple inquiries: she just waited and prayed that she would not notice any tell-tale, but easily explainable, signs about him when he did eventually come home. Frequently her prayers went unanswered, and she would suffer agony, when she saw a tiny smear of lipstick on his cheek ('Didn't take my make-up off properly, darling') or detect a waft of perfume on the shoulder of his tweed coat ('Always use this jacket for rehearsals, darling').

Once or twice, he did not come home till very late; then he took a sleeping pill before falling into bed, and at breakfast the next morning, he swallowed a benzedrine tablet to wake himself up again before going off to work.

Ann no longer visited John at the studio during the day—she was not invited. When she had hopefully suggested it herself, he had told her that he found the part so difficult that he was afraid she would make him nervous if she were watching him. . . . Ann knew enough about working in front of the cameras to admit to herself that this, too, contained more than a modicum of truth; but she had difficulty in forcing into the back of her mind the thought that she could, at least, have been asked.

With sadness and hurt, she realized that she had never seen the dressing-room; there had been such gay plans, once, about how they were going to decorate it. She wondered what it was like.

John was never anything but kind and sweet to Ann, but this was harder for her to face than a tangible enemy: she felt that she was slowly being drained of all vitality, as though a vampire bat were nightly sucking out her blood as she slept.

On many mid-week evenings they went to parties and every Saturday night, with no work for John the following day, they invariably stayed out late. John had hit his stride as a social lion, and appeared to have made friends on every hand; at the parties he drank a great deal and was the centre of every noisy group. Often Ann drove the car home, and John, with nodding head, would sit silently beside her. She noticed, with a pang, that his face was becoming just a little bit bloated.

Marie Davenport was present at all the parties to which they were invited, but Ann found, to her surprise, that she was not consumed by hatred or even by jealousy. She experienced the bitter, heavy feeling of someone battling against overwhelming odds. It all seemed so unfair, so desperately unfair. So hopeless really.

'I have only myself to hold him with,' she reasoned. 'And

I have not changed from the first moment I met him. . . .
I have been the same person. . . . I'm *sure* I have. . . .
The change he sees, therefore, can only be in comparison to
someone else, and the other person has him to herself for
far longer in the day than I do. . . . How unfair that a
husband should spend practically all his waking hours in the
company of another woman, intimate hours too, with all
the fun and excitement of a common creative effort. At least at
night I have him to myself.' But at this last thought the icy
fingers closed again round her heart, for the last three weeks
of the picture she would *not* have him to herself, even at
night. For the last three weeks of the picture John would be
going three hundred miles away to beautiful Golden Pine
Lake. Ann felt more helpless than ever as she visualized what
life up there would be like for the film company. John and
Marie Davenport would work together all day long, but when
the sun sank low and the light became yellow, the cameraman would shake his head and work for the day would
cease . . . then. . . . With a tremendous effort, Ann
forced these thoughts out of her mind, but they would always
return; no matter how hard she tried, they always crept back,
and she knew that the three weeks' 'location' at Golden Pine
Lake would be her supreme test.

Slowly the weeks dragged on towards the fateful date.
John came home from the studio at a different time each
night. Ann noticed that the closer his return was to her zero
hour of seven o'clock, the more likely he was to be fidgety and
nervous. On these occasions he would eat little supper, and
once when he had come home early and had been particularly
upset and uncommunicative, she had sought to help him.
'Johnny darling, was it very difficult today?'

'That Davenport woman is unbearable . . . hopeless to
work with.' A thrill of excitement had passed through Ann.
'Why? . . . how? . . .'

'Oh, I dunno. She's just so damned spoiled she can't see
straight . . . I can't stand her much longer—'

Ann looked at his unhappy face and wondered with rising

hope if this could be the beginning of the end of whatever Marie Davenport had meant to John.

The telephone bell rang in the next room and John hurried out, shutting the door behind him. Ann did not want to hear what he said, so she went out into the garden for a few minutes. When she came back, John was a changed man, smugly happy. He was adjusting his tie in the mirror over the fireplace.

'What was that?' asked Ann with a sinking heart.

'Oh, nothing,' he answered with exaggerated casualness. 'Just . . . a message from the studio.'

When they went up to bed that night John fell almost immediately into a deep sleep, and Ann lay for hours on her elbow, searching his face.

'Oh, Johnny, come back! . . . Don't go away from me! . . . Come back! . . . Please God make him come back. . . .'

At last the day came for John's departure to Golden Pine Lake. Ann helped him pack his things into the car. He had said nothing about her going with him, and when, swallowing her pride, she herself had finally suggested it, he said, 'Oh, the studio doesn't allow that; besides, it's much too rough . . . just dreary little cabins, that's all.'

So this was it! The dreaded trial had arrived. With leaden heart Ann put John's fly rod on the top of his other baggage.

'You haven't said good-bye to Christopher Peter.'

'Oh, you do it for me, darling,' he kissed her on the forehead, 'and take great care of yourself . . . I'll soon be back.' He climbed into the Cadillac convertible which had now replaced the Buick, and drove away. As he rounded the corner at the end of the street he waved back gaily. Ann stood for a moment beside Hengist in the driveway, then turned and ran into the house and flung herself onto her bed: she buried her face in her pillow and all her pent-up unhappiness flowed out unchecked. Two hours later Clarabel found her there and brought her a cup of tea. . . . 'There now, honey, don't take on so, it's always the same after you have a baby. . . . Sometimes the let-down comes right away, sometimes it comes a year later, but sure enough—it comes.'

After a while Ann went downstairs in the house that seemed so empty, and sat like a waif curled up in a big chair in front of the fire.

The front door of the little house opened and Ann gasped aloud with delight, for there, stooping slightly to avoid bumping his head, stood . . . Oglethorpe.

CHAPTER ELEVEN

Now THEN, M'DEAR,' said Oglethorpe when Ann had finally disengaged herself, 'pop upstairs and put on your best tin hat—we're going into action.'

He refused to explain how or when or why he had arrived until they were seated at a small table at Ciro's. Carefully and deliberately he ordered their meal and then he spoke.

'I've been here for a couple of days, m'dear, staying with an extraordinarily intelligent feller called Milton Myers.'
Ann was amazed.

'But why didn't you come and stay with us? Johnny has only just gone away, he'll be terribly disappointed. . . .'

Oglethorpe covered her hand with a huge brown paw.

'Johnny is going to be a great deal more than disappointed by the time Myers and I get through with him. You see, m'dear, I know all about it. Myers has spent two days bringing me up to date and making a plan. . . .' He paused as the waiter came and delivered the first instalment of dinner—rolls, butter, ice water and napkins. . . . 'So to save you pain allow *me* to tell *you* what has happened. Correct me if I am wrong. . . . It seems that this Hollywood place is pretty strong meat, according to Myers only a microscopic number of people who get to the top in it manage to remain unchanged and unspoilt during the ascent. According to Myers some people lose their sense of proportion and sense of humour quite early on in the proceedings and it seems obvious, though a pity, that our boy is one of these—'

Ann made a little noise of protest but Oglethorpe would have none of it: 'Now then, m'dear, don't you start sticking up for him or I shall get straight back on that aeroplane and return to my orchids—'

Ann looked at him incredulously. 'You mean you came all the way out here because of *us*?'

'Of course I did. Myers cabled me that trouble was brewing and I'm very glad I came.' He kissed her hand with old-world gallantry.

Ann found it hard not to cry.

'Now,' said Oglethorpe, 'back to business. . . . I gather that our boy is currently behaving like a half-wit and needs a good fright to put him straight. By the way, I take it you do want him back, don't you?'

'He is my whole life,' said Ann simply.

'Good. Now here is the plan. It's not very original, but nor is the patient's disease, and Myers and I felt that it would just about handle his case.' He glanced at his watch. 'It's nearly zero hour: the photographer feller will be here in a minute.'

Ann, though somewhat lost at this point, felt happier than she had done for weeks. It gave her great strength to know that two devoted friends were fighting side by side with her, and she listened excitedly as Oglethorpe issued instructions.

Milton Myers, it appeared, had found a tame photographer who had been given three assignments.

The first was to photograph Ann and Oglethorpe dining intimately at Ciro's that very night, the second was to take their picture the following morning arm in arm and smiling happily at Santa Anita race-track, and the third and most important was to snap them once more in the afternoon complete with Christopher Peter and a lot of luggage standing beside an American Airlines machine about to take off for New York.

'Myers is with our boy in the mountains now, he is going to feed these pictures and stories to match to a woman named Argus who he says will jump at them and plaster the newspapers with them,' explained Oglethorpe.

'But what about you?' cried Ann in dismay. 'I get the idea perfectly, but if Johnny sees you and me together he's not going to come rushing home in a panic.'

Oglethorpe smiled indulgently.

'I could be very hurt, m'dear, by that remark, but I'll let it pass. Apparently this tame photographer feller can fiddle the negative—it won't look like me at all when the picture comes out. I suppose it will be some dull-looking character with no moustache and a chin, anyway John will never know that it's me. Incidentally, I shall get off the plane just as it is leaving, but you, m'dear, you and the baby are going home to North Carolina.'

'I see,' said Ann doubtfully. 'Oh dear, I hope it works.'

'This may sound brutal,' said Oglethorpe, 'but it's better to find out one way or the other, you can't just stand about and hope for the best. "Don't stand about" is the Oglethorpe motto—"Don't stand about . . . crack about." If you crack about something is bound to happen—' He looked up. 'Ah, here comes the photographer feller.'

It required some pretty delicate timing on the part of Milton Myers once he had the necessary pictures in his possession.

First he had to sow the seeds of sedition in the mind of the chief of publicity of Meadowbrook Pictures, Inc. This was just in case Annie Argus should do any careful checking up— an unlikely event at the best of times.

He did it quite casually when the office was full of people.

'I wonder if any of these rumours are true about Ann Windsor getting into the sack with a Swede,' he murmured.

'What Swede is that?' asked someone.

'Oh, I dunno, I just heard tell there was some big blonde Scandinavian guy making time while Hamilton is up at Golden Pine. . . .'

'. . . making Davenport,' somebody filled in, and in the ensuing laughter Milton Myers slipped out of the office.

His second piece of staff work was to ensure that John saw the result of their handiwork at a time when it would do the most good.

Ann, who was more than a little relieved to discover that Annie Argus' column was not syndicated in either the *Tryon Bulletin* or the *New York Times*, which were the only two newspapers her parents ever read, had been home in North Carolina for almost two weeks before Milton Myers judged the time to be ripe.

John had only three more days left at Golden Pine when the first round of the photographic barrage was laid down.

Already 'softened up,' as Oglethorpe had put it, by the fact that he had received no letters from Ann since he had been away, and more than a little worried by the fact that, on the two or three occasions upon which he had taken himself ten miles to the nearest telephone he had been unable to get any reply from his house, John's defences were soon breached.

Annie Argus had risen like a giant salmon to the bait.

'*It hurts me just terribly to report this,*' she gushed, '*but this is a real scoop! A week ago I received a distracted letter from a Swedish Countess in San Francisco saying that her husband had gone to Hollywood because he was in love with of all people—Ann Windsor! Now, as readers of this column know, I never print a rumour unless I am sure it is absolutely true. For a long time this reporter has known that all has not been well in the Hamilton home, but we never suspected that THIS was the cause of it (remember what the little bird told us about Marie Davenport?). Now here is my scoop . . . a photograph of Ann Windsor with her handsome admirer—Count Morgen Tignigen and, as you can see, Ann looks as though she is thoroughly enjoying the Smörgasbord ! ! !* '

John had finished work for the day and was just about to go fishing. As he left his little log cabin beneath the pine trees Milton Myers approached.

'Read this,' he said.

John saw it was open at the columnist's page.

'*Now* what does the old bag say about me?' He gave the column the usual actor's reading—his questing eye soon caught his own name and his interest quickened perceptibly. When he had finished, John stood stunned, then he sat down heavily on the doorstep of the cabin and read the item through again. He turned a face the colour of putty towards Milton Myers. 'But what is she doing? . . . Who is he?'

Milton Myers adopted an air of exaggerated calm. 'I wouldn't know, Johnny Boy, but I should imagine quite a bunch of the fellows down there were glad when you left town for three weeks.'

'But . . . but . . .' John exploded, 'she mustn't do that sort of thing . . . it's . . . so unlike Ann.'

A twig cracked and Marie Davenport appeared round the side of the cabin. She was dressed in carefully pressed tailor-made blue jeans: a white turtle-neck sweater clung lovingly to her high breasts: on her head was a red stocking cap from the end of which dangled a white woollen ball: she was carrying a brand-new fly rod.

'I'm all ready, darling,' she announced.

John eyed her with distaste. 'I can't go fishing.'

'Why not?' she asked sharply. 'I thought you were going to teach me how to cast?'

'Well, I can't tonight I'm afraid . . . er . . . I have to talk business with Milt.'

'For Christ's sake,' said the blonde idol of millions, 'don't you get enough publicity as it is?' Her eye caught the newspaper still open in John's hand. She grabbed it. After a few seconds she threw it back on to his knees.

'Well, what's wrong with that? . . . You can't expect to have it all your own way, can you? She's probably been cheating on you all the time . . . the mousey ones always do.'

John was on his feet in an instant. 'Don't you dare talk about Ann like that. . . . She's never cheated on anyone in her life and . . . she's not mousey, either.'

Marie Davenport's lip curled in a sneer. 'Okay, Sir Galahad . . . what are you going to do about it anyway?'

'For a start,' said John, 'I am not going to take you fishing tonight or any other night.'

Miss Davenport switched to the tactics of the jilted scullery maid. 'I thought you were a gentleman,' she said.

'Well, I'm not,' snapped John.

Miss Davenport could never resist a good exit line.

'You can say that again,' she said with a toss of the head which lost a certain amount of effect because the woollen ball flew round and hit her in the eye. 'You're a goddamned lousy egotistical heel.'

She flounced away.

'The next two days up here,' said Milton Myers, raising innocent eyes to the heavens, 'should be fraught with interest.'

John did not hear him. 'What am I going to do, Milt—? What am I going to do? I must find out who this man is— I can't get away from here till the day after tomorrow. . . .' He started pacing up and down. 'I just don't believe it. Ann? . . . She wouldn't do this . . . she *couldn't*.'

Milton Myers busied himself knotting two pine needles together.

'If you like, Johnny Boy, I'll run down for you and find out what gives . . . I could be back by midday tomorrow.'

John grabbed his arm fiercely.

'Would you, Milt? Would you really? God! what a good friend you are—'

Milton Myers never drove the three hundred miles to Hollywood. Instead he took John's Cadillac to Reno, eighty miles in the opposite direction, and there spent a profitable night with an old friend who ran a heavily weighted roulette wheel in the 'Dirty Dollar Saloon'. He had a long telephone conversation with Oglethorpe. Oglethorpe listened with approval to Milton Myers' report and in his turn told of his talk with Ann far away in North Carolina.

'All I could do to stop her sending him a wire saying that we were a couple of lunatics, but I finally got her calmed down . . . promised to let her know how things go tomorrow.'

'Having any fun down there?' asked Myers.

'Well, old man, I'm off to the beach in a little while to reconnoitre . . . "don't lie on the sand and look at the stars— come to Hollywood and do the reverse. . . ." Good-bye, old man.'

The next morning Milton Myers bought a Reno paper and looked at the happy photograph of a much-altered Ogle-thorpe and a radiant Ann hand in hand at Santa Anita races. He read with approval the succinct observations of Annie Argus on the whole subject, then he drove back in a leisurely way to Golden Pine Lake.

Late that afternoon an assistant cameraman brought him up to date. 'Oh, brother! . . . have you missed a ball up here! . . . Hamilton has pulled the quick switch on Daven-port and the dame is going crazy! . . . Something must have happened because he suddenly started acting like he hated her guts. First off, she gave it right back at him, but when he didn't react like they usually do, she nearly went out of her mind. . . . She's as nutty as a fruitcake at the best of times, but this is the first time some guy has really given her the brush . . . she just doesn't know what's hit her!'

When John saw Milton Myers he rushed over to him. . . . 'Where the hell have you been?' he hissed. 'I thought you were my friend. . . . I've been going mad up here. . . . What's happened? . . . Who was he . . . the man she was with?'

Milton Myers shook his head. 'I'm afraid it's bad, Johnny Boy—just packed up and left—took the baby and walked out. I found the house all locked up. . . .'

John clutched his arm. 'What are you saying?' he croaked. 'What do you mean, she's left?'

Milton Myers continued. 'I finally tracked down Clarabel at her home, that's why I've been so long, and she told me that when she came to work yesterday, Ann and the kid had gone. Oh, yes, and there was an envelope with a month's wages in it and a little note. . . . "Thanks for all you've done for us"—that sort of thing.'

John went chalky white. 'But she can't have gone just like that, not saying where she was going . . . she couldn't— not Ann.' He almost whispered the words.

The next day was scheduled to be the last day of 'Logger-heads.' The picture very nearly never got finished at all.

Marie Davenport marched over to John just before they were going to start the final love scene and thrust the morning paper under his nose.

'Get a load of this,' she said, and stood waiting expectantly with one hand on a carefully balanced hip. John, already fore-warned by yesterday's report from Milton Myers, looked with sleepless and tormented eyes at the beaming picture of Ann, Christopher Peter and the tall blonde stranger. A giant silver airliner with a smiling stewardess at the top of the loading ramp completed the composition.

Supremely conscious of the ring of interested faces around him he tried hard to sound nonchalant.

'Why don't you mind your own business?' he asked.

Marie Davenport, always a girl for the quick switch in tactics, tried something new. 'All you lousy British are the same—no guts and no manners. Yeah! even Churchill. Why, I wrote him a fan letter once during the war, told him I thought he was the greatest guy alive and asked for an auto-graphed picture. I didn't pull rank on him, mind you. I didn't do it through the studio.' She tapped her high bosom several times with her thumb and her bosom wobbled aggres-sively. 'I sat down and wrote it myself . . . the bum never had the decency to answer.'

John was trying to decide whether it was worth while putting her over his knee when the director bustled up.

'Okay, break it up folks and let's get this last scene in the can . . . now John, you grab hold of Marie and remember in the clinch this is what you've been waiting for and what the audience has been waiting for for fifteen reels . . . all right, let's go.'

John groaned inwardly and pulled Marie Davenport to-wards him. Waves of hatred swept between them.

Somehow he struggled through the day. Several times he almost decided to give up—just walk out of the place, get into his car and drive away. But Milton Myers was always on hand to persuade him to see the day through.

It seemed like an eternity, but at last the final love scene

was completed, at last came the order from the director—
'Okay, cut! . . . wrap it up and send it back to Bengy.
. . . That's it, folks.'

John released Marie Davenport so suddenly from his arms
that she fell to the ground. Then he dashed for his cabin.
'Come on, Milt, hurry up. . . . Let's get going.' He started
piling his belongings into the back of the car.

'What's the hurry, Johnny Boy?' asked Milton Myers,
innocently.

'I want to go home,' said John. 'I'm going to find Ann if
it takes me fifty years.'

'She'll show up, Johnny Boy. . . . Don't forget she's got
your son along with her.'

'I don't want her to show up in a divorce court,' said John
between his teeth. 'Come on, let's get moving.'

After a few miles of silent furious driving John gave Milton
Myers his opening. 'Oh hell, Milt, why did I ever let them
make me an actor? . . . We were so happy before. This
would never have happened—it's all the fault of that bloody
Hollywood and everyone connected with it.'

Milton Myers did not spare him. 'Oh no, it's not the
fault of Hollywood, Johnny Boy, and you know goddamned
well it's not . . . the fault is yours and nobody else's.'

John half turned to him. An angry flush spread across his
face, but he kept silent.

'Shall I go on?' asked Milton Myers. 'Do you think you
can take it, or are you so puffed up with your own importance
that it won't penetrate?'

'Go on,' said John grimly.

'When I first met you,' said Milton Myers, making every
word tell, 'I reckoned you were just about the swellest guy
I'd ever run across. So did Ann, I guess, or she wouldn't have
married you. All through the pony racing you were swell.
From what I hear, you were swell when you first came out
here—then one piddling little success in a bad picture and
you fell apart. It used to make me want to throw up . . .
the studio paid me a hundred bucks a week to make up

254

publicity stories about you, and you, you poor sucker, you started to believe them—to believe your own publicity, for Christ's sake! Then you let some broad give you a goddamned great scrapbook and you started collecting the crap I wrote about you! . . . Then you get yourself a secretary! You!—a secretary . . . and an agent! . . . and a business manager! What the hell do *you* want with any of those? Who do you think you are—Gable? And all through this, Ann never said a word—just took it on the chin, but you were so dumb that you didn't see what you were doing to her, or such a bastard that you didn't even care. Then comes the topper! You meet "the sexual terminus". . . . I don't know whether you got there or not, and like a lot of other people, I just don't give a damn. . . . But the great Mr. John Hamilton has to fall for the same old line she's given every actor on the lot, and you wind up making a horse's ass out of yourself and just about breaking the heart of one of the sweetest little girls in the world, who incidentally happens to be the mother of your baby. . . .'

Milton Myers paused for breath and took a sidelong look at John. John was very white and his knuckles gleamed through the skin, so tightly did his hands grip the steering wheel. He still remained silent.

'Swimming pools!' continued Milton Myers. 'Cadillacs!' He banged his foot down on the floorboard. 'And then you have the goddamned gall to blame Hollywood because your wife couldn't take it any longer! . . . Why don't you blame yourself? . . . I'll say this—you're not the first by any means who couldn't take Hollywood. It's happened to hundreds before you, and it'll happen again, long after you're forgotten, but for Christ's sake, realize that Hollywood is full of good, honest, hard-working people who *can* take it, and who think that people like you, who fall apart so easily—just plain stink! . . . For every Bengy there are three dozen fine honourable men in those big front offices. . . . For every Annie Argus there are several hundred honest and truthful newspaper people, and thank God for every John Hamilton there are several thousand ordinary sensible folk earning an honest living, looking after their wives and rearing their kids in happy, sensible homes.'

Milton Myers paused for the last time, then he spoke more quietly. 'Obviously I wouldn't have got all that off my chest if I didn't know that you could still snap out of it if you wanted to—I've been in show business all my life, and I've pretended to be a lot of things that I'm not, but I've never gypped anyone, least of all myself, and I don't like watching my friends do it either.

Milton Myers sat back and waited: a shrewd judge of men, he knew that pride can be highly indigestible when it has to be swallowed: much mental saliva has to be generated: many glands of reasoning and common sense, atrophied by disuse, must start once more to function. It is a painful process, and, to be successful, it is bound to be a long one.

Milton Myers waited for almost two hours. During that time John never uttered a word. He drove the car; and in the method of his driving, Milton Myers was able to follow the outline of his thoughts. Long bursts of furious speed, flying round hairpin bends with smoking tyres, would be followed by short periods of careful, even decorous driving. Gradually the periods of careful driving became longer and the bursts of speed less frequent. Finally, the Cadillac settled down to a good steady pace, then, out of the corner of his eye, Milton Myers stole a look at his companion's face. John saw the look: he turned his head and smiled wryly.

'Thanks, chum,' was all he said.

It was five o'clock in the morning before John and Milton Myers arrived at the little house in Brentwood.

Oglethorpe opened the door to them and John stood transfixed as his old friend addressed him.

'Hello, old man. I hear you have been making a four-star, first-class, ocean-going twat of yourself. . . .'

Milton Myers spoke up. 'It's all taken care of, Ogle, our boy is in great shape now. I think we can relax.'

'That's a relief then,' said Oglethorpe. 'You've given us

quite a jumpy time, old man. Let us open a bottle of something and celebrate your return to normal.'

John's mind was in a turmoil as he followed his two friends into the living-room. He could hardly bear to look around the little house; it seemed so cold and deserted. He longed to ask them for news of Ann and Christopher Peter.

Milton Myers saw the entreaty in his eyes.

'It's okay, Johnny Boy, Ann's with her folks in Tryon, North Carolina—if you step on it you'll be able to hop the midday plane—'

A great gasp of relief forced itself from John. Before he had time to frame the other question, which was half choking him, Oglethorpe spoke again.

'Ann will tell you all about that Swedish feller when you see her. I wouldn't worry about him too much if I were you—poor type of feller really. Looked as though he drank his bath water. . . . Welcome back, old man.' He raised his glass in an elaborate salute. The whole subject was never referred to again.

Milton Myers and Oglethorpe drove John to the municipal airport. As they travelled swiftly down the broad 101 Highway, past the celery beds and the oil derricks, past the hundreds of billboards banked in solid phalanx along each side of the road, John caught a glimpse of a man in a Mexican hat: he was seated beneath a large yellow umbrella; behind him was a sign which pointed in the direction from which they had just come: 'THIS WAY TO HOLLYWOOD. BUY YOUR MAP HERE. GUIDE TO THE MOVIE STARS' HOMES.'

John heaved a great sigh of relief.

As the airliner roared away eastward Oglethorpe and Milton Myers turned slowly towards the bar.

'Have you got any dough, Ogle?' asked Milton Myers.

'I have enough to stand you a nip, old man, if that is what you mean.'

'No, I mean real jack—around twenty-five grand.'

'What have you in mind?' asked Oglethorpe.

Milton Myers settled himself comfortably on the bar stool.

'Ogle . . . I've been thinking about that orchid set-up of yours in Bermuda. . . . I've been thinking that maybe we could dehydrate them and can them and then ship them all over the world.'

Oglethorpe looked thoughtfully at his new-found friend. 'What would you like to drink, old man?'

Milton Myers' expression was that of a dreamer. 'I guess it's time for an Orange Blossom cocktail,' he said.

CHAPTER TWELVE

ANN AND CHRISTOPHER PETER were returning from their afternoon walk. Christopher Peter liked to watch the four o'clock train cross over the wooden trestle bridge just outside Tryon, and the engine driver always looked out and waved and blew his whistle especially for Christopher Peter. A hint of early frost in the air had brought the roses to the little boy's cheeks. Ann had to push fairly hard to reach the top of the hill, and the cold, clear air felt good in her lungs. Below her the little township of Tryon lay cradled snugly in the hollow: blue wood-smoke from the chimneys spiralled straight up in the still evening air, and on the other side of the valley the setting sun turned the trees on the foothills, now at the height of their autumn glory, into a blaze of yellow and russet and red and gold. Above them towered the Smoky Mountains, a soft, milky blue. Ann sighed. It had never been so beautiful. She was happy and content here surrounded by the red earth of the fields and among these soft-spoken gentle and kindly people—this was home. Happy and content up to a point, but always in her heart was the aching gap that was—John.

'There's another wire for you, honey,' her mother called from the living-room as Ann opened the front door of the white frame house.

'Thanks, mother.' Her parents had no idea of what had

been going on in California: as far as they were concerned, it was a most sensible arrangement that their daughter should bring their grandson to visit them, and all the more so since her husband was working away from home for three weeks.

Ann tore open the envelope with shaking hands: she dreaded these bulletins, yet she waited feverishly every day for them to arrive.

When she had read this one, she knew it would be the last one she would recieve.

'PATIENT DISCHARGED COMPLETELY CURED AND ARRIVING TRYON TOMORROW STOP HE'S ALL YOURS STOP LOVE
DOCTORS MILTON AND OGLETHORPE'

She sat down on a chair in the hall and cried softly.

Mr. and Mrs. Windsor threw themselves with feverish excitement into preparations for John's arrival.

The day dragged on interminably for Ann, but at last came bed-time. She could not sleep: she lay there building plans for their future and, being Ann, never once considered that there could be any discussion of, let alone recrimination over, the past. She was far too happy for that.

John loosened his seat-belt and looked down on the sprawling city of Los Angeles falling away below him.

In his mind he visualized his meeting with Ann. What could he possibly say to her?

His insides gave a sickening lurch whenever he thought of all the intimate little things they had done together, all the gay and wonderful happenings they had shared. Had he ruined everything? Was he too late? 'Please, plane, go faster! . . . don't let me be too late . . . go faster . . . I must see her . . . go faster, plane!'

The flight to Asheville was supposed to take ten hours, which meant, allowing for the change in time, that he would arrive there about two in the morning. He would still have to make his way twenty miles or so to Tryon, but he was sure he could get there somehow. All through the long afternoon John urged the plane forward with every fibre of his being. It seemed to crawl across the landscape. At last it grew dark inside the plane, and below the earth composed itself to sleep. The first lights winked up from the little townships and farms. John's head nodded: he was very tired.

'. . . ashville.' The word filtered through to his brain. John had been in a deep sleep. He leapt up from his seat, grabbed his hat and his suitcase, said a sleepy good-night to the plane hostess, and went in search of the wash-room. There he freshened himself up with much splashing of cold water; took a long time straightening his clothes and climbed into a high chair while a young negro smeared and rubbed and polished his shoes. 'Where would I find a taxi to take me to Tryon at this time of night.'

'Tryon, boss? . . . never heard of it!'

John smiled deprecatingly. He never failed to ask directions from people who assured him that they were strangers there themselves.

'It's only twenty miles from here.'

'Well, I don't rightly know, boss . . . I've lived here all my life and I never did hear of no Tryon.'

'Tryon, North Carolina,' explained John.

It was the bootboy's turn to smile. A huge grin lit up his black face.

'Just where do you think you are right now?' he asked.

'Asheville, North Carolina,' said John.

'Man, you sure are off your course!—you're in Nashville, Tennessee!'

John leaped to his feet. 'Nashville! . . . Oh, my God!' He dashed outside. The Asheville plane with its red, green and white lights made a slow turn a thousand feet above him, then it straightened out and headed due east for its destination over two hundred miles away. John watched it with loathing.

It had been so warm in California that he had forgotten to bring an overcoat; now the cold night air of Tennessee made him shiver inside his thin grey flannel suit; he turned up his coat collar and with shoulders hunched in despair walked slowly back towards the administration building.

He adjusted his watch to the time shown by the big clock—it was almost midnight.

Dispirited inquiries at the information desk confirmed his worst fears—there was no other plane that night that came down at Asheville and there were no buses that went that way and no taxi company would undertake the two hundred mile trip over the mountains at night. He cut a disconsolate figure in the huge empty over-heated waiting-room.

'Boss,' said a voice at his elbow. 'I'se been lookin' all over for you. I'se aimin' to close up my little old shoe shine parlour but I thought maybe you'd like to have your suitcase first.'

John smiled his thanks and tipped generously. As he watched the grateful back departing he had a sudden idea. 'Hey!'

The negro swung round.

'What is it boss? Can I help you?'

John was excited now. He spoke rapidly. 'Are there any used car dealers open at this time of night in Nashville?'

The negro was dubious: he scratched a woolly head, but an hour later in an old 1923 Pierce-Arrow and eighty-five dollars poorer John was headed in the right direction once more. His spirits soared again as he wheezed and rattled along the broad highway. The first hundred miles were not too bad. The road was fairly straight, the gradients not too steep, and the surface was splendid. John discovered that by pressing the accelerator flat against the floorboards the ancient car, on a level piece of road with the wind behind it, could achieve and maintain a speed of about forty miles an hour.

The springs at each side of the driver's seat were broken, but the strain of sitting at an angle of forty-five degrees helped John to overcome the drowsiness which was a natural result of the blue oil fumes and the carbon monoxide gas which billowed up from the cracks in the flooring.

It was shortly before three o'clock in the morning when he

started the ascent of the western slopes of the Smoky Mountains.

The old car churned up the steep ascents in second gear, and every half an hour or so clouds of steam from the boiling water in the radiator fogged the windshield.

It was bitterly cold but the fumes inside the car were so bad that John had to keep all the windows open to save himself from asphyxiation; occasionally a squirrel or an opossum or a fox ran across the road and often the dim head lights were reflected in the eyes of other animals peering out of the darkness between the trees. It seemed as if the climb would never end, but at last the twisting road levelled off: John glanced at his wrist watch—it was six o'clock; the sky was perceptibly lighter straight ahead. He lit a cigarette and shifted his position to ease his buttocks, numbed by the position in which he had been forced to sit.

Slowly the grey streaks of the early light appeared through the clouds, and after a while he could discern the red dirt mountain road stretching ahead of him, the puddles on its slippery surface reflecting the pre-dawn light. With a sigh of relief he switched off his headlights and settled back to the blissful contemplation that the worst must surely be over: that in two or three hours he would be in Tryon, and then . . . Ann! He urged the ancient car to further effort.

As he sped round a bend a small signpost on the right-hand side of the road caught his eye—TRYON 4½ miles.

He stamped on the brake; the wheels locked and with a sickening lurch the top-heavy old car skidded across the slippery surface of the road. Frantically John spun the wheel. He had a momentary vision of a huge moss-covered tree trunk rushing towards him, then there was a grinding, splintering crash.

Towards morning Ann dozed fitfully, but was much too excited to get any real rest. When the cocks started crowing and the first grey fingers of light showed through the curtains of her bedroom she got up and dressed.

She was soon across the fields and mounting steadily the gentle slopes of the foothills. She looked over her shoulder: the sky was beginning to glow in the east; it would be a glorious sunrise—the dawn of a truly perfect day. Smoke rose lazily from the chimneys of the little houses in the valley far below. Some Jersey cows started to crop their way slowly across a meadow, and from a pond, in the middle of a small wood, a flight of wild duck rose circling into the sky. A tiny speck of a man came out of his cottage to chop some firewood; the noise of his axe strokes reached Ann a full second after he had made them. Her heart was full. Today Johnny would be home!

Slowly the great crimson orb of the sun rose majestically above the horizon, touching the ground mists of the valley, as it did so, with a delicate rose pink: even the steam from the little local train, puffing importantly across the trestle bridge on its early morning mission, was tinged with the same soft and reassuring colour. As the sun climbed higher Ann felt the warmth of its rays reach out and caress her cheek and she realized how long she must have been standing there, gazing down. She did not know what time John would be arriving, but she had no intention of being absent when he did. With a last look at the valley she turned back to the leaf-strewn path up which she had climbed.

The track joined another in a clearing surrounded by a thicket of dogwood and holly; the berries hung in great red clusters on the bushes.

In the years to come John and Ann disagreed over this—it was one of the very few arguments they ever had. Each claimed that they saw the other first. In point of fact they stepped into the clearing at exactly the same moment. John was limping and his clothes were in tatters, he was also bleeding from a small cut above his eye, but he stoutly maintained that, in spite of all this, he still ran faster than Ann as they raced towards each other over the golden carpet of leaves.